THE JUDAS TREE

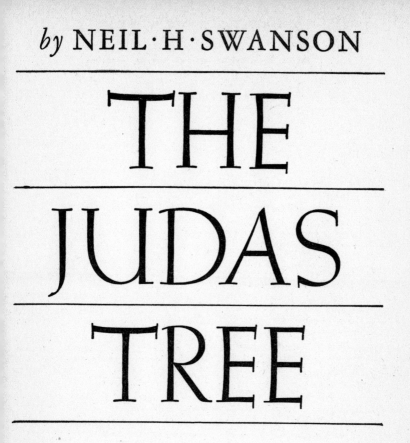

by NEIL·H·SWANSON

THE
JUDAS
TREE

GROSSET & DUNLAP

PUBLISHERS   NEW YORK

MANUFACTURED IN THE UNITED STATES OF AMERICA
AT THE VAN REES PRESS

TO MARGARET DIANA

who made this book

possible

YOU STILL CAN SEE IT:

IT looks like an outhouse—a fashionable one, when such things had their day; but an outhouse.

It is grimy; and it is all but lost in a clutter of railroad tracks, sheds and warehouses.

It stands near the apex of what men call, pridefully, the Golden Triangle. The wealth of the steel magnates centers there.

On one side flows the Allegheny river, on the other the Monongahela; they make two sides of the triangle. The base is a street called Grant, after a soldier as miserably unlucky as Braddock.

Past the brick outhouse rushes the traffic of a great city. Around it, within twenty miles, live one million five hundred thousand people. Some of them know what it is: it was once part of a royal fortress. Not one in ten thousand knows what really happened there.

So....

This is the story of what happened—an epic of courage that America forgot.

THE
JUDAS
TREE

CHAPTER I

In Which a Young Man on the Way to His Wedding Buys a Red-Headed Woman—and Finds Himself Obliged to Let a Baronet Shoot at Him:

ARNETT LESLIE, major of militia in my lord Baltimore's colony of Maryland, straddled the brass twelve-pounder in the cabin of the merchantman *New Adventure,* and beat time with his bombo glass to the ribald chorus of a London song.

Mr. Leslie was supremely happy. The *New Adventure* was forty days out of Southampton, and the green shores of the Chesapeake were slipping by at last. In an hour, if the breeze held, the anchor would be splashing into the green water of the Patuxent; in ten, he would be home. The bombo party was his farewell to the shouting group around the captain's table—or else it was their farewell to him. The toddy bowl had been filled and emptied so many times since noon that no one remembered, now.

Not even at my lord Baltimore's Christmas rout had there been half so much to laugh at—nor had the bombo been half so good. Mr. Leslie swayed back and forth, gripping the barrel of the cannon with his white satin knees, and laughed at Robin Stuart's red knees waggling hilariously under his highland kilts, and at Stuart's long face, more solemn than ever as he sang the tavern ditty of "The Juniper Tree."

Captain Stuart had his arms around the Swiss, Barent, and Todd, who was master of the *New Adventure.* Over at the end of the table, Dick Lawless and his friend Kildane were slopping bombo into their glasses with a ladle and swaying in time to the song. They were all very serious. Leslie thought he had never seen a funnier sight. It struck him, all at once, that they looked very much like the gaudy parrots he had seen in a cage in London, teetering solemnly on one perch. Todd was a fat blue parrot, in his seaman's coat, and Stuart a red and black one, in his funny short jacket and kilts. Barent, the Swiss, in his scarlet and blue regimentals of the

Royal Americans, was the gaudiest of the three; but Dick Lawless and his friend outdid them. Sir Dick was all in purple, like a plum, and Kildane had a buff silk waistcoat under his pale blue coat. Major Leslie, in the white satin coat and smallclothes he had donned for his homecoming, felt by far the most conservative.

Robin Stuart took a deep breath and pulled Todd and Barent closer to him. With a sway and a swoop, they started off on another verse:

> O-o-oohh, *my sweet Phoebe,*
> *How merry were we,*
> *When we lay under the juniper tree!*

Leslie looked over at Lawless and Kildane, and saw that they had stopped singing. Both of them were staring at him in a fuddled sort of way. Major Leslie's glass had made as many trips to the bombo bowl as theirs, but he still had enough of his wits about him to know that Sir Dick was doing his unpleasant best to force a quarrel upon him. Between them, the young baronet and his friend had devised a number of slurring remarks, in the course of the afternoon, which Mr. Leslie chose to ignore. Sir Dick had no head for Antigua rum; it made his manners worse than usual. They had been especially bad since Major Leslie told him, smiling, that he would not fight.

And he wouldn't: he had made up his mind to that. There was no sense in taking offense at Lawless, and Kildane merely aped his friend. Leslie flipped one leg over the cannon, and swung his buckled shoes in restless arcs. In all his twenty-six years, there had never been a day in which he had liked the world half so well as he did today; and that, he told himself, applied to the people in it, even including Dick Lawless. But the day was almost over. Through the gun-port, opened to the breeze, he could see Point No Point shrinking into a golden haze astern.

He leaned over, elbows on knees, to watch the wake; the breeze, he thought, must be freshening, for the ripples spreading behind the *New Adventure* seemed sharper and longer. The sunset, slanting over the wooded shore, was gilding them; they lay like the ribs of a gold-laced fan on the green-satin lap of the bay. Leslie smiled to himself, thinking of a fan he had bought in London for Evelyn Gentle. His feet took up their impatient swinging again: this homeward voyage had been endless, and now the ten hours that lay between him and Evelyn seemed suddenly longer than the forty days at sea—longer even than the eight months in London.

In ten hours, there would be an end of exile.

There would be Leslie Hall ... candles on old mahogany ... white stars of the dogwood blooming like a milky way along the dark wall of pines ... his father's eyes pledging him over the rim of a sangaree goblet ... the black Nancy mare nuzzling his cheek ... the ride to Gentle Hundred ... Evelyn....

The hours seemed to be lengthening, like the stretch of sunset water that lengthened slowly behind the *New Adventure*. He leaned far out over the cannon muzzle and eyed the packet's wake, trying to follow it back into the golden haze. He had, for a moment, a queer feeling that Evelyn was somewhere in that golden haze, and that she was going farther and farther away. There was no sense to it. He looked suspiciously at the almost-empty bombo glass in his hand, and it occurred to him that perhaps Dick Lawless was not the only one who had tasted too much rum-and-sugar. But there was no sense to that idea, either. Major Leslie felt certain that he could sit the Nancy mare over the stiffest jump in Maryland quite as steadily as he was sitting on Captain Todd's twelve-pounder.

Except for the intoxication of being almost home, he was perfectly—at least *almost*—sober.

He peered out again at the haze astern. It was dancing and golden, as the haze enveloping Arnett Leslie's future had always been; it was even tinged a little with roseate light as the sun went lower. But it was dwindling and dwindling. It was behaving exactly as if it were the haze over the past, instead of the future.

Leslie smiled and set the bombo to his lips. It had been a happy past; it deserved its golden haze and its tinge of rose. The future ...

Behind him, somebody else's glass clinked on the toddy bowl and shivered with a sloppy sound. A chair scraped across the planks, and a body fell against the table and hung there, scrabbling and grunting.

He turned slowly on his gun-barrel and saw that it was Dick, and that Dick was looking at him, as straight as he could for weaving and swaying. The young baronet's flushed face was working.

5

"You...Leslie," the twisting mouth managed to say, "you're a rich man's son. You're rich, but you're like everybody else in this plagued country of yours; you're all snobs. Think you're too damnation good for indented folk. Blast me, it's all 't other way around. They'll run you out o' your plaguey colony, and serve you proper when they do."

Leslie grinned and slid down from his cannon. Indented folk were a sore point with Sir Richard; there were sundry bond women on board the *New Adventure,* coming out to Maryland to serve their five years under articles to pay their passage, and Todd, who knew Sir Dick, had practiced divers schemes to keep them beyond his reach. Leslie walked to the table and held out his glass to be filled. He would not be forced into quarreling. Not today.

"Why, then, it's a plagued country, Dick," he said. "Stuart, have you hid the ladle? We'll drink to this blasted Maryland of mine, and confusion to all the top-lofty people in it." It occurred to him that the only way to be rid of Sir Dick and his bad manners was to drink him completely under the table and put him to bed.

Dick made a face at him, and splashed his glass full to the brim. They drank the toast, and Leslie, setting his glass down and wiping his wet fingers on his handkerchief, looked speculatively at Stuart and the Swiss. By their looks and by the feel of his own head, Dick Lawless and Kildane would not be the ones who were put to bed. Between their quarrelsomeness and their capacity for toddy, Sir Dick and his friend were more likely than not to ruin this last evening on shipboard. Arnett Leslie gave thought to reinforcements.

"Come, another toast," he suggested. "The indented folk. You can drink to that, Captain Barent. You'll find many a redemptioner enlisted in the Royal Americans." He raised his drink, and set it down again. "Todd, before we drink to our passengers of note, what do you say to having the indenture fellow in to drink it with us? Watson is adding a round forty to this colony of ours."

Todd stirred heavily in his chair and rumbled disapproval. Leslie looked expectantly at Sir Dick; he more than half hoped that the young baronet and his friend would refuse to drink with the man Watson, and take themselves off to their own cabin. But Lawless was nodding and sputtering with eagerness.

6

"D'you mean the soul driver, Leslie? Rabbit me, now, that's a thumping idea. I'd thought he would not be good enough for you. Damme, I did. I keep forgetting you are all tradesmen out here. That makes Watson one of you, eh? He's a respectable tradesman in live merchandise, what? Damned sweet merchandise, some of it. Look you, Todd, have him in, have him in. And tell him to bring that red-headed wench in with him."

Leslie instantly regretted his suggestion. He saw Todd frowning ponderously, shaking his head to rid it of the bombo fumes. There could be trouble in plenty from Sir Dick's meddling with the bond women. Dick cut his objections short.

"I knew you would be crawling out of it," he said truculently. " 'Fraid she'll dirty you, aren't you, Leslie? English gentlemen know better. Not 'fraid pretty wench will dirty 'em. Tha's it; can't dirty real gent'man, Leslie. Tha's diff'rence between dirty colonials and English gent'men. Todd, go fetch them."

The master of the *New Adventure* got reluctantly to his feet and lumbered to the cabin door. Lawless and Kildane clamored after him.

"The red-headed wench," Dick babbled. "The one i' the blue gown, Todd." He laughed and winked elaborately at Leslie. "Pinch me, we've been singing wenching songs all afternoon, and no wenches! 'S pity, Leslie. 'S damned pity."

Leslie put his glass down on the table and went back to his cannon. He wished Todd had told Lawless no, flatly. But Todd, he knew, had certain orders from my lord Baltimore respecting Sir Dick and his precious lordling, Kildane; he could scarcely refuse an order from either of them, so long as it had nothing to do with navigation. Sitting on the gun carriage, Major Leslie looked at the unsteady pair, busy filling fresh goblets for the new guests. Across the table, Barent was shifting restlessly in his chair and casting glances toward the door. Sir Dick, Leslie thought, was not the only one anxious to play host to the red-headed girl in the blue gown.

She was pretty enough to set them all to ogling the first day out of London. Todd had done a miracle to keep Lawless away from her so long. Leslie shrugged; he was tempted to take Robin Stuart up on deck for a look at the bay. Now, ten hours from home and Evelyn, he had no liking for a drinking party with an indentured woman. But he decided to stay; after all, it was his party. He objected to being driven away from it.

For a few minutes after Watson and the girl came in, he was glad he had stayed. It was not because the girl had red hair in a loosed cloud on her shoulders, or because she had freckles more deadly than beauty-patches on a skin that was more cream than white. It was not because the soul driver who would sell her for her passage money at Annapolis looked so ridiculously like a buzzard, with leathery wrinkles where his hair should be and a very beak of a nose. Dick and Kildane, bowing and sweeping the deck with their handkerchiefs, were funnier than any of the comedy gentlemen he had seen on the stage of Mr. Foote's Little Haymarket theater. He laughed and enjoyed himself, and saw even Stuart's long face soften at their antics. He laughed when Kildane plucked the girl by the sleeve and pulled her toward the cannon, waving a goblet as he came.

"Mistress Gail," he was simpering, "come look at the bridegroom. See him, all in white? Going home to be married, Di. Rich, and going home to marry beautiful girl...."

"Rich," Sir Dick said loudly in her other ear, and guffawed at Leslie. " 'Fraid you'd dirty him if you had drink with us."

Leslie stiffened. The girl, looking at him with gray eyes that were frightened and curious at the same time, saw his black eyebrows draw down into a straight line, and the skin of his dark face drawn up over his cheekbones until his eyes stared blackly out of narrowed lids. Between his powdered hair and his white stock and collar, the black brows and eyes were startling. She drew back a little, and Kildane put his arm around her.

"Sweet little baggage," Kildane smirked. "Here it's your last night 'way from home. Goin' home to beautiful bride an' flithy ... *filthy* money. Here's brisk wench, Leslie ... red hair ... neatest ankles west of London ... rest of her to match, I'll wager. Whyn't you find out, eh, Leslie?"

Leslie stood stiffly beside the gun-carriage. He knew that, across the table, Captain Stuart had gotten to his feet and was watching, his thin face alert. The agent, Watson, was twittering helplessly, his wrinkled face twitching. Todd set his untouched glass down on the table with a jerk. Leslie wondered why he himself was standing there without a word, gaping at the red-headed girl. There

8

was no reason why he should take offense at Kildane's last words; they were no more rude than the mildest of the gibes Lawless had flung at him during the afternoon. And the girl herself did not seem to resent them; she had not moved from the circle of Kildane's arm. She merely looked at Leslie with gray-green eyes.

Leslie smiled, stiffly.

"Mistress Gail," he began, "I . . ."

Kildane cut in with a new notion.

"I have it, Leslie," he said, and laughed loudly, "*buy* the wench!"

Sir Dick swore thickly, and reached out to clap him approvingly on the arm. He missed the arm, and his fingers struck the girl's bare back above the low-cut dress with a sharp spat.

"Rabbit me, there's a thought!" he gloated. "Heh! Buy her an' take her home to your lovely bride, Leslie. Prettiest lady's maid in all dirty colonies. An' you'll have her handy, Leslie, after the honeymoon, eh?"

Leslie bowed to the girl.

"Mr. Lawless is drunk," he said clearly. "I apologize for him."

He expected Lawless to resent it, but Lawless merely guffawed again.

"Drunk! Best idea I've had in fortnight, an' he says I'm drunk! D'you hear that, Watson, old soul driver? He says I'm . . . By God! I'll buy her myself!"

Leslie stepped quickly past the two, swaying and gabbling with the girl between them. He walked to Watson and spoke sharply.

"The price of the girl, Mr. Watson. I will pay it now."

The servant-trader's face seamed itself into a net of wrinkles as he gaped up at Leslie. He tried to find the table with his glass, missed it, and sent it crashing to the floor.

"Let be," Leslie told him bruskly as he dabbed at the stuff on his breeches. "The price—now."

Watson's thin lips moved soundlessly. At Leslie's back, a clear voice said:

"I do not wish to be indented to Mr. Leslie."

He wheeled on her.

"You were not asked, Mistress Gail."

Lawless chortled noisily, and came unsteadily across the cabin to put his arm around the girl's waist. His face bent close to hers. She did not move away, nor try to avoid the arm, or the murmuring lips. She looked at Leslie.

9

"I do not wish it. I am no concern of yours."

Leslie turned his back on her and touched Watson impatiently on the arm.

"I will not be your mistress," the clear voice told him, and Lawless laughed again.

"You will not be my mistress," Leslie answered her without turning his head. His hand went into the skirts of his coat and brought out a wallet. "You are no concern of mine. I shall pay Mr. Watson your passage and court charges. You will sign the indenture. I shall then set you free."

"Free ... ?"

"After that, what you do does not interest me. If your taste runs to Lawless and his kind, please your taste. You see," he looked at her briefly over his shoulder, "I am pleasing my taste. It is distasteful to me to see a woman *forced* to amuse Sir Dick in Maryland. It is our custom here, Sir Richard Lawless, to use the dirt in these dirty colonies of ours to grow tobacco, and to bury our dead." He turned full around and faced them; behind him, he heard Robin Stuart telling him, urgently, to sit down. "We do not care overmuch for your kind of dirt, Mr. Lawless."

He stared at the baronet for a moment, his eyes black between their tightened lids, his mouth flat and hard. Then he looked at the girl, and smiled broadly.

"Forgive me," he said, and bowed a little. "I should not have used you to convey my thoughts to Mr. Lawless. I should have told him what I thought several hours ago. I think perhaps you should go now. Mr. Watson will bring you the needful papers."

He saw that her bright face had gone suddenly the color of pale ivory, and that there were freckles on her nose. Her arms were straight down at her sides, stiff, as if her fingers were tightly closed. Her nose had a tiny, quivering flare about the nostrils. She looked, he thought, a good deal like the Nancy mare when she was excited—head up, eyes questioning, tense, more curious than afraid.

She moved away from Lawless and Kildane as if they were not there, and walked to the door, her arms still straight at her sides, her back like a small drum-major's. As she passed Robin Stuart, Leslie noticed that the top of her red head came barely to the bottom of the black facing below his shoulder. He grinned at Stuart. Spunky girl, she had walked out on them without a word;

she put them all in their places, he told himself, for bringing her into their rum-and-sugar affair at all. Stuart was gaping at him, and Leslie continued to grin back cheerfully as he plucked notes from his wallet and tossed them down in front of Watson.

He heard feet shambling across the deck, and kept his back turned toward them. The table shook as Lawless came against it and leaned there, muttering thickly.

Stuart's voice overrode the mutter.

"I say we all go on deck," he was saying. "Dick? Come along?"

Leslie felt a surge of warmth toward the Scot. Barely over the wound he had taken with the Black Watch at Havana, he was trying to draw Sir Dick's attention to himself, away from Leslie. Leslie shook his head at him over Watson's wrinkled poll. Stuart looked grave.

"Come along, Dick," he persisted.

But Lawless was ignoring him. He mouthed at Leslie, and raised his glass in a furious gesture. A few drops of rum thick with sugar flew out in a row, with a fine spray between them, and settled in a ragged brown line across Leslie's satin waistcoat. Stuart and Todd leaned forward together. Lawless clung wavering to the table edge, smirking at the stains on the white silk. At his back, Kildane cried out at him in a high, wild tone:

"Call him out, Dick! Call him out, and kill him!"

Major Leslie pulled his lace handkerchief from his sleeve and dabbed at the sirupy stains. There was a flush high on his cheek-bones.

"Mr. Lawless is in no condition to fight, Kildane," he said, "and I have other business. There was no insult in what I said to your friend; it was merely the truth, and no more offensive than a dozen things he said to me. These spots are the serious affront, sir, and it is my privilege to call out Mr. Lawless. I shall not call him out. You see," he smiled at Stuart, "I have more waistcoats, but very little more time."

Lawless stood at a slant against the table, his mouth contorting as if he could not make it fit around the words he wanted to use. Then, with a scream, he threw his dripping glass into Leslie's face.

"Coward!" he raved. "You'll not call me out, you coward! You'll not fight, because you're going to be married!" His voice began to tear, like coarse cloth, in jerks. "You'll hide behind a woman's panniers! Bah, you filthy colonials are all cowards. If you weren't, English gentlemen wouldn't have to come over here to fight your stinking battles for you. Why, you ... you ... that wench you bought is too damn' good for you! She's English. Go bed with that colony slut of yours...."

Major Leslie's hand struck him across the mouth.

He reeled away from the table, slipped on the sopped planking, and fell. Leslie caught him, and dragged him to the bench under an open port. He writhed up on one elbow as Leslie laid him down.

"Coward!" he screamed. "Coward!"

Stuart and Barent got him out of the cabin between them. The master of the *New Adventure* went lumbering up the companionway after them, and Leslie heard him shouting for a boy to come with a bucket and a mop. The boy came running, and fell to picking up pieces of broken glass.

Leslie went back to the gun-port. The breeze, he saw, had all but failed; the ship was moving so slowly through the green water that the wake had narrowed, like a fan that was almost shut. The golden haze had darkened; it had, now, the look of a cloud bank low on the horizon. A dark ending for a gorgeous day; an unpleasant ending for the voyage home.

He turned away from the darkening gun-port as feet clattered down the companionway. Stuart and Barent were coming across the cabin together.

"What possessed you, Arnett?"

"You'll have to fight him," Barent added, and wet his lips. Leslie looked at him curiously.

"Why?" he asked.

"Why?" the Swiss bleated in astonishment. "He will brand you a coward everywhere."

"And you would be obliged to confirm it?"

Barent's blunt face congested. "Damme!" he said plaintively to Stuart. "He strikes a baronet, and does not wish to give him satisfaction."

"I do not wish to murder him, Captain Barent."

"I stand with Major Leslie," Stuart's calm voice came in. "Mr. Lawless delivered the first insult, and many insults, which Major Leslie overlooked, out of consideration for the fellow's condition. It is my opinion that Major Leslie conducted himself with admirable restraint, and that what he did was done under unbearable provocation. I do not consider...ah, Captain Todd," as the shipmaster came lumbering back..."I was just saying that I do not consider Major Leslie under any obligation to meet Mr. Lawless."

Todd looked from Stuart to Barent and back again, combatively.

"Are you explaining Major Leslie's conduct to me," he growled, "or his courage?"

Barent cleared his throat. Todd swung on him, his shoulders thrust forward.

"Don't," he blurted. "I am no gentleman, to toe a peg and take pot-shots on a dueling ground. But I saw Major Leslie fight a gun here on the *New Adventure,* when the Frenchman caught us on the eastward passage, and their first broadside knocked a whole gun crew into the scuppers like so much mush. He fought that gun for three hours, sir. Don't explain Mr. Leslie to me."

He poked his big hand at Leslie, grumbling, and squeezed Leslie's fingers.

"I misdoubt you'll be a fool, and give him a shot at you," he growled. "It's a relief to be no gentleman, major."

"Oh, I'll fight him," Leslie said wearily.

"And fire first," suggested Barent. "That will be safe enough. The boy's no soldier."

"Barent...Barent!" Stuart protested.

The Swiss shook his blond head stubbornly.

"I consider that Major Leslie...how do you say?...egged the boy on. Sir Richard Lawless has asked me to be his second." He bowed stiffly to Captain Stuart. "You will be Mr. Leslie's, I presume?"

"If Major Leslie will have me," Stuart said warmly, and slipped his arm through Arnett's. "I am afraid we have different ideas of insults—and courage, Captain Barent."

Stuart pulled Leslie with him toward the companionway, and up to the packet's poop rail. Dusk had closed down upon the Chesapeake. The *New Adventure* was scarcely moving through the still water. Down in the waist, a girl hummed snatches of a tune. Feet scuffled, and a pulley creaked; something solid thudded on the deck, and rolled over with another thud. Leslie nodded toward the sound.

"My baggage," he told Stuart. "We are in the mouth of the

Patuxent river now. Todd was going to send a boat to Solomons Island to get a barge for me. I might have been home before morning."

"A pity," Stuart answered slowly. "Somehow I think you knew it would turn out this way. You held your temper, and yet at the end, you were...um...relentless."

Leslie put his elbows on the rail and stared off up the shadowy river that came down to meet the Chesapeake.

"Yes. I was."

"Why? You have so much to lose."

"I am not sure I can tell you. I knew this afternoon, I think, that this would happen. I felt it...you are right about that. Why? Too many months in London, perhaps, listening to men like Sir Dick. What he said this afternoon was nothing but what is said about us colonials by others, by many others, more important and more powerful than he. You will hear it, too, Stuart, at Annapolis, among the governor's friends there, and in Philadelphia, among the Quaker merchants.

"We get tired, sometimes, of being called cowards."

The highland captain leaned on the rail beside him.

"What does it matter," he asked, "when it is not true?"

"It does not matter. We get tired, that's all. It did not matter about that girl, and Lawless. Twenty miles up that river there, Stuart, is Gentle Hundred, and the girl I am going to marry. All at once, this afternoon, I could not see Lawless paw and maul that red-headed child, when she could not help herself. I made her free. If she wishes to be his plaything, she can choose. Perhaps it is just that we do not like to be forced, here in Maryland."

"Um. And what is it I am to hear at Annapolis, and from our round-hat friends in Philadelphia?"

"Why, that we hang back like cowards and cry for the king's troops to come and fight for our homes. You will hear that we Marylanders, in particular, will not even levy taxes to support the king's troops when they come. Well...

"The governor honored me with command of a company of militia, sent out to the frontier in '58. We were at Fort Cumberland, three companies, trying to guard a border ten thousand men could not guard effectively against scalping parties. We went to Bedford as garrison there when Forbes marched against the Forks of the Ohio. When he took Fort Duquesne, we came back to Cumberland. My sixty men served fourteen months without pay, without clothes, without shoes, without food except what they killed themselves. Twelve died, seven of them with their scalps ripped from their heads; five more I know are cripples, and will die cripples."

"That was when you were wounded?"

"Nothing. A tomahawk across the shoulder. Hundreds have done more, and been worse wounded. And for what? *This* is what makes Maryland men loath to hear themselves called names in Annapolis, at the governor's house, and in London, at my lord Baltimore's:

"My lord Baltimore, whose whole fortune comes from his proprietary of Maryland, declines to pay one farthing for the defense of the colony. He declines to permit our delegates to put upon his estates the same taxes they put upon their own. He will not pay tuppence to feed or arm or clothe the cowardly colonists who risk death at the torture stake to build a colony.... A colony? My God, an empire! For him!"

Leslie ran his fingers through his hair, careless of its powder and its ribboned queue.

"That, Captain Stuart, is the other side of the story. I think Mr. Lawless must have picked at my nerves a little." He laughed shortly.

Stuart laid an arm across his shoulders.

"Men used to speak like that about Scotland," he mused, half to himself. "Now we fight London's battles around the world. Havana...heat...plague...hell. Now this. What will this be like, I wonder." He shook himself, and tightened his arm on Leslie's shoulder. "Don't look so glum at your river, Leslie. A day or two more. You must fire first, major. You cannot risk even Sir Dick's wobbling hand; you mustn't be late for the wedding."

Leslie laughed, a clear happy laugh.

"I'll not be late. Somehow, I feel fortunate tonight. Do you notice, Stuart, how clean this new world smells?"

CHAPTER II

*In Which Major Leslie Aims at a Silver Button on a Baronet's Coat,
and Shoots a Leaf Out of an Elm Tree Instead:*

S IR RICHARD LAWLESS fired first.

The ball whiffed the sleeve of Major Leslie's brown coat,
and he heard it flick through the leaves of the crepe myrtle
behind him. He raised his own pistol deliberately.

Ten paces away, Sir Dick stood with his empty weapon clutched
in front of him, waist high. He looked at it, and then over his
shoulder toward the group of his friends under the honey locust.
His mouth worked. In his strained face, it was not pleasant to see—
his lips, loose, shuddering; his jaw muscles, tense, white, in unnatural ridges. Against the bright green of laurel and young locust
trees, his plum-colored coat made a perfect target. He had left it
unbuttoned and hanging loosely, to conceal the outlines of his body;
but there was a silver button just below the wide lapel, just over
his heart....

Like a bright new shilling set up as a mark in a shooting match
on court day, Leslie thought, and glanced at it along the barrel of
the pistol.

Then, abruptly, he raised his pistol hand straight up above his
head, and pulled the trigger.

The wooded banks of the Severn river threw the sound of the
explosion back and forth, until they shook out of it the last faint
echo. A twig from the elm overhead came slanting down and
struck the grass at Leslie's feet; a baby leaf no bigger than a squirrel's ear wandered erratically behind it and clung to the rough
stuff of his coat. Mr. Leslie plucked it off and put it between
his lips.

Sir Dick's friends were hurrying across the sparkling grass to
gather in an excited, gesticulating group. Captain Barent's cocked
hat jerked vehemently back and forth, and his scarlet sleeve waved;
once it pointed toward Leslie. Major Leslie nibbled reflectively at
his elm leaf.

"Will they ask another fire, Robin, do you think?" he asked his second, standing alone at the edge of the clearing. Stuart came slowly toward him, and Leslie saw that his face was whiter than it had been since the first day of warm sun on the *New Adventure's* deck.

He realized, with a feeling of warmth, that Stuart had been afraid for him. Under the sunburn, his skin was bloodless. He shook his head gravely as he approached.

"Ye're a middling fool, Arnett," he said, and took the empty pistol. "No, they'll not ask a second fire; look at him ... ye know they'll not. But ye might better have killed him than shamed his friends by making him tremble so. Why, in the Lord's name ... ?"

"I'll tell you at breakfast, Robin. Go talk to Barent, and have it over."

"If they insist on a second fire?"

"I'll not give it," said Leslie shortly. "See ... his ball drew blood." He pulled the stuff of his coat sleeve around where Stuart could see it, and thrust his forefinger through a neat round hole in the cloth. Probing, the finger found another hole to match the first, and poked its way through. Leslie waggled the end of it, calling attention to the smear of blood along the knuckle. "He drew blood. There's no obligation to fire again. I have reasons why I do not wish to kill him."

Stuart's face brightened a little.

"Ye're a fool for all that," he persisted. "Get down to the boat. I'll finish with them."

Major Leslie lifted his black tricorn and bowed to the noisy group around Lawless. Stuart plucked him impatiently by the sleeve.

"Be gone, now," he urged, tugging him toward the river. "Have a care for yourself and that sweet lady waiting for you. You've made an enemy in Barent; get you gone now, before we have him quarreling with you. His manners are no better than Sir Dick's, but his aim is steadier."

Leslie blew out the remnant of his nibbled leaf.

"Why, then ..."

But Robin Stuart brushed past him and stepped out across the grass toward Lawless and the knot of bright gentlemen around him. They turned to look at him, and their chatter quieted. Mr. Leslie considered whether he owed it more to Lawless and Barent to stay and be quarreled with than he owed it to Robin Stuart to go, since Robin was so urgent about it. He stood watching the Scot's swinging kilts and perky bonnet marching to meet Barent. The backs of Stuart's bare knees, he saw, were criss-crossed with scratches from the blackberry brambles he had stumbled into, coming up the path from the boat to the dueling ground. One of the scratches was deep enough to be edged with drops of blood. It struck Leslie suddenly that Robin Stuart, a stranger in a strange land, might well lose more than he in this quarrel with Sir Richard Lawless. For Lawless had powerful friends in Annapolis, in the governor's clique, and Maryland governors had a way of making life difficult for royal officers whom they disliked.

It occurred to Major Leslie that for Robin's sake he must let this quarrel end quickly. It had, he realized, an endless possibility of trouble for Stuart. For himself, it was not especially serious; the name of Leslie was powerful enough in Maryland to be protection against such minor lordlings as Lawless and Kildane. But Robin Stuart was a soldier; in spite of his scars, a vicious word spoken in the proper place might ruin him and his career. Leslie regretted that he had asked Robin to be his second; it would have been simple enough to find, at one or another of the plantations above Annapolis, some friend to do that service. Tom Yeardley, for one, would have pranced with delight, and put twenty guineas on the outcome.

Leslie smiled at the thought of Yeardley, who had been his right hand, and his left hand too, on the Cumberland patrol. It was hard to imagine two men less alike than Tom Yeardley and Robin Stuart. And yet, Leslie realized with a surge of affection for both of them, Stuart had become in a month and a half as close a friend as the other. He knew that Stuart, arranging the duel with Lawless, had been doing a piece of work as distasteful to him as it would have been pleasant to Tom. These swashbuckling affairs of pistols at ten paces were contrary to his nature. A waste of talent, he called them glumly.

Still, Leslie concluded, watching him stride up to Sir Dick's friends, he would undoubtedly fight Barent, or Kildane, or Lawless if any one of them spoke slurringly of Arnett Leslie. That was one consequence of this quarrel which must not be allowed to follow.

Leslie turned his back on the grass plot and pushed through the myrtle to the path that ran down to the Severn. It might delay him another hour on his homeward journey, he told himself, but he would stay in Annapolis until he had seen Robin Stuart into the saddle and on his way to Philadelphia.

He was sitting in the punt, whistling away at "The Juniper Tree," when Stuart came swishing through the brush and stepped aboard.

"I was afraid they had prevailed on you to eat breakfast with them, instead of me," he told Stuart gravely.

"Afraid!" Stuart picked up an oar and thrust it against the bank. "Afraid! You haven't the sense to be afraid of man or devil." He snorted reproachfully, and pushed the punt clear. "I hope the good Lord makes you afraid of your wife, Arnie Leslie."

Leslie reached out soberly for the oar and set it between its pins.

"My wife!" He glanced up at the face glowering from the stern seat. "It has a strange sound, Robin." His face and his voice took on a shyness that made Stuart's grim mouth relax a little. "Do you know, Robin, that is the first time any one has spoken of *my wife?* There has been no woman at all at Leslie Hall these five years. My mother was dead when I came back from Cumberland in '59."

He hesitated, his eyes following the ripples as he moved the oar aimlessly backward and forward through the crinkling water. He had, quite unexpectedly, the feeling that he was approaching a tremendous event. It was a feeling apart from anything he had experienced before, a feeling wholly apart from the thrill of home-coming, apart even from the imagined moment when he would feel Evelyn Gentle's welcoming kiss, and the pressure of her hands on his face.

"You know, Robin," he said again, more to himself than to the man who was beginning to smile at him, "it does have a strange sound. Plague me, I'm afraid already!"

Suddenly in a furious hurry, he snatched up the other oar and thrust it between the thole pins. The current swirled into eight green whirlpools behind the tugging blades. Stuart's blue eyes laughed at him and his red cheeks creased into deep wrinkles.

"Daft!"

Leslie's laugh rang out happily as he threw his weight into the oars. The punt shot out toward the south bank of the Severn, where the broad Annapolis chimneys were beginning to send slow streamers of smoke drifting across the elms and locusts.

"Not daft," Leslie told him, "but fortunate. Remember, I told you two nights ago that I felt fortunate? I am just beginning to realize how fortunate I am. We're going to celebrate, Robin. A Maryland breakfast—wild turkey, and sea bass, and corn pone, hot from the oven. And peach brandy and honey for your stirrup cup."

Stuart lay back on the seat and laughed outright. His voice burred.

"Ye're daft, a'right, Arnie Leslie. Ye're daft as a loon. And ye'll no more stickit in one place than yon weathercock in y'r wee town. One minute ye're wild to be havin' a wife, and the next ye're wild to be havin' y'r breakfast. Which will ye...?" He sat up sharply, his lower lip thrust out. "May the guid Lord...Arnie Leslie, what may *that* be?"

Leslie let the oars trail.

Stuart was gazing with a bewildered air at something ahead.

"I think ye're all daft in this wild place ye call America," he said, so plaintively that Leslie turned to look.

A low, weather-beaten boat with a chopped-off triangle of sail was wallowing stolidly across the bow of their punt. It was pointed at both ends, and from its unpainted gunwales on each side projected outriggers that had the look of clumsy, sprawling legs. With its outstretched legs and its sharp nose and tail, it was like a huge waterbug crawling across the harbor; its sail, close-hauled, might have been a water-insect's folded wings.

"That?" Leslie turned back to the oars again, grinning. "That's Maryland for you, Robin. That's a pungey—made of hollowed logs. That's an Indian dugout canoe, after white civilization got through improving it."

"Ay, ye may call it a pungey or whatever outlandish name ye wish. But for what are the wheels? I have no tasted the peach brandy and the honey, Arnie, but I see a prince's carriage out for a sail, I do."

"Ay," Leslie mimicked him, beaming, "so ye do. Master Todd has been unloading my baggage for me the morn'. It's a brave, blue carriage, is it not, Robin?" He let the oars run again and sat gazing at the pungey and its queer cargo as it ambled by. "It's my wedding present to...ay, laugh at me, ye sour Scotchman...it's part of my wedding present to my wife."

"Part of it?" Stuart protested, looking up at gilded moldings, bright glass, and a gay crest on the blue-paneled door of the traveling coach.

"The biggest part," Leslie conceded. "There's a dressing table Master Chippendale made, somewhere in those boxes under the carriage." He pointed, boyishly eager. "In the big box, below the boot, I think. And a spinet from a musicker's shop my lord Baltimore knew of, and a bed with blue harrateen to the curtains, and a gown or two I got in London, and a fan...."

He blushed, slowly, painfully, as he caught the twitch of Stuart's lips. The water gurgled around the oars, and the punt shot under the pungey's stern, where a negro steersman ducked his head and grinned. Stuart stretched out at full length and shook with laughter as the blood climbed up Leslie's temples among the roots of his black hair.

"Ye've taken a fearful bad case of sun-scald," he told Arnett, between fits of laughing. "What was it ye told me to daub on me when the sun burned *me* red? Bear's grease?"

And he would have his joke out, and laughed until his lean jaws ached as he dragged Leslie into an apothecary's shop in King George Street and paid a shilling for a burnt-earth jar of goose grease.

It took him half through the breakfast in the taproom of Mr. Sandys' ordinary to finish his laughter. It kept bursting out in spite of his best intentions, between mouthfuls of sea bass and wild turkey, until Leslie had to laugh, too, though his face burned with the heat of the blood in his cheeks and forehead. Master Sandys, shuffling across his sanded floor with their brandy and honey, thought them the merriest pair he had served since the house of burgesses adjourned three months ago.

Master Sandys' bald head reminded Leslie of an errand he had still to do in Annapolis. Across the skeleton of the turkey on its wooden trencher, he inquired whether Master Watson was still asleep.

"The soul driver, Major Leslie?" asked Master Sandys. "I'll have him down by his spindle-shanks if you want him, sir. He'll be down three steps at a jump if I tell him you wish to buy a brisk lad or two for Leslie Hall."

"I'm buying nobody."

"Oh. Ay. There'll be no need, eh? Plenty of indented folk, and slaves too, now that Leslie Hall and Gentle Hundred will be one manor."

He bustled away up the stairs, and went bawling down the hall for Master Watson.

"Can they tell a bridegroom by the color of his face, here in Annapolis?" asked Robin slyly. "And the name of the bride, too?"

"Oh." Leslie scrubbed the grease from his fingers onto one of Master Sandys' towels. "The whole colony knows it. We have been betrothed these three years, and would have been wed, too, but for the crack I took of a Shawnee tomahawk. D'you see, her father would not have her wed a cripple who was like to die and leave her with children...." His face went redder than before. Sobering, he leaned impulsively across the table. "Come with me to Leslie Hall, Robin. Stand up with me at the wedding, as you did this morning."

Stuart's face sank back into its wonted gloom. His bony fingers reached out briefly and touched Leslie's hand.

"I canna," he burred. "Ye ken the colonel is waiting in Philadelphia, an' my lord Amherst will be havin' me go look at this will woods of yours. I'll gie ye mony a thocht while I'm crossin' the mountains ye've fought in, Arnie." He fished out his handkerchief and snorted into it. "Atten-*shun*...here's Master Watson."

The indenture agent looked more like a buzzard than ever. His wrinkled neck rose out of his shirt-band without a stock to hide it; when he stood bowing beside the table, it gave his thin cheeks and round eyes the look of a hungry bird. His pinched nose pecked and pecked at the air as Leslie told him to sit down, pushed a pewter mug and the brandy bottle toward him, and took out his wallet.

"You gave the girl—what's her name...?"

"Gail, sir. Diantha Gail, sir."

"You gave her the proper paper?"

"Ay." Peck, peck at the air. Peck, peck into the mug of brandy. "Ay, indeed, sir. Before we came ashore, sir."

"She is not with the indented servants now?"

"Oh, no, sir. You said as she was to come ashore a freed-woman, sir."

"Free, Master Watson. Not a freed-woman; *free.*"

"Oh. Ay." Watson's eyes peered at Leslie over the rim of the mug. "Entirely free, sir. She is stopping at the Sign of the Three Blue Balls, sir. I assured the landlord, sir, that I...that you, sir..."

"Quite so. She has no money. Here." Leslie took a package from the wallet and pushed it across to Watson. "Ten guineas for her, and one for yourself. And a paper with my address; give that to her, also, and make a note of it. I wish you to send me a receipt, in her hand, to Leslie Hall. I wish you to tell her that if she is in need of friends, Mistress Leslie and I..." he smiled at Stuart... "will be glad to know of it. Make clear to her, Master Watson, that she is under no obligation. You understand?"

Watson's beak lifted out of the brandy.

"No obligation? Oh, a great obligation, Major Leslie, if I may say so. I feel it, and I hope the red-headed chit feels it, too, sir. She must feel it."

Leslie's eyes narrowed.

"I say, no obligation, Master Watson. Mistress Gail is no longer indented. Leslie Hall will welcome her as a guest at any time."

A great light dawned in Master Watson's birdlike eyes.

"I understand. I understand." Peck, peck over the pewter mug.

"I doubt it," said Leslie, his nostrils tightening as if at a faintly unpleasant odor. "Send me a receipt in her hand, if you please."

"If the chit...if Mistress Gail has learnt the art of writing." Watson bobbed up as Leslie rose and pushed back his chair. "Happiness to you and your lady, sir." He bowed and scraped, his shoes gritting on the sanded floor.

"The girl's mark, then, sworn by a notary," Leslie told him sharply.

He went quickly to the door and out into the street. Watson bowed again as the major and the highlander turned into the stableyard.

"Ugh," Leslie said. "I'll feel cleaner when the *New Adventure* has taken him back to London."

"You gave him ten guineas," Stuart reminded him.

"Eleven. Pho, he'll not dare cheat. It would mean hanging."

"If he could be hanged. By the look of him, he would fly away with the rope. A proper gallows bird. Ye're a lovable fool, Arnie, and a trusting one. For a' that, I'm glad ye took the bit lassie out of his claws, and out of Master Dickie's claws, too. I ken the money means nought to ye, but God bless ye for a daft one."

He fell to bawling for a stable boy to fetch his saddlebags and his horse.

"The money," Leslie repeated, and laughed a little. "I promised to tell you why I let Sir Dick fire first."

"Not for *money....*"

"Ay, for money, Robin. I'm not such a sentimental fool as you think. D'you remember Sir Dick calling me a rich man's son? I am just that. Some day—a far day, I hope—Leslie Hall will belong to me, with its thousand acres, and all that. But by then, Robin, there'll be another Leslie Hall, if all goes well. And that is why I shot a leaf out of an elm this morning instead of the heart out of Sir Dick's plum coat:

"I've warrants from my lord Baltimore to three thousand acres out beyond South Mountain. That is my fortune—three thousand acres, and the coach you saw, and some gear to fit a room or two for a woman. Father will lend me the slaves to clear a little of the land, and build us a house. From that on, Robin, I am a poor man." He laughed again, apologetic, "I chatter like a barmaid. You see, I do not wish you to think me altogether daft. I cannot afford to have my lord Baltimore snatching back my land grants because I have killed his precious Lawless for him."

Stuart snorted.

"An' ye give ten guineas to a girl whose name ye canna remember. An' ye buy her free for a whim. How much did that cost, now? Eighteen pounds more! No, Arnie, ye are not daft. Ye're just God's fool, so ye are."

There was a saddled horse waiting for him in the stableyard of the Duke of Cumberland tavern. Mounted, he leaned across the nag's neck to assure Leslie again:

"Ye're no' daft. Any daft one is a wise man along o' ye, Arnett Leslie." He flapped the reins. "Gie the sweet lady a kiss for me!"

Leslie flung the pot of goose grease after him. At the corner, Stuart turned to wave; his short jacket perked up behind; his feather bobbed out of sight behind the red brick wall. Leslie faced about and went briskly toward the harbor. In some ways, he told himself, this unpleasant morning when he had let Sir Dick shoot at him had been the pleasantest he had ever spent.

Swinging into Main street, past the white stone stoop of the Indian King tavern, he began to whistle. Master Norris, busy with sanding his taproom floor, looked up and hailed him through the open door, and would have stopped him. But Leslie flourished one hand in greeting and kept on; the affair of Sir Dick had wasted too much time already. He quickened his stride, and changed his tune to match it. He was whistling "The Juniper Tree" as he came by the leaded windows of John Ball's public house, and saw the three blue balls like overgrown, impossible plums hanging above the door. The door was closed. Overhead, somewhere, a shutter creaked, and a kettle banged and clattered.

Leslie veered out into the middle of the street, lest some chamber wench busy with pitchers and basins douse him from the upstairs windows. Looking over his shoulder, he saw the blue shutters ajar at one dormer window, and a bare arm waving. He waved his hand at it, and blew it a kiss in sheer light-heartedness. Master Ball's hostelry, he thought, must still be housing some of the gay ladies who made the winter interesting at the theater down the street. They would be glad that Sir Dick and his friend Kildane had come to town.

His lips puckered to whistle merrily again as he hurried out along the wharf where the log canoe waited for him.

CHAPTER III

*In Which Mr. Leslie Tastes a Kiss from a Scarlet Mouth, and a Flower
from a Scarlet Tree, and Finds Both Bitter:*

A BARGE lay moored to the pilings of the wharf. Arnett
Leslie jumped down to its broad stern seat, climbed its gunwale, and sprang recklessly to the outrigger of the log canoe
beyond it. In three quick steps he was up the arm of the outrigger
and aboard the pungey.

The black boatmen gaped at him. The outrigger was wet and
slippery; running along it in his heeled slippers, he should by
rights have slithered off into neck-deep water. He laughed happily,
and shouted to the negroes to cast off; he had never felt, before,
quite so sure of himself; even in the red heels, he knew that he
could not have missed his step on the outrigger—not on this day
certainly. This day was his.

The slim pungey was crowded with his baggage. There was
barely room to squeeze through between the wheels of the traveling
coach and the gunwales on either side. Leslie stood a minute beside
the boat, his hand on the blue paneling, while the boatmen loosed
the ropes and pushed the clumsy canoe clear of the wharf in a
flurry of splashing oars used paddlewise. Bending to try the silvered
handle of the door, to make sure that it was tightly shut and
latched, he caught his reflection in the coach window. The reflection smiled at him, and he smiled back and nodded. *Daft!* It felt
good to be daft. In a few days, now, he would be looking in through
that window at Evelyn Gentle. In a few weeks, at Evelyn Leslie.

He looked down with satisfaction at the red and gold and black
crest on the door—the bearings of the Gentles and the Leslies,
quartered together. Before he knew it, his fingers were touching the
hawk's head of the Gentle crest. The combined bearings pleased
him much more than the Leslie crest ever had; the heraldic lamb
was honorable enough, of course; it went back, he knew, to the
days of the great crusade when a black lamb on a golden shield

26

had ridden into battle at the left hand of the lion-hearted Richard himself. But a lamb—even a lamb approved by the heralds—was still a lamb. He smiled again at the reflection in the window, and then smiled at himself for smiling.

The bob-tailed mainsail spread itself to a shrill creaking of its sprit and a sing-song, muted chorus of Negro voices. The pungey turned its sharp nose to the Chesapeake and its sharp tail to the high gable of John Ball's tavern and began to crawl out of the harbor. Leslie walked aft, among the piled-up clutter of his London boxes and trunks, and sat down on a seat covered with leather cushions. The leather was stiff with salt and stained with grease from many wallowings up and down the Chesapeake; there were fish scales plastered on some of the cushions. A trickle of water ran between his feet as the pungey heeled to the first strong breeze beyond the point. Leslie spread his legs wide on a brass-bound trunk and his arms along the stained pillows, and let his breath run out in a long grateful exhalation.

Home...the log canoes were always wet. They were heavy, awkward things, crude as the new world was crude; but they had a way of doing their work, no matter how much they leaked or how much they wallowed. Smoked deerhide cushions, fish scales, hushed voices chanting, water slapping the stolid bows that were hewn from whole logs...it was home...it was Maryland.

A gust of wind came darkling down the bay and struck the towering sails. Green water came piling over the gunwale as the canoe dipped. The sing-song chant broke off in a high cry. Up over the higher gunwale scrambled two black boys, barefooted, shirtless, fingers and toes gripping the arms of the outrigger. Agile as monkeys, they ran out over the foaming water to the slim sapling trunk that formed the outrigger itself, turned and squatted there. Slowly, stodgily, the log canoe righted itself. The buried gunwale emerged; the log on which the Negroes crouched swung down until it skimmed the crests of the waves and the water boiled across their bare feet.

Leslie's arms stretched happily along the stiff, smelly cushions, and his heels began to tap on the brass-bound trunk as the chant took up again:

> 'Possum's in de co'nfiel',
> Buzzard's on de limb....

Leslie looked at the moving shore and at the green water racing by, and spoke to the Negro at the tiller behind him:

"If this wind holds, we'll catch the turn of tide at Solomons."

"Yas, *suh*. Dat right."

The wind held; in mid-afternoon it swung into the north, and the pungey changed its gait; instead of galloping, it began to run with the smooth ease of a pacer. The waves ran with it, but the pungey was faster; it caught them, one foaming white-cap after another, climbed their green backs, and rode them. The sails puffed themselves out like cheeks. No, Leslie decided, watching them, they were too big for cheeks. They looked more like fat, sleek tavern-keepers, with stomachs that bulged above and below their belts; the sprits across the middles of the sails made them look amazingly like fat bellies too tightly belted. The crew sat on the spray-wet thwarts and sang, and one of the boys came with a woven basket full of oysters and crouched at Leslie's feet to shuck them. Leslie ate an amazing quantity, with a square of crisp corn cake on his knee and a bottle of apple wine tucked between the cushions beside him, and felt still nearer home.

Corn cake...apple wine...oysters in their own plates...*home*. He wanted to spring up, to fling his arms, to shout. My lord Baltimore was an idiot to stay drinking and gambling and wenching in London, when this paradise of a new world belonged to him. Zooks, what a gift the king gave the Calverts when he gave them Maryland! And they would not so much as look at it now. Leslie brushed the crumbs from his knees and stretched out again on the deerhide. 'Y *gad,* Lord Baltimore could have his England; it was cold and plagued with fogs, and it smelled vilely, and strewed garbage underfoot in its best streets. Arnett Leslie, he told himself fervently, would make better use of his three thousand acres than Frederick, Lord Baltimore, had made of his whole colony.

He fell to planning the limestone manor house that he would build on the westward slope of South Mountain. It would be broad and ample, tall and gracious, strong and gentle all at once; downstairs, the windows must be shallow, and high above the ground, with stout shutters and iron bars, and loopholes like thin slots below them; if the Indian nations rose again, the settlers along the Cumberland trail need not flee pell-mell into Baltimore; his house and Tom Yeardley's, on the next spur, would be their

28

rallying places, stone-walled, impregnable. He began to smile to himself. They would mean something, those two manor houses. They would mean a new frontier for Maryland—not a flimsy frontier of log cabins and truck-patches, to be abandoned at the first whisper of danger, but a fortified frontier, ready to fight. *Lord...Lord...*it was worth fighting for, this paradise called Maryland. It had been good to the Leslies, and the Leslies had been ready, always, to fight for it. He would be only carrying on the traditions of five generations when he built his new Leslie Hall on South Mountain; the Leslie Hall where he was born had been a fortress, too, a hundred years ago.

He began to wonder whether another five generations would come to dwell in the new one. Taking himself as the first generation, he began to count with his fingers, raising them, tapping them down on the leather cushion. If he had a son, his name would be Amidon; and *his* son would be named Arnett; and *his* son would be Amidon again. It had been so since the first Amidon Leslie had taken his grant from the first Lord Baltimore, and come out from England with the prescribed "twenty able men, each with musket, sword, belt, and bandolier, ten pounds of powder and forty pounds of bullets." He tapped down another finger, and smiled again: a hundred years from now there would be another Arnett Leslie. Perhaps on such a day as this, that great-great-grandson would come sailing home to take a bride as lovely as Evelyn....

Gadzooks, that was expecting a bit *too* much.

He laughed aloud, and looked at the shore. It was climbing already into reddish banks; the sun was almost down, but those rising bluffs meant that Solomons Island was not far ahead. The pungey would catch the turn of the tide, and the tide would bear it up the Patuxent; he would be home before dawn; in the morning he would see Evelyn.

He dozed on the leather cushions, missed Solomons altogether, and woke to find the moon a silver plate in the sky behind him and the Patuxent a polished pewter platter on which the pungey lay.

The sails, he realized, were down; the wind was gone. The stars were out, thick as powder on the shoulders of a blue-cloth coat. The four boatmen swayed backward and forward in slow rhythm, bent above the oars. They were chanting softly, a chant that was only hushed sounds far back in their mouths, with only a word here and there. Away to right and left, solid black smudges stood between the river and the spangled sky. Somebody, Leslie thought drowsily, must have set the pewter platter down between two charred sticks; the smudges looked like charcoal; they were uneven along their upper edges, with projecting points that might have been stubs of burned-off limbs. Studying them, he saw the lowest stars slide backward out of sight behind the highest of the black points, and decided that the points were trees—pine trees. They marched across the stars, slowly, almost stealthily; but they moved. That, he assured himself, meant that the pungey was moving, too; he sat up to make certain of it. At his back the steersman spoke softly:

"Time to sleep mo', Majo' Leslie. Us los' de win' bouten a hour ago. De tide he still pushin' good an' strong."

Leslie peered at the moving smudges against the stars.

"Where are we, Bob?" he asked finally.

"Us jes' pass Mist' Allenden's wharf, majo'. Hit's behin' de trees on de high hill, so de lights don' show no mo'."

"Twenty miles," Leslie said.

"Yas, suh. A little risin' twenty, river way. Home fo' breakfus'."

He slept again, and felt a hand nudging his shoulder, and heard the same muted voice:

"Pret' near dere, Majo' Leslie. Yo' kin see de chimleys."

He started up eagerly. The river had gone dark, and the four rowers were a moving blur. The moon had traveled while he slept and gone on ahead; it hung now far down the sky, just to one side of the masts. Against it rose four black rectangles, like toy blocks on end. Leslie drew a deep breath. Home....

He spoke to the Negro behind him:

"Did they row all night?"

"Yas, suh. No, suh. Dey spelled off like. Home *befo'e* breakfus', Mist' Leslie. Bouten a hour yit."

The nose of the pungey swung a little and the four chimneys marched across the moon and disappeared. Leslie stood up and took off his coat and laid it on the seat, unbuttoned his waistcoat and laid it on the coat, loosened the stock about his neck.

"I'm going to swim a little while," he said. "Keep on rowing."

Undressed, he stood on the gunwale, and dived into black water between the arms of the outrigger. *Ugghh,* he had forgotten how cold the Patuxent could be; it made the breath shrink in his lungs. He came up gasping, his long hair in his eyes; he had forgotten the jerk and swing of the head that plastered it back smoothly, and dived again to get it into place. He had not, at least, forgotten how to swim; the pungey had crawled a dozen lengths ahead, but he caught it without effort and swam alongside. A glow spread through his body; his body stretched out, glorying in the thrust of the current against it, thrusting back joyously; his arms reached out for more and more of the river. It was his river; he had fallen into it when he was three, swum across it when he was seven, fished in it, sailed on it; it had borne his barge when he went courting to Gentle Hundred. Now it was bearing his bridal gifts home to Evelyn. *By zookins,* it was doing more than that! It was bringing Evelyn her husband. Mustn't forget himself. He arched his back and dived, deep, deeper. Turned, and pulled himself up, swimming with powerful strokes, an explosion of energy. Shot, head and shoulders, above the surface. Whooped like a boy; whooped again, like a red Indian, and heard the eerie quaver of it come back across the water.

He knew, by the echo, that he and his boat were close under the yellowish bluff that marked the down-stream boundary of Leslie Manor. It was invisible, but he could see it, every rain-cut seam, every bush, every low cedar at its brim, every locust and elm behind the cedars. Sobering, he began to scrub himself with his hands. Pudding-head! He should have shaved; his face was like a pin-cushion.

He overhauled the canoe and the Negro, Bob, helped him up over the stern. He had no towel, so he rubbed himself with the brown coat, and used the breeches to dry his dripping hair. Then, standing on the deerskin cushions, he dressed himself in the white satin he had donned three days ago for his homecoming, and swore a little when his fingers touched sticky spots on the front of the waistcoat. *Lawless* ... he should have spanked the tipsy fool for throwing the bombo at him, instead of wasting time on decorum and pistols. There was a raw place on his elbow where Sir Dick's ball nicked him; he minded the spots on his waistcoat much more.

The pungey swung sharply to the left. Leslie, busy with tying a ribbon to his damp club of hair, saw the chimneys of Leslie Hall come marching back across the moon. They were tall, arrogant chimneys, broad, deep chested, square shouldered. They stood above the dark bulk of Leslie Hall like grenadiers on parade. *Home....*

The pungey crept toward them, into the darker darkness under the ancient willows that lined the shore, a single oar stroking slowly. The outrigger touched a solid object, slid, bumped again. Leslie saw the dim shape of a piling, and stepped to the gunwale. The outrigger nosed past the post; the wharf came level with his chin. He put out his hand and touched it, gripped it ready to spring. The Negro Bob stirred and came scrambling over the seat.

"Majo' Leslie, heah. Ah fo'got de box. Mist' Capt'in Todd give it to me to hand yo'. Heah." He pushed a shallow wooden case against Leslie's arm, and Leslie took it. It was quicker to take it than to put it down. He sprang for the wharf and began to run.

Dark as it was, he could see. He could have seen with his eyes shut; the very noise of the planks under his heels was familiar; he could tell by the sound that he was half way to the shore; the water became abruptly shallow there, and the drumming of his feet was also shallower.

Even the smells were as they should be: just at the water's edge, a nose-prickling odor of wet soil, of water weed, a suggestion of decay; then the smooth smell of grass; then, where the path dipped, a faint tang of tobacco from the storehouse at the foot of the rolling road—it was always there, on still summer nights, a band of scent as tangible as the first terrace of the lawn was tangible to his feet. And then a smell that was not a smell at all, but a presence in the air, a feeling of flowers everywhere: the Judas tree was blooming. Passing it, he looked up, and saw its branches lacy against the sky. Just beyond it, his heels rang on the brick walk.

He could not see the walk at all, but he knew every brick of its herring-bone pattern. Felt, with a tightening of every nerve, the soft ridge of moss that grew in a long crack across the walk. It had been there twenty years. Queer that he should step on that; it gave the last fillip of sensuous pleasure to these perfect minutes.

He ran up the broad steps, between the ghosts of white pillars, and put his hand on the latch. The door swung heavily open. Ponderous old door, its four-inch oak was hewn a hundred years ago to stand against ravaging Senecas and Nanticokes, with iron sockets to keep it closed. He'd like to have that door for the new manor house on South Mountain. Amidon Leslie would like the notion, too.

He crossed the great hall between the fireplaces and took the dark stairs two at a time, and never thought of stumbling. This was his day; another day, but still his. He went eagerly to the second door from the stairway head, pushed it lightly, and strode to the canopied bed between the front windows. His voice shook a little:

"Father. Father."

His hand touched Amidon Leslie's shoulder.

He stepped back.

There were two heads on the wide pillow. Arnett Leslie turned and went on tiptoe to the door and closed it behind him. Standing in the hall, he thought that perhaps he should go to his own room and go to bed. Anything else would be quite unmannerly. Embarrassing. He was, himself, painfully embarrassed. He stood and stood. After a while it occurred to him that there was no necessity, actually, for being uncomfortable. *Gadzooks,* he had been to London; he had learned somewhat of the ways of gentlemen there.

And he had been away almost a year. He desired to see his father now, not three hours from now. If Amidon Leslie wished not to be alone in his great bed and had found himself a mistress to share it, he was setting no precedent. He had, his son reminded himself, been five years a widower. He had been utterly faithful to his wife; he had been faithful to her memory for a long time. He would have no apologies, feel no embarrassment. The Leslies were like that. They went ahead in their own way. Arnett Leslie put up his knuckles and rapped loudly on the door. Instantly he heard his father's voice:

"Yes. Wait a moment."

Footsteps came unhurriedly across the room, the latch clicked, the door opened, and closed.

"You're back, Arnett."

"Yes, father. I'm back."

"Romney Clawther came up river yesterday from Solomons. He had heard that you were on the *New Adventure.*"

"Yes."

It was all strangely stiff and unnatural. Amidon Leslie pulled

33

his bedgown more tightly around him. It struck Arnett Leslie that his father was, after all, acutely embarrassed.

"Your room is ready, Arnett. Shadrach made some sangaree. It is on the table. Warmish, I'm afraid. I'll come in a minute."

Arnett found himself bowing, a slight inclination, formal and absurd. It was too dark there in the hall to see a bow. He realized that he, too, was embarrassed, ridiculously embarrassed. He should put his arm around Amidon Leslie's shoulders and say:

"Come along. We'll drink to her. I'm home. Nothing else is important."

He did not say it. He went, instead, down the long hall, around the turn, to his own room. Fumbling, he found flint and steel in their old place on the mantel, found tinder in its box, and his particular clumsy iron candlestick alongside it. The wooden case under his arm was in his way, and he went across the room to his trestle table and set it down; even the silver punch bowl was in its rightful place; his hand touched it familiarly. Everything was familiar, except Amidon Leslie ... and, he added, himself.

Lighting the candle on the mantel and the three in the brass stand on the table, he undertook to deny that admission. If there had been an uncomfortable moment, it was past. It was not important that his father had brought a woman to Leslie Hall. As a matter of fact, it would have been proper and natural if he had married a year ago, two years ago. He frowned, and dipped the ladle into the sangaree, and filled two goblets. He was not at all surprised when Amidon Leslie, standing in the doorway, said quietly:

"She is not what you think, Arnett. She is no light-o'-love."

Arnet smiled at him across the table, and raised a goblet.

"I didn't think so, father. You are married."

The older man's lips twitched once.

"They told you at Annapolis."

"No." He felt awkward again at his father's awkwardness. Desired, somehow, to tell him that it was quite all right. "Come. Here's your cup. A toast to the new lady of Leslie Hall." Was that disloyalty to the woman who was dead? He did not know; it was, rather, loyalty to the man who lived. "Who is she, father? Do I know her?"

Amidon Leslie's eyes met his son's straightly.

34

"Yes. It is Evelyn."

Arnett Leslie's eyes met his father's straightly.

"To Evelyn Leslie," he said, and put his cup to his lips.

When it was empty, he set it down. He had not realized that the table was so high; the pewter rang loudly on the wood. He had not realized, either, that the room was so wide and long. It seemed to grow immeasurably, to have no walls at all. He had, for a moment, a queer sense of being alone in a high place. The high place was cold, and the cold had gotten somehow into his bones. Amidon Leslie said steadily:

"We were married two months ago."

Arnett's fingers touched the wooden case on the table beside the sangaree bowl. There was, it appeared, a key tied to a heavy cord around the box; he looked down and saw it in his fingers. The box and the key were tangible. Gazing at them intently, he put the key into the lock and turned it, and put the cover up. From the doorway his father said:

"Very well."

Arnett looked at him curiously, and then back at the opened case. The candlelight shone on dark metal and rich wood. Todd, he saw, had given him a pair of dueling pistols. No, not dueling pistols. Boarding pistols. He slipped his fingers around the mahogany butt of one and lifted it out.

"I never saw these before," he said, and smiled. "Captain Todd gave them to the free Negro Bob along with my baggage this morning, and Bob forgot to give them to me. Look...." His thumb pressed a catch at the side of the grip. From the top of the barrel, a slim, three-edged knife flew up like the opening blade of a clasp-knife; with a click, it settled into position like a bayonet, projecting a foot beyond the pistol's muzzle. "D'you see, it has a misericord fitted to it on a hinge and spring? They're boarding pistols. I saw one like them on the frigate *Royal George;* her lieutenant of marines had one." *

Amidon Leslie walked to the table and leaned over it. Arnett handed him the weapon.

"Why did you do it, father?"

---

* Commodore Joshua Barney, distinguished officer of the American navy in the Revolution, owned a pair of boarding pistols similar to those presented to Arnett Leslie by the owners and master of the *New Adventure.*

Amidon raised the pistol and sighted it at the wall, past his son's shoulder.

"They're not loaded?"

"I haven't looked. Not likely. They are not primed."

They smiled at each other.

"I thought you were about to kill me," Amidon Leslie said.

"I ought to. And her, too."

"No. You asked me why I did it. Because I wanted her."

They smiled again. The smiles deceived neither; it was the Leslie way. The first Amidon Leslie, tradition had it, smiled gravely to himself as he pulled his oar in Captain Cornwaleys' pinnace in the first naval battle fought on the inland waters of the new world, and kept on smiling when a slug from the Claiborne galley's first volley took him in the back.* Rowing into action with his bloody back to the enemy, he had smiled broader and broader until his lips drew back and left his teeth bare. He helped beat Captain Claiborne's men very badly, and haul them prisoner to St. Mary's. Now, these younger Leslies, the third Amidon of the line facing the third Arnett, stood and smiled at each other with grave courtesy. The son pushed the untasted goblet toward his father, and ladled his own full again.

"You wanted her," Arnett said, and nodded slowly. "You knew she did not want you. She wanted Leslie Hall and forty slaves and a thousand guineas a year."

"No doubt."

"Are you fool enough to think she loves you?"

"My son calls me a fool...."

"No. Not your son."

"I see. I am disinherited, is that it? No, I am not fool enough to think she loves me. I am hungry; you are greedy. Youth always is greedy, and must have surfeit water to cure it. Evelyn does not love me; she preferred me. Therefore, being hungry but not greedy, I took what she offered. You are young, Arnett...."

The son struck the table once with his knuckles.

"Let be! I like you better without excuses. I even admire you.

---

* Fought on the Pocomoke river in Maryland, April 23, 1635, between the pinnaces *St. Helen* and *St. Margaret*, commanded by Captain Thomas Cornwaleys, and the pinnace fitted out by Captain William Claiborne to dispute possession of certain Maryland territory.

It is difficult for a white man to be more treacherous than an Iroquois."

"You do not let me finish," Amidon Leslie complained. "Being young, you were greedy of this indigestible pasty they call love; it has not agreed with you. You will be very sick for a little while, but it will not kill you; you will eat again."

"I think it would stick in my throat," Arnett said, not intending it for an answer. The situation had, he thought, made him actually a little ill. His head felt like beef jelly in a dish. If he took it in his hands and shook it, it would quiver with the thick, stiff motion of jelly. He held it still. Amidon Leslie's voice began again:

"If you had been content to stay here, it would not have happened." He saw his son's teeth between drawn-back lips, and his speech quickened. "No. No. I do not mean London. I had no idea, when I urged you to go to London.... I mean you would not stay here, live here at Leslie Hall; you would go out into the wilderness like any Dutch farmer, like any bond servant when his indenture is up. It was that crazy scheme of yours to dig and hew a new manor out of South Mountain that frightened her. You cannot blame her."

No, he could not blame her. Arnett Leslie saw that quite clearly. She had been very sensible. Evelyn, he realized, had not married his father; she had married the fourth largest estate in Maryland, a thousand acres, a manor house, forty slaves, eighteen horses, a yearly crop of excellent tobacco. Amidon Leslie was incidental. If the girl who married the first Amidon Leslie had been as sensible as Evelyn Gentle, there would have been no Leslie Hall for Evelyn to marry. He wondered whether that stout Amidon who fought against Claiborne and his pirates would have married his own son's betrothed. He felt, for some reason, closer to that first Amidon than he did to the third who stood opposite him, watching him over the rim of his sangaree goblet. He felt, for some reason, stronger than his father.

It was not that there was any sign of weakness about the face behind the goblet or about the hand that held it; Amidon Leslie's hand was perfectly steady, his eyes coolly alert, his mouth smiling. The weakness was inside, a flaw no one else would think of as a flaw at all. On the contrary. Arnett Leslie could visualize the delightedly scandalized smiles that greeted the news of his father's marriage in the manors along the Patuxent, and in the governor's house and the coffee house and the taprooms at Annapolis. *Life in the old dog yet. Headlong, romantic devils, these Leslies.*

It would occur to no one, Arnett assured himself, that Amidon Leslie had compromised with softness. It would occur to no one that he had been dishonorable. Clever, rather; and a gay, dashing fellow to sweep the beautiful Evelyn Gentle off her feet when he was past fifty, and she not yet eighteen.

Arnett Leslie fumbled behind him for the chair that should be there, found it and pulled it up.

"Sit down," he suggested, and felt in the skirts of his coat for the pocket hidden there. He brought out a folded paper, sat down, and spread the sheets on the table.

"There was a balance of twelve hundred pounds to our credit with Galt and Son," he said, naming Amidon Leslie's agent in London. "The tobacco added to that eight hundred sixty-two pounds, three shillings, tuppence. I wrote you that," he appended, glancing at his father. Amidon Leslie was frowning. "I drew on Mr. Galt for six hundred guineas, for myself; it is set down here." He pushed a creased slip across the boards. "You will want to enter the items in your accounts."

"Yes. Yes. Certainly. Tomorrow...."

"Then, on this sheet, there is the sale of the lodge at Romsey, and of the farm, the cattle, the horses; I wrote you, I think, that it seemed best to sell the horses, since our Maryland breed is as fast on the flat, and surer on the jumps. It brought, altogether, not quite a thousand pounds. It should be set down, I suppose, on the clerk's record at Annapolis."

"Yes. Yes." The older man's fingers put new creases in the columns of figures, fussing with the crisp sheets, turning dog-ears in their corners. "Tomorrow, if you like...damme, it *is* tomorrow, is it not? Well, then, after breakfast...."

"I shall be away by then."

"Away?"

Arnett's smile widened.

"You thought I would stay?"

He saw, with relief, that his father did not intend to lie.

"No. I made a settlement. Twenty thousand pounds, in cash or kind. Governor Sharpe tells me Lord Baltimore gave you your grants; you will want some of the nigras...."

"God's breath," said Arnett Leslie softly, and stood up, "you thought to buy her of me."

His father's smile matched his.

"She was not yours to sell," he said as softly.

"But for sale." And then: "Strike, if you like. It is quite safe."

Amidon Leslie's clenched hand descended slowly and rested on the table edge.

"You are a fool," he said.

"So I perceive," his son agreed. "Suppose we end it. Good night."

Amidon closed the door behind him. The latch clicked; Arnett picked up the ladle and filled his cup, drank, and filled it again. Thank the Lord they had gotten through it with a show of decency; that far, at least, the Leslie tradition had not been violated. Cool in anger. 'Gad, he was cool enough; he was cold; his head felt thick; it was stiff enough inside now, he thought, so that it would not shake like beef jelly. Putting up his hands to shake it, he found his fingers wet with cold sweat. He finished the sangaree in the silver bowl.

When it was all gone, he tried to think what to do. It took him, considering how little he had to do, an unreasonably long time.

He took out of the cuddy his leather camp trunk. It had been too scuffed and shabby to go to London; it would do very well now. From the hooks in the wardrobe he took down his scarlet major's coat with its yellow facings, the buff waistcoat and breeches, and put them in the trunk. On top of them he laid the uniform he liked better—a brown linsey hunting shirt with its own ravelings for thrums and a mended tear across the breast, breech clout and beaded clout belt, fringed linsey leggings, a pair of worn moccasins. On top of them, his tomahawk and knife in leather sheaths with Cherokee beadwork, his pouch and powder horn, a stiff leather flask of bullets.

He stood looking down at the half-filled trunk, and around the dim room. There was, it seemed, very little that he could truthfully call his own. The trunk was a fair sum of his life; he had been a rich man's son, and a soldier. Now he was poor.

The idea interested him. He counted the money in his pocket, and smiled: six guineas sixpence; when he paid the hire of his pungey,

he would have three guineas sixpence, a blue traveling coach and
the rest of the gifts he had fetched home for his bride, and three
thousand acres of wild land—that was his fortune. He fell to wondering whether Evelyn would have the grace to blush when he
gave her the coach and the gowns, and the boudoir flummery. It
would be amusing to watch her. *Amusing.* He swore abruptly,
aloud. God's breath, he would sink them in the river before she
should touch them. He had bought them with his mother's legacy.

The sangaree bowl, he saw regretfully, was completely emptied.
He dropped the boarding pistols into their case, and put the case
into the trunk, took his sword from its peg by the mantel and laid
it beside the pistols, lifted his rifle from the antlers and loaded it
and primed it. Tapping the ramrod on the ball, he smiled at
himself, a curl of the lip that had no humor in it, but only mockery.
A loaded rifle would go well with his blue chariot and his boudoir
furniture. It struck him that Arnett Leslie would cut an incongruous figure; would be, he added, a useless one. The treaty signed
a few months back in Paris had put an end to the seven years' war
in which he had grown up; the rifle and the uniform were out of
date. And the linsey hunting dress…*'y gad,* he could see the
blushes and the grins his naked thighs would fetch him if he
ventured into Annapolis in clout and leggings. There had been a
deal of change in Maryland since the first Leslie, in his old age,
saw his son lay the foundations of Leslie Hall. The colony had
changed its linsey shirt for one of linen with ruffles, and covered it
with a satin coat, sleek and soft.

Soft … he slammed down the cover of the shabby trunk. That
was it: *soft.* Queer he had not realized before how few of the Maryland officers on the Cumberland patrol were tidewater men. Cre-
sap, Evan Shelby, Tom Yeardley, they were all hill men now,
aliens to the gay manors. *Dammit,* he, Arnett Leslie, was an alien
too. He looked around again at the room. It had been his room
for more than twenty years; even the trundle bed he had slept in
until he was six still stood in the far corner; it had pleased his
mother to keep it there, with his first small saddle, his first pair of
boots. He was conscious only of an overpowering desire to get
away.

The trunk went easily to his shoulder; the candle, blown out,
left an evil smell in his nostrils as he went down the broad stairs,

rifle in hand, and out between the white pillars. He saw, from the portico, that there was a light in the kitchen wing, and set the trunk down on the brick walk. Shadrach, weazened, shuffling, lifted his wrinkled poll from the fire he was kindling on the hearth.

"Misto Arnett!"

"Shadrach ... good morning. Is there a boy about? I want Nancy quickly." Plague take the old fellow, must he stand there like a mourner, twisting his mouth, twisting his withered hands? Shadrach's hands had lifted him into that small saddle upstairs, the day he rode his first pony.

"Yo' ... yo' is goin' 'way?"

"Yes. Never mind feeding her. Half a bucket of water. No grain in the saddle bags." He would take nothing that was not wholly his. They could get along with foraging, he and Nancy. The old slave came shuffling toward the door, his fingers fumbling and fussing with each other.

Arnett Leslie turned and walked with long strides back to his trunk, swung it to his shoulder, and went quickly down to the wharf. The steep banks of the terraces were thick with the blue stars of periwinkle. Beyond them, the three old chestnut trees stood in full bloom, like altars, every branch a candelabrum with its tall white candle; even in the thin dawn, he saw them spreading a soft glow, pale yellow, pale maroon, as if the flower candles were alight. He looked for the dogwood, and found only a strip of darker shadow banked against the pines; a little farther down the slope, he realized that he would not see the dogwood blooming—the dogwood never hung out its galaxy of stars until a week after the Judas tree was in full flower. And the Judas tree, he saw, was thick with blossoms, its slim, bare branches smothered in pink-purple lace.

The five boatmen were asleep, the steersman on the leather cushions, the rowers on the hewn log bottom, between the carriage wheels. He woke Bob, and slid the trunk down to him over the edge of the wharf.

"Take everything," he commanded, "up to Baltimore, to Mr. Burke's brick warehouse. Tell him I'll come for them presently. Here." He dropped three guineas into Bob's hand. "You understand?"

"Yas, *suh*." He did not understand, Leslie saw, and repeated his instructions.

Turning away, walking back along the sounding planks, he found that he was still carrying the long rifle. He shrugged. It made no difference; he went on up the herring-bone walk.

Under the Judas tree, he stopped. Evelyn Gentle—Evelyn Leslie—standing there, blocked his way. She held out both hands to him, a remembered gesture. Lace fell away from her round arms to the elbow; it was light enough to see the pattern of blue veins in her wrists. He had kissed the upturned palms—here—when the Judas tree bloomed last. He looked down at them intently, and put the rifle in front of him, between himself and the low, bright bodice, and set his hands one upon the other on the muzzle.

"Arnett, you would not really go?"

He said something, in his throat, but the sound did not get to his lips. *Dammit ... dammit ... dammit.* He knew instantly that he had told her, more clearly than if he had spoken, that he loved her. She took a step toward him, the bright panniers of her dress swaying, her arms lifting. Under the lace cap, her bright, blond hair caught a dart of sunrise level through the pines; she tilted her chin so that the light fell across her eyes and showed the lashes damp.

"Arnett ... Arnett...."

He managed, stupidly, hoarsely:

"Good morning, Evelyn."

"Good morning, Arnett, my dear, my dear." Her voice trembled. Her hand, very certain of itself, came out and took the rifle by its barrel and put it to one side. "Oh, Arnett, will you not understand? Will you not? It is all so simple."

"Simple...." Ay, it was simple enough, if she meant plain.

"Do you not understand? I could not go and be a bond woman in a linsey gown, barefoot, to grub brush and milk cows." She laughed, a soft trill, very sure of itself. Her voice ran on sweetly. "I should not be beautiful in linsey, with dirty feet and sunburned nose, and blisters to my hands; and you would not have loved me so. You will not go, will you, Arnett?"

"Yes."

"But you will come back ... often ... very often."

Her quick rush took him by surprise. He felt her arms warm

42

against his neck, her full breasts soft against his body, her full lips hot against his mouth. Touching him, her lips murmured.

"Now d'you understand, Arnett? Now d'you understand? I shall be here for you, when you come back, whenever you come back. Stay...stay...I will love you so; you will not mind...at all...what happened." Her mouth was hot again on his mouth.

Arnett Leslie let the rifle fall. His fingers plucked her soft wrists down from his neck and flung them. His tongue came out, licking; there was a bitter taste on his lips. And a bitter word:

"Strumpet!"

She was, he saw, utterly amazed. Her mouth was open, and it was not beautiful. The tight bodice seemed too tight; above it, curving flesh rose and fell with her breathing.

Leslie stooped and picked up the rifle. Straightening, his head brushed a low branch; the sun, he saw, had turned the pink-purple blossoms scarlet. His free hand reached up and pulled one blossom off.

"A proper setting, Evelyn," he said smiling. "Had you forgot they call it the Judas tree? The blooms have a bitter taste."

He put the flower to his mouth, nibbling it, still smiling. The calyx, crushed, set his tongue puckering. He said, politely:

"Would you like to try it?" And plucked another of the gaudy flowers. Evelyn struck at it, flattened it, and left his fingers tingling.

Arnett Leslie bowed and stepped off the brick walk. When he had passed the first terrace and it would not be rude to spit, he spat out the unpleasant petals in his mouth and licked his lips.

CHAPTER IV

In Which Mr. Leslie Is Laughed at and Comes Close to Murder, Kicks a Landlord, and Kisses Another Woman:

IT was Shadrach who came near to making Arnett Leslie a murderer.

Shadrach, waiting on the stable path with the black mare, muttered and grimaced as Leslie set his foot in the stirrup and swung himself up, and pointed his gnarled finger at the saddle bag. The bag bulged.

"I told you ... !"

"Jes' peach brandy, Misto' Arnett, what yo' allus like'. Peach brandy what yo' gran'poppy make."

Leslie slapped the saddle bag. There were three tall bottles pushing against the flap.

"Here." He thrust his hand into the pocket of his breeches and jerked it out. Shadrach's stiff fingers missed the coin when it fell. "Give that to Mr. Amidon Leslie. It will pay for the brandy."

His heels shot the Nancy mare away in a flurry of flung gravel. The rifle jerked against his thighs and he put his hand on the barrel above the pan to steady it. The low, white-washed cattle byre, the sheep sheds with their bright green paddock, the swine runs, the hay ricks all flashed past him, and he hardly saw them. Under the cedars on the knoll, the rattle of gravel changed to a muffled drumming. Dark fields fell away on either side, ridged with seed rows freshly planted; the ridges whirled by like the spokes of a wheel, turning; the mare stretched out into arrowy speed over the smooth dirt of the rolling road.

Subtly, and yet suddenly, the earth changed. Leslie saw that it had changed; it gave him, in his present mood, an acid pleasure. The gray-black earth of the garden gave place to brownish-yellow; across the fields the jade of young tobacco ran in tenuous lines. Leslie's mouth, smiling, left his teeth bare. He had never realized, before, how the tobacco gave its own color to the earth that bore it; between the jade-green rows the dirt was high-yellow, like tobacco leaves just beginning to dry in the sheds; where the leaves shadowed it, it was darker, like the cured leaf ready for the casks; where the dew had wet it, it was dark as tobacco juice, dark as spittle. Paghh!

He rode for hours at that furious speed; the planters' pace was bred into the black mare. As he rode, he drank.

Getting the cork out of the bottle was not easy, with Nancy galloping, but there was a bitter, sickly taste in his mouth. The peach brandy, when he got at it, tasted much better; he rolled his tongue in it, and then swashed his tongue over his lips. He swallowed slowly, and put the bottle to his mouth again. When it was empty, he worried the cork out of the second bottle with his teeth. By the Lord, old Grandfather Arnett had been a master hand with his odorous peach mash and his copper still; he had turned out a man's drink. And drunk it, too. There had been, old Arnett's namesake told him, no softness about *him*. No treachery, either; when he wanted a woman, he did not trick his rival into going to London, and steal her behind his back. No, damme, he fought for her, bare blade to bare blade, in the room over John Ball's taproom in Annapolis, and took his wound, and killed his man. It had been a pretty scandal, even in those stout days. And while the tongues clacked and the governor tore his wig, Arnett Leslie II had married the girl and carried her off to Leslie Hall, and got a son, and named him Amidon. Amidon's son curled his lip, and rolled his tongue in old Arnett's brandy, and let the black mare run or walk as she would. He acquired, after a while, the notion that he would not be Amidon Leslie's son. By God, he would not be; he would be old Arnett's grandson; old Arnett's blood was in his veins; he could feel it pumping, warming, glowing. That galloping blood, he told himself confidently, could not be Amidon's; there was nothing treacherous about it. It would not, he insisted, content itself with a woman who had no love to offer, who exchanged herself for a manor house, and forty slaves, and eighty cows.... No, it was eighteen cows....

He did not remember how many cows it was. The third bottle, he saw, was empty; he could look right through it when he tilted it to his mouth. Looking closely, he discovered a log wall. He put the bottle down, holding it by the neck, and found that the log

45

wall was still there, and that Nancy had stopped at a place where the road forked. Between the forks stood a log tavern, its plank door propped open with another log. He shouted.

The mare started, and danced a few steps. He spoke to her sharply, and shouted again. *Damned lazy...*

He swung his arm, and saw the bottle sparkle into a bright shower against the log wall.

God's breath, that brought them! Three men came crowding into the doorway, gaping out at him, jostling. They moved and shuttled together, a blur of white faces and white wigs, and Leslie leaned forward to see them better, trying to pick out the tavern-keeper. One of the faces, he decided, was familiar: long fox-like nose, wide mouth, not too much chin. The mouth spread out into a grin; opened, in the middle, into a laugh with long creases at each end. He recognized Romney Clawther's laugh. What was it he knew about Clawther? Oh, yes. It was Clawther who had come up the river from Solomons and told Amidon Leslie that his son was coming home. He frowned elaborately, wondering whether the laughter he heard and saw in the doorway had anything to do with that home-coming.

Romney had left the other two men and was moving toward him. The wide mouth was still deeply creased at the sides, and roundly open in the middle; Romney, he saw, was laughing and calling out to him at the same time. He bent his head to listen: "Where away, Arnie?" Plague take the fellow, he had no call to be so cousinly. What was he bawling? "I'll be bound I know what drives you, Arnie. It was too crowded, sleeping three in a bed, eh?"

There was a galloping in Arnett Leslie's brain. Old Arnett's blood, or old Arnett's brandy, it made a pell-mell roaring. His hand, lying on the barrel of the rifle across his thighs, slid back and cocked it. His trigger finger slid past the guard and pressed. The mare jumped and stood quivering.

Leslie, suddenly cold sober, saw Romney Clawther standing with his mouth uncreased, wide open from jowl to jowl, and behind him, on the doorpost, a long white scar where the rifle ball had gouged out a splinter. Staring, he saw Romney jerk in all his limbs, spin about, and run for the tavern door. The two who had stood there were already gone.

Leslie flicked the reins, and turned Nancy into the right-hand road.

He slept that night in a clump of stunted pines, lying on the ground in his satin coat, and woke cramped and nauseated to call the mare and saddle and bridle her. She nosed against him, nibbling first at his shoulder and then, delicately, at his ear. Without thinking, because it had been the custom between them, he went to the saddle bag for sugar, and found there beside a double handful of sugar lumps a square of corn cake and two turkey legs wrapped in a white towel. Shadrach....

When he had eaten, he felt better, mounted, and rode slowly out of the woods into the road again. It was not much of a road. Wheel-tracks, rather, where Nancy's hoofs sank deep into the red dust; a woman's fingers dipping into the powder box on her dressing table might have made as loud a sound. The dust rose knee high and hung there; the mare's black legs moved through a moving cloud of it. By midday she was rusty roan from hocks to ribs; the man's white stockings were the color of old bricks.

The ruts deepened. At another fork, a great oak with three blazes on its trunk marked the turning toward Baltimore Town and the Patapsco ferry. He took the three-notched road.

A stake and rider fence emerged from the scrub and kept them company for a while. At long intervals, other ruts unwound themselves out of the locusts and the runt pines and joined them. At longer intervals, tobacco fields pushed the woods aside and gave distant glimpses of curing sheds and slave quarters, and once of a white clapboard house with end walls of red brick. Leslie's lip curled at it: *counterfeit!* Romney Clawther had such a house, imitating with sawed boards and a thin dab of brickwork at the ends the massive authority of the real manors. But before the Nancy mare had carried him out of sight of the white house, his lip was curling again, at himself: he was counterfeit, now, too. He might, except for blind chance, have been a murderer.

He roused twice that afternoon—once when the mare stopped midstream of a shallow ford and turned her head reproachfully until he loosed the reins to let her drink; and once when he saw red dust rising in a tall swirl over a ridge ahead. He pulled Nancy sharply off the road through bright sumach, and waited in a clump of pines while a cream and gold traveling coach wallowed past, four horses at a gallop, coachman in scarlet livery on the box, three gentlemen on horseback in a red smother behind it. He knew the coach; he could guess the riders. Mary Lee Hallett hurrying home to Upper Marlboro from Baltimore race day and the rusk-and-tea ball that followed it; three swains panting and sweating and chewing dust to wheedle her favor at the next. He sent a taunting laugh after them. He was done with wheedling; he had gained that much.

He let Nancy pick her own way back to the road, and choose her own speed. She, at least, took no feminine advantage; she trotted and galloped as often as she walked. The dust cloud trotted and walked and galloped with them, and settled in fine powder on black satin neck and white satin breeches alike. When, near sundown, the suck of the mare's hoofs in mud roused him again and he straightened in the saddle, Leslie saw his white waistcoat criss-crossed with red streaks at every crease.

The Patapsco ran blue between vivid marsh grass just ahead; beyond it, the houses of Baltimore village straggled over rolls of hills.

He swung stiffly out of the saddle and let Nancy follow him aboard the ferry, and stood grimly self-conscious, hands clasped on his rifle muzzle, while the black crew poled across. It suited him to trudge through the swampy track on the farther bank and up the first slope where the dust lay thick again in the ruts. He knew he made an incongruous sight, London slippers smeared with red muck, rifle atrail under lace cuff and satin sleeve, the horse at heel. It pleased him to have her following, with reins dangling; a horse could be trusted.

The wheel tracks crossed the ridge and wound amiably down the gentlest curve of slope. Wooden houses appeared here and there, and the road swerved good-naturedly to amble past their dooryards. Fields bright with young tobacco sprawled themselves down toward the bright blue bay; rail fences wandered among the painted houses; the spire of a brick church rose like the spike of a dragoon's helmet on a shaggy hill, and beyond it a brawling torrent spilled itself noisily through the town. It monopolized all the energy in sight and made the only sound of life there was.

Against the clapboard wall of the Seneca Trail Inn, a high

wheeled gig lay on its side. One red wheel was crumpled like the frame of a half open parasol; the hub had gouged a black scar along the tavern wall. Whoever had wrecked it there had left it and gone about his business.

His business, by the sounds from the open windows, had to do with sangaree and toddy, and he had much help. A deep voice was bawling:

> *"So come you all and go with me*
> *Over the hills and far away...."*

Leslie felt a dark tide of nostalgia rising in him. The Maryland men had worn that ballad ragged, marching to help Forbes chase the French out of Fort Duquesne. He touched Nancy's nose to let her know he had not forgotten her, and went into the tavern. A 'prentice in a linsey smock drowsed with his arms on the bar and his head on his arms, and stared with open mouth when Leslie jogged his elbow. Through a half-open door came the slap-slap of cards, and a wheezing tenor worrying at "Over the Hills" where the deep voice had left off. The tenor, Leslie noted with curling lip, was far away enough from the key. He gave the 'prentice brusque orders, and saw the Nancy mare led away to the stable yard. He had no will to follow and see the orders he gave obeyed.

Upstairs, he sat on the clean sheets in his dusty clothes and drank peach brandy and honey until it was easier to lie down than to sit up. Hours later, a table in the card room went over with a thump and crashing of glass, and he opened his eyes. The room was dark. He kicked off his slippers and closed his eyes again.

When he woke, sunlight lay level across the red smears of dirt on the bed. He got up and undressed, and stood naked in the middle of the room to finish what was left of the brandy and honey. Then he drank a great deal of the water from one of the buckets by the wall, and doused his head in the rest; and then, standing in the iron kettle, lifted the bucket overhead at arm's length, looked up at it, and tipped it. The deluge made him blink and sputter, but his head felt better. He emptied the kettle out the window, and tried it again with the second bucket. After that he turned his attention to the white satin clothes; all the water in Baltimore harbor, sparkling through the window, could not help

49

them. He shook the worst of the red dust out of them, and began to dress.

With his smallclothes on one leg and nothing on the other, he heard a horse stamp and harness jingle below his window. Looking out, he had some doubts that two buckets of water had been sufficient for his head:

His blue paneled coach stood at the tavern door, hitched behind four white horses. The top of the coach was heaped with his trunks and boxes. At the foot of a hitching-post a ragged black boy lay asleep, curled like a 'possum in the dirt, his kinky head six inches from the leaders' hoofs. Mr. Leslie split the white satin breeches in his astonished haste.

The stable-boy uncurled and scuttled away on all fours at the prod of his toe, and wriggled and rolled his eyes when Leslie collared him.

"Whose coach is this?" he demanded.

The rolling eyes took in the coach, the horses, the sky and the grim gentleman who had forgot to tie his stock above his ruffled shirt.

"Da's Mist' Majo' Leslie's coach," he gurgled.

"And whose horses?"

"Whose ho'ses? Yo' means whose ho'ses? Dey's Mist' Capt'in Yea'dley's ho'ses, suh."

Leslie's hand came away. Yeardley's horses—there would be no trick about it, then.

"Where's Captain Yeardley?"

" 'Deedy I donno, suh. 'Fo'e de Lawd I dunno, He tol' me: wait heah, or I skin yo' 'live. Dat was las' night, right aft' de gemmen had dey suppeh."

Last night?

"Yassuh. He say wait heah or he skin me, an' goes in de tave'n."

Leslie turned and ran up the tavern steps. He did not need more than one guess to know where Tom Yeardley would be.

The card room was a wreck, but of those who had wrecked it only one pair of boots remained. The boots protruded beneath the settle, and Leslie, looking behind it, saw Tom like an overgrown cherub peacefully asleep, his tousled blond head pillowed on the ruins of his tricorn hat. He had to drag the overturned table away before he could get at Tom to shake him. Tom slept on. Leslie's lips curled a little, but they were neither cynical nor scornful. Tom Yeardley was a mighty sleeper. There was the night Tom gave his bachelor supper in this same room; it had been touch and go to get Tom waked up in time for his own wedding. They had been an hour late, at that, and the bride had sworn at him under the parson's very nose....

There was never any doubt about what Anstice Yeardley thought or felt. Leslie's mouth tightened. His voice, as he jerked the landlord half out of bed, was deliberately hostile.

"...plagued hostler, so you are, John Grannis. If you've served my mare no better than you've served Tom Yeardley, the pillory's too good for you."

Grannis sat sputtering, his bare shanks tangled in his quilts.

"But, Major Leslie, there was nought...you know how't is... all very merry 'til past three, and the night watch poundin' on the door. Strip me, major..."

"I'll strip you," Leslie promised him grimly, and dragged him off the bed.

"Swizzle me, Major Leslie, there was not one of the gentlemen could help me lift him. I got the rest o' them to bed, and their boots off, too. But Mister Tom, you know how heavy he is. Strip me, 't is a wonder he did not kill himself i' the gig." John Grannis fumbled for his breeches.

"Let be," Leslie told him curtly. "I'll help you lift him."

"I swear, major, I never saw the likes of it. They come down Long Street here, Mister Tom and young Foreman Wight, four horses tandem to their gigs, hell for leather. Young Wight beat Mister Tom's white filly at six furlongs on race day, and Tom would have his money back again. So they raced i' their gigs, and Tom's leader shied at a petticoat just down the street there, and into the wall he goes. Pitched him out, it did, and he rolled end for end till he hit the stoop...."

"Let be," Leslie said again, and pushed him into the card room.

"He was a-waitin' for you, Major." Grannis shot a look over his shoulder. Leslie's face gave him no encouragement. "There was a deal of talk, race day, on how you were back from England...." He fiddled at the overturned table.

"Well...?"

"Come noon yest'day, the free nigra Bob brings a pungey in wi' your baggage and all. Mister Tom, when he had wrecked his gig and had a toddy on it, swears he will have your coach up and his horses harnessed, ready and waiting to take you home with him when you should come."

"Um. His feet, there, John. No ... not upstairs. The coach."

They bundled Tom out through the taproom door, and into the carriage among the bales and boxes, and Grannis tumbled up the stairs to fetch Leslie's clothes and hat and rifle. Leslie felt an ugly impatience with the man. The guineas Tom had wasted across the Seneca Trail bar warranted him at least a pillow to his head and a quilt to cover him while he slept on the cardroom floor. Grannis was a slovenly fellow; an unpleasant fellow, Leslie decided, who would kick a horse and twist her bit if he had a grudge against her master. Leslie went out to the stables himself to get Nancy. She followed him round the corner of the tavern and stood curiously at his shoulder while he tossed her bridle into the coach and then, because there was no room for it elsewhere, set the saddle firmly across Tom Yeardley's knees. When he stepped back to close the door he found John Grannis bending over, hands on thighs, gaping and grinning at the coat of arms on the blue panel.

The night rail bulging above John's bare shanks was poor protection. He bellowed so loudly that the four horses jerked against the harness, and the coach rocked on its leather straps. Leslie, climbing on the box, sorting out the reins, regretted that he had kicked the fellow quite so hard. He had been, for an instant, as blindly angry at the grin on Grannis' face as he had been at Romney Clawther's taunting laugh. They could keep their laughter and their grins to themselves. By God, they could. He snatched the whip out of its pocket and sent it curling over the four white backs. The horses sprang forward. In ten lengths he had them galloping. The coach heeled like a fat blue boat in a squall as he swung the leaders out of Long Street into John Digges' wagon road.

Leslie approved of John Digges. He had built his own road westward through the hills and woods to his plantation; Baltimore drowsed and danced and drank and drowsed again beside its red ruts, but Digges was a gentleman of energy; he crushed a whole hill of stone and covered his road with it. His wagons did not have to wallow hub deep in dust or mud; his ladies rode to the

Baltimore races with their coach windows open; it was only when they came to Long Street that they had to close them to keep out the choking red clouds. Approving John Digges, Arnett Leslie found that he disliked Baltimore. The lift and warmth he had felt when he realized Tom Yeardley had come to seek him spent themselves; his spirits drooped and chilled. He rode hunched over in the seat, the reins loose in his hand, his eyes on the green ribbon that flowed toward him between the horses, between the crushed stone wheel-tracks where their hoofs rattled away like a militia drum, with a beat missed here and there.

He remembered other things about John Digges. It was John Digges, in the last Indian alarm, who stuck to his plantation and vowed to fight for it, while the foremost gentlemen of Baltimore and the manors around loaded their silver and their women pell-mell on the ships in the harbor, in a panic to save their own skins. They had not been heroic; they had been no more heroic than John Grannis, bellowing, with his hands to the tail of his night rail. Leslie smiled, an unpleasant twist of his set lips. Grannis, he told himself, did very well as a personification of Baltimore. And Romney Clawther, with his shallow laugh and his shallow life, would do as well for the tidewater gentry.

When he had a manor of his own, he decided, he would have a whole row of china figures on the mantel, made to his order. There would be Grannis in his night shirt, for Baltimore; Clawther, swizzling from a goblet big as his body, to represent the younger generation of Patuxent gentlemen; Sir Dick Lawless for London...and Leslie wondered whether a china figurine could be made to show Sir Dick's hands and mouth shaking with terror. Then there must be a figure in a gown cut very low on a plump, wanton bosom; a figure with very red, lying lips....

He shook his head. No artist could paint such lies on china lips.

He saw rail fences coming to meet the coach. The road ran between them past Digges' barns and granaries, and swung to the right under great locust trees toward a house with pillars. Leslie twitched the reins. John Digges would do well on the mantel, a sturdy china figure to shame the rest; but Leslie's mood rejected him in person. He swung the horses into the left-hand fork. The coach began to jounce. The road, twisting down between bulging hills, degenerated quickly into two gouges in the rooty soil. The carriage tipped and swayed; overloaded, it floundered down upon the wheel horses; the tongue thrust up like a bowsprit between their noses; dust rose thick from their sliding hoofs. Rocks projected into first one rut and then the other, and the wheels sliced sparks into the dust as they heaved themselves up and jolted down. Leslie stood up to drive, finding a sullen pleasure in fighting with the rocks and potholes. The bales and boxes on top of the coach slid and tumbled; the leather slings creaked and groaned; trace chains clunked and strained. Through the commotion, he heard Tom Yeardley beginning to groan also, and then to curse in the plaintive key he used when puzzled or surprised.

Leslie flicked out the whip. The coach plunged and rocked down the last stretch of slope; hoofs and wheels ran like a burst of gunfire over a log causeway and a bridge; after them, like answering shots, Nancy's shoes cracked upon the corduroy. The five horses stretched out across a green valley at full gallop; the carriage, bucking in its slings, seemed to gallop too. Inside, Yeardley set up a tremendous bawling. He was still bawling when Leslie pulled the team into a trot and eased the leaders down the bank that led to the Patapsco ford. Even here, twenty miles from the Chesapeake, the stubby Patapsco had almost ceased to be a river; it had to gather itself up against the rims of the wheels before it had depth enough to run over between the spokes.

Leslie brought the coach to a halt half way between the banks, and jumped down. The water filled his slippers; that, too, gave him an ingrowing pleasure; the sooner he ruined this silly love-plumage he had fetched from London, the better. He pulled open the carriage door and said:

"Good day, Tom."

Tom was sitting on the floor, the Nancy mare's saddle hugged against him with both arms. He had a corded box upon his shoulders and the brass-bound trunk on his lap; his big head wagged uncertainly.

"Did ye beat 'em, Arnie?"

Leslie lifted the trunk off his knees and pushed it onto the seat.

"Come out, Tom. You need a drink."

"God! Same Arnie. Glad you're home; missed you, Arnie." He tried to get up with the saddle still clutched to his chest; his face wrinkled with a prodigious effort to think. "Had to see you, soon's you got home. Can't remember why. Where's drink?"

Leslie took the saddle away from him, and pulled him out.

"There," he said, and let him drop on all fours in the sandy shallows. Tom bellowed again, and lifted first one hand and then the other, found no place but the river to put them, and put them there.

"Go ahead. Drink."

Tom drank, and sat back on his haunches, his face streaming.

"You did this once before, Arnie," he said, and looked up reproachfully across his shoulder. Solemn, his big face was bovine; above his heavy features, his forehead bulged at the temples, as if horns might some day push through his thatch of blond hair. Leslie, sitting on the coach step, remembered how that placid face could take on a solid fury, how the great head could lunge forward from the mighty shoulders, how Tom Yeardley had lowered his head and charged like a bull one afternoon in the wilderness beyond Fort Cumberland. Leslie was a little surprised that he still felt grateful to Tom; he shouldn't be grateful; if Tom had run away, as more placid men had run, Arnett Leslie would never have come back from Fort Cumberland, never gone to London, never come home to find Evelyn Gentle in his father's bed. *Pagh! Damn thinking.*

Tom's face lost its solemnity. He smiled, and looked abruptly like a pleased baby.

"You did this once before, Arnie," he repeated, and wagged his head. "On the way to my wedding. 'S breath!" His forehead creased again. "You were coming home to *your* wedding. That's why I had to see you."

"You be damned," said Leslie quickly.

Yeardley's face cleared. He beamed.

"'S all right, then, eh? Glad. Damme, I *am* glad. Worried about you. Wanted to tell you she's well lost, Arnie. Tell you not to fret. Went down to fetch you home with me. You know, over the hills an' far away...." He began to sing:

> *"Whoe'er is bold, whoe'er is free*
> *Will join and come along with me...."*

55

He stopped and peered over his shoulder at Leslie.

" 'S all right, is it, Arnie?" he asked again urgently. "Worried about you. 'Fraid you'd go jump in river, forget to swim. R'member how you fished me out o' the Potomac? Never could swim in deep water." He brightened, his face like a happy cherub's. "I can swim this river!"

He lay down on his stomach and flailed vigorously at the inch-deep current. Leslie got down from the carriage step and held Tom's head in the water and sand until, between fright and choking, he was a little more sober. They were both dripping when they climbed to the box and the coach rolled up the westward bank. The water gathered in puddles on the leather cushions and dribbled down the blue panels; Leslie watched it with approval. Mixed with dust, the water was leaving brown stains on his white satin breeches, and that, too, pleased him.

He was helping Tom sing as the coach climbed the spur of South Mountain in the late afternoon:

> *"Over the hills with heart we go
> To meet the proud, insulting foe."*

Leslie cracked the whip savagely; the coach lurched ahead. *He* was not going to meet the "proud, insulting foe"; he was running away. Running away from insulting friends; running away because Romney Clawther laughed at him for a jilted lover. The whip cracked again. The horses were galloping as they swung through the limestone gateway of Tom Yeardley's manor, just over the crest of the mountain. They did not need the rein; they whirled the carriage up to the flagstone steps, and stopped. In the doorway, between peeled locust trunks that served as pillars for Tom's unfinished manor house, Leslie saw Anstice Yeardley in sprigged cambric and a ruffled cap. She came quickly down the steps:

"I'm glad you're here, Arnett."

Leslie said stiffly:

"Good day, An'." His mouth felt frozen. *Dammit,* had she done *that* to him, too? Would he always feel spiteful and awkward when he looked at a woman, because Evelyn . . . ? He dropped over the wheel and stood.

Anstice Yeardley put out her hands.

"You're not afraid of *me,* Arnett?"

56

"No, An'; no." *Plague on it,* he was afraid. She knew it. Romney Clawther knew it. He must carry the brand of it on him, like a thief in the stocks. A brand....*Here is a fool.*

"Arnett, you're not afraid of *me*. 'T is not every woman would hurt you so. You ought to know that."

Her arms went strongly around his neck and pulled his head down. She kissed him firmly on the mouth.

"There, Arnie. That didn't hurt, did it?"

"No, An' . . ." He began to laugh. Three days ago, with Evelyn Gentle's kiss acid on his lips, he had sworn he would never kiss a woman again. He ran his tongue along his mouth,

"No, there's no taste to it, Arnie." Anstice began to laugh also. "There's no need for lip-red here in the wilderness. Go along in; I'll fetch Tom. He's in a state. There's peach brandy on the table, and wild honey syrup."

Leslie heard his slippers squushing up the flagstone steps and the stir and creak of loose puncheons. Lip-red. Perhaps that was what had left the evil taste on his mouth, and not the blossom he had plucked and given to Evelyn. That, he decided, would be one more joke on him; Evelyn would not have noticed any difference between the taste of the Judas flower and her own lips. He considered the matter soberly over his brandy cup. No, the joke was on Evelyn; but she would never know it.

CHAPTER V

*In Which a Woman is Flogged and a Dog is Kicked, and Mr. Leslie
Comes to the Rescue of One but Not the Other:*

"QUARREL with him!" Anstice Yeardley told Tom, while
she stripped off his bedraggled clothes and doused his
head with water icy-cold from the spring under the house.
"Quarrel with him?" Tom, dripping, blinked at her. His voice
rose plaintively. "Pinch me, An', he thinks we're the only friends
he has."

"I'll pinch you!" she promised him sharply, and dizzied him with
her vigorous rubbing at his drenched head. "Maybe you'd not
mind if *I* walked out on *you*. But Arnett minded it when that
flibbertygibbet walked out on him. He's sick and sore, I tell you,
and like to do some devilish fool thing. Here, get your breeches
on you and go quarrel with him. Anger him, Tom. Make him
furious. Make him forget."

"Gadzooks, An', what can we quarrel on?"

"Gadzooks, Tom, you can call him a coward if you like. Or a
horse thief. And don't mention women!"

"Women?"

"Put on those breeches, or I'll women you, Tom Yeardley! And
I'll not say a word if you drink him under the table, and yourself
with him. I'll see you to bed."

"You're coming to table, An'."

"I am not." Anstice smiled at him, rumpling his damp hair.
"Maybe if Arnett had needed Evelyn much as you need me, she'd
not have jilted him. A woman knows when she's needed. D'you
have to be told he despises women just now? Yes, silly, me along
with the rest. When I kissed him, it but reminded him of her.
He hated it. Get along with you."

So Yeardley quarreled with his guest, though the guest was
his dearest friend.

It was a difficult quarrel to start. Leslie sat slumped in his chair

58

at dinner, his hand more often on his brandy cup than on his knife. Tom talked and talked. He was everywhere, skipping from subject to subject like a man crossing a stream on stepping stones. He did not dare to stop; upstairs, Anstice was listening. Between sentences, he asked questions; sometimes Leslie answered them, and when he did, the answer was as likely to be wrong as right. After each answer, he sank back into his own gloomy silence, and had to be hauled out; he made it clear that he preferred to sink.

Tom gave up trying to irk him; turned, instead, to London and Lord Baltimore.

Yes, he had dined with my lord. Twice. And gone in his carriage to the Drury Lane, and to the Christmas rout.

Yes, my lord drank more than was good for him.

Yes, every one in London did that.

Yes, he had brought back Lord Baltimore's grants to three thousand acres in the Conococheague.

"Pinch me and pull me! Did you so?" Tom was up and out of his chair and around the table, pounding Leslie delightedly on the back. " 'Y gad, Arnie, I hated to speak of it, thinking it might not have gone through. How does it lie? Is it close? As we planned it, Arnie, along the spur here, next to Near-the-Navel?" *

Leslie nodded, and pushed out his cup to be filled again. Tom bubbled with enthusiasm. He forgot that he was trying to pick a quarrel. The French peace just signed at Paris, he said, had added much value to this strip of the Conococheague valley along the road to Fort Cumberland.

"Lord, Arnie, the mere wind of it started settlers pouring back across the Monocacy and the Catoctin," he said. "Remember how they went pouring the other way, scared to death, when the war began? Three hundred wagons over the Monocacy in one day. Well, Arnie, they'll be coming back as fast, now that there's peace again. They'll fill our valley here, and spill out to Fort Frederick. Ay, and to Fort Cumberland. There'll be a fortune here, man. Look you, Arnie, already they're coming east every summer from the fur country, pack trains and wagons, fetching skins to Balti-

* Near-the-Navel is no imaginary name. It stands on the colonial records of Washington county, Maryland—the name of a tract of land duly granted to its holder under that title.

59

more, fetching salt and powder and cloth and iron back to the settlements beyond the mountains."

He leaned across the table, thrusting out his pipe to tap Leslie's fingers.

"Look you," he urged, "we'll move Baltimore Town out to South Mountain. We'll build warehouses here; we'll have their iron and their salt and their flour and everything here waiting for them; we'll buy their furs. We'll save them that forty-five miles in to Baltimore. We'll have a town of our own, man, and we'll have more money than grows in all the tobacco plantings from Patapsco to Potomac.

"I tell you, Arnie, we didn't realize it then, but when Forbes' Highlanders stamped Fort Duquesne into the mud, they did more than stamp France out of America. They opened up the whole Ohio country."

Leslie stirred, and put his cup to his lips. He drank it empty and set it down with a thump.

"Ay. Ay. They opened up the Ohio when they signed in Paris," he said loudly. "Opened it up to what? To the gentlemen of the Ohio company. To a dozen rich Virginians to grow fatter on. To a dozen Quakers to wheedle settlers into, and bring the Indian nations down on the border again."

Tom sat silent, astonished at his heat.

"Mark you, Tom, the treaty of Paris may have taken the Ohio country away from the French, but it did not give it to the English. If the English want it, they will have to take it. If they take it, they will have to pay for it."

Tom found his tongue:

"Thunder! They have the money to pay for it."

"Money! When did a white man pay for Indian land with money? He pays for it in blood—somebody else's blood."

He hitched closer to the table and sat with his elbows on it, staring moodily while Tom filled his cup. When Tom set the decanter down, he drained his drink and asked for more.

"Somebody else's blood," he burst out. "D'you mind who started the last war—this war they've just ended? Who was it but this same Ohio company with its fine ultimatum to the French kindly to step off the earth, to clear out of the company's private fort at the Forks of the Ohio? Who fired the first shot? Who but the

60

Ohio company, with its blundering Colonel Washington, ambushing a French ambassador and killing him?"

" 'T was the governor of Virginia sent Washington out," Yeardley told him, and hoped An' was listening.

"The governor of Virginia! And who pullled the strings that made the governor of Virginia dance? Why, the precious Ohio company, and you know it."

"But Washington went out and fought. You'll have to grant the Virginia gentleman that."

"Oh. Ay. He fought, and lost, and surrendered, and signed a confession he had assassinated an ambassador. And pulled the Indian tribes in upon the frontier like a swarm of bees behind him."

"They say he saved all that was saved of Braddock's . . ."

"Braddock! And why did Braddock lose weeks and months taking his fine army out through Alexandria, when there was a road through Maryland, fair and clear, bridged and forded for sixty miles? Because the Ohio company is Virginian, and the army must go by the way the Ohio company desired."

Delightedly, Yeardley egged him on.

"You're blind and obstinate as Braddock himself," he shouted, and thumped the table in counterfeit anger. "You'll say, I suppose, that it was for the Ohio company that Bullet and his Virginians saved Forbes' advance guard at Fort Duquesne?"

"By God, I do say it!" Leslie smashed his fist down in anger that was not counterfeit at all. "I say Virginia and Pennsylvania profit by what Forbes did. I say the Ohio company paid for the Forks of the Ohio in blood that day—somebody else's blood. Duncan Cameron's, for one. Maryland blood. Ay!" He thumped the table again, and sent his cup rolling. "And I say if the Ohio company had its way, Forbes would have done Braddock's folly over again, and the Forks would still be French.

" 'T was Washington and his Ohio company gentry did their worst to block Forbes and thwart him at every turn. By God, Tom, if you or I had done it, 't would have been mutiny, and a court-martial, and our buttons cut off with the regiment looking on."

"You talk like a fool," Yeardley said, and hugged himself with delight at the success of his quarreling.

Leslie, flushed with anger and brandy, was out again on the Cumberland patrol, fighting his way through the wilderness to help hold the Forbes road while the army slashed its way across the mountains to capture Fort Duquesne. For the moment, Evelyn Gentle meant as little to him as she had five years ago.

"I tell you, Tom, if you or I or any Maryland man had done what Washington and his Virginia friends did, they'd have drummed us out to the 'Rogue's March.' God's breath, Tom, when Forbes had got the army a hundred miles through the mountains, when he had it on the Loyal Hanna, and a fortified camp built, and the road almost cut across the Laurel Ridge, Washington and his Ohio Company friends were still nagging him, pulling his sleeve, telling him that he must give it up, drop all that he had done, and use their precious Braddock road.

"There was Forbes, with only half a year to live, too sick to walk, too sick to ride, going back and forth over the mountains in a hammock between two horses. And Washington? There, forty miles from Fort Duquesne, Washington is telling Forbes he can't go on, he can't get his guns over Laurel Ridge. . . ."

He drained his cup again, and waved it at Yeardley.

"By the Lord, there was a man! There was a man they couldn't stop! Dying in his hammock, he told Washington to shut up, and get his Virginia troops up into Pennsylvania, and remember he was a soldier. Yes, sir, Old Iron Head twigged your precious Washington and brought him to heel, and went and took the Forks of the Ohio in spite of the Ohio company. And paid their purchase price for them by dying. And Maryland paid more of it, year after year, in a war it didn't seek. Paid for it in burned settlements and blood and scalps, and children with their brains smashed out on tree trunks, and wives stolen..."

He stopped, staring at Yeardley, his hand in mid-gesture.

His mouth worked, and the color ran out of his flushed cheeks. Instead of the sentences racing in remembered anger, he spoke two words again, his lips fumbling with them:

"Wives...stolen..."

The cup crashed on the table. He looked at it dully, and then at Yeardley, and then, uncertainly, at the dwindling fire. His shoulders slumped back against the deerhide chair, and his chin sank into his stock.

Yeardley shook his head heavily, and dragged his watch from his pocket. Two in the morning...they had all but emptied the second decanter. He shook his head again, to clear it, and heard Leslie talking to the fire, his tongue laboring over indistinct words, his hands limp along the arms of the chair.

Tom bent and slipped an arm behind his shoulders.

"How about bed?" he suggested, and made to lift Leslie to his feet. "Tomorrow we'll find us a fox, and we'll have such a run as the tidewater never saw. And then we'll ride over these grants of yours, and pick a place for the house—there'll be a spring..."

Leslie's mouth smiled briefly. His eyes, half hidden behind the narrowed lids, stared steadily into the fire.

"There was a spring at Leslie Hall," he said.

"Zooks, we'll have you another like it, and a manor like the Hall."

"No." Leslie got up quickly. Except for the flush burning on his cheek bones, he gave no sign of the decanter he had drunk. His tongue had stopped fumbling. He said again, sharply, "No."

His hand clapped Tom's arm.

"No, Tom. It's no good." His voice was decisive. "I want no spring, no lands, no manor house. That's gone—dead; and I do not care to sit and look at the corpse. I've been thinking—thinking on this Ohio company I railed about so. Why do these Virginians want the Ohio country so badly? Why but to make money? Land and furs. So. If a Virginia gentleman can make money out of fur, perhaps I can too. It would be a pretty jest to take some of their blood money, eh, Tom? How do you fancy me as a fur trader?"

Yeardley's arm along his shoulders urged him toward the stairs.

"Pish, Tom, I'm not drunk. Nor sleepy, either. Look you, now, there's sense to this. You did your best to quarrel with me tonight, trying to make me forget. I knew it. Ergo, I will make myself forget, instead of sitting here on your mountain, Tom, and looking over my shoulder at the tidewater, and the tobacco fields, and Leslie Hall."

He clapped Tom gayly on the arm again.

"Heigh ho! A drink on that, old friend." He reached for the third decanter on the stone mantel, and ran the cups over. "I'm cut to the pattern for a trader. I have such gewgaws and trade gear as would make the Ohio company's mouth water." He pressed the slopping cup into Yeardley's hand, and drank gustily. "Listen, Tom, and think you how the redsticks' eyes will bulge when I

63

offer them Master Sheraton's own dressing table with three mirrors to see the war paint in, and a crystal necklace for Chief Dog-Meat's seventh squaw, and silken hose for leggings, and satin shoon for moccasins, and a fine lady's bridal bed with blue harrateen to its curtains. By zooks, Tom, you must ride in when the burgesses sit, and tell them of it in Annapolis!"

He sent the pewter cup crashing into the fire. It hissed and sputtered on the charred logs, and the rank odor of wet smoke eddied out.

"Ay, and tell them at Leslie Hall that I will send Mistress Leslie the price of her bed in prime beaver, because I did not give it to her after all. 'T was kind in her, was it not, to teach me how a bed may be traded for? By God, if I can get such a price for my bed as she did for half of hers, I'll come back rich as hell. A drink on that, too, eh?" He took Tom's cup with steady, insistent fingers, and passed it back brimming. "A toast . . . to the cleverest trader in all America: she bartered half her bed for Leslie Hall and forty slaves and a thousand acres, with Amidon Leslie to boot."

His eyes on the strained face, Yeardley drank, and took the decanter out of Leslie's hand.

"Let's go to bed," he said again.

"A whole bed?"

"A whole bed," Yeardley told him gravely.

"A whole bed. . . . I am honored, sir. Honored, and in your debt, sir."

When Tom Yeardley stumbled and wavered on the first step, his guest put an arm around him and steadied him up the stairs.

It seemed to Leslie that he had hardly been asleep at all when he was half awake again, sitting up in bed. Something had jerked him upright, but he had no notion what it was.

He had been sleeping, he realized, for hours. The windows were gray with mingled sun and mist. Thin wisps of fog trailed over the limestone sills; the topmost quilt was clammy with it. He put his hands under the covers quickly.

Then, with a motion that was more instinctive than voluntary, he was out of bed, the puncheons damp and cold under foot. Somewhere a woman screamed.

Running to the nearest window, he heard her again—a short, sharp cry, bitten off. After it, a man's voice, cursing.

64

The window looked out over the stables and the wagon yard. Leslie put his hands on the wet sill and leaned out, and saw why the woman screamed. She stood with her back to the house, her face to a peeled post; her hands were tied and raised above her head; the rope that bound them ran through an auger hole at the top of the post. A man with a black beard stood behind her, with a whip. As Leslie looked, he drew back the whip and swung it; this time the woman made no sound. The whip dropped; the man stepped closer to the post.

There was something familiar about him, so familiar that Leslie watched for a glimpse of his face; watching, he missed the swift jerk of a hand that stripped the dress from the woman's shoulders and let it drop in a heap about her feet. The whip swung and licked at her naked back; swung again and coiled around her hips. She cried out, short, sharp, and broke the cry off, as if she had set her teeth against it. Leslie saw that the blows had left red lines on her white skin. He saw, too, why the bearded man looked familiar: he was dressed in breech clout and leggings, in frontier fashion, with a checkered shirt stuffed inside the clout string at his waist.

Leslie shivered; the fog was cold around his bare legs. His head ached. He wondered, going back across the clammy planks to the bed, what the woman had done to be whipped. An indented servant caught pilfering a trader's packs, most likely. Laws were queer: they set up whipping posts for petty thieves and for loose women who bartered a night for a shilling or two; they said nothing about stealing a man's whole life, nor about a woman who bartered herself for forty slaves, a thousand acres and a manor house. He dreamed that the woman in the stableyard had stolen a house with four chimneys and run away with it, and been caught and flogged; and woke to see Anstice Yeardley standing beside his bed.

She had a tray in her hands, and told him briskly to move over so she could set it down. It occurred to him that he had no recollection of undressing; he realized, now that An' was here, that he was wearing one of Tom's night-rails, and that it was built on a grand scale. Trying to sit up in bed for the tea and hoe cake An' had brought, he found that it was a very manor house of a night-rail. Anstice leaned over and buttoned it under his chin to keep it from falling off.

"D'you hate having me stewing about you, Arnie?"

"I like it, An'. You are..."

"Let be. You're lying. I know you; you hate anything in petti-coats just now. That's good; 't will teach you not go away and leave the next one. Pho, Arnie, don't tell me there will be no next one. Here, give me that cup."

She poured it full of tea again, and passed it back, and plumped herself down on the edge of the bed.

"I know I'm making you grit your teeth to keep from swearing at me. Swear, if you want to. I swear a deal at Tom. I did it this morning, though it is my fault he is in a state again. Didn't you know? You've lost your head as well as your heart, I'll be bound. Did you think Tom Yeardley would pick a quarrel with you an I had not driven him to it? Pshaw, Arnie, you know him better. 'T was I told him to make you angry, and get you a night's sleep by forgetting your sore head...or heart...or both. Now I shall finish the stint: I vow 't is more sore head than sore heart. Will you throw the tea at me? No? Oh, la, you quarreled grandly with Tom last night; I listened and applauded."

She pulled a long face at him, and filched a bit of hoe cake from the tray.

"How do I do as a surgeon for broken hearts, Arnett? I am no quack with the same pill for earache and for a mad dog's bite. If 't were Tom, now, I should cuddle and cozen him; he is but a baby, for all his height and breadth. But you, Arnett—you're a fighting man; all the Leslies have been. You are angry, but not fighting angry. D'you see, Arnie, I would have you fight, even though you fight with me. I almost called you this morning." She looked at him, and hesitated.

Leslie washed down his mouthful of corn cake.

"To stop the execution?" he asked coolly.

"You watched?" Anstice let him see a faint contempt in her face.

"No. I went back to bed."

"You *are* bitter, are you not, Arnie?" The gentleness in her voice surprised him much more than the contemptuous look.

"Ay. Would you not be?"

"Toward every one, and everything? I misdoubt that. What if I

66

had been the girl he whipped? Would you have gone back to bed, pleased that *some* woman should suffer?"

He smiled at her calmly over his tea cup.

"I knew it was not you, An'. She was too thin."

"Damme, Arnett, I shall throw the tea at you, instead of you at me."

"Who was he?"

"Who was *he?* La, have your way. Set your bitterness to brew on the hearth, like tea; 't will turn your insides to leather and make a mean, old man of you."

"Why, then, I need but turn myself inside out, and I shall have me a new hunting dress, all leather from head to toe."

"May the devil bite you, Arnett Leslie! Look you, I would have taken the whip to that hairy oaf myself, an his wife had not come and stopped him. Who is he? Bond, he calls himself; a trader in the Ohio country. He bought a slip of a girl, indented for seven years to pay her passage and gaol charges. She tried to steal a horse last night, to get away, and Bond caught her. That bullock whip of his drew blood before his wife heard the child screaming, and made him loose her."

"Stealing a horse, and trying to run away. 'T is the whipping post and pillory, and maybe branding for that, is it not? She should have stolen Tom and the whole of Near-the-Navel. Then she would have had no punishment, and *you* would be bitter, too, An'. D'you see? The slipper never pinches..."

Anstice got up quickly.

"You would not have spoken so to me, or any woman, a year ago."

"No, nor a week ago, An'."

"Nor stood like a sultan to see a girl flogged, and never lift a hand!"

Leslie put the last of the hoe cake into his mouth and licked his fingers.

"I didn't stand to see her flogged," he protested mildly. "Not like a sultan, nor like anybody. I went back to bed."

"A gallant gentleman!"

" 'Y gad, no! You use me ill, An', except in corn cake and tea."

His mouth flattened and his brows drew down into their straight, black line; Anstice realized that the raillery was in his voice only.

"You've not seen the gentlemen ogle and gloat when the sheriff has some poor light-o'-love to flog on market day. I did not ogle, An', nor gloat; but ..."

"God help any woman, for you'll not," An' finished for him. "Is that it?"

"I hadn't thought of it," said Leslie, smiling, "but it is near enough."

"Fiddlesticks!" An' took up the tray. "I know you better than you do, Arnett, or I'd have Master Bond's bullock whip to your back myself. I dried your clothes. And there's a shoulder of beef on the spit. Come down to the kitchen when you are hungry."

She made a face at him as she backed through the door.

Leslie took his time about dressing. While he dressed, he thought. And having cramped his feet into warped London slippers, and shaved a three-day beard that caused him far more shame than An' Yeardley's lecture, he came to the conclusion that there was nothing to think about. Tom and Tom's peach brandy, he decided, had settled the future for him.

He went downstairs with his mind made up: all the fortune he possessed was in those London bales and chests; until he sold his bridal gewgaws, he could not buy so much as an ax to build a cabin; they would fetch pretty prices in Annapolis or Baltimore— and set the gentry and the very post boys laughing at him from Head of Elk to the Potomac. Ergo, he must sell them elsewhere. Elsewhere, in his mind, had become the Ohio; he had never seen those bloody Forks for which he had helped to pay with a hatchet gash in his ribs. He would go look at them; and if there was no officer or gentleman trader with the cash to buy his flummery, there would be some Shawnee chief to covet the necklace that Evelyn might have worn, and some greasy Mingo to admire himself in Evelyn's London mirrors and sleep in Evelyn's bed.

He felt quite happy, in a miserable, unhappy fashion, when he came down to the kitchen seeking Anstice and more breakfast.

An' was not there.

The shoulder of beef hung sizzling on the spit. It wanted turning, Leslie decided. But when he had found a wooden skewer to turn it with and came briskly toward the hearth, the roast began to revolve on its own account with a clatter and a creaking and a sputter of grease flying into the fire. The spit, he discovered,

68

was no ordinary household affair. Tom Yeardley had brought it, cog-wheels, tread-mill, chains and all, from some tidewater tavern. Peering over the back of the settle, Leslie saw a white terrier guiltily busy in the tread-mill, and saw, too, why the tread-mill had stood still and the roast begun to burn before he came into the kitchen. Sitting solemnly against the wall was a dour little Scottie, beburred, bewhiskered and bedraggled.

He looked up briefly at Leslie and cocked his head and sidled an inch or two toward the door. Then his eyes went back to the tread-mill.

A courtship, Leslie concluded, and spoke to the busy white terrier. The tread-mill stopped. With misanthropic humor, he cut off a toothsome slice of the roast and tossed it to the Scottie. The glum fellow sniffed it; perhaps it was hot, for he lifted his nose and sniffed again at Leslie, waggled his whiskers to shake off the grease, and trudged purposefully back to the tread-mill. The terrier gave him her nose between the slats. The Scottie, overcome with emotion, turned three dizzy circles on the floor. The last of them sent him skidding into the wall, legs braced, paws scratching at the scoured puncheons, a comic figure of lost dignity.

Leslie observed him with growing disgust. Like all other lovers, he did not know how comical he was. He sorted out his feet and marched back to the tread-mill with an air. The lady turned her back on him and the tread-mill began to whir.

"There," said Leslie, and smiled grimly at the dismayed, dour face, "d'you see?"

The Scottie stood on his hind legs and put his forepaws on the tread-mill pen. When the kitchen door swung open, he turned his head and Leslie heard him whimper to himself. An arm in a checkered sleeve reached for his nape.

"By cuffee, I'll learn ye!"

The Scottie whined and edged along the pen. The reaching hand closed on a nest of burs matted in his hair and snatched him up. Teeth flashed under the grim whiskers; the dog dropped; the hand came away streaked with blood. Oaths came roaring through the black beard above the checkered shirt. A boot swung and missed.

"By the holy hell, I'll kill ye f'r that! I'll kick ye t'mush! I'll..."

Leslie came around the end of the settle.

"I wouldn't," he said gently.

"Th' hell you wouldn't," Bond roared at him, and kicked at the dog again. The heavy boot caught him in the ribs and hurled him against the limestone wall. He dropped, yelping, and scuttled for the door again.

The man Bond reached it first, backward. His boot heel caught on the flagstone sill and threw him. He struck the ground on his back, grunted, and lay still. Leslie rubbed the knuckles of his right hand on his satin breeches and left a smear of blood.

"Arnie!" An', in the cellar doorway, set down the skimming pan she carried. "Have you killed him?"

"I hope so," Leslie said softly. "Help me catch the little fellow."

They cornered the Scottie in the dark angle between the tread-mill and the stone oven; his right foreleg hung dangling; trapped, he wrinkled his lips over desperate teeth.

"He's just a puppy!" An' crooned over him when Leslie laid him, trembling, in her lap; and trembled herself when he whimpered at Leslie's probing fingers.

Then, watching the man's somber face intent on whittling splints from kindling in the wood box, she began to smile. He did not look up when the man Bond got muttering to his feet and shuffled away, nor when the rumble of wheels announced that he had gathered up his wagons and his bull whip, his drab wife and his horse-thief servant, and taken the road to Hager's Town.

When, hours later, Tom Yeardley came lumbering downstairs, he heard from An' that Arnett Leslie was on his way to being cured of his broken heart.

Tom had his doubts; and Leslie strengthened them. For nothing could shake him out of his decision to go trading to the Ohio with the wedding gifts that he had bought for Evelyn. For a week Tom argued and pleaded, his big face puckered like an unhappy baby's with his concern; the peach brandy did not help him, and An' would not. In the end, he traded five pack horses for the blue traveling coach, and went with Leslie into the woods to cut tree crotches and trim them into pack saddles. He traded an ax and a mattock, powder and balls, blankets and flour, for silk stockings, lip salve and powder, and the one London gown in Leslie's trunks that would fit Anstice; and swore and blew his nose furiously when Leslie insisted that An' should have the dainty sewing cabinet he had meant for Evelyn.

Two weeks from the day he rode away from the Hall, Leslie rode out through the limestone gateway of Near-the-Navel, and turned in his saddle at the first dip of the wagon road to wave good-by. It pleased him to wear his fine white satin and his cracked slippers, incongruous at the head of a pack train; though the train itself was queer enough. One of the horses was blooded and trim, two were big boned and plodding, and two were just horses. From the stolid gray mare with the bell on her neck to the shabby brown pony without much tail, they carried packs that bulged and stuck out at unexpected angles. The crude saddles themselves were padded with odds and ends of old quilts gay with impossible flowers. There were wallets and sacks of cornmeal and rye wheat flour, and feather beds lashed into tight rolls and shaped like cradles to protect the more precious baggage. From the gray mare's back, four spindly mahogany legs stuck up into the air, and over the bundles on the pony's saddle four more legs bobbed in military unison. All eight legs were elaborately carved in the form of leaping dolphins. Between them a fat brass roaster thrust out curly iron legs from another pack.

Leslie's mouth set itself in a black line as Tom's rumpled head dropped out of sight behind the limestone wall. Tom and An', he thought, might have come to the gate.

Twisted about in his saddle to watch how his pack train followed, he saw why An' had stayed behind and kept Tom with her. She had sent the dour little Scottie to follow him; he was coming down the road, running with his queer crabwise gait; stubborn pup, he insisted on holding his splinted leg straight out ahead of him. Every so often it overbalanced him. He came down now on his whiskers in one of the wheel ruts.

Leslie rode on. When the road turned he pulled Nancy in and went back. The dog was not too clean, and he had been into the burrs again, and he wiggled. The burrs pricked through the white satin breeches and Leslie swore. It was a damned nuisance.

CHAPTER VI

In Which Mr. Leslie Undertakes to Improve the Manners of His Majesty's Army, and Acquires a Family Thereby:

LESLIE traveled slowly. There was no need for haste; his horses were new to the clumsy pack saddles; easy marches at first would save him trouble with sore backs later on. He reasoned it out very plausibly with himself. And knew, when he had it done, that all the reasons were pretense; the truth was that he was running away, and he did not like it; the truth was that he was afraid to face the open laughs, the covert smiles, the contemptuous sympathy that would be waiting for him at every rout and hunt and manor table. No, it was not fear, he insisted; it was simply that he chose not to invite insults that must be resented. It was simply that if he stayed in tidewater he must be forever on the alert for offenses to his pride; he must go about always with his cheek held out ready to be slapped. He would become a swashbuckler, with Todd's pistols always in his saddle bags, a quarrelsome, chip-on-the-shoulder Ishmael. He misliked the rôle; there were no good reasons why he should stay to have it thrust upon him.

Gadzooks, he was not running away. He had met an enemy, and the enemy had beaten him by treachery. He was retreating in good order, with his baggage. He had not surrendered.

It occurred to him then that the enemy had been a woman. He spoke harshly to the black mare. The pack train struck Conococheague ford at a trot and went floundering across.

He made his camp that night in a shallow valley rimmed around with pines, where in the dusk his small fire set a red gloss on rhododendron leaves, and a gossipy stream talked breathlessly through the bell mare's tinkling. Weary and morose, he grilled bacon on a stick, and tossed most of it to the dog. The dog regarded it as an overture as well as a meal, and came wriggling and nuzzling against his arm, until Leslie cuffed him into understanding that he was not welcome.

Leslie did not bother to undress. For a time, lying in his blankets, he listened to the hobbled horses cropping grass along the forest edge, and to the small remembered stirrings of the wilderness. He was glad there was no moon; he would have seen against it four broad-shouldered chimneys on parade. The four chimneys made one of the pictures he wished to forget. Trying to forget them, he fell asleep.

Toward morning, he dreamed that he had come to a ford where water clear as the air slid swiftly over shining gravel. He was thirsty, and laid his rifle across a stone, and stooped to drink from his cupped hands. Standing ankle deep, he drank, and drank again, and shook the last drops from his hands in a flying circle that sparkled like a necklace before it spattered on the alder leaves.

Behind the alders, he caught a flash of vermilion that should not be there, reached for it, and flushed a Shawnee warrior crouching in the bushes. In the dream, the savage sprang at him and they wrestled across the ford, the water churning cold to their knees and the gravel shifting underfoot. He got the Indian by the scalplock, and felt the coarse hair slip through his hand. He twisted his fingers in it; the shaved and painted head slid across his wrist, twisting and jerking to break his grip. Then a pain shot down his fingers and up his arm as the Shawnee sank his teeth into the tendons of his arm.

He woke, struggling with the blankets. They were wadded around his middle. His legs were bare, and it was raining—a cold, slow rain that was half fog.

His right arm was asleep and prickling with hot twinges. Eyes glowed at him, close to his face; he felt coarse hair slip through his fingers, and a shower of sparks burning along his arm. Then a hot, moist tongue licked eagerly at his chin, and the terrier wriggled along the twinging arm until he got his nose against Leslie's cheek. The whiskers he found there made him sneeze. In the half light, Leslie saw the little fellow's dour mouth open as if in a self-conscious grin. He reached out the arm that was not asleep and pulled the wet, wriggling body over against his chest.

When he got the blankets back into place and lay down again

to sleep in the drizzling rain, the Scottie inched himself up until his nose could burrow down between arm and shoulder. Then he sneezed again, and sighed, a long-drawn sigh that ended in a contented nudge.

Arnett Leslie and the pup slept late that day; at least, Mr. Leslie did.

When he awoke at last, the rain was gone; but the terrier was still there, plastered tight as a wet shirt to the man's body, with his chin-whiskers on the lapel of the white satin vest and his puppy eyes soberly on guard.

At the first stirring of the long body under the blankets, the small body huddled against it began to tremble; in a moment the tremble turned into an ecstatic wriggle, and the after-thought of a tail went furiously to work. A pink tongue slid out tentatively, and flicked back again as Leslie turned his face just in time. The tail stopped. Leslie put out a hand to push the pup away. Instead, he took the dour jaw between thumb and finger; there was something queerly familiar about that long, sad face, with its thickety eyebrows and its solemn eyes. The man lay drowsily looking at the sober little fellow.

"Plague on it," he said at length, and the sound of his voice set the pup to squirming again, "you look like Robin."

The eagerness in the half-hidden eyes made Leslie swear softly to himself, it was so much like the eagerness in Robin Stuart's eyes when they forgot to be somber.

"Damme, you *are* Robin," he told the dog, and waggled the be-whiskered face back and forth between thumb and finger. "You've got a name, beastie. Robin. Do you understand, sir?"

He flung off the damp blankets and got to his feet, stretching ruefully as he discovered how stiff and cramped he was from that first night on the ground. The pup, beside himself, shot across the glade on three legs, turned two crazy circles around a stump, and shot back again, barking and grinning.

Instinctively, Leslie's eyes went to the forest that ringed them round, and his voice rang sharply:

"Here . . . stop that!"

The gleeful barks stopped short. Through narrowed lids, Leslie searched the rhododendron and the shadowy woods, and found nothing. The puppy, head cocked, sat down in the wet grass to watch him; after a while, the pup, too, began to scan the under-brush, looking back now and again, hopefully.

But the man did not speak to him.

His sharp order had been sheer habit. It was still hard to believe that a piece of parchment signed in Paris could make it safe for a white man's dog to bark in the wilderness beyond the Conoco-cheague. Somewhere along this Cumberland trail, a dog's excited bark at a squirrel in a locust tree had brought a Delaware scalping party down upon John Simpson and his family as they fled to the settlements in the last fierce outbreak; it was barely two years ago that a patrol from Fort Frederick had come upon the bodies of John Simpson's wife and daughters, stripped, staked out upon the ground, with the fire that had killed them still smoldering upon them. John Simpson's nine-year-old son had ridden a packhorse into the all but deserted village of Frederick, gibbering and sobbing with terror. Leslie wondered, casually, what had become of the boy.

Bound out to some German farmer, most likely. . . . Well, it was not a bad lot for a poor boy. A girl, now, bound out to a rake like Lawless . . .

Leslie shrugged his shoulders impatiently. It was nonsense, he told himself testily, to let every passing thought pick him up and carry him back into places he wanted to forget. When he rode through Tom Yeardley's gate, he had closed a gate against the past. And he had closed his mind, too. It must stay closed. He began slowly to take off the satin vest, noting with satisfaction the stains that one day of wilderness travel had left upon it. When he had it off, he rolled it into a tight bundle and laid it on the ashes of last night's fire.

The white breeches followed it. When he threw the wet silk stockings after the breeches, the dog thought it was a game, and fetched one of them back to him, and then sat back in pained be-wilderment when Leslie jerked it out of his mouth and ordered him angrily away. He tried it again, after a while, and was cuffed for his pains. Leslie, going barefooted across the glade to his leather trunk, felt again a surge of resentment. The plagued dog wouldn't let him even destroy the tangible things that were re-minders of what lay behind the gate. Dammit, the beast's sad wisp of a face, following him reproachfully beyond arm's reach, wouldn't let him so much as vent his spleen in a blow without making him pay for it. He spoke gruffly to the pup.

"Robin!"

Instantly the bedraggled body was wriggling between his bare ankles. Robin sat on a corner of the blanket while Leslie, in shirt and drawers, opened the worn trunk and took out the linsey hunting shirt and leggings, the breech clout and the moccasins, and slowly dressed himself.

This day the pack train did not trot. The road it traveled was only two wheel tracks cut deep into the sod. Grass divided them, and young shoots of oak and locust grew hopefully between. Now and then there was a stump; in the bottom of the ruts, roots sprawled nakedly; the covered wagons, Leslie realized, had dug the wheel tracks much deeper since he had seen them last. The slashings of limbs and brush beside them were grayer, more weather-beaten; at the crossing of one nameless stream he missed a great bowlder that had forced his forage wagon to swing in a half circle in mid-ford. But these were trifling changes; the road was the road he knew; every dip and turn had its memories.

Twice he passed burned cabins in stump-dotted clearings. A spring bubbling up through mossy rocks brought back a hot, bright noon, a file of Maryland hunting shirts black with sweat, thirsty militiamen muttering angrily because he would not let them stop to drink; ambush had been deadly close that day; Tom Yeardley's patrol had pried two greased and painted Indians out of the cedar scrub on the hill just ahead, and shot and scalped them both. Three miles farther on, he saw bare sapling trunks slanted like rafters against a ridgepole set between two tree crotches—the skeleton of a half-faced camp, and he nodded to it gravely. He had almost died there, lying on a pile of ferns, blood seeping from the hatchet gash in his chest. The rain, he remembered, had soaked him through before the men got the saplings cut and thatched with brush; he had lain awake all night, wondering whether he was about to die; he had wanted to live long enough to see his mother and Evelyn.

He put Nancy to a trot. In the late afternoon he turned off the trail, and camped in a spot where he had never been before. After supper he set Robin hysterical with joy, playing tug-of-war with him with the stock that matched his ruffled shirt. Robin crawled into the blankets that night as if he owned a half interest in them, and the man let him stay.

Day after day, the pack train ambled deeper into the wilderness. The Tuscarora loomed black against the sky one night, and in the morning Leslie saw it glowering down at him like some Indian manitou, swathed to the chin in a white blanket of fog, its feathered pines a barbaric war-crest. The next night it lay behind, purple below, dull gold and green above in the level sunset.

At the lazy pace he set, Leslie found that spring was catching up to him. The hills were drenched with white dogwood; blossoms banked themselves like drifts along the dark trunks of pine in every open space; climbing the slopes, they blended with locust trees so massed with bloom that they were tight bouquets. There were acres of those living nosegays, whole plantations of them. Where the trail dropped down through swampy meadows, violets and buttercups grew so thick they looped gold and purple love-knots around the stems of the bouquets. The pines began to trick themselves out in fresh green points of lace; the poplar groves took on a bronze glow in the sun. Leslie rode with the strings of his hunting shirt loosed, the flaps open on his chest; he was conscious, at times, of a loosening of tightly drawn strings within him.

Then the strings tightened again. Coming within sight of the brown Potomac bluffs, he saw the stone ramparts of Fort Frederick white against them, and turned perversely aside. There were men he knew in the barracks there; they would squeeze his hand sore and talk him deaf, and do their best to drink him under the table. And they would ask questions. Leslie plunged northward through the forest, under the afternoon shadows of Sidling Ridge. His face set itself into hard lines. Robin wriggled uneasily on the blanket roll, and got curt orders to be still.

The wilderness lost its healing. The moon came up full, and Leslie, sleepless, hated it for the chimneys that took shape against it. He began to lengthen the day's march, catching the hobbled horses before daylight, setting out without breakfast, driving himself viciously. He took an ugly pleasure in fighting the forest, slashing a passage through vines and deadfalls with the ax when a little searching might have found an easier way. His moccasins wore thin, and split, and he had no others; brambles and underbrush tore his shirt and leggings, and plucked the thrums from sleeves and cape; he came to Forbes' road a surly, ragged figure. He knew this road, too; its very familiarity offended him. Sooner or later, this wagon track would remind him of what he wanted to forget.

Just ahead, in the valley below, lay Fort Bedford. He thought of avoiding it as he had avoided Fort Frederick, and swore at himself for thinking of it. *Damnation,* let them laugh at his mahogany dolphins and his brass roaster and his feather beds.

He rode deliberately at a walk through the cluttered log cabins of Fort Bedford, and past the stockade and earthworks of the fort itself. A lounging sentry in the green of the Pennsylvania Provincial regiment gawked at him from the open gate, and yawned. In front of the trading shack, a blanketed Indian sat with two white men in tow shirts and osnabrig breeches; they had a keg between them, and dipped into it with gourds. The contents of the keg interested them more than the pack train. In a field beyond the town, a woman was scratching the dirt with a sharpened tree fork hitched behind two cows; she pushed back her sunbonnet to stare as Leslie passed.

The road swung around the grass-grown rifle pits dug by Old Iron Head's army on the way to Fort Duquesne. They, too, were familiar; they had been thigh deep in water when the Maryland militia took them over from Forbes' regulars. Leslie swore. The damned road had done what he had known it would do; it had jerked him back to Evelyn; he had stood just there, in that caved-in embrasure, to read her Christmas letter. He had not loved her then. *Dammit,* he did not love her now.

He rode on up the wooded slope, around a turn, and saw six green-coated Pennsylvanians busy around a forage wagon.

Robin got up recklessly on three legs on the blanket roll and barked. Two of the soldiers looked over their shoulders; between them, Leslie saw that they had a boy and a bear tied to the wheels of the wagon. The bear was hitched to the low front wheel by a chain around his neck; the boy, bare to his waist, was spread-eagled by wrist and ankle to the rim of the tall rear wheel. His back ran with blood. The green-coats made a circle around him and a sergeant; as Leslie rode up behind them, the sergeant brought a black whip hissing across the bloody flesh. The boy yelped, and the six soldiers laughed and stamped, and pounded each other on the shoulders. The whip rose again.

"Sergeant!"

The colonials stiffened with a jerk.

"Us caught a flour thief, zur," the sergeant said quickly, and then saw that the man who snapped at him was no officer at all, but only a backwoods trader in a ragged hunting shirt. His red face flushed redder. He roared:

"What you do here? Py Gott, get out! Get along!"

Leslie smiled.

"Has that boy been tried?"

"You heardt me! 'Raus!"

Leslie's lips drew back faintly over his teeth.

"Sergeant, I asked you: Has that boy had a trial?"

The Dutch sergeant opened his mouth and shut it again; the grim man on the black horse had an air about him that went with sabers and gold sashes. Then he looked at the pack train jumbled up behind the black mare, and his whip came up truculently.

"Ve do not haf trials for voods-runners, *oder* for t'ieves," he blustered, and thrust himself through the ring of privates to brandish the whip in Leslie's face.

Leslie picked Robin up by his scruff and leaned to drop him into the grass. The whip went back over the sergeant's shoulder and cut, hissing, at Leslie's head. It struck, instead, an open hand that wrenched it out of the Provincial's grip and slashed it across his open mouth. The sergeant bellowed and threw up his arms to shield his face; the whip beat them down. Leslie slipped from the saddle, caught him by one sleeve, spun him, and laid the cat three times across his back.

A private sprang for his musket, leaning against the wagon box, got it, and whirled it like a club. The ragged hunting shirt twisted under the descending butt; the whip slashed twice at the soldier's wrists; he dropped the musket and backed into the wagon, ducked under it and ran on all fours. The lash bit at the nearest green tunic, raised dirt out of it, and found only air when it struck again. Leslie looked at the rout and smiled, and drew the lash through his fingers. *Gadzooks,* the thing was heavy as lead, a bullock whip cut short. No wonder the boy's back was like a chopped beefsteak.

He drew his knife and cut the thongs.

The boy stood swaying.

"Look you, did you steal their flour?"

Pale blue eyes flickered from side to side.

"Be they gone, zur?" Leslie's lip curled a little; the boy had a hang-dog look, loose lipped, loose chinned; he was unpleasantly dirty. A very rabbit of a boy. He whimpered: "Be they gone?"

"Ay. Did you steal their flour?"

"No, zur. Da bear it was, zur; on his behind legs he stand oop, and take da flour from da wagon out."

"A trick, eh?"

"No, zur." Tears ran weakly down the caked grime on his face; he snuffled. "When I sleep, he take da flour out."

"Woods-colt, are you?"

The boy gaped.

"Where's your father?"

"He be kilt by Injuns, zur. By Red Stone dey kilt him, and keep me wit' dam. Yust now dey let me go."

The old story, Leslie thought; God alone knew how many stolen white children were still alive in the Shawnee villages. He put a hand under the boy's arm to steady him.

"D'you know your name?"

"Ay, zur. It be Fritz Van Buren." He snuffled, and licked at his upper lip.

"Didn't you tell them the bear took the flour?"

"No, zur."

"No? Why not?"

"Berhaps if dey know dat, dey kill him."

Leslie's eyes narrowed. A very puling rabbit of a boy....

"Here." He pulled Fritz toward the mare. "Get your foot up to the stirrup there. Get a hold on the saddle; I'll not hurt your back so much if you can haul yourself up. Steady. There's a spring a little way up the road; we'll camp there."

He stooped for the boy's shirt. Holding the linsey garment, he looked sharply up at him.

"You got this from no Indian."

"No, zur. By da trader dey give me it; to da trader dey sell me, by Carlisle, zur. Da trader he will da bear kill; on da back he w'ip me. I do not stay by him."

Leslie saw that the shirt was criss-crossed with dark stains. *Damme,* a pretty welcome for a white boy set free from Indian captivity. He stooped again to pick up the Scottie, and led Nancy back into the trail. There was still one queer thing about the business.

"Why'd you come this way from Carlisle, Fritz?"

"I be going back to da Injun town by Wenango, zur." His thin voice rose shrilly. "Da bear, zur! Da bear be tied."

Leslie went back and unfastened the chain from the wagon wheel. Gad, he would have the whole pack train shying into the underbrush. He told himself brusquely that Arnett Leslie was a plagued fool. At the spring a mile up the road, he had proof of it: while he cleansed the weals on the boy's back, the bell mare's clapper set up a hysterical jangling. Turning, he saw Robin lunge crabwise for the bear's fore-paw, nip it, and scuttle away; the bear, snubbed short by his chain, reared up on his hind legs and frightened the brown pony and one of the nondescript horses into a poplar thicket. Before he could catch them, a meal sack burst and half a bushel of ground corn went sifting to waste in the trampled leaves. He saved a little of it; three days later, in the abandoned cantonment Forbes' army had built below the Laurel Ridge, he cleaned the dirt and charred sticks out of a mud oven, made a fire and baked journey cake.

"Tomahawk Encampment," he told Fritz as they sat cross-legged in the dusk, munching the hot pone. And told him how the English general, Forbes, rode in a blanket slung between two horses to fight the French and Indians at the Forks of the Ohio, and how, just over Laurel Ridge, Captain Evan Shelby of Maryland fought a duel with an Indian chief and killed him between the battle lines of the two armies. While he talked, the boy went fast asleep; and Arnett Leslie, disgusted, rolled himself into his blankets and chirruped to Robin to come to bed.

Some time in the night the mangy bear uprooted the sapling that held his chain, and stole the rest of the journey cake.

CHAPTER VII

In Which Mr. Leslie Brings His Feather Beds and His Sore Heart to a Place Called Fort Pitt, and Finds It Just as Ugly as He Expected it to Be:

THE month of May was all but gone when Arnett Leslie and his queer cavalcade climbed the last of the bluffs, and Leslie saw the Forks of the Ohio.

There it lay—the meeting-place of two great rivers, the birthplace of a third river greater than either. Armies had come three thousand miles across the sea to fight for that bit of land between the two parent streams and their lusty offspring, the Ohio. Two British generals had died to take it. The prisoners captured in the Braddock massacre had shrieked their lives out at the stakes set up on the green bank of the Allegheny. Here on the bluff that overlooked the Forks, the Maryland riflemen had stood and fought while Major Grant's Highlanders ran vainly from the Delaware hatchets and the Shawnee scalping knives. Somewhere near by, young Duncan Cameron had died.

Leslie let the long rifle slide slowly through the crook of his arm and the butt drop into the beaten grass between the wheel tracks. Duncan Cameron's life had been too big a price, he thought, to pay for that triangle of land; and Duncan was only one of a thousand who had died.

Sitting on a hummock of muddied grass, he contemplated the fact that he had come to the place where his journey ended—and ended, he realized, in vain. Elbows on knees, with the rifle cradled between them, he stared moodily at the sweep of green slope below him.

First there was a marshy pond; then a town; then a fort on the point where the rivers met. Down in that straggling town, he was going to forget certain unpleasant matters. While he sat and looked at the nearest log huts set hit-or-miss in the meadow, the reminders he had brought with him across the mountains came ambling up the hill behind him, hoofs sucking noisily in the wet clay, little bell tinkling, pack saddles creaking, ears jerking and nostrils twitching to be rid of the gnats that swarmed in the damp, hot sunshine. Six horses, the boy, and the dog, the procession bunched up in the road and halted at the brow of Grant's Hill.

There were burrs on the dog, and shapeless linsey-woolsey garments on the boy. From the stolid farm horse to the brown pony without much tail, the packs bulged and stuck out more unexpectedly than they had even on the day Leslie rode out through Tom Yeardley's gate, and the rags of gay quilt that padded the saddles were more ragged.

The boy wriggled through the bunched-up horses and came to a halt beside Leslie. He let the Nancy mare's reins trail through his hand and slip to the ground. With one slow finger he reached out and touched the tall rifle leaning against Leslie's knee.

His voice droned:

"Us bant need that no longer. That be Fort Pitt down yander."

Leslie's head moved irritably. The high, spiritless voice had a nerve-rasping quality; there was an exasperating patience about it.

"Us be eatin' darackly," said the boy's old-man tone.

Leslie slapped at the gnats about his neck.

"Will you ever get enough to eat, Fritz?"

"Berhaps."

The man's long fingers ran restlessly through his black hair, and the short club at the back of his neck burst from its ribbon and hung dangling about the open collar of his hunting shirt. He fished impatiently in the grass behind him.

"Here, zur," said the droning voice, and the boy's slow fingers dropped the ribbon on Leslie's knee.

"Aren't you afraid to go on down?" Leslie probed at him. He glanced up at the parallel stains across the boy's ragged shirt; they were fading into the coarse cloth, but the long weals of the whip were still marked in blood.

"No, zur," droned the waif, "you bant let they w'ip me again."

Leslie swore so loudly that even the dog stopped short in the fascinating business of chasing a slim, green snake through the grass and looked back with one ear apprehensively cocked. But Leslie was not looking at the dog, nor at anything else in particular.

He was finding Fritz Van Buren's outspoken faith in him more than a little embarrassing.

"They'll have to whip me first, Fritz," he promised, knowing that he possessed very slight means indeed to make the promise good.

The boy's drooping shoulders straightened.

"They'll not!" he shrilled.

Leslie smiled in spite of himself. Somewhere in this rack of bones was a spark of spirit after all. Not, he assured himself quickly, that it made any difference to him; nothing made any difference to him.

He slipped his hand up the barrel of the rifle and used it as a staff to pull himself up off his tuft of grass. Then, on impulse, he thrust the weapon toward the boy.

"Carry it," he ordered curtly.

Under the beads of sweat, the boy's face lighted. And then the light went out, as Leslie strode to the black mare and plucked out of the blanket roll the shortened bullock whip he had wrenched from the Dutch sergeant. He made it swish and slap against the threadbare leggings. The rag-tag dog scurried gayly around his feet and nipped for the flying lash; but Fritz looked apprehensive. Leslie, cutting at the air, caught the youngster's appealing eyes.

"I'll be skewered and basted if you're not afeared!" He said it sharply, but the boy found nothing in his voice, at least, to frighten him.

"Not of the w'ip, zur. You bant goin' to fight with the sojers in Fort Pitt, zur? Not for me, zur?"

Arnett Leslie's brows drew down blackly over his narrowing eyes. He cast a glance around his baggage train, and his lips took on the hardness that was years older than his thin face.

"No, not over you, Fritz. They'll not be touching you; I promised you that. But there is that about our baggage, Fritz, may amuse some of them down yonder more than is polite. I'll not be laughed at."

"Laughin' don't hurt, zur."

"No? You'll not be a man until it does. Look you: you do not wish to be beaten; I do not wish to be a clown. Come along, Fritz."

He slipped the Nancy mare's reins into the crook of his arm

and started down the mud track toward the pond. Behind him the bell tinkled and the packs jostled and creaked. The terrier set up a high-pitched barking, and the pony snorted.

"That be the bear, zur," Fritz murmured at his elbow. "Excuse, please."

Before Leslie thought to stop him, he was slipping off into the brush, the rifle trailing. He was back in a minute, with the gaunt beast's chain twisted into his belt. Leslie's lips shut on an angry protest. It was quite enough to go marching into Pitt's Town with mahogany dolphins bobbing above his pack saddles, without this scuffed and scraggly bear in tow. But he looked at Fritz, and said nothing.

Fritz had taken on dignity and stature; the long rifle in his hands had straightened his sad shoulders and kept them straight; he had an air of confidence about him as he fell into step beside Leslie. Robin came scurrying out of the bushes and elected to trot in the wheel track just across from the bear. The cavalcade moved slowly down the slope.

Fritz marched with the long rifle clutched across his body in both hands, his eyes staring past its barrel toward the red and black fort squatting in the lowland a half-mile down the slope. He leaned forward a little as he walked, as if his shoulder itched for the feel of the rifle butt, and his arms ached to throw up the long barrel and let fly. Leslie grimaced. Heigh-ho, the boy had little enough reason to love the troops in these back-country garrisons. The Indians had been kinder to him. If he wanted to play at attacking Fort Pitt, let him.

Leslie realized, as the cart tracks wound down the hill toward the shining blue pond, that Fort Pitt was no mere backwoods stockade. It lay there in the arms of the two great rivers, sullen and stolid and strong, an old-world fortress transplanted into the wilderness. Arnett Leslie was soldier enough to appreciate the massive strength of the sprawling walls, and the strategic power of the solid bastions with their cannon-ports looking out on both rivers just at their meeting-place.

The Highland regiments that built those walls had taken heed to the painted stakes atop Grant's Hill. Here, where the road wound past the pond, the kilted boys of the Seventy-seventh had been tomahawked and scalped, trapped and helpless in the muck.

Yonder, on that little stretch of level meadow, Forbes' main column had found the heads of those boys set up on red stakes and their kilts draped like skirts below them. No wonder the survivors of the Seventy-seventh, with their own tortured dead a grisly vision in their minds, had piled the walls of Fort Pitt high and thick.

They lay there now in the hot sunshine, a huge five-pointed star that glowed dull red on the two sides that faced the town. Those two landward flanks were faced with brick, molded and baked by Forbes' army on the spot where the captives of Braddock's tragedy had been tortured. A little beyond the red and black fort, Leslie knew, the French fort called Duquesne had stood at the very apex of the triangular peninsula. But now there was not a sign of it. Forbes' Highlanders and Royal Americans had stamped its burned remnants into the earth in their hate, and left it a legend.

There were log shacks now where Grant's boys had died along the shore of the pond. The road curved around the south end of the pond and dipped down to a muddy ford across a creek. With swishing whip and jingling bell, the cavalcade came down through the scattered hog-pen cabins into the Lower Town.

Major Leslie, eyeing it, found little enough about it to please him. It was a very slattern of a town.

Slovenly cabins stood hit or miss along the way, each one with a patch of beaten, bare earth around it as if the fresh spring grass had shrunk away from these unlovely habitations. Some had windows of greased paper, and some had shutters, and some had only gaping square holes where the planks that had covered them through the winter had been taken down. The roofs were stone and clapboard; which is to say the clapboards were laid on from ridgepole to wall, and held more or less in place by a motley collection of stones and bowlders strewn over them.

Dirty children dressed in a single garment of linsey-woolsey played and quarreled in the muddy dooryards; an unkempt woman came out of a cabin door, scattering a mob of wild-haired youngsters, and went padding down the road on bare and dirty feet. For the most part, except for half-naked children in their shifts, and now and then a woman staring from an open door, the Lower Town seemed lifeless. Major Leslie's lips curled a little, as if he sniffed something unpleasant in the air.

A cow and a calf came out from between two cabins and fell

in behind the barefoot woman. The three of them, like an advance guard, scattered six somnolent hogs from their wallow in the road. The hogs fled, squealing and spattering mud, straight through an open door. Arnett Leslie nodded to himself, as if the pigs had confirmed an opinion he had already formed.

The road swung off to the right on a lazy curve; the slattern and the cow and calf paid no heed to the road, but went on past a well-sweep toward the fort. The black-haired man and the tow-haired boy, the harum-scarum dog and the nonchalant bear went on down the ruts between two more or less regular rows of log houses. At the left, toward the river, the red walls of Fort Pitt showed at intervals between the cabins, and through one gap Leslie had a long, curious look at a hewn-stone bastion and the muzzle of an eighteen-pounder glowering down upon the town. At the right there were glimpses of green meadow land, and one broad, irregular field where the black earth was tinted with the pale green of young spelt. A little farther on, the log cabins fell away altogether on the right, and Pitt's Town took on its first appearance of order and cleanliness. Spreading up the gentle slope and away to the broad blue reaches of the Allegheny, the King's Garden lay basking in the sun, ridged in black furrows here and there, and again marching neatly in parallel ranks of bright green lettuce, and again in heavy columns of grape vines marshaled to stout stakes and supported by whole phalanxes of corn.

It had a look of gentility about it that made Leslie think of other gardens in the Patuxent lowlands; it made him, for a moment, feel almost kindly toward Pitt's shabby town. And then, as always happened, the memory of those Maryland gardens clutched him round the heart, which was sore enough already, and he fell to disliking the steaming black mud and the sullen black cabins and the swarming black gnats more bitterly than ever.

And so, hot and pestered and more than a little lonely and sick at heart, Major Leslie came to the last turn of the road where it swung in toward the earthworks and the drawbridge of Fort Pitt, and saw above him the Great Union of England drooping lazily against its staff.

The sky was so hot and blue, the air so still, that the bright blue field of the drowsy flag melted into the sky, and left the crimson crosses of St. Andrew and St. George burning like a smoldering fire. As the pack train swung around the turn, the great fort came suddenly to life. Beyond the walls, unseen, drums rolled thunderously; at the crest of the brick redan that guarded the gates, two sentries in scarlet coats stiffened into statues, their muskets at *present*. On the staff, the drooping crosses stirred into a flicker of life, and the flag slid slowly down. A soldier in a green tunic caught it in his arms and drew it out of sight behind the gray stone angle of the bastion.

There was too much of the soldier in Leslie for him not to feel the pulse of the rolling drums and warm to the fire of the burning crosses in the bright blue field. He stood with his moccasins in a half-dried puddle and gazed with a grudging admiration at the brick redan and its rigid sentinels, at the log drawbridge and the massive log gates beyond it, at the passage through the solid walls, and the glittering muzzles of cohorns and carronades thrust out from their red-brick embrasures. Old Iron Head had built well; this fort of his had an air of power about it, and an air of disdain as well. Behind its earthworks and its moat, it stood aloof and withdrawn from the squalid town. Down in the moat, a group of officers in white waistcoats were bowling; when the drums stopped, the click of the balls sounded just as Leslie had heard it sound on the bowling green under the locusts in Annapolis, and under the oaks on my lord Baltimore's London lawn.

For a moment, the moving color and the easy laughter made Arnett Leslie forget that they were part of a life he had put behind him. A wrist with a froth of lace about it flipped open a snuff box, and offered it, with a flourish; and Leslie's nostrils twitched. Zooks! It was five weeks since he had taken snuff. He stood with the black mare's reins hanging loose in his fingers, and gazed down at powdered wigs and polished boots, laced hats and dangling fobs. They were a whole world away from the shabby town. For the first time since he gave Tom Yeardley's gate the kick that closed it decisively upon the past, he felt homesick, and admitted it to himself. Not homesick for Leslie Hall, he amended the admission brusquely, but for people of his own kind—*men* of his own kind. After all, there was no reason why he must wear linsey and osnabrig where other gentlemen wore linen and silk.

He jingled his few silver shillings in his pocket. They would make just as much noise in fashionable breeches as in those bedraggled things he was wearing. They might, he added wryly, go even farther if he claimed the hospitality of Fort Pitt than if he went bargaining for room and board in some log cabin. And the pretty luxuries in his baggage might fetch a better price if sold as a favor by Major Leslie than if bartered as a matter of necessity by plain Arnett Leslie in the rôle of mendicant trader. He brought his whip down on his leg with a decisive· *spat,* and swung around to Fritz.

"Hardships, eh?" he rallied the solemn youngster. "D'ye suppose, now, they'd invite *us* to play at bowls with them?"

"No, zur," Fritz answered gravely. "They be gentlemen, zur, and officers."

"And you'd say I am no gentleman, is that it?"

"But you bant, zur."

Leslie laughed shortly, and slapped his leg again.

"No, thank God. Just a merchant, with an eye to the best market. Here," he flipped the mare's reins into the boy's hand, "lead the beasts off the road a bit and wait for me. I've a mind to call on the commandant. Mayhap he'll have us to dine with him, and we can sell him a featherbed over the wine."

He turned briskly toward the drawbridge, stopped for a moment to glance again at the squat town and still again at the bowlers, and drew back to make room on the narrow drawbridge for two girls who came out from one of the pig-wallow alleys and passed him on their way to the fort.

Trailing behind them, he grimaced at the contrast they made—shabby town and arrogant fort personified. From head to foot, they were as different as the Forks of the Ohio were different from London. One, the taller, wore her hair piled high, with a chip hat perched saucily aslant; the other wore a faded blue sunbonnet with a shapeless frill which failed to quite hide wisps of damp red hair. Plump brown shoulders rose from a frill of lace above a wine-red gown that was puffed out with side hoops and its own stiff ruffles, and under the brocaded hem a pair of red-heeled slippers flashed in and out. Step for step with the gay slippers, a pair of dirty bare feet moved in and out beneath a flounce that might once have been blue; it was faded now into streaks and splotches of gray and white, with unexpected strips of blue where the seams ran and the stuff had faded less.

Leslie grimaced again. Every fourth step or so, the bedraggled flounce hitched up and revealed slim ankles, and there was a generous splash of mud on one of them. A camp-woman, fetching home the garrison laundry, by the look of her and the bundle she kept hitching up in her arms. Phaugh! She might at least wash the dirt from her ankles before she delivered the washing.

The red heels seemed more worth while. Whoever had the money and the desire to buy red-heeled slippers for a woman at Pitt's Town might be tempted to buy a bed with blue harrateen curtains, or even a mahogany dressing table. Even, perhaps, a virginal, if the wench with the plump brown shoulders had the wit to play it. Leslie shrugged disgustedly at his own thoughts as he followed the oddly-matched feet over the log drawbridge and into the covered passage that led under the wall of the fort.

There was a ten-yard stretch of shadowed coolness, and then a white-gaitered sentry in a red coat, a square brick guardhouse with iron bars at its single window, and beyond that an acre of bare, baked earth—the parade-ground of his majesty's stronghold of Fort Pitt. Around the square of black earth stood red-brick barracks with square holes for windows, and solid wooden shutters swung back against the walls. Soldiers lounged on benches in front of them, or leaned from second-story windows to shout ribald comment at the girls. Leslie looked again at the wine-red gown; enlisted men would scarcely be shouting at even a camp washwoman if the girl beside her, in hooped and panniered gown, was an officer's wife. By the jokes and the loud laughter they provoked, she would be something else than a wife. If the officer who had bought those red-heeled slippers happened to be some lordling with money in his pocket, the jests and the laughter promised a good market for boudoir furnishings. Mr. Leslie's shoulders said *phaugh!* again as distinctly as if he had said it aloud.

The sunbonnet and the saucy hat went steadily across the parade, past the open well and windlass in its center, toward the last of the red-brick barracks. Watching them, Leslie spoke to the sentry at the guardhouse door. The soldier jerked his thumb toward a taller building that stood apart. The commandant, he volunteered, was much engaged.

"If you be one o' them traders he sent for, ye're late," he added.

"He'll have y'r hide. He's skinnin' 'em alive in there f'r tradin' guns to the Injuns."

The wine-red dress vanished through a door in the barracks, and the faded blue dress stopped at the door next to it. Leslie went up the steps of the commandant's house and into the orderly room just inside the door. A clerk told him briskly that the commandant was busy, and a gruff voice storming angrily behind a closed door bore him out.

"Who is officer of the day?" Leslie inquired, and smiled a little at the answer.

"Captain Arnold," the clerk said, "but he's gone to his quarters. First door in the officers' barracks—next building."

"Perhaps," Mr. Leslie ventured, "I had best leave him to himself, if he is busy."

"Busy?" The clerk yawned at the open window and the lounging soldiers across the parade. "In this hell hole?"

"A lady..." Leslie suggested. "With red heels to her slippers...."

The clerk closed one eye in an elaborate wink.

"Must be you've just come in," he leered, "not to know Sergeant Peggy."

Mr. Leslie's eyebrows went up.

"You make them sergeants in Fort Pitt, then? I wonder, now, what my lord Amherst would say to that—making sergeants out of the enlisted women."

"Oh, she's no enlisted woman—not Sergeant Peggy. She's an officer's lady, by the left hand, see? Peggy Sargent, her name is. Captain Arnold hadn't been at the forks a month before she came. Followed him across the mountains from Philadelphia, she did. Followed him into the fort today, did she, now?"

He winked again, and went to the window and leaned out.

"No," he pulled his head in and shook it, disappointed, "he's taking it very quietlike."

"And what," inquired Mr. Leslie confidentially, "may he be taking?"

"Why, her following him about. He cursed her last time, very noble. Gave her a proper cursing, he did, and threw her out. He has other fish to fry, he has."

"And she keeps getting into the pan, I take it," Mr. Leslie

prompted him. It struck Mr. Leslie that he was acquiring information which might well prove invaluable to a merchant with goods to sell.

"Ay, into the pan, and into his wig, too, I'll warrant you. She'll not let him go, nor so much as look at any one else. She's a queer one, that Sergeant Peggy."

"And who," prodded Mr. Leslie, "is the other fish Captain Arnold wishes to fry?"

The clerk winked again. Leslie, watching him in huge disgust, marveled that Captain Arnold's clerk should talk so freely and so unpleasantly about his officer.

"She's a new one. Red-haired, and a howling beauty she'd be, in that red gown the other one wears."

Mr. Leslie's soul curled at the thought of red hair against that wine-red dress. Red hair required a gown of sea green, or perhaps of jade, or gold, or a deep, rich brown—he laughed abruptly, thinking how amused my lord Baltimore would be to know how Arnett Leslie was using certain lessons in how a lady should be dressed. The clerk looked blank.

"You mean the washer-woman?" Leslie asked him.

"Ay," the clerk answered shortly. There was something about this shabby stranger's manner of laughing that made him suspicious and a little fearful that he had said too much.

"Do you think," Leslie persisted, his mind on a certain bargain he might drive with this sorely beset Captain Arnold, "that the washer-woman has surrendered?"

"Why not?" the soldier countered, and blinked at him. "He's at Hellward Bound's place every night oglin' of her; there's money that fair burns in his pocket, and he'll be a lord in his time."

"A lord." Mr. Leslie's lip twitched a little at that. "And what," he wanted to know, "is Hellward Bound's?"

"Hellward's? God, you passed it; it's the log tavern in King's Highway. Hellward fetched the wench over the mountains for a barmaid." He smirked and winked. "An' for bait to draw custom, too."

Leslie's nose testified to something unpleasant. He looked the clerk down from his dirty scratch-wig to his half-buttoned gaiters and back to his pasty face. His voice took on a wire edge.

"You will present my compliments to Captain Ecuyer," he

directed sternly, "as soon as he has finished with the gentlemen he has with him, and tell him that Major Leslie of Maryland will pay his respects this evening."

He turned his back on the startled sloven and marched out. For an amateur merchant, he told himself, he had not done at all badly. He went quickly down the steps, intending to call forthwith upon this captain who had money to burn, a discarded mistress to soothe and a new mistress to win. Captain Arnold should be an excellent customer.

He stopped, instead, at Captain Arnold's door, and looked with amazement at the scene in front of the door beyond. The girl in the sunbonnet stood like an embattled small fury behind her bundle of washing, her hands clenched at her sides and her chin as angry as a chin could be. The washing lay at her feet, and across it a captain of Royal Americans was doing his best to argue and cajole. When the red-coated captain reached out an eager hand and got it slapped for his pains, Mr. Leslie permitted himself a crow of delight.

And then, the delight growing on his face, Mr. Leslie was bowing very low, his leg perked out at the most fashionable London angle behind him, and saying:

"Captain Barent, we meet again!"

The captain glanced at him, and glanced away. Mr. Leslie's smile grew broader and broader. He looked expectantly at the half-open door of Captain Arnold's quarters; but if Captain Arnold was aware of the little drama on the next doorstep, he made no sign of it. Perhaps, Leslie told himself, Captain Arnold was busy.

When he looked back again, the familiar red face of Captain Barent was wearing an impatient look, and his cajoling voice had become a match for the anger in the wash-girl's chin.

"You're damnation full of virtue today, aren't you?" he was snarling. "I know your pot-penny virtue! Holding it for a price, eh? There's a price for washing, but there's none for the lips of a camp wench. There's your shilling!" He tossed a coin down on the dirt beside the bundle, and with the same gesture his hand shot out and gripped the girl's bare arm above the elbow. With the brutal jerk, he dragged her toward him, lifted her over the bundle on the ground, and kissed her roughly on the mouth.

"There!"

His angry thrust sent her stumbling. The bundle burst open. Leslie, starting forward, looked for the first time at the girl's face under the blue sunbonnet. Then, with a mouth that was flat and stiff, he was saying to the flushed redcoat in the doorway:

"My congratulations, Captain Barent! Those who told me I should find Fort Pitt a crude, uncivilized place disclosed a most amazing ignorance. Truly, it is as civilized as London, or Annapolis, or the cabin of the *New Adventure* where I met you first. I see you have the same sports here that you indulged in there." He knew his voice was harsh, and his words insulting. He meant them to be. He looked across the sprawled-out washing into the astonished eyes of the girl Dick Lawless had wanted to buy.

"My congratulations, indeed, Captain Barent," he pressed on, and felt a furious longing for a weapon to be pressing home instead of words that could not hurt. After all, Barent had had his way with her. Barent, and Lawless, too, no doubt, and God knew how many more. He spoke again, brutally, "Captain, I fear I underrated you. Three hundred miles is a long way for a girl to follow a man across the mountains—and leaving a lord behind her, too."

He glanced at Barent. There was no sign of hurt in that congested face, but only a choking fury. Leslie sought viciously for the word that might hurt him, too.

"Or did Sir Dick hand her on to you when he had done with her?" he suggested softly.

He thought that, at least, must send Barent's hand flying to his sword.

It brought, instead, a slap that stung his own cheek.

He heard the girl say a single word in a hard, clear voice:

"Vile!"

And then, on a sob:

"Vile!"

She rushed past him, her hands clenched against her mouth, her skirt swishing against his leg. Leslie put his hand against his cheek; the skin still tingled. He saw that Barent had gotten his sword clear at last. His lip curled. With his fingers still rubbing his cheek, he turned his back on Barent to watch the blue dress and the bare, flying feet.

The girl of the *New Adventure* was half way across the parade. Much closer—so close that one anxious hand reached out and plucked him by the wrist—was Fritz Van Buren. Fritz had the bear by the chain looped up in his hand, and the little dog between his feet.

"Please, zur," he was begging, "please, zur, come away." Leslie sensed the fear in the thin face, but his eyes looked away again toward the fleeing girl. Fritz' voice, frantic now with alarm, rang unheeded.

"Please, zur, he'll kill you! He'll . . ."

Fritz threw his frail body into the jerk on Leslie's arm. It pulled Leslie off balance, so that he staggered two uncertain steps before he caught himself. Barent's thrust hit only air. Three voices cried out together. One was Barent's, hoarse with anger. One was Captain Arnold's, sharp and querulous. But the boy's was higher and louder than the others. He shrilled at the little dog:

"Sic 'im, Robin! Sic 'im! Sic 'im!" And pointed at the scraggly bear.

With a delighted yelp, Robin flung himself pell-mell at the bear's hind leg and nipped it. The bear grunted and jumped, a shambling leap that took him to the barrack wall. Fritz dropped the loops of chain, and Robin nipped the bear again. The lean brute lowered his head and ran; snubbed by the chain, he swung in a short arc that took in the burst bundle and the furious captain. The chain caught Barent behind the knees and jerked his feet from under him. He sat down with a jarring thump.

Mr. Leslie, slowly taking in the scene, saw Captain Barent's sword hand fly up stiffly, so that for an instant his saber presented itself to him in a perfect salute. That Captain Barent was sitting down in the midst of ruffled shirts and stocks and cotton drawers made the salute no less acceptable to Leslie. He answered it with the politest of bows.

"Here, zur." Fritz was pressing the long rifle into his hands. Leslie, smiling more happily than he had smiled for many weeks, put it back into Fritz'.

"Keep it. Captain Barent . . . eh, and Captain Arnold, I presume," and he swept another bow to the hawk-faced officer who stood staring at him with expressionless eyes, "may I present my body-guard, my corps of riflemen?" He gestured toward Fritz, standing with feet wide apart and the long rifle clutched across his chest, and then, with a wide smile, swung his hand to include the bear

95

and the rag-tag terrier. "And my heavy cavalry and my light cavalry, too? You see," he beamed at Arnold, "the heavy cavalry wears the bearskin, in the approved style of the Guards; and the light cavalry ... well, gentlemen, the light cavalry has fleas. That is not unusual, is it, Captain Arnold, in His Majesty's service?"

Arnold's cold eyes appraised him.

"Who in the devil are you?"

Mr. Leslie stooped over and plucked Captain Barent's sword from his astonished hand.

"Please, Barent, introduce us, won't you, now?"

Barent leaped to his feet, his hands reaching with fingers hooked. Leslie laid a hand on his own throat and smiled.

"No, no, Captain Barent. There is a decency about these affairs. Whenever ..."

"Barent, who is this fellow? Have you gone crazy, gabbling at him there? Who is he?"

"Major Leslie," shouted the Swiss, and added other titles not in any military tables.

Leslie bowed mockingly.

"The Major Leslie," he told Arnold, "who, as Captain Barent doubtless has informed you, was so cowardly that he refused to give Sir Richard Lawless a second fire. Ah," he added, as he saw recognition in Arnold's face, "I *thought* Barent would be telling it that way."

"Do you think of any reason why you should not be put under arrest?"

"Several," Leslie returned coolly. "First, my rifle corps would almost certainly object." He smiled gayly at Fritz, and patted him on the shoulder. "Second, the heavy cavalry may get beyond control; you know how difficult it is, captain, to control troops when they have been once committed to an action. Third, I have business with the commandant of Fort Pitt, and I should dislike to have to invite him to the guardhouse to hear of it. You follow me, Captain Arnold?"

"You are insolent!" Arnold snapped at him.

"Very," Leslie agreed. "On the other hand, if you were at the door in time, you were witness that I was the object of an unprovoked and murderous assault—for which I shall ask Captain

Barent to offer explanations later. I suggest that before you arrest me, you escort me to the commandant."

"Captain Ecuyer is occupied."

Leslie bowed again.

"Will you convey to Captain Ecuyer," he asked, "the compliments of Major Leslie, and say that Major Leslie will be at Mr. Hellward Bound's tavern, ready to call upon him at any time he finds convenient?"

Captain Arnold bowed slightly. To Barent's loud beginning of a protest, he said one short, unpleasant word.

Major Leslie bowed again, smiling a thought too widely, turned sharply on his heel, and marched for the gate. Behind him came what he was pleased to call his rifle corps, very pale of face and very short of breath; and the heavy cavalry lagging on its chain. Midway across the parade-ground, the light cavalry sat down and scratched a flea; then, after duly sniffing, it paid its compliments to a corner of the guardhouse wall.

CHAPTER VIII

In Which Mr. Leslie Discovers Why a Barefoot Washer-woman Thinks Him Vile, and Takes Extraordinary Steps to Make Amends:

THE bowling was proceeding merrily in the moat as Major Leslie, the boy, the bear and the dog crossed over it on the drawbridge. But Major Leslie no longer cared about bowling. His heels came down with angry thumps upon the logs, and his strides lengthened as his anger swelled.

The red-headed hussy! He should have let Lawless buy her when he wanted to. How Lawless and Barent must have laughed at him for a soft-headed colonial! All he had done was to turn her over to Sir Dick and the Swiss as a gift.

Fool . . . fool . . . fool, said his heels on the bridge. By the Lord, she must have gone to Lawless with her ten guineas still chinking in her pocket. *Fool . . . fool . . . fool,* he had literally paid Lawless a bounty to take for nothing what he had been more than willing to buy. Leslie's whip cut viciously at his leg.

His furious strides took him over the drawbridge and through the muck of the King's Highway far ahead of Fritz and the bear and the dog. He untied the mare's reins and the halter ropes from the sapling that Fritz had turned into a hitching post, and stood waiting.

The boy came slowly, his shoulders bent as if the weight of the heavy rifle was too much for his thin strength. Leslie watched him impatiently. Dammit, the fellow was blubbering again.

"Here!" Leslie thrust a halter rope out at him, and Fritz took it, fumbling, without looking at it. His pinched face stared up anxiously.

"You bant angry, zur?" The childish mouth quivered, and the pale eyes watered.

Leslie felt suddenly ashamed.

"No." On impulse, he put his hand on the ragged shirt, and felt

98

the bony body under it trembling. "Didn't you know they might whip you if you went in there?"

"Ay, zur."

Along with the uncomfortable sense of shame, a sense of gratitude and liking crept around the raw soreness of Leslie's spirit. There was unexpected warmth in it. His arm slipped around the shoulders of the ragged shirt. His voice was gruff, but his lips smiled a little.

"Tell me, Fritz, d'ye always blubber when you fight?"

"I never fought none, zur."

Mr. Leslie said "Zooks!" softly. Then he said it again, not so softly, and his mouth closed tightly on the smile and shut it out. His eyes looked bleakly over Fritz' head toward the passage that ran past the redan to the drawbridge. Along the passage, the girl in the wine-red dress was coming, one bare arm raised in a gesture that said *wait*.

She was walking rapidly, so that the stiff skirt billowed out behind her like a plump mainsail and the gay slippers went plunging heedlessly into ruts and puddles. She crossed the King's Highway, almost running, and turned into the alley.

"Major Leslie...."

Leslie bowed faintly, and waited.

She was younger than he had thought she was, and darkly beautiful. Her long black lashes hid her brown eyes better than her kerchief and ruffle hid her full brown bosom; but even in their shadows, her eyes were urgent.

"Major Leslie... you *are* Major Leslie, are you not?"

"Yes," curtly, without a trace of warmth.

"I want to... I must talk with you."

"Yes?"

Anger twitched at the girl's full lips.

"Are you always rude, Major Leslie?"

"Not always."

"*Oh-h-h!*" A flush welled duskily over neck and breast and up through the gypsy-brown cheeks to the roots of the black hair. "You make yourself very plain."

Mr. Leslie indulged in another faint bow.

"It seems to be a custom in Pitt's Town."

"You have made yourself learn its customs quickly," the girl

99

shot back at him. "Most gentlemen require longer. Oh," her fingers clasped in the ruffle of her breast, "I must not quarrel with you. Please, I must talk with you, alone."

"Alone?" Mr. Leslie let his eyebrows go up and his mouth curl.

"It is hardly a subject to discuss where a child may hear, sir."

"If that is the subject," Mr. Leslie shrugged, and flipped the reins to start the mare, "it hardly needs discussion, Mistress Sargent."

The wine-red dress swayed and shook on its side-hoops and a red slipper stamped in exasperated anger.

"Pitt's Town could teach you nothing," the girl told him furiously. "Even Barent is a gentleman beside you!"

Another ironic bow.

"I could not believe there was a man so vile, so cold, so cruel. When she told me what you had done to her, I told her she lied. Not even Barent would have done what you did! Not even an Indian! Barent would have bought her for himself; he never would have bought her to make sure another man might have her." Peggy Sargent's voice took on a breathless sound; her eyes, staring at him, were black with anger, but Leslie, grimly amused, felt suddenly that there was even more fear than anger in both voice and eyes. The tirade swept on, and Leslie ceased to smile. "I think there is a name for what you are. A man who procures a girl for another man—a pimp, is it not? Major Leslie of Leslie Hall"... the dress crumpled into the alley dirt as she swept him a bitter curtsey... "gentleman, and pimp!"

"Fritz!" Leslie thrust the mare's reins into the boy's hand. "Go find this Hellward Bound's tavern. Unload the packs and get them under cover. Feed the horses. Tell Hellward Bound, or whatever his name may be, that we want his largest room. Now, Mistress Sargent..."

Mouth grim and eyes blackly hostile, he slipped his hand between bare arm and tight bodice, and turned the girl quickly toward the King's Highway. Whether angry or afraid, Peggy Sargent was astonishingly concerned with Mr. Leslie and his doings. It struck Mr. Leslie as being, at the least, unreasonable.

Where the King's Highway turned left to climb the slope to the Upper Town, he led Peggy Sargent off the road into a dooryard where a fresh-killed doe hung by the heels from the eaves and dripped slow drops of blood into a dirty pool. Between the cabin and a sapling stable ran a narrow space littered with chips, with stones fallen from the roof, with broken gourds, and cast-off wooden frames still stained with blood from beaver skins that had been stretched on them to cure. Grass hung in frowsy patches from the stable wall where the saplings sagged. Leslie, stalking behind, smiled humorlessly at the red heels picking their way through the noisome litter, and at the bare brown shoulders shrinking from the rasp of the bulging hay walls.

The mud was a little deeper back of the stable, but beyond that was grass, and beyond that the river. On the first bit of grass, Leslie stopped and said curtly:

"Well?"

The girl faced him, her back to the town. Under the angle of the saucy hat, the sun fell across her face, and Leslie saw tears shining on her lashes. So quickly that they took him entirely by surprise, her hands flew out and closed on his arm as if she meant to hold him there by main force and make him listen. He pulled back his arm, but managed only to pull the girl closer to him.

"Major Leslie, I beg you—be kind to me."

Leslie frowned. It occurred to him, now that he was here, that the whole business might be some device of Barent's or Arnold's.

The girl's hands tugged insistently at his arm.

"You are not listening. Please! Did you follow Diantha Gail to Fort Pitt?"

Leslie laughed, mocking, but amazed.

His "No!" was clipped and bitter.

"Oh. I thought perhaps it had been arranged in the beginning."

"Thought what had been arranged, Mistress Sargent? I am not good at riddles."

"Then you did buy her, for Captain Barent? It was just a trick? Oh-h...." The girl's eyes loathed him, and her hands dropped limply into the folds of the panniered gown.

Leslie's voice had a cutting edge when he answered.

"I did not buy her for Captain Barent. I bought her and gave her her freedom. It was not a trick. And Mistress Diantha Gail does not interest me. I am sorry." He bowed, and turned bruskly back toward the town.

A hand plucked him by the arm. Peggy, a whirl of silk and a whirl of words, fairly threw herself upon him.

"I knew it! I knew it!" Utterly astounded, Major Leslie felt her arms go around his neck in a fierce hug and her mouth press itself softly, and then warm and hard, against his cheek. Too startled to find a word to say, he gaped at her, and saw that she was laughing, and that tears were spilling down her face.

"I knew it. I knew it," she cried again, and her hands reached for his shoulders.

Leslie stepped back, and heard her laughter ring out gayly.

"You think I am touched, don't you?" she asked him, and laughed again. "I am. La, I am, indeed. Listen to me. . . . No, no, I will not kiss you again. Not until . . ." she dimpled and curtsied . . . "not until you ask me. Oh, I am almost happy. Listen, now:

"Do you know why Diantha Gail is here, in Pitt's Town?"

Mr. Leslie's expression made it clear that he neither knew nor cared to know.

"Because she is bond maid to Hellward Bound."

Leslie shrugged.

"Wait. She told me you pretended to set her free. Was there a man named Watson? And Lawless—Sir Richard Lawless?"

"Yes." Distrust and suspicion crowded themselves into the word. Minute by minute, Leslie was growing more certain that Valentine Arnold's mistress was trying to make a fool of him.

"Yes. She thought you had set her free. She was taken up by a constable and put into Annapolis jail. Watson swore she had run away. She said you had bought her freedom, and Watson swore it was a trick, a lie. She named witnesses—Barent, and the baronet, Lawless, and the ship captain. The justice who heard the case called Barent and Lawless, and they swore you had never bought her, that it was all a jest at a drinking bout at sea."

Leslie at last was interested.

"They sold her again?"

"Yes. Yes."

"Todd would have testified," Leslie said hoarsely, his eyes narrowing as he looked at this evil picture of deceit and cruelty. "Todd was the ship captain. He . . ."

"They wouldn't call Todd. They turned her back to Watson, in

102

the jail. They added two years to her term, for lying, and for trying to escape. And then Lawless found a buyer."

"Lawless?"

"Yes. Oh, yes, don't you see, major? Barent wanted her. He was going out to the Ohio, to the garrison here. Between them, Barent and Lawless found a trader from the forks, come to Annapolis to load trade goods for the Indians. Bond bought her."

"Bond?"

"Oh, yes; yes! Bond, the Indian trader. Halbert Bond—the one they call Hellward Bound."

Peggy Sargent shrank a little from the fury in Arnett Leslie's eyes.

"I should have killed him," he said thickly. He felt the cold stiffness that came to his lips in anger, the cold stillness that came to Leslie men in moments of stress and deep emotion. Pictures took form before his eyes, changed, and gave way to others. Barent, staring and mouthing at the girl in the cabin of the *New Adventure*. Sir Richard facing him across the dueling ground. An elm leaf fluttering down. *I should have killed him!* A girl, stripped, bound to a post in Tom Yeardley's stable yard, and the bullock whip cutting at her legs. A girl with bare, muddy feet struggling in Captain Barent's arms, above a bundle of laundry. *I can kill Barent. I will find Lawless and kill him; and Watson, and see him to the gallows. No, Lawless should hang too....*

His hands reached out and took Peggy by the shoulders and shook her. His eyes, blazing between lids so narrowed they left barely a slit, searched her face.

"That is the truth? The truth?"

"Yes. *Yes!*"

"Then why...? Has no one told the commandant?"

"No. What use? He has no power. Bond has her indenture papers. Barent would swear again...."

"And why do *you* tell me? Why not Diantha?"

"She believes you never intended to buy her and set her free. She believes it was a trick, a cruel, drunken game."

"Ah-h. And why do *you* come to me? What is it to you?"

His face, tight with anger and suspicion, came close to hers. Bloodless, the windburned skin was yellowish-brown; under the tangled black hair and the meeting brows, it was a deadly, frightening face.

His hands shook her again. Peggy cried out at him:

"Because Valentine Arnold loves her!"

"And you want him to have her?"

"I?" The girl stared at him wildly. *"I want him to have her?* Oh God, no...no...no! While she is here, a bond servant, he can force himself upon her. Because Barent pursues her, Captain Arnold is crazy with jealousy. He will do anything, anything. Oh, if you have any pity, major, take her away...*take her away,* and let me keep him."

Leslie looked down curiously at the shaking shoulders.

"You love him so much?"

"Yes. Oh, *yes.*"

"Even if he loves a bond maid more?"

The dark head against his arm shook convulsively.

"Yes. I don't care. I love him. Don't you know what that means?"

Arnett Leslie found that he did not. Looking at the gay ribbons on Peggy's chip, he saw instead a girl's face against a mass of purplish blossoms. Instead of Peggy Sargent's sobbing breath, he heard another woman's voice say softly, "If you want me, I am still here." Damnation! There were times when the one you loved was the last person on earth you could want. Or take. Out of the pain of a wound torn open again he rasped angrily at the girl weeping in his arms.

"A man would be too proud to act so...."

"A woman who loves has no pride," Peggy's stifled voice told his sleeve.

Roughly, Leslie pushed her away.

"Will you...?"

"I'll see that Mistress Gail goes free. Perhaps you can persuade her to run away from Captain Arnold." He did not for a moment imagine that the girl Diantha would go away unless it suited her. As he thrust his way angrily through the littered path between hay-stuffed stable wall and hog-pen cabin, he was telling himself that, in cold fact, Mistress Peggy Sargent's concern for Hellward Bound's bond maid was as selfish as any other emotion a woman was capable of feeling. If it were only Barent, and not Arnold, who was hounding the red-haired girl, Peggy Sargent would be watching the chase with greedy eyes, ready to laugh and applaud when the quarry was caught.

Coming out again into the King's Highway, he considered briefly the wisdom of going at once to Captain Ecuyer, and dismissed the idea. The sale of a bond maid was a civil matter in which a soldier would hesitate to interfere. And even if Ecuyer chose to concern himself with Diantha Gail, his own captain, Barent, would swear again that Leslie never had bought the girl and never set her free—he would swear that at most the sale had been a jest around the bombo bowl. Besides, Halbert Bond would have his papers to prove that the girl Diantha was bound to him for five years—with the punishment for trying to escape, for seven years.

Leslie brought his whip down with a thwack on his legging. Whatever might be done to undo Captain Barent's very dirty trick, Mr. Leslie realized he would have to do himself. Walking briskly up the road among the draggle-tail cabins, he thought of what might be done. He might, for one thing, frighten the truth out of Barent; unless Barent was more of a coward than he appeared to be, only extreme peril to his life would frighten him enough. That, however, might be accomplished; to provoke the Swiss captain into a duel without benefit of seconds or witnesses should not be impossible.

Leslie thought of the boarding pistols Todd had given him. How white his father's face had gone when the lid of the case swung up and he saw the shining barrels, and the hinged bayonets glittering.

Busy with his planning, Arnett Leslie did not realize that for the first time he had thought of that scene in the north wing of Leslie Hall without a fierce thrust of pain. Let Barent face him with those bayoneted pistols, and the chances would be excellent, he assured himself, that there would be a confession of the perjury that had sold Diantha Gail back into servitude. And, if that failed, there was always the possibility of buying her from Halbert Bond. And that, in turn, meant that Arnett Leslie must turn trader as he had intended, or he would have no money to buy this red-headed bond maid for the second time—nor to buy so much as a gourd of Madeira, or a place to sleep. Jingling the six shillings in his pocket, he came briskly around a bend of the King's Highway into a wider place where the earth was a little muddier and a little more deeply trampled, and Hellward Bound's tavern sprawled along the road.

The tavern was little more than a big log cabin with a loft, and a series of wings and lean-to's. Like most of the cabins of Pitt's Town, Hellward's hostelry had the rough and ready air that went with the hog-pen finish; at the corners, the logs stuck out helter-skelter, some a foot beyond the rude mortise, some twice that length, and their ends were just as the ax had left them when they came off their stumps. The roof was of clapboards laid on loose and weighted down with bowlders. Greased paper windows in clumsy frames hung sagging on leather hinges, and two Mingoes, greasy as the window panes, sagged against the cabin wall beside the open door. Hot as it was in the glaring sun, the Indians were swaddled in blankets to their cheekbones, and their eyes glittered at Leslie out of daubed patches of vermilion, as emotionless as the eyes in the sign that swung in the tavern dooryard.

It was a fine, carved sign, big as an eagle, but shaped as no eagle ever was except, perhaps, in Master Hellward's nightmares. It looked, to Leslie, much more like a dropsical buzzard. It hung by two chains from its wings to the branch of a dead scrub oak a few feet in front of the door, its claws so low that a tall man passing underneath might find his hat scratched off his head, and its eyes glaring blankly into the sun. Even with his mind fixed on the business of undoing Sir Dick's unpleasant handiwork and making Barent smart for his part in it, Leslie had to smile at those staring eyes. Some backwoods wag had spared a pair of shiny brass hip buttons to provide Hellward Bound's wooden eagle with his eyes.

Past the sickly eagle and the blanketed Mingoes, Leslie stepped into the hubbub of Hellward's taproom.

It was rough inside as out, a long, low room with unbarked logs for walls and a puncheon floor thick with tracked-in mud. It buzzed with flies and the talk of a dozen men; green tunics and tow heads of Pennsylvania Provincials lined a puncheon table; men in linsey shirts or long-skirted blue coats, with a leather hunting dress or two among them, pushed a bottle from hand to hand on the swinging bar across one end of the room. Behind the bar a huge figure that was more bear than man leaned forward with his hands on the swinging slab of oak. His arms, short and powerful, were covered with a mat of black hair; crooked at the elbow, they looked like the bowed forelegs of Fritz' pet preparing to pull himself up onto the bar. Between the furry arms, a beard big as a shovel all but hid a grimy deerskin shirt, and climbed up a round, red face to meet black hair in a tangled thicket on cheekbones and ears and just above the small, darting eyes.

The buzz of talk stopped. Mugs bumped on the puncheons and stools scraped as the Provincials pushed back to gape at the hatless stranger. Somebody laughed, smothered the sound quickly, and then laughed again. Leslie, stiffening, guessed that in the last quarter hour all of Pitt's Town had heard how a washwoman had slapped his face. His heels planted themselves with uncompromising thuds on the heavy planks, and his voice rang sharply in the low room:

"I sent a boy to see my horses watered and baited, and order your best room."

Bond snorted into a pewter mug and wiped his beard on his forearm. He gave no sign that he recognized the man who had knocked him unconscious in Tom Yeardley's kitchen.

"The best is taken. Y'r boy's in the stable yard. He'll show ye. Y'r name Leslie?"

"It is," coldly, with the insolence that seemed to spring up whenever, in these last weeks, he must bandy words with any one. "What of it?"

Bond's left eye closed in a wink that agitated the underbrush around it.

"Nothin'," he leered. "On'y wanted t' know whut t' put onto y'r headboard."

Leslie's hand closed tentatively on his whip. Bond ducked his head again into his whisky mug and came up dripping.

"Reg'lar fightin' cock, ain't ye?" He made a rumbling in his throat that did not quite break into a laugh. "Ain't aimin' t' fight ye. But if ye start in by knockin' Royal Americans on their backsides on their own parade, ye'll be makin' the weeds grow out yonder in the frog-eaters' buryin' ground." *

* The graveyard laid out by the French garrison of Fort Duquesne lay between Lower Town and the Allegheny River, north of the gardens, on the Allee de la Vierge, which the English translated into Virgin Alley. It is Oliver Avenue in modern Pittsburgh.

Leslie half turned to make sure the greencoats at their table would not miss his answer.

"You got the tale wrong, Bond. It was my horseboy knocked Barent down. I doubt you'll need the headboard; Captain Barent picked his own laundry to sit down in."

That, Leslie told himself with satisfaction, should make it certain that Barent would be sending a challenge before many hours.

Mr. Leslie tapped his leg and smiled, and thought of another remark for the gawking soldiers to carry back to Barent.

"I need this laundry wench of yours, Bond; after a hundred miles of old Forbes' road, I have a deal of washing. Send her to my room, and bid her make up my bed."

He stalked past the tableful of Provincials and down the dim passage to the rear.

In the stableyard, shut in on three sides by the hodge-podge wings and angles of the tavern, Fritz had the horses stripped of baggage and pack saddles, and was watering them with bucket and windlass at an open well. Robin came waggling his whole carcass in delighted welcome, and Fritz' thin face lighted with relief.

Leslie waved the whip at him, and stooped to scratch behind Robin's ear. The dog vibrated in happy hysterics between Leslie's legs, and Fritz set the bucket down and came trotting eagerly.

"That be your room, zur, beyont the kitchen." Leslie looked casually past the sapling shack that served as cook house to the tavern, and wrinkled his nose at the whitish-gray muck of dish water at its door. "Shall I hopple the horses, zur? There be grass out beyont. I'll sleep out an' watch tham, zur."

"Sleep out? You'll not." He smiled gayly at the orphan dog and the orphan boy. *Zooks!* There were compensations in having an evil temper. Hadn't he gotten Robin because a backwoods freighter had infuriated him, and Fritz because it had pleased him to turn a Dutch sergeant's cat against his own loutish shoulders? Draggle-tail and measly as they were, these two companions of his suited him; they never presumed upon his vile moods. "Get along, now. Get the nags watered and turn them out. I'll be wanting a hand to lug this baggage in."

"Ay, zur." Fritz scurried back to the windlass. The handle whirled as he shot the bucket down. His eyes adored Leslie's shoulders swinging past the cook shack to the door of Halbert Bond's second best room.

It was not much of a room, Leslie saw as he stooped through the low door frame. Its walls were the same unbarked logs, its floor planks were splintery with hasty ax work, its windows mere holes in the wall, with solid shutters in place of greased paper for window panes.

The floor, at least, was clean; there were not so many flies as there were in the taproom. They were over at the cook shack, most likely, he grimaced, and established himself as a guest of the Golden Eagle by tossing his whip onto the table.

The table was a single slab split from the heart of some huge oak; four round poles in auger holes did duty as legs, as unsteadily as if they had spent the day in Hellward's barroom.

Leslie picked up the whip and threw it into a corner, dragged the table to the door, and rolled it out into the dirt. The three-legged stool went flying after it, and Leslie strode toward the bed in the corner, meaning to send it after the table and the stool. But the bed, he found, was as much a part of the cabin as the walls and shutters. It had only a single post, but the post was a five-inch tree, with its butt sunk through a hole in the floor and its other end mortised into a log beam overhead. Two feet above the floor, a limb had been cut off to leave a crotch. The crotch held the ends of a long pole and a short one; the poles, thrust solidly into cracks between the wall logs, formed a side and the foot of the bed. The head and the other side were the cabin walls; loose clapboards laid lengthwise served as spring and mattress both. A dingy bearskin and a ragged blanket left them half exposed.

With a gesture of disgust, Leslie lifted the blanket and tossed it under the bed. Behind him, a cool voice mocked him:

"Always the ruffler and the swaggerer, Major Leslie?"

Leslie whirled, anger instinctive on his lips.

In the doorway, chin up and eyes scornful, the girl Diantha stood with the stool in her hands. Against the sun, her hair made a shining aureole around her face. For some incomprehensible reason, her bright hair annoyed Leslie more than the stool she was bringing back. His voice slashed at her:

"I threw that out!"

"I brought it back." She set it down beside the door, and leaned against the wall, watching him. Smiled faintly. Added: "You see, Halbert Bond is not a gentleman; he cannot fight you; he would only wring your neck."

Arrogance. Mr. Leslie, who understood so well the art of being arrogant, warmed with admiration at the cool insolence. He smiled.

"But it would give you so much more pleasure to wring it yourself, Mistress Gail."

"But I shan't."

"I was never," said Leslie, and meant it, "so inclined to let my neck be wrung." He smiled gravely. "If you will listen, I have something to tell you."

"I listened once."

She saw by the look on the man's face that that cut had gone home. The look surprised her, it had so little in it of anger or arrogance. Leslie spoke in a low, dogged tone.

"I came to make my apologies...."

"Apologies!"

"And such amends as I may....No, listen to me. You are right to be bitter. But I did not do what you believe I did. I shall see that what was done, is undone, and that those who did it are punished. Believe me"...to his own amazement, his voice shook uncertainly; there was something pitifully gallant in the slight figure and the scornful, distrustful face..."believe me, had I known, I would have come back....I would never have gone without making sure...."

Still on guard, but doubtful, the girl's voice cut in:

"Making sure of what, may I ask?"

"That Watson gave you the certificate...the money."

"Money?"

Leslie shrugged. He was acutely uncomfortable. It was not his wont to fumble for words, but he fumbled now.

"I told him....I gave him money...."

Diantha Gail laughed and came slowly toward him. There was an expression about her mouth that made Leslie think of the cold stiffness that came to his own lips when he was white with anger. Measured, deliberate, like strokes of a whip, she lashed him with bitter phrases.

"Oh, you need have no fear. He gave you all you paid for. No painted Indian could have done better. Indeed, you should not have missed it, Major Leslie. Oh, it was sweet torture while it lasted. Do I disappoint you that it no longer hurts?"

"Mistress Gail..."

Her face had gone dead white, as it had in the cabin of the *New Adventure*. Across her nose, the freckles stood out in sharp brown splotches. Her hands were clenched at her sides, her arms straight down and rigid.

"They told me in London this was a savage country," she rushed on. "They said the beasts were fierce, and men worse than the beasts. They said Englishmen turned savage in a year in America, and that colonials took scalps as greedily as Indians. And I thought they knew not what they talked."

Her laugh was shrill, her clenched hands beating the poor panniers flat against her body.

"You didn't take my scalp, Major, and you did not wait to see the torture. Shall I tell you of it? Or did you enjoy it, in your thoughts, while you went to your wedding?"

On that word, she stopped. Her hands came up to meet her mouth. Behind them, she asked a question in a hushed voice:

"Why are you here? You were going to be married."

And then, staring at Leslie's face:

"Oh, what is it?"

Leslie stepped quickly past her and picked up the stool and dropped it beside her.

"Sit down," he told her, "and listen. Watson had the price of your passage; he had ten guineas in gold to give you; he had my address, and a message that you would be welcome at Leslie Hall. He embezzled the money, and perjured himself because Dick Lawless and Barent told him to. Wait! You have said your say; now I say mine:

"I shall see Watson hanged. I spared Lawless at Annapolis; I shall not spare him next time. I shall fight Barent within two days, and either kill him or have the truth, to free you with it. If that fails, I shall buy you again, and see you freed."

Now, at last, she dropped onto the stool, her hands limp in her lap. Her throat quivered.

"I want to... I want to believe... that."

Leslie's hands turned out in an empty gesture.

"It is true. I cannot prove it, except out of Barent's mouth."

"You followed me? You came here...across the mountains...to undo their evil? You..."

The empty gesture answered her.

"No. Peggy Sargent told me, an hour ago."

"Then why...?"

"Chance. Sheer, blind chance."

"It is so strange. No one...seven years...they added two years, for lying...."

"I know. All I can do is to apologize, and make what amends can be made. I was hasty to leave without being sure."

"Hasty!" Diantha's lips began to tremble. "You were on your way home, to be married. Of course you were eager."

Trying to hide the tears on her face, she bent over the crumpled calimaneo gown and pressed the ruffles to her cheeks.

"Eager!"

Leslie's steps thudded across the floor. Diantha, raising her head above the damp flounce, saw him striding across the stableyard, jerking the sailcloth from his piled-up baggage, lifting a roped and padded crate to his shoulder, coming back.

He slid his burden to the floor in the middle of the room. Without a word or a glance for the girl, he jerked off the ropes. The slats of the crate resisted him, and he went back to the stableyard to wrench loose one of the legs of the slab table. Under its leverage, the crate burst open; out of it Leslie's impatient hands pulled wadded paper and rolled cloth and strewed it in a heap about him. When he had finished and stood back, Diantha's breath caught in a gasp of amazement.

Standing in the wreckage of the crate was a mahogany dressing table. On its shining top, shepherds and shepherdesses danced and flirted in mother-of-pearl, inlaid with intricate skill. From its four tiny drawers, brass rings dangled. On each of its two front legs, a plump, carved cupid gazed upward adoringly at the lady who should be sitting there.

"Master Chippendale," said Leslie, and dived again into the crate. More knots, more wadded paper, more rolls of coarse cloth. When he stepped back again, the girl on the stool looked up at three red-haired girls who gazed back at her with amazed gray eyes, and let their lips part and their hands fly up to their throats as if the breath was caught there. Above the inlaid mahogany rose a mirror with three leaves; over the top of each, a small, gilt cupid looked down roguishly.

Diantha took her hand from her throat and held it firmly with the other one, in her lap, a fold of the blue gown gripped tightly in her fingers.

"It's beautiful," she breathed. Leslie, looking down at her, was conscious of a feeling that was new to him. There was so much hunger in the girl's voice that he felt the hurt of it himself. He spoke gruffly, without looking at her again:

"That is part of my pledge that you will not be deceived again. I brought this to sell. If Barent will not tell the truth, this baggage of mine will pay Master Bond whatever he paid for you."

"But this...surely not this? This is a lady's...a great lady's. It is"...she got up quickly and stood beside him, her eyes searching his moody face..."it is your wife's, is it not?"

"I have no wife," he answered crisply.

"But you were going home..."

"She was—gone. That, you see, is why I am here."

"Oh-hh. But this. Surely you would not sell what was hers. Why...?"

Leslie turned to face her squarely. He felt, for the moment, not unhappy. His lips smiled, and they were not, this time, alone; his eyes, with fine wrinkles running together at their corners, lost something of their somber depth.

"Why? Faith, it's simple. I did not like things at Leslie Hall any longer, so I came away. I have," and he jingled the coins in his pocket, "six shillings and some London bridal fripperies."

"And that is all?" The gray eyes looked and looked, trying to see behind the smile and the crinkled eyes.

"And that is all. Eh? You think, I suppose, that because I have six shillings and some trade goods, instead of a thousand acres, some slaves, and five hundred casks of tobacco, ergo, I cannot ransom you? I thought so. Look you, Mistress Gail—I am a trader, a pack-a-back peddler, with six shillings and a bedroom suite. Shall we trade?"

"Trade?"

"Aye. Trade the price of your freedom for—um—washing and ironing, brushing and furbishing, such as one cannot get at Master Bond's once his bond maid is set free. And mayhap, when business

113

picks up, selling and bartering and keeping accounts in a fine log trading house with a fashionable mud portico and three fat pigs to keep the style of Pitt's Town."

Leslie was smiling as he put his bargain, but Diantha had tears in her eyes once more.

"I believe you," she told him, and put her sleeve hastily across her face. Muffled behind it, he heard her saying: "Oh, I believe you. I vowed I never would believe a man again, but I believe you."

"Then you will work for me?"

"Oh! Yes. And yes, *yes!* Though they say I am your mistress, as they say now I am Captain Barent's. Or Halbert Bond's."

Leslie felt a rush of anger.

"Bond's?"

"Poof, what difference does it make? Bond has been far kinder than Barent, or Lawless, or even Captain Arnold. Oh, an arm around me when I must go behind the bar, or a finger to my chin. I am become used to all that. And Master Bond has a wife to keep him in his place."

"Ah." It was a little illogical that the existence of a Mistress Bond should ease his mind so much. An hour ago it had been Barent's treachery that had concerned him, and not the plight of Diantha Gail. The difference did not occur to Mr. Leslie. He waved his hand briskly toward the baggage in the yard, and went out for another bundle with a lighter heart than he had carried for many days. When he saw Fritz and Robin coming across the meadow behind the inn, he waved and shouted, and brought them on the run. With Fritz to help, and Robin to hinder, he rushed the rest of his London furbelows into the Golden Eagle's second best room with the gayety of a boy. Robin barked and raced and chased his tail, Diantha sat on her stool and laughed and wiped her eyes and laughed again, and even Fritz burst out in a high-pitched laugh that startled him into breathless silence.

In an hour, the log room stood transformed. In one corner was the virginal, from the London musicker my lord Baltimore had recommended. Its dolphin legs, scratched here and there but still steady enough, stood up on their tails and held its dainty body on their noses. Diantha, on her knees like an entranced child, crowed and laughed at the more reckless dolphins on the stool that matched the virginal; one of them wabbled a little, but they stood on their heads with the rush seat on their tails, and balanced themselves on the round balls under their chins.

In the opposite corner, across from the post and clapboard bunk, stood the bed that was to have been Evelyn Gentle's bridal bed. Its blue harrateen curtains glowed in the sunlight through the open door, and its sheer mosquito netting softened the sheen of blue satin quilts above the highpiled feather beds. Between bed and dressing table was a gay chintz chair, and beyond, by the virginal, a sophisticated boudoir seat in Russian leather.

Diantha stood with hands clasped, in the center of the room, and looked from mirrors to virginal, from chair to valance, from shimmering curtains back to the mother-of-pearl flirtations on the dressing table, as if she could not look enough.

"Arnett Leslie," she whispered miserably, "you cannot sell these things." And then she amended it: "Precious heaven, who in this swamp-hole town would buy them?"

Leslie glanced at her with narrowing eyes, and probed deftly:

"Why, perhaps Captain Arnold. Even the rank and file in Fort Pitt gabble that he keeps Mistress Sargent as his light-o'-love, and that he has gold burning in his pockets."

Hm. Perhaps Captain Arnold was caught in the golden web of Diantha Gail's bright hair; but neither his name nor his affair brought either light or shadow to Diantha's face. She answered serenely:

"He might. He has money enough, and Peggy followed him when he came to Pitt's Town. And then, there's Captain-lieutenant Carroll; he has a brand new wife, and money twice a year from home. But..." Her face, childishly wistful, turned again to the virginal.

"May I... may I play on it?"

The question surprised him. Diantha Gail, immigrant bond maid, asking to play a virginal.... He nodded, and pulled out the stool.

The girl sat down on the very edge of the rush seat, and her fingers touched the keys. At the first tinkling notes, she snatched them back again.

"Oh-*hh!*" A queer, startled sound. As if the keys had burned her finger tips. She glanced hastily at Leslie, and then laid her hands again on the keyboard.

"Do you remember?"

Two hundred miles of mountain trails had not improved the strings, but the light, pattering notes, falling into the stillness like small, separate drops of music, brought back a bombo bowl, a long brass cannon, and Robin Stuart's long, red face.

Oh, sister Phœbe, how merry were we....

Across the stable yard, a woman's strident voice shrilled, and the girl's hands stopped on clashing keys.

"Di! Di! Where be ye?"

"It's Mistress Bond." Diantha smiled faintly as she stood up, very straight, with her hands at her sides. "I...I..."

"Don't," Leslie smiled at her.

The girl shook her head.

"I must," she said stoutly. "I'm...I think I should thank you. I want to try. I...Oh, I *believe you*, Arnett Leslie!" She rushed past him. From the stable yard he heard her calling an answer to the strident voice.

CHAPTER IX

In Which Major Leslie Turns a Tavern Maid Into a Fine Lady for an Evening, and Wipes a Wandering Tear from the Lady's Nose:

AN hour after dusk, Arnett Leslie sat at supper in a dim corner of the Golden Eagle's taproom.

On the puncheon table, rough as the broad-ax had left it, a homemade candle smoked and smelled. Across a wooden platter, a drowsy spring fly crawled sluggishly in search of whatever scraps Major Leslie had left of his dish of beef and bacon; and two more flies balanced tipsily on the edge of the wooden noggin just drained of applejack.

At the hand-hewn bar across the room, Halbert Bond drowsed likewise, with his furry elbows in a pool of slopped rum and his beard between his fists. Pitt's Town seemed as quiet and empty as the tavern, the soft passing of moccasined feet in the mud road outside scarce loud enough to blur the restless buzzing of the two flies on the empty noggin.

Leslie, motionless in his corner, puffed somberly at his long clay pipe and eyed as somberly the wisps of blue smoke curling up through the candle flicker. He was finding a great deal to think about.

Bare feet whispered on the puncheons, and Diantha came to stand at his knees, a beech bowl between her hands. Through the dusk their glances met and held each other, friendly, but still faintly doubtful. Diantha flashed a look at Bond. Her voice, when she spoke, was much gentler than her words:

"If you will move your feet, Major Leslie, I can set your dessert down."

Perhaps it was the little-girl slimness of her white wrists above the wooden bowl that made him feel a twinge of shame at the rudeness of his muddy feet, thrust out on a stool of their own. He brought them down with a promptness that surprised himself, and moved the empty platter to one side. Diantha put down the bowl, gathered up platter and noggin, and went softly away. Leslie set his iron spoon into the sago cream; it was cool and good; he had no means of knowing that sago cream was not a dish on the menu of the Golden Eagle. As he ate, he speculated on just how long it would take Captain Barent to send a challenge, or to come quarreling in his own person.

Feet clumped and scuffled in the mud outside. A broad voice said "Halt!", and the clumping feet came irregularly to a stop. At the open door, a round-faced corporal in Pennsylvania green thrust head and shoulders into the taproom and bawled at Halbert Bond.

"Hey! Where at is da faller wit' da whip?"

Hellward stirred, opened his eyes solemnly, and solemnly closed them again.

"Here," Leslie called.

The corporal tramped across to the corner and handed him a note.

"Froom da commandant," he said, and saluted with a grimy hand. Leslie returned the salute; the corporal ambled out; the town patrol scuffled away.

Bending across the sago bowl to bring the candlelight onto the crabbed writing, Major Leslie failed to hear Diantha's feet as she padded back from the kitchen. He sat back abruptly, and all but knocked a steaming pewter mug out of her hand.

"Be careful!" she flashed out at him.

He looked at her silently, from her bare feet, a white blur in the shadow of the table, to the shining halo of her hair. The most brazen officer of the Royal American regiment would have been hard put to it to outdo that long, rude stare; but Leslie outdid it himself. He snatched up the smoking candle and held it so its light fell on the shabby dress, that no amount of washing would ever make fresh and dainty again, and on the slim bare arms holding the steaming mug.

Diantha flushed.

"Truly, sir, it is not worth so much excitement," she protested coolly. "It is not really coffee, but only our make-believe—sassafras root and roasted rye kernels."

"Lord!" exploded Mr. Leslie, oblivious of the candle dripping on his knees, and got slowly to his feet, and set the candle down.

"I'm sorry I stared," he apologized, and held out the note.

The girl bent over it in the circle of candle light.

"Oh-hh! The garrison ball. They have them every fortnight."

"Have you been there?"

"In bare feet, with only a night-rail to my back, except for this elegant blue gown I wear?"

"Tonight you are going. I ask you to go, not just to please yourself, nor to please me. I have a reason. Will you?"

"Why? I do not see..."

"Of course you do. I want to go to that ball tonight, in uniform, an officer whom Captain Barent cannot ignore. I want you with me, to anger him beyond endurance. I want to make certain he will quarrel with me; I want to force him, if I can, to fight me without the fuss and feathers of a duel. I mean to prick a confession out of him. In uniform, he will fight me."

"You mean, you would provoke a duel..."

"A fight."

"He may kill you."

"He'll not." A short, harsh laugh. "I am fortunate at fighting. More fortunate than at most things. Will you come?"

"I can't. In this rag-bag of a gown?"

Leslie looked at her soberly.

"I have a trunk," he said. "I think, perhaps, we shall surprise our friend Barent. Come."

He picked up the candle and took her bruskly by the arm, pushing her toward the back door of the taproom, down a dim passage, out into the courtyard.

"Here." He thrust the candle into her hand, and stooped over the heap of pack saddles and baggage that still lay beside the wing of the inn. From under a sailcloth he plucked out his brass-bound trunk, and swung it to his shoulder. "Where is your room?"

She pointed: "There. Just across from yours."

He stalked across the court and through the doorway. The girl, a little breathless with hurrying to match his long strides, raised the candle at his shoulder to throw its light on a clapboard bed, ill furnished with sleazy blankets. The bed was all the furniture there was, except for another of those three-legged stools, and a row of whittled pegs thrust into the wall. All but two of the pegs were bare, and the two held only a linsey shift and a night-rail of some coarse stuff that was neither dainty nor new. With an angry word,

Leslie brushed past her and crossed the courtyard again to his own room.

"They'll gabble anyway," he said, as he set the trunk down at the foot of the curtained bed. "But they'll scarcely say that you've taken Fritz for a lover. And he's fast asleep."

He looked sharply at her and saw the bewilderment in her face, and the smears of dried mud on her ankles.

"We'll want water," he told her. "Is there any hot?"

"Yes." Diantha's hand shook a little as she set the candlestick down on the shining dressing-table. "A great pot of it, on the crane in the kitchen."

"Wait."

He swung out, and she heard him among the cluttered noggins and pannikins in Bond's sapling lean-to. When he came back, he had the iron pot on a stick thrust through its handle, and set it down incongruously enough between the flashing mirrors and the virginal. Still stooping, he threw back the lid of the brass-bound trunk. In spite of herself, Diantha cried out at the shimmer of silk that lay revealed, and knelt to touch it with fingers that snatched themselves away as if they feared a touch would prove it all a dream.

Leslie had to urge her, bruskly, to take out the satin stuff and try it on. She got them out at last, three billowing gowns, and laid them side by side on the coverlet, and stood with clasped hands, silent.

There was a shining green that shot out glints of changing light under the flicker of the candle, reflected a dozen times from the mirrors; and a quilted green petticoat to match. And there was a flowered and ruffled gown of yellow silk laced across the stomacher, and another of stiff, quilted sarcenet, all stormy blue with a laced false front of paler blue instead of the stomacher.

Crumpled as they were from the trunk, they filled the shadowy log room with a radiance of their own, and made the girl's face amazingly sober as she looked from one to another and back again. Beneath them in the trunk there were satin shoes to match the gowns, and a huddle, too, of daintier silks.

She came at last for help to Leslie, kneeling on the floor to take out his uniform, and poking ruefully at sundry warps and dents in the laced tricorn hat. She stood before him and begged him to pick the gown that he liked best. Smiling at her puckered forehead, he tossed the scarlet coat and the buff breeches across the lid of the trunk, and looked at her and at the three shimmering gowns, and back at her soberly. And at length strode over and picked up the green silk by its two tiny shoulder puffs and held it in front of her with mock solemnity. Flushed, shining eyed, she gazed up at him and down at the gay dress with its frothy eschelle of gayer green ribbons cascading down the bodice, and then reached out for it with a passionate, hungry gesture and hugged it to her.

Two tears rolled down her cheeks, one to splash into dark green on the bright green dress, and the other to wander over to her nose and cling there stubbornly, though she tried to sniff it away; until Arnett, between laughing at her predicament and blinking his own eyes, wiped it away for her with a lace handkerchief pulled from that magical trunk of his. Then, because her lips were trembling so, he snatched up his coat and his smallclothes, his packet of razors, and his hat, plundered the chest of his sash and his shoes and his hose, and fled to the kitchen.

He wished for a mirror while he shaved; but there was not even a candle in that mud-floored lean-to. He shaved by touch, and buckled his plain white stock by guess, and made a hopeless job of tying his short, unruly hair with a ribbon that kept slipping off each time he had the bows and the ends adjusted to his liking. He gave it up at last, and went back across the court to tap softly at the door behind which small, rustling sounds told of an excited struggle with petticoats and hoops.

She came running, still in her bare feet, and when she had let him in, she lifted the frothing flounces to show him that toes and ankles were scrubbed until they were pink. Her hair was piled high in a golden crown that made her face seem older and more slender, and gave it a shy dignity.

Fritz, rousing sleepily on the bearskin in the dim corner, blinked amazedly at Arnett Leslie resplendent in scarlet and yellow. And blinked and rubbed his eyes when the brilliant uniform bowed low before a vision of gold and green, and Leslie kissed the hand of Hellward Bound's serving maid. Squirming noiselessly to the edge of the clapboard bunk, he lay smiling eagerly as the gloomy, unhappy man he had followed to Pitt's Town knelt at Diantha's feet. And squirmed in delight as Diantha, bare shoulders shining above the froth of green, leaned over to smooth and tie Mr. Leslie's stubborn hair into a proper club, and at last, impatient, gave a final fillip to the ribbon ends and pulled a boyishly grinning Leslie to his feet by thumb and forefinger on one of his ears.

CHAPTER X

IT was pitch black in the streets of Lower Town when the tall major in scarlet and the fine lady in green came out on the log doorstep of the Golden Eagle. The lady came out first, and sidewise, because the sidehoops of that shining gown were so wide and flaring that Hellward Bound's doorway was not half wide enough to let them pass.

They stood a minute together on the log step, while their eyes got used to the darkness. Pitt's Town was all but blotted out; only the glow of candlelight through open doors and the duller glow through greased-paper windows marked here and there the erratic wanderings of the King's Highway. Out in the blackness somewhere, a violin wailed softly, and at intervals a dog wailed also, not so softly. Bursts of shouting gushed up from some boisterous group around a whisky keg; there was the vague murmur of the town, unseen, crouching there in the dark, holding this bit of low, muddy dirt in the name of the white race.

By day, with the red ramparts of Fort Pitt rising above its slab roofs, it seemed to thrust back the wilderness. By night, the wilderness closed in around it, as if to smother, to choke it, to blot it out. It pressed now about the two on the door log as they stood in a little pool of light from the taproom candles, and the candlelight, futile in that surrounding darkness, showed how the wilderness forced its ways on these would-be conquerors. For all her silk and ribbons, the girl was barefoot, and the man held her satin slippers and stockings in his hand.

Major Leslie slipped his free hand into the lace at Diantha's elbow. Diantha picked up the billowy green silk and held it high, and set one tentative foot into the mud of the dooryard and felt it sink. Outside the light from the door, they were lost in utter blackness.

Floundering through ruts and pools and blundering into unlighted doorways, they came at length to the bend where the highway turned to follow the line of earthworks to the gate. It was lighter here, for the guard had a roaring bonfire in the street just opposite the drawbridge. In the firelight, men in homespun and buckskin squatted on their heels and threw dice on a blanket spread in the middle of the street itself. The cubes lay forgotten while the officer and his lady passed, and Diantha giggled.

"How would a Maryland gentleman answer this question of conduct and etiquette?" she asked and giggled again. "Am I to drop your beautiful dress into the mud and be modest? Or hold it up while the populace stares at my legs, and be nice and clean for Captain Ecuyer's ball?"

"Neither," said Leslie promptly, and surprised himself with a very macaroni of a foolish notion. "I saw, in London, a fine lady come riding to a rout in a chair all scarlet and gold. D'you see?" He spread the lapels of his major's coat wide to show the buff waistcoat underneath. "Will I do for your chair?"

While she laughed at him, he picked her up, flounces and hoops and muddy feet, and swung her breast-high against him. Striding between the sharpened stakes of the outer palisade, he passed two red-coated sentries who presented arms soberly and then winked at each other over their musket muzzles.

A bare arm tightened round his neck.

"Truly, Major Leslie," the girl murmured, "I had never thought to go to any ball in so handsome a riding-chair."

So they passed through the log gates of Forbes' great fortress, down the brick-faced passage through the walls, where the log firing steps on the ramparts made a roof overhead and flambeaux in brackets on the revetments filled the covered way with a red and smoky light. The parade ground was hard and firm, but Leslie did not set Diantha down at all until they had crossed it and come close to a chattering group clustered around the doorway of the commandant's tall brick house. There was light enough here —long yellow shafts of light falling through tall windows with real glass in them. And music, slow and stately at the moment; and beyond the pillared doorway glimpses of scarlet and green, gold saber knots and bright sashes, the flash of polished scabbards and the gleam of bared shoulders, full skirts twirling slowly, powdered heads dipping in curtsey and bow.

Diantha seemed not to know when Leslie swung her down. She stood gazing, her hands clasped at her lips, the silken flounces, forgotten, brushing the dirt. Watching her, Leslie felt as he had felt when he found Fritz Van Buren on the Bedford trail. He had to take her by the arm before she even thought to take a step toward that scene of gay color and stately music, and draw her back again at the doorstep lest she walk in barefoot as she was.

There was water in a wooden tub beside the step, and a green-coated private on duty with strips of clean towel. Arnett knelt on one knee and set Diantha on the other, the while she dipped first one foot and then the other into the tub, and dried them on the towel, and slipped on the white silk stockings and the satin shoon fetched from London and never meant to dance on the verge of nowhere in the wilderness.

He felt her hand trembling on his arm as they went in, and she whispered something, so low he did not hear her and leaned closer.

"I said I wished she had not died; she would have loved it," Diantha murmured, and pressed his arm. "I feel so queer about it."

"Died?" Arnett repeated, puzzled.

"I feel so strange, wearing her lovely clothes. As if I ought to run and take them off. You meant to keep them—and you are so generous you give them away to me...."

Arnett Leslie laughed, a hard sound—too loud in the crooning of the violins.

"Died! She did not die." Diantha's hand went to her mouth again, and her eyes were frightened. "She married my father."

"Oh-h!" And again, "Oh-h! How terrible. I am so ashamed. What a terrible thing to say to you—you have been so good to me. I—I can't go in now. Take me back, please. Oh, I am so sorry."

Major Leslie, looking down soberly enough, softened at the woe in her face.

"Why," he said calmly, "it's time I was forgetting it. It was very simple. I went away to England, and when I came back to be married, *she* had decided that there was no reason why she should wed the heir to Leslie Hall when she could wed the owner."

"Truly, I am sorry."

"Why be sorry? Besides, Mistress Gail, I think the gown and

slippers are far more handsome on you than they would have been on her. And much more welcome, too. The music's stopping; we should speak to Captain Ecuyer."

They caused a buzzing and a nodding as they came down the long room together, the threadbare vagabond and the barmaid from Hellward Bound's pothouse. Major Leslie was smiling; he had just made a remarkable discovery. He had discovered, for the first time, that it hadn't hurt to talk about the girl whose silken gown was rustling across the ballroom floor in the Pitt's Town garrison on the slimmer, lovelier body of another girl. The lovelier girl was not smiling; she walked with her eyes straight forward and her chin up. The knot of older officers over against the farther wall was conferring busily.

Major Leslie saw them, and saw, too, the tall figure in scarlet and blue that broke away from the knot and came quickly toward him. They met in mid-floor.

"Captain Barent," said Major Leslie stiffly.

"Your pardon, Major Leslie," said Barent, just as stiffly.

"For what?" asked Leslie, and smiled to see the flush spreading up until it crept under the edge of Barent's powdered wig.

"If Mistress Gail will excuse us, I am instructed to speak to you alone."

"Your instructions, Captain Barent, have not been extended to include me. I can guess what you have to say, and suggest you do not say it. Since you are acquainted with Mistress Gail, I also suggest that you make her welcome, sir. She is my affianced wife."

Leslie had counted on making a sensation with that announcement, but not on such consternation as flashed across Barent's reddening face. He looked at Leslie, standing there with that cool, sardonic smile of his, waiting. Looked at Diantha, though Diantha did not know it because she was staring, pale-faced and startled, at this man who claimed her as his fiancée without troubling to take her into his confidence. Looked over his shoulder to the group by the wall as if for help. Looked back at Leslie, waiting . . . waiting, he felt, for the slightest excuse to refer the whole matter of the day's unpleasant doings to that plain straight saber at his hip.

And then Leslie pressed him, as if they already were talking with bare steel on the parade ground instead of veiled words on the ballroom floor.

"Make Mistress Gail welcome, sir, so we may pay our respects to the commandant," said the Marylander softly.

And Captain Barent bowed, his throat and face as deeply red as if the black string of his wig, twined about his neck, had tightened and were choking him.

Whereupon Major Leslie bowed with grave courtesy, and Mistress Gail dropped a haughty small curtsey without ever taking her eyes from the amazing gentleman who had chosen this place of all places to announce his betrothal to a girl who hadn't yet been told about it. There was a louder buzzing as the scarlet uniform with its yellow facings and the green silk with the imperious small face and the pile of gold hair above it moved down the long floor to bow and curtsey again before Ecuyer and his staff.

The bluff Swiss governor acknowledged bow and curtsey, the powdered pigeon-wings of his wig bending so low they all but brushed the green ribbons at Diantha's breast. His sunburned face smiled briefly as he took Leslie's hand with a cordiality not quite necessary. Perhaps, soldier of fortune that he was, he liked the combative challenge of this fortuneless soldier's black eyes. Perhaps, none too happy in the responsibility for holding this fortress of his in a hostile world, he took a certain pleasure in the presence of a vagabond bold enough to bring a tavern wench to the officers' ball.

Whatever the motive, his welcome to the red-and-buff stranger was a signal to every young ensign and lieutenant in the place that they might go ahead, and they went. They came swooping down upon Mistress Gail until she was ringed around with the scarlet and blue of the regulars and the green tunics of the Pennsylvanians; and the wig-bags bobbed and the tightly wound pigtails waggled and jerked above high collars and flowing lace jabots as Ecuyer's subalterns bowed and scraped, and begged for dances, and pressed cups of punch upon this girl who had served them all with whisky or toddy or Antigua rum across the bar at Hellward's in the last fortnight.

Arnett Leslie found himself put neatly out of the way. Humorously resentful, he looked on at Diantha's little triumph. *Affianced wife!* He chuckled. *Zookins,* she was his property, if not his betrothed; he had paid eighteen pounds for her. Nor could he complain that his property was not duly admired; the bobbing and the ogling and the prinking declared that he had bought with excellent judgment. He stood there outside the circle, with his cocked hat tucked into his elbow, and had to be asked twice before he heard an amused voice at his shoulder:

"Come away, Major. There's a bucket of bombo behind you, and I can give you professional assurance that it will warm your blood quite as well as those pretty shoulders!"

The Leslie Hall stare he turned on the owner of that impertinent voice met one quite as cool and forthright.

"I'm Boyd," said the redcoat beside him.* "Come away. We've sunk a whole wallet of our precious sugar lumps into more Barbados than three garrisons can swizzle. Sugar and fire, Leslie. And that's all you can say for the liveliest lady." He threw his head back and grinned impudently. "Pish, Major, don't be so hoity-toity. They think I'm an arrogant fellow, too. No offense, sir—but why not wet your muzzle in good bombo instead of letting the whole fort see that you're jealous as hell, sir?"

Strangely enough, Major Leslie laughed. This impudent Royal American had a friendly truculence about him that claimed kinship with Leslie Hall and its prickly pride. He let Boyd swing him around and go burrowing arrogantly through the crowd around the puncheon table until they stood in the noble presence of a wooden horse-bucket all splattered about with sugared rum and flanked by a moist odd-lot of noggins and glasses, tin cups and dried gourds with peeled sticks for handles.

There were bare shoulders clustered around the bombo table among the gay tunics and sashes. Across the bucket a rawboned woman with two black patches on her flushed face waved a dripping gourd at him.

"Faith, Major Leslie, ye're welcome among the ladies in Pitt's Town," she rallied him. "Ye're the first excitement we've had since the hothead beside y' tried to crack poor Donnellan's topknot with a tree."

Boyd waved his cup at her.

"Here's to all of us hotheads," he shouted, with his arm across

---

* Boyd was the surgeon in the Fort Pitt garrison. Captain Ecuyer's journal recounts that Surgeon Boyd quarreled violently with one Lieutenant Donnellan, and that they belabored each other with fists and sticks in a fight that lasted intermittently for three days until both were disciplined for it.

Arnett's shoulders, "and may the redsticks never make them hotter by skinning the topknots off altogether!"

"Redsticks! Poof!" snorted the rawboned person, setting down the empty gourd and wiping her lips on the back of her hand. "We'll let you at them, Master Boyd—you with your club and Major Leslie with his one-tailed cat, his dog and his bear, and that lovely young hellion from the pothouse." Leslie stiffened, and Boyd's arm closed warningly on his shoulders. "Lud knows she routed the pack of ye 'til young Lucifer came to town with his bedroom on his back and took her off her feet—and Barent, too—between retreat and the troop!"

"Don't mind her, Leslie," murmured Boyd, "I told you there was gunpowder in that bombo bucket. And Mistress Jones is paying you a double compliment—to your own irresistible charm, my dear major, and the unquestioned virtue of your betrothed."

Arnett Leslie's lips went flat.

Boyd clapped him roughly on the back.

"Pish. Poosh. Posh, Leslie. You can't quarrel with me. We're too much of a piece; 't would be a grievous waste of our talents, sir."

A French horn from the orchestra in the balcony cut through his hearty voice with a single mellow note. Leslie saw a familiar figure. The captain who had glowered at him while Captain Barent sat down in the midst of a bursted laundry bundle was standing alone in midfloor, his hectoring tone demanding attention. Boyd waved his gourd and nodded.

"He'll be your first—Arnold. And, if you like, I'll be your second —with apologies for a most vile wit—when you fight your first. He dropped the wench he had and went wooing the new one the day she came to Pitt's Town. Now that he has seen her in silk ... *law!*" He marked the grim twist to Major Leslie's mouth, and changed his course quickly: "I warn you, now, keep a hand on that temper of yours. Arnold's calling for the hurly-burly, and I'll lay you a pistole to a shilling somebody kisses your lady before it's over."

Up on the balcony the red-coated orchestra burst into the striding music of the "Pioneers March." Laughing and giggling, skirts swishing and swords a-clatter, the crowd swirled into a hilarious circle in the middle of the floor. There was a furious rush of green and scarlet coats toward the shimmering green gown, and a boisterous struggle, half serious, half in fun, for places in the chain on either side of Mistress Diantha Gail.

With Boyd's hand insistent on his arm, Leslie found himself thrust into line and holding hands with the rest. Arnold, his voice a little shrill, was calling for quiet, beckoning out of the effervescent circle a brisk young ensign all adangle with fobs and seals beneath his sash, and a pretty minx powdered and patched and rouged, and laced into a pink dress so tight she seemed to have no waist at all. The orchestra dropped the "Pioneers March" and whirled into the lighter music of "Beauty, Retire." The pink minx and the befobbed ensign pirouetted across the circle to its farther side and went whispering down the line. Giggles and protests followed them as they went, the officer bending confidentially to the hidden ears of the ladies, and the girl beckoning with mock coyness and a crooked finger to the officers to bend down to her mischievous lips.

She came at last to Leslie and slipped a bare arm around his neck.

"Do you know our hurly-burly, Major?" she whispered, her arm pulling his head down a thought closer, it seemed to him, than was strictly necessary. "You see, we give each one sealed orders—something funny to do, or something very nice. I hoped somebody would give me something nice to do—with you, Major Leslie. But I have no luck at all. See, the best I can do is whisper to you, when I *might* have had a chance to kiss you." Her arm tightened. "Oh, well, if I can't, no other girl shall—not here—not even this pretty servant girl you jest about wedding...."

"That," said Arnett courteously but very definitely, "is not a jest."

The girl flashed a mirthful look at him, and set her arm more firmly about his neck.

"Oh, la, Major Leslie, we are not so witless, though we do not come from Maryland. How can you wed a bond maid every one knows dare not wed at all? Your orders, Major Leslie, are given in the interest of peace and good will in our little garrison. When the drum rolls, you will go to Captain Arnold and embrace him and kiss him on both cheeks!"

With a taunting laugh, she whirled away. Next to him, Arnett heard the ensign whispering and chuckling in the ear of the sallow-faced captain's wife whose hand he was holding. As he minced away, the woman pulled Arnett toward her and whispered, between simper and giggle:

"This will be a merry to-do—Helene has told every man in the circle to do the same thing. It will be a miracle if there are no broken bones, or a duel in the morning. She's told them all to kiss your charming companion, Major."

The fifes gave a final flirt to the tune of "Beauty, Retire" and went prancing into the rollicking "Juniper Tree." Up on the balcony, the orchestra leader was singing:

> *O, my sweet Phœbe, how merry were we,*
> *The night we lay under the juniper tree....*

The gay circle, rocking back and forth in time to the bleat of the horns, flung back the catch:

> *The juniper tree, I, oh!*

Arnold drew his sword and held it overhead. The leader sang:

> *Take this hat on your head,*
> *Keep your head warm;*
> *Take a sweet kiss, it will do you no harm,*
> *But a great deal of good, I know!*

Arnold's blade gleamed and fell. A fife squealed. A drum rolled. And the hurly-burly broke into a swirl of bright colors mingling, voices rising, laughter shrilling.

Across the crazy hubbub of it, Leslie saw a jostling eddy of scarlet tunics and beribboned wigs, and in the midst of them a pile of gold hair tossed helplessly about. Clumsy, pawing boors! He pushed toward them through the crowd.

Out of nowhere came a girl in sprigged muslin, with wild flowers in her hair, to throw her arms around him and kiss him on the lips and run away. The faded lady on his right tweaked at his hair ribbon; it came off, and dropped his hair about his ears. Behind her, he saw the brisk young ensign chuckling at his own mischief.

Leslie's heels rang resentfully on the puncheons as he thrust by. Confound them all, with their backwoods gamboling. He could guess how thoroughly Ecuyer's young officers would be taking advantage of the hurly-burly to maul and kiss Diantha. He put out his arm and set aside, with decisive rudeness, a Dutch lieutenant who got in his way.

When he had pushed through the hilarious crowd, Diantha had disappeared. The eddy of subalterns that had tossed and jostled her was breaking up, turning away from the door. He caught an angry phrase and a name: *"Barent!"* An ensign of artillery came running up the steps, his face flushed. He caught sight of Leslie and said something in a smothered tone. A laugh went up, and the bag-wigs turned curiously to look. Leslie's annoyance rose quickly toward anger. He said, sharply:

"Where is she?" And heard them laugh again.

"Ye did her no service with your jest about marriage," the ensign told him, grinning. "Old Bond came chasing her. It means a year on her service, and a flogging too; ye should have thought o' that."

"You let him take her...." Leslie's voice was deadly. His shoulder spun the stammering artilleryman against the wall as he went by, running.

He was still running when he came to the Golden Eagle. He stood an instant on the doorlog, staring.

And then whipped his saber clear.

Crumpled against the bar, her shoulders bare, the green gown and the chemise beneath it torn away, Diantha faced Hellward Bound and Captain Barent. Across one shoulder ran a bloody weal.

The furious swing of Leslie's saber struck his own whip from Bond's lifted hand. The second, though the blade struck flat, brought the blood in a red line through the back of Bond's shirt. He smiled as he struck, as the Leslies were wont to fight. Barent, his weapon half drawn, found something unpleasant about the smile, something more deadly than the point of Leslie's blade, level with his throat. He stood unmoving while Leslie stepped backward and set himself against the bar.

"Why?" asked Leslie. He spoke to the girl, but his eyes held Barent's.

"Master Bond would have me kind to Captain Barent."

Leslie marveled at her voice. Her shoulders quivered beneath his arm, but her voice was steady. "I declined the honor, for which Captain Barent already has paid well. They offered to have me whipped for it. Truly, Major Leslie, Captain Barent is an impetuous lover."

132

Leslie spoke to Barent:

"Will you answer to me now, or in the morning, with seconds?"

"In the morning, if you ..."

Leslie caught his eyes, and leaped. His arm flung Diantha headlong on the floor. His saber hilt drove for Barent's jaw and sent him reeling.

The puncheon table shook. Upright in the middle plank, with a long white crack running from it half the table length, a rusted frow * stood quivering.

Behind the bar, Hellward Bound reached for a skinning knife stuck in a crack between the logs.

"I think," said Arnett Leslie, smiling gently, "that you both die here. You have lived too long."

"Throw it!" gasped Barent, staggering back from the table edge. Shrilly, frantically: "Throw it!"

Bond's hand went back over his shoulder, the long blade lying along his fingers. Barent's sword rasped clear.

On the lip of the noggin by the candle, a drowsy fly buzzed restlessly.

"Throw it!" shrilled Barent again, and took a step outward from the wall.

Across his high voice ran another sound. A drone, as of a great fly, bumbling and buzzing. A short, uncertain sound.

Somewhere a woman screamed.

The drone rose to a rumble, the rumble to a low, rolling thunder.

Over the dark town, crouching on its bit of earth, the thunder swelled and rolled louder. Drums ... alarm drums ... all the drums of the guard beating together. From the Flag bastion of Fort Pitt, the long roll sent its warning down the walls. It was thunder, but the thunder trembled, as if the hands that beat the drums were shaking.

* Frow—a heavy cleaver.

CHAPTER XI

In Which Arnett Leslie, Having Forsworn All Women, Invites One Into His Bed—but Sleeps on a Plank Himself:

IN the taproom of the Golden Eagle, three blades hung motionless.

It was Barent who moved first. After the first shock of alarm, his eyes said that he was glad to go. He ran awkwardly, like a man with wooden legs. Leslie, before he followed, rapped with his saber point upon the bar:

"We'll have an end of pretending, Bond. I know your vile bargain with Barent. If I say so, you hang for it."

The saber point flicked out. Bond snatched his hand back with a yelp of pain, and dropped the knife. Leslie took Diantha's hand and led her quickly out.

The parade ground of Fort Pitt, when they came back to it, was a grotesque of red and black. Soldiers with flambeaux ran back and forth. Shadows crouched in the angles of the walls; when the torches passed, the shadows pounced out upon men and women huddled around the windlass and the well. On the brick well-frame, a man in linsey hunting dress flung his right arm in wide gestures as he talked.

"I tell ye," he was shouting, "I seen them!"

A question angered him. His hand slapped down on the other where it lay on the muzzle of his rifle.

"Means?" he cried. "I'll tell ye what it means! It means ye've let Bond an' Croghan an' th' rest o' y'r Injun traders cater to th' lousy redsticks till they've got more beef an' flour an' powder an' shot stored up in their villages than ye have in y'r fort. Ye've given 'em licker, an' th' run o' y'r towns. Now ye'll pay for it. They've wiped out Clapham's plantation, an' they'll soon be here."

Diantha's hand closed tightly on Leslie's arm. The red light fell on the tall, egg-shaped head-dresses of officers' ladies and on the sober coats, the linsey shirts and the bed-gowns of village folk. The officers who had danced in the governor's house were herding their companies into line along the barracks. Commands cracked out. A platoon of greencoats swung into column and came past the well at the double, bayonets clinking in their scabbards, breaths sharp with haste and excitement. In the windows of the governor's house, the musicians who had played for the hurly-burly were leaning out, their violins and flutes, their cornets and their snare-drums still hugged against their scarlet chests. The woods-runner on the well drew an arm wearily across his mouth.

"A lot o' ye ain't seen an Injun war," he said. "I tell ye, take heed. It's the first massacre since Forbes whipped 'em on the Loyal Hanna. If ye'd seen what I seen...."

"I was two miles away when I seen the smoke, an' I found the first o' them a mile out o' Clapham's. They'd been scalpin' him when he broke away, an' the flap o' skin was danglin' down over his face where he lay acrost the trail. His back was feathered like a porcupine with Delaware arrows.

"An' when I come to Colonel Clapham's, I seen old Clapham dead acrost his grindstone, with the scythe he had been sharpenin' drove through his back an' stickin' up out o' his chest, an' his head peeled. There was two women an' a brat, too. They'd taken the young one up by the heels an' bashed his brains out on a tree, an' they'd taken the women over by that picket fence Clapham had around his garden an' stripped 'em an' set 'em up on the palin's.

"There they was.... *God!*" He drew his sleeve again across his face. "It had taken 'em a long time to die...."

Leslie heard pent-up breath run out in a sigh that was like wind across dry grass. A man's voice, high and angry, told the man on the steps to hold his tongue, and cursed him for a fool.

"Ay, I'm a fool, an' so are all of ye, dancin' an' friskin' it, with Injuns lickin' their lips an' whettin' their knives f'r y'r scalps."

The man who had shouted at him thrust through the press, and Leslie saw that it was Arnold, coming back from the muster of troops at the barracks, with an ensign of the guard.

"Take him back into headquarters, Mr. Baillie; he'll have the town in a panic," Arnold ordered in his high, sharp voice.

The crowd swayed and gave back; in place of the fascinated silence with which it had heard the news of the massacre at

Clapham's, a buzz as of an overturned hive rose over the rustle of silk; louder, sharper with alarm as dazed minds took in the presence of deadly peril, the voices of women clamored at each other.

Diantha said nothing at all. Leslie, seeing all too vividly the things that had happened at Clapham's, forgot for the moment that she was there. Then he saw Captain Arnold, self-possessed in the turmoil, turn and come toward him. Red light and dark shadow accentuated the hawklike look of his face as he glanced at a woman who ran to meet him. Leslie saw him stiffen and quicken his step; the woman caught him by the arm, and they stopped together where the light from the doorway fell on the woman's wine-red dress. Arnold's voice came in an angry murmur. There were tears in Peggy Sargent's voice when she answered him, and his impatient arm drew away.

"Oh, stay, then," Leslie heard him say. "Barent's room. He's gone." Then he broke away and came quickly over to Leslie and Diantha, his bow to Leslie rigidly polite, his question to Diantha eager and more than polite.

"Will you not stay the night in the fort?" he urged her, and put his hand on her wrist. "Like as not it's a false alarm, but you'll be safer here. 'T will be a nervous night in Pitt's Town."

Leslie felt Diantha's fingers slip out of his hand, and realized for the first time that she had been holding it so tightly that two of his own fingers were numb. She had been terrified, he reproached himself, and he had not had the wit to give her so much as a word. Terrified, but brave enough, too; she had not made a sound in all the hubbub of frightened women. Now she put her hand quite calmly on the cuff of his sleeve; and gave Arnold an answer that amazed Leslie as much as it did the captain.

"Thank you, Captain Arnold," she curtseyed faintly in a stir of satin flounces, "Major Leslie is my plighted husband, and I will go with him."

Arnold's shoulders went stiff, and his eyes glared at Leslie. His voice was insolent:

"Mistress Gail, you do not know this man...."

"Better than I know you, Captain Arnold."

"Have you thought why he followed you here?"

Diantha's laughter trilled out.

"Why, to wed with me, to be sure. Can you think of a better reason?"

Arnold's voice was hoarse with anger. He bowed stiffly, his hand on the hilt of his sword.

"You'll be here in the fort right enough, this time tomorrow. If we are attacked tonight, Major Leslie, you will be responsible for what happens to Mistress Gail."

"I have been responsible for some little time," Leslie told him, and wondered whether Arnold had any inkling of what he meant. "And when Captain Ecuyer wishes us to come into the fort, we shall be glad of your hospitality, captain."

It pleased Leslie mightily, for some reason he did not trouble to explore, to leave Arnold standing there. Diantha put her hand on Leslie's arm as if to hasten him. With stiffly polite words, the two men said good night. Diantha drew her hand away to pick up the green skirt in her curtsey, and then tucked it back again quickly. They walked in silence across the parade and through the covered way. Below the redan wall, where the flambeaux flamed redly over the roadway, Leslie looked down at her, curiously.

"Afraid?"

"You are not?" she countered.

"Why, no, not particularly." And then he added, mostly to himself: "I feel too good to be afraid, tonight."

"Good?"

Leslie laughed softly.

"Diantha Gail," he told her, "you are not the only one who has been set free. But you did better with me than I with you. I bought you out of bondage and let you go straight into it again; you bought *me* free, and free I am, and will stay so."

"I do not understand? *I* have brought *you* free?"

"Ay, and whatever I may do to serve you would be a small enough reward. You see, I ran away because the girl whose dress you are wearing married—some one else. And I thought the world had died, and was buried somewhere inside me. Now I find," he said it easily, "that the world has come alive, and is like to be amusing and even exciting again."

"Oh," said Diantha in a small, doubtful voice. "I see."

"*See!*" Leslie scoffed as her foot went down in a rut and she staggered against him in a billow of skirts. "You see like a blind man in this dark. Here, I'll have eyes for both of us."

He scarcely recognized this merry fellow who suddenly had sprung up inside him, nor the reckless gayety with which he stooped and gathered up Diantha Gail, hoops and flounces and flying ribbons, and held her tightly against his breast. At that, he acknowledged, he was a more pleasant fellow than that grim, sardonic Leslie in linsey who had trudged down across the Blue Ridge a week ago.

And so they came again to the Golden Eagle, and the girl slid down onto the doorlog in the dark. The door of the taproom stood wide, but the place was black, and reeking with smells. Somewhere inside there were grunts and snores that might account for Halbert Bond. Diantha fumbled for his hand, found it, and pulled him into the room.

"You may know your outdoors," she whispered, "but I know my way in a barroom, sir."

Then, contrarily, she barked her shins on a clumsy slab of a stool, and swore like a very barmaid, in a small, stifled voice, so that Leslie pretended to be shocked and Diantha flashed back at him:

"I dare say your fine Maryland ladies do it better."

In the courtyard between the two wings of the tavern, hoofs stamped and bodies stirred, and the boy Fritz came softly to meet them.

"I fetch in da beasts an' hopple dam by da long rope," he reported to Leslie with shy eagerness. "Da soldier down by fort say Injuns come, zur."

He stood yawning and blinking in the light of the candle Diantha found in the familiar kitchen, and Diantha, seeing Leslie with his arm thrown over the boy's shoulders, thought she saw a different man. The drawn, brittle look was gone, though he was sober enough as he followed her into the room where the dolphins sported under their stool and the triple mirrors threw dancing lights over the shaggy walls.

"We'll take turns watching, Fritz," he said, and looked curiously at the musket leaning beside the door. "Whose is that?"

"I got him from da storeroom out, zur, whan da soldier say Injuns come. Powder I got, too, zur, an' much bullets." He showed proudly the horn and pouch hanging from a peg above the clumsy trade gun.

"Bond let you have it?"

"Bond were gone, zur."

"Who's sleeping in the bar?"

"One of da fallers w'at turn himself into whisky barrel, zur. Like a barrel he lay dere, on his belly on da floor."

Leslie chuckled, and then laughed outright at Diantha's rosy face. A mild enough word, he thought, for a bond maid to blush at. She stood hesitating by the dressing table, one finger tracing a mother-of-pearl shepherdess, her face wistful.

"Look you, Fritz, climb back into bed and get to sleep. I'll watch till dawn; then it will be your turn."

"Please, zur, it should be my turn now. I slept much, before da drum begin. Please, you should to bed go now."

Leslie looked over at the girl.

"He is no help at all, is he?" he teased her. "You want to sleep in your London bed, and this Fritz, who is a fine soldier but no diplomat, insists that I must go to bed at once. What to do? What to do?"

Her face was rosier still, and she looked down gravely at the tip of a slipper. It struck the man, suddenly, that she was scarcely as old as Fritz. His voice was gentler than she had heard it before:

"Well, then, you might ask me to share your bed."

And, at the quick lift of her head and the sobering of her mouth, he added:

"I mean—the bed in your old room. Diantha Gail, do you mistrust *every one?* Is there no one . . . ?"

She looked at him for a long moment, her lips parted, her eyes startled. Then, to his amusement, her hands flew to her face and she sat down quickly, her elbows on the dancing shepherds and shepherdesses, her shoulders quivering in the green, quivering silk. Leslie took a doubtful step toward her, hesitated, and said gently:

"I was but teasing you, child. I did not mean . . ."

She flung around to face him, the tears shining on her cheeks. Her hands dug into the stuff of her dress where it lay across her knees and closed tight upon it, her arms tense in that rigid, childish attitude that went with her moments of deep stress. Her tight small hands and her tense slim arms kept her body straight and steady, but they could not stop the quiver at her lips.

"Oh!" And again, "Ohh! Can't you see? Can't you see?"

Behind him, Leslie heard the faintest shadow of a noise as Fritz picked up his musket and slipped out.

"See what, child?"

"Child! I am not a child. Can't you see I would not have you kind? Anything—*anything* but kind!"

Clumsily, because he was deeply moved, Leslie pretended not to understand.

"Why, now, 't is simple to be rude. Here, we'll fix it this way. I'll not sleep in your old room; I shall sleep here, on Hellward's bearskin across from you, and catch a plague of fleas."

She shook her head at him, a fierce, small shake.

"Did you never feel you could not *bear* a gentle word or a kindness?" She bent her head to the puff of one sleeve to brush the tears from her lashes. Muffled against her shoulder, her strained voice confessed: "I am afraid. I am so afraid. And you make me weep when you are kind. Oh, curse me... drive me out to my own bed and my corn-husk mattress and tell me it is all a jest ... tell me I shall never be free. I can bear that."

And Leslie, knowing so well what it meant to dread a kind word, and how it was that a man, and a woman, too, he supposed, might run and hide because the pain of sympathy and pity was too keen to bear, sat himself down on the edge of the clapboard bed and told her about Evelyn Gentle, and about his homecoming to Leslie Hall.

He lost himself, after a little, in the telling; and realized, as the tale went on, that he could tell it now without bitterness. He began to smile as he told her of Tom Yeardley's red gig lying with its wheel through Master Grannis' tavern wall, and of how Tom had seized the coach that would have been Evelyn's and hitched his own horses to it, and then forgotten them and drunk himself fast asleep. He told her about the wild journey to South Mountain, and how he and Tom had howled bawdy songs, and how Tom had tried to swim up the creek that was only deep enough to wet his belt buckle.

He heard the girl's laugh ring out in delighted and shocked amazement when he told her the name of Tom Yeardley's manor on the mountain side. He told her how he and Tom had ridden down the western face of the mountain to see the lands he held by the new patents from Lord Baltimore, and why he had decided to forget the limestone manor house he had planned to build. About the morning when he leaned out of his window in the fog and saw a girl bound to a post in the stableyard and a bullock whip curling around her bare body, he said nothing. He was, at last, ashamed that he had gone yawning back to bed; the sheen in Diantha Gail's eager eyes would go out if she knew he had been more concerned for a dog than he had been for her.

But he did tell her how he found Robin tagging after him along the road, and how he had named him. They both smiled at the thumping that set up beneath the curtained bed when Leslie said "Robin." But Robin was too sleepy to come out, or to applaud for long; the thumping died away drowsily. Leslie finished the tale with a word or two of Fritz, and none about the slashing fight with the greencoats who had been flogging him. It seemed, in this happier mood, a foolish and unnecessary fight; he had taken out on those luckless Pennsylvania soldiers his bitterness toward the whole world.

"So," he closed the story, "I came to Pitt's Town and found a lovelier lady to wear my bridal gear." It did not hurt, he discovered, to say even that.

"But will you stay here always in the wilderness? Surely... surely some day you will go back, and build the limestone manor house."

He looked up, smiling quizzically at the eagerness in her voice. "No." His hands turned themselves out to show her how empty they were. "It takes more than sixpence to build it; more than six shillings, too. 'T will take too many beaver skins to lay the stones, my dear...."

My dear. He stopped at that. He wondered what trick of mind had made those words come out. They meant, he felt, a great deal more in the second-best room of Halbert Bond's backwoods tavern than they did in the ballroom of my lord Baltimore's London house. He would see to it that they did not slip out again. But Diantha Gail did not seem to notice them. She was leaning toward him, her hands clasped tightly before her knees.

"But if you had the beaver skins, or the money, surely then you would go back?"

Leslie's long, expressive hands pleaded ignorance of what he

141

might do in that impossible case. The next question was far away from beaver skins or manor houses.

"What will you say when they know, down at the fort, that you were merely jesting when you said...when you introduced me as your fiancée?"

"Why, by then," Leslie smiled and leaned back with his shoulder against the post of the bed, "you'll be free beyond any man's questioning, and the whole garrison will be at your feet."

Diantha moved uneasily as he got up, stretching, pulling at the stiff collar of his tunic.

"Will you not..." she began, and flushed. "Will you not sleep in that bed, Major Leslie? I am more afraid than I should be. Indians seem like...like cannibals." She shuddered. "Or like queer monsters in old folk tales. It seems strange to have them close enough to *reach* us. Truly, I wish you would not go away tonight. Oh," she smothered his half-hearted protest with a lift of the chin and a faint smile, "you have made it very clear that you would not look at me. I am much more afraid of the Indians than I am of you."

Leslie yawned again, and did not even wonder why she turned away so quickly. He unbuttoned the long, gold-laced waistcoat and stripped off the bright tunic, and hung it side by side with the waistcoat on pegs along the wall. Then he picked up his rifle, snapped the pan to glance at the priming, and went to the door.

"I'm going to see Fritz a few minutes," he told Diantha. "If I give him this rifle to do sentry-go with, he'll feel like a field marshal. And I'll close the shutters, and the door. If you blow out the candle when you are ready, I'll come back."

He went out, and the shutters banged cheerfully.

When he came back, the room was dark.

Presently Diantha heard the snick of flint on steel, and saw the candle flame spring up again against the triple mirrors. The man's shadow danced against the farther wall, but his boots came closer to the curtained bed. He stood between the looped curtains and looked down at her.

"You said I made it clear I would not look at you," he smiled. "I came to prove you wrong—and to say I am very sure there will be no Indians tonight."

She squirmed under the rustling quilts, curling up into a childish ball, and smiled up at him with parted lips.

"You are...you are..." Suddenly grave, her lips trembled faintly. "Oh, I am glad you came to Pitt's Town."

Out from the covers came a slim bare arm, and a hand to touch his arm shyly.

"Good night." The hand lingered on his wrist.

The candle light fell in a pool of gold on the spreading waves of her hair across the pillow. Her face, childishly solemn, seemed childishly small also. Her gray eyes blinked sleepily at the candle. Leslie bent suddenly toward her, and saw her lips part again in a smile. His lips touched the hand where it lay on his wrist.

"Good night."

The candle went out, and she heard his boots go steadily across the room. After a while, they dropped on the floor, first one, then the other. Then the clapboard bunk creaked and cracked.

CHAPTER XII

*In Which Major Leslie Is Caught Napping, Although Wide Awake;
and Pays for It with a Sore Head, Bound Hands, and an Aching Heart:*

THE bed that went with the Golden Eagle's second-best
room was far less comfortable than many beds Arnett
Leslie had made for himself on the bare ground. The fur
robe thrown over its hewn planks smelled of the bear that had worn
the fur, and the blankets outdid the bear. The blankets and the robe
together could not soften the clapboards or smooth out their uneven
joints. But Leslie slept.

When Fritz woke him in a dawn that was white with fog, he
realized that he had slept deeply, dreamlessly, and that it was pleasant to be awake. He slid out onto the damp floor, and stood shivering, running his fingers through his tumbled hair, and fumbling
along the pegs for his breeches.

Fritz, whispering his report of his hours on watch, seemed reluctant to go to bed. He stood leaning on the rifle in boyish imitation
of a *coureur de bois* to whom Indian alarms were an old story,
to be taken with a grain or two of salt. The patrols from the fort,
he said, had been hopping about all night like rabbits; there was
not a sign of an Indian. Even his whisper had a swagger about it,
and Leslie, pulling on breeches and boots, smiled to himself as he
listened. The long rifle and a little friendliness had worked a miracle
with Fritz; now, to Leslie's amusement, he proposed to go and
milk cows instead of sleeping.

"Da big fur face..." Leslie chuckled at the boy's description of
Halbert Bond..."make *her* milk dam efery morning bafore br'ak-
fast." He jerked the muzzle of the rifle toward the curtained bed.
"She told me, last night, whilst she make zupper."

It was on Leslie's tongue to tell him that Diantha Gail need milk
no more cows for Hellward Bound, but he did not say it. If Fritz
Van Buren had it in him to be chivalrous as well as courageous,

Arnett Leslie would not be the one to hold him back. So he said instead:

"Go it, Fritz. Ye'll be a macaroni with an eye to the ladies before ye're as tall as that gun."

Fritz, with his chin stretched up to rest on his clasped hands on the rifle muzzle, grinned delightedly at the chaffing.

"I be taller already, zur," he said solemnly, and startled Leslie by adding: "We be lookin' out for she now, bant we, zur?"

Leslie glanced at him sharply. Fritz was a different boy indeed; there was something in his tone that suggested he was already including Diantha Gail as a member of the family, along with Robin and Nancy and the bear. He padded over to the clapboard bed and laid the rifle down on the blankets and drew one of them over it to shield it from the damp.

"There be fresh powder in pan, zur," he whispered as he tiptoed to the door. "But no Injun come in fog lak blanket." He gave Arnett a shy smile as he went out, and Leslie heard him chirruping to the terrier, and Robin's paws scudding across the court. A little later the two of them were rummaging among the cluttered cooking gear in the kitchen lean-to; Leslie chuckled again at the little dog's politely-stifled yelps of eagerness. Boy and dog came out of the kitchen on the way to the fenced common where the cattle grazed, below Massacre pond; moccasins and scurrying paws whispered in the weeds, and the fog eddied a little behind them and then was still again. The man went softly across the room, found his pipe, filled it and lighted it, and sat down on the doorlog with his back against the wall. The trade gun that Fritz had taken from Bond's storeroom leaned against the logs beside him, but he barely glanced at it; Pitt's Town, with that fog swaddling it like cotton-wool and the patrols on guard, was safe enough for the moment. And for the moment, there were things on Leslie's mind more serious than Indian raids. These things required thinking.

There was, for one, the matter of Diantha and the uncouth Bond. It might be best, he considered, puffing at his pipe and cradling his knees in the crook of either arm, to go straight to Ecuyer with the whole affair. There was always the chance that Barent would kill him in a duel—Leslie frowned, annoyed to find that particular thought bobbing up in his mind. He blew out smoke in an impa-

145

tient jet, as if to be rid of the notion. But it came back and insisted on being examined.

He looked across the dim room to the blue curtains, just beginning to take on shape and color as the pale light strengthened. Diantha Gail had been afraid; she had not screamed or moaned or even asked a question, in all the hubbub of panic-stricken women on the parade last night. But she had confessed she was afraid, and had asked him to stay. It struck Leslie that he had acquired a fresh responsibility, along with Fritz and the draggle-tail dog. Confound the boy, with his knowing air. It would not be taking care of Diantha Gail to go get himself shot by Captain Barent, Leslie acknowledged wryly. And, after all, the girl had had enough of fear and heartache for a while. He bit down on the stem of the long clay, concerned with just what story he should tell to Ecuyer.

The commandant was, in effect, governor of the town; and if his authority did not extend to the property rights of civilians in ordinary affairs, it certainly could be stretched to cover serious crimes. False swearing was a grave enough crime, when it involved the liberty of a young and beautiful woman in a frontier groggery; Ecuyer, as royal governor, would scarcely risk the injustice of keeping Diantha Gail in bondage to Hellward in the face of a charge of false oathtaking and unlawful sale.

And if, to cap the charge against Barent and Bond, the commandant should be given guarantees ample to satisfy a civil court....

Leslie hugged his knees and puffed contentedly: He would offer Ecuyer his whole pack train as pledge of his good faith and the truth of his charges; before the day was over, Diantha Gail would be free, with the protection of the garrison around her. If, after that, Barent wanted a duel, and the duel went wrong, Ecuyer would still be standing between the girl and the Swiss; Ecuyer would insist on proofs before surrendering her again to Halbert Bond.

Leslie drew deeply at the fragrant smoke and let it wander out in a slow cloud. Elbows on knees and hands hanging lazily between them, he tapped the pipe against his teeth and considered the problems that came after that of Diantha Gail.

They were a little more difficult. Diantha Gail, too, seemed to keep on appearing in the midst of them, although her problem was neatly disposed of and laid aside. *If you had the money, or the beaver skins, you would go back?* That was *her* question. Leslie admitted that today he was not sure of the answer. It would have been simple yesterday; today, he was not nearly so sure that the answer was *no*. He pondered it, not too seriously. There was no hurry about it. And no hurry, either, about building the limestone manor on the spur of South Mountain. Tom Yeardley would welcome him; between them, they could make the South Mountain the new terminus of the Cumberland Road; no freighter would plod the extra eighty miles to Baltimore and back, if he could trade his furs at Yeardley's for powder and shot, cloth and tools, flour and alum salt.

Leslie's thoughts raced along unchecked. With a trip or two across the mountains every year, trading on his own account, he could add enough to the business of Yeardley's depot to rebuild his own fortunes. Enough, he assured himself, to build the limestone manor house as he had dreamed of it, with loopholes in the lower walls, fireplaces vast enough to take whole logs, and wide windows high enough in the lofty rooms so that Indians could not scale them, but not too high to let the sunlight into the corner where the virginal stood on its dolphin legs. *Great zooks!* He glanced again at the curtained bed. He had all but forgotten the girl who lay sleeping in Evelyn's bed.

What a laugh Tom Yeardley would cut loose when he saw all that bridal gear coming back through the stone gateway, and a whole family with it....

Leslie took a grip on his reckless thoughts at last and reined them in. There were some trails on which he had no mind to let them take him.

Somewhere in the fog, a horse nickered, and one of his own pack beasts tethered in the courtyard answered. Out on the King's Highway, a patrol marched by with a muffled cadence of boots scuffling through the soft dirt. The hobbled horses stirred; hoofs trampled; Fritz and Robin would be coming back from the common, stopping to look to the tethers. Too late, Leslie saw other horses looming up through the fog, and riders, with guns slanting down at him across the saddle horns.

The riders were white.

Leslie threw himself backward through the open door. Sprawled on the floor, his hand reaching for the trade musket against the wall, he heard a low voice growl from the far end of the room: "*Lay* there!"

Across the window sill, a musket barrel pointed at his head; behind it, a bearded face cuddled the stock. There was a rush of feet at the door. A fringed leg kicked the trade gun and sent it clattering on the puncheons. Between the bed curtains Leslie saw Diantha Gail's face, and her hair in a gold cloud on her bare shoulders. A hand closed on her arm and dragged her out. Leslie flung himself forward, his hand groping for the musket on the floor. He got it; saw the man who held Diantha thrust her body in front of him as a shield; saw a hand clap itself across her mouth.

On his knees, Leslie aimed into the press of bodies above him. The flint clicked on the steel, but the dampened powder in the pan took the spark without exploding.

Diantha was struggling, writhing in the arms that held her to the breast of a fringed hunting shirt. A rifle butt whirled up... down. Leslie met it with the barrel and parried it, staggered to his feet, struck at a dark, shapeless face outlined against the doorway. Bond! The face drew back and the blow missed. Hands clutched at Leslie's shoulders from behind; he shook them off, struggling forward to strike again at the bearded, gloating face of Hellward Bound. The hands on his shoulders slipped, but other hands caught the musket as he raised it for another blow. He let it go, and sprang with empty hands.

Bond met him with his rifle leveled. A blow on the neck from fist or gunbutt behind him drove Leslie headlong. Bond's rifle, thrusting, smashed its muzzle into his forehead. He went down in a black smother that flashed with red lightning.

The blackness engulfed him, gripped him, carried him along. It was like a river, sweeping him in a current that swayed him from side to side, dizzily, and jostled him against rocks. He tried to fight against it, to swim up out of the smother, but the red lightning flashed blindingly, and he went down.

When he had the will to fight again, the current was still swaying and jostling him, but it had lost something of its rushing speed. It might be an eddy, a pool below those rocks on which he had been bumped and dragged. But he was not in water, he realized dimly; it was hard to breathe, but whatever it was that smothered him, it was dry and tight, and not wet at all. Somewhere a voice said: "Here."

The swaying and jostling stopped.

"Over with him," the voice commanded.

"Wait! Finish him first."

"This will finish him."

The swaying began again, more violent than before. It brought back the dizziness, and the flashes of red against utter blackness. The dark current that bore him plunged downward in a sickening swoop. Something struck his face and stung him into consciousness; he knew he was falling.

A blow on his chest and side drove out his breath. The current closed over him completely.

When it let him go at last, the sun was in his eyes. His head burned inside, and he closed his eyes quickly to shut out the fire; but the burning was just as intense, and he opened them again. For long minutes he lay trying to understand what had happened. With every minute, the realization of pain grew and grew until the dizziness came back, and brought with it the memory of that black current that had swayed, and bruised him on rocks, and finally leaped with him over some nauseous cataract.

But there was no current, and no cataract. He was warm, and thirsty. He was lying on something rough and hard, and his arms seemed to be gone. For a while, the missing arms bothered him more than the pain in his head and the new pains he kept discovering all over his body.

Then he tried to move, and found his arms; they were under him—bound at the wrists, and numb. There was a gag in his mouth, stuffed in so firmly that his jaws ached. He could barely see out of one eye. His legs, too, were lashed together at ankles and knees, by the feel of them. Lying on his back, he struggled to lift his legs high enough so that he could see them. They were bound with rope, he saw when he accomplished it.

The effort made the pain worse, and he lay limp until it eased again. Then, trying to see where he was, he rolled over to the right and came up against weathered brown rock. When he rolled to the other side, he felt nothing under him but space, and the sensation of falling; black vertigo rushed over him, and he squirmed desperately back against the rock. Lying there on his numbed arms, he had the feeling that hands had reached out and pushed him back just in time. He lay still until the nausea left him. As his brain began to clear, he tried exploring with his eyes only.

The left eye would barely open; the harder he tried to raise the lid, the sharper were the thrusts of pain through his head. The jets of pain seemed to start near that stubborn lid; they brought back, finally, the flashing vision of Halbert Bond's rifle stabbing at him, the shocking blow on his temple, and the flash of red. He wondered whether Bond had shot him.

And then realization flooded over him. Bond had crept up on him as he sat day-dreaming on the doorstep. Bond had surrounded him with a gang of his taproom cronies. Bond had dragged Diantha out of bed. He was taking her away! Leslie groaned, and struggled at the ropes, threw his body against the rock wall, beat with his full weight upon his numb and helpless arms. *Bond was taking her to Barent!* He fought madly, threshing, writhing, sickening himself with the pain of his struggles. He rolled, and felt only empty space under him, and then felt invisible hands push him back.

At last, spent and ill, he lay as he had come back to consciousness, and tried to think.

There was rock at one side and rock, apparently, under him. Staring up along the brown wall, he saw it jut out a few feet above him; beyond that, there was blue sky, laced with leaves. His eyes followed the leaves down. Some of them were ash; some were sumach; some were leaves of the wild grape. It was their vines, he saw, that had caught him and pushed him back when he tried to roll away from the wall; they grew in a tangle of their own twisting trunks and those of scrubby trees and bushes. Turning slowly, he saw that the rock on which he lay was a narrow shelf, hardly the width of his shoulders, and that the wild grapevines climbed up over its edge as if their roots were just below it. The trees into which they clambered stood on another, wider ledge many feet farther down. Beyond them, blue water sparkled. The water was moving.

Through the screen of leaves, Leslie tried to follow the drifting sparkle. Most of it was shut out by the tangle of vines and scrub. Painfully, stopping again and again to let the waves of sickness subside, he hitched himself up along the rock, supporting himself with his shoulder against it and his weight on his bound wrists. Half-lying, half-sitting, he could see a broader reach of water, and a strip of level shore. There was a cabin, a crude wharf of logs and stone, and a man in a green coat sitting on the wharf.

Near him, three other men bent over the frame of a half-finished boat; and beyond, a long line of unpainted flatboats lay afloat, their noses to the bank.

For the first time, Leslie realized where he was.

Bond and his men had thrown him over the bluff of the Monongahela.

The wild grapevine, growing tight against this shelf of rock, had saved his life, catching him as he rolled, and literally throwing him upon the ledge. While he struggled with his bonds, the vines had held him there.

Hellward Bound had intended murder. Leslie set himself desperately to work on the thongs around his wrists. If Bond had ventured to go so far, he would stop at nothing. He had taken Diantha....

But this time, he would be miles away from Pitt's Town, taking her somewhere. It had been barely dawn when he led his men to the room where she lay asleep—the room where she had asked Arnett Leslie to stay because she was afraid. And Leslie, dawdling over pipe and dreams, had been helpless. He groaned again, his heart as sick as his burning brain. Now it was past midday.

The leather about his wrists was sunk deep in the swollen flesh; when he tried to chafe the thongs against the rock, he only cut his skin. In an agony of fear and self-reproach, he drove his arms savagely against a jutting angle of the ledge; the blood began to run down his fingers as he dug at the lashings and the raw flesh. Bond had taken Diantha; *by this time....*

He could bear the pain of his bleeding wrists; but the tightly drawn leather did not yield. He hitched himself along the ledge until his feet hung over. He did not know how far he would drop if he plunged through the vines, off his shelf of rock. But there was no other way. He threshed his legs about in the matted creepers and brush, trying to clear a space in them so no stub or branch would catch his arms and hold him dangling there. The noise he made shut out the first startled cry from the man sitting on the wharf three hundred yards downstream; but it could not shut out the screech of the Delaware warwhoops or the scream of the carpenter who went down in the first rush of savages out of the underbrush around the sawmill.

Leslie froze on the lip of the rock ledge.

His eyes saw a dozen naked, painted bodies come down the Monongahela bank in panther-springs; saw one of the boatmen crouch shrieking against the unfinished gunwale; saw two swinging hatchets chop him down; saw the other three white men running frantically out along the wharf.

One of them turned desperately, an ax uplifted in his hands. A hatchet glinted in the sun; the ax wavered, dropped; between his lifted hands, the soldier's face turned suddenly and hideously red. Before his sagging legs could let him drop, the Delawares were on him; his body fell away from his scalp, ripped off as he staggered and died still on his feet. On the frame of the unfinished bateau, a clouted Indian broke the wounded carpenter's back across the gunwale, his knee on the screaming man's chest, his knife already at the dripping hair. As he rose, bounding and flourishing the scalp, the two survivors of the working party plunged from the end of the wharf into the sparkling river. Behind them, the Delawares fired at them until their guns were empty. Then, howling, they plunged back into the brush. Leslie heard them pass along the edge of the bluff above him, their yells like the yip-yipping of a frenzied dog.

A little later, a platoon of Royal Americans came running up the river bank. Leslie squirmed to the edge of his ledge and let himself go. A sergeant, pushing a squad in vain pursuit of the marauders up the Monongahela, found him unconscious, head down on a slope of shale, his bound legs caught in dead willow stubs.

CHAPTER XIII

In Which Diantha Gail Rides North, with Her Feet Tied Under the Belly of the Black Mare; and Captain Barent Comes to Do His Wooing:

THE scalping of the Pennsylvania soldiers at the garrison sawmill, under the very guns of Fort Pitt, was the first blow of the Pontiac Conspiracy on the Ohio frontier.

Arnett Leslie, hearing the screams of the Provincials dying under the Delaware knives, was witness to the first of those successive attacks that in a single fortnight blotted the white race out of existence on the middle border, from Du Troit to the Forks of the Ohio. When, near sunset, greencoated men carried Leslie and the mutilated bodies of their dead through the gates of Fort Pitt, their sergeant handed to the captain of the guard a stone war-ax smeared with red.

The captain handed it gingerly to Ecuyer on the Flag bastion.

"It's not blood," his gray lips formed the words stiffly as he saluted, "it's paint."

Ecuyer dandled it a moment in both hands.

"Gentlemen," his eyes in their bristle of blond lashes traveled steadily from man to man in the gaudy group around him, as if he would weigh them, too, and balance them against the war club, "we have a war. It is so they declare war—with a head breaker, yes." The long hickory shaft bent in his blunt fingers, and sprang straight again. "Adjutant, double guard tonight. Every soldier to sleep in his clothes. Captain-lieutenant Carre, a detail to warn the inhabitants that they shall move into the fort. Captain Phillips, working parties with wagons to bring in their goods, and all the food. The militia for fatigue duty.

"Gentlemen, tomorrow—no more Pitt's Town."

His stout cheeks wrinkled in grim humor at the murmur of the officers around him.

"No more fiddles, also. Those big cabins, they make good palisades, I think, on top these mud walls we got. The rest we burn

—so these red devils they do not hide in them, and burn us."

It was hot on the Flag bastion, but a young subaltern of the Royal Artillery shivered. He put his hand quickly behind him, groping for something to lean upon; his fingers touched the brass carronade in the embrasure; the brass was hot. Sweat stood out suddenly on his face in a rash of little drops, and he shivered again.

The sun hung half way down the brown river bluffs. Under it, the blue water was kindling into a red-gold that danced and shimmered like flames; a whole green island in the Ohio vanished, licked up into the glare; over it, like whirling ashes above a fire, a flight of cliff swallows dipped and swirled just under the crest of the bluffs.

Ecuyer looked at the setting sun, and then at the mud walls of his fort. The brick bastions that faced the town were stout enough, but those mud walls along the two river banks were far from impregnable. There were rents and gaps in them where the spring flood had ripped away the sod, and the dirt was sliding into the moat. They were not difficult walls to climb. A quick rush of savages under cover of darkness....

His face set. His thick hands bent the handle of the Delaware ax and snapped it.

In two hours, it would be dark.

.   .   .   .

It was dark already on the Venango road.

Twenty miles to the north, Halbert Bond led a train of a dozen horses along the old Delaware war path to the lakes. Just behind him, on one of Leslie's pack beasts, rode a dark-skinned woods-runner whose black hair hung loose over his shoulders; at the rear of the column, Bond's wife rode likewise with black hair hanging loose, her linsey bed gown tucked about her knees, a rifle across her thighs.

Midway of the winding file, a drooping figure in rumpled green swayed listlessly in the black Nancy mare's saddle.

Diantha Gail had stopped watching the trail; there was no use to watch it. Arnett Leslie was dead; Bond, laughing his rum-stenched breath into her face as he thrust her backward out of Leslie's room, had told her how he died.

"Begged, he did. Screeched like a lousy Mingo when we got

him to the Mon' bank an' started aswingin' him. Ye c'd hear him ascreechin' after we heaved him over, 'tils he hit the water—*splash*. The sturgeons are eatin' him by now, ye little slut. Will ye come easy? Or will we gentle ye?"

They had had to gentle her. It took Bond and two of his friends to get her into the saddle and tie her there, with a flounce of the old blue gown stuffed into her mouth to stifle her screaming. Bond's cronies had laughed and gloated, their hands making free of her struggling body as they hoisted her onto the mare's back. Even Bond's wife, who had been kind enough on the journey from Baltimore to Pitt's Town, gave her a harsh look. When, miles into the wilderness north of Shertee's, they had taken the gag out of her mouth, the woman had turned coldly away when Diantha pleaded with her.

She rode now in slumped despair. Her body swung limply with the motion of the horse. Her mind was numb, as her arms were numb with the cords that bound them behind her. She was not even afraid; there was nothing left to happen—nothing, now, that mattered. She had stopped caring whether Bond or the slouching woods-runner or Bond's woman saw her weep; she had lost the desire to keep back the tears; they ran unheeded down her cheeks, through the bits of leaf dust and wisps of spider web that had caught and clung across her face, and made dark spots on the crushed ribbons at her breast.

The rasp of a blackberry vine across her bare leg scarcely hurt her. Both of her legs were scratched where the brambles had raked them, but she cared neither for the pain nor for the shameless exposure, though the vines and the underbrush had pulled and torn at the dress until her legs were naked to her hips. Riding with bowed head and eyes that saw only the sweat-darkened neck of Leslie's mare, she did not know that the day was almost over, or think that night might bring some new climax.

The trail ran down into a steep valley between eroded hills, where roots of oak and elm trees lay bare along the slope. The horses hugged the western side of the ravine, jerking uncertainly along in a green twilight. Through the dusk rose the drone of insects. Since Halbert Bond had stopped his drunken singing, the winged humming and the scrabble of hoofs was all the sound there was.

The path swung out around a shoulder of the hill, and dipped across the stream that slid through willows and rank swamp grass. The horses sank deeply into the marshy shallows, their feet sucking as they pulled them up, their bodies swaying and lunging as they went down into the sliding current. The water splashed loudly.

"Ye could hear him ascreechin' 'tils he hit the water—*splash*." That much was a lie. Diantha knew Arnett Leslie had not screeched, or begged. He had died silently, fighting.

The Nancy mare stumbled in the mud. The lurch of her body was agony to the girl's bruised legs. The cord under the mare's belly jerked at her ankles, wrenching her. Her eyes closed tightly on tears that ran faster with the pain. Her mind fled back into numb resignation.

The trail swung away from the willows and the swampy stream, and climbed a lower hill. In a swale above the valley, where the twilight was paler green, Bond slipped heavily from his saddle.

The horses came crowding up, nosing at the grass. The woman rode through them, swung herself down, set her rifle against an oak, and busied herself with hobbles. Bond bawled at the woods-runner still swaying on his mount, and dragged him out of the saddle, cursing.

"Take her down," he ordered. "Let the old woman hopple her, too." He pulled a bottle out of the bosom of his shirt and pawed his beard aside to get his teeth at the cork.

The *coureur de bois* moved towards Diantha with weaving legs and began to fumble with the knotted cord at her ankles. One of his hands closed around the tight thongs with a torturing pressure; then it slid slowly up, past her knee. Bond's woman passed behind him, her arms heaped with blankets, bridles dangling from the crook of her elbow.

"Cut it, you fool," she told him hoarsely, and went on.

The fellow looked after her, groped for his knife, and jerked it out. He leaned against the mare's shoulder, thrusting at the cord without looking, his hand still lying on the girl's thigh. When the thong parted, he pinched her, his nails digging into her flesh as he dragged her off Nancy's back and held her to him. His wet mouth smeared her cheek, and his hand came up to seize her by the hair and force her face away from her shoulder. Somewhere in the dusk, Bond bawled at him again, furiously.

"Drop her! She's none o' yours, y' weasel. Barent bought her." The thick voice ended on a gurgle.

"Bahh! What's the odds? He haint here, an' we are." His hand in her hair wrenched her head up again. Bond spun him around, bellowing and mouthing at him.

"I told ye—drop her! He'll cut the guts out o' ye! The gammy fool wants t' marry her."

"Jesus!" The arm jerked away from Diantha's shoulders. "The little slut bedded wi' th' other bloody-back las' night."

"He don' know that." Bond's maudlin laugh bubbled around the bottle at his mouth. "Hain't goin' know it, neither. C-c-c...." He choked and spat, retching, and came wavering toward his ally with the bottle held out. "C-c-cowbird in his nest afore he crawls in himself. Can't have *two* cowbirds ahead o' him, can we, now? Take drink; drop her." He thrust the bottle into the fellow's hand and wandered away.

Diantha followed him. After three steps, she fell, her numbed legs unable to hold her up. The woods-runner stumbled over her and swore and kicked her; but he left her lying in the grass, her face pressed hard against the ground to keep back hysterical sobs.

After a while, she felt hands turning her over on her back, and an arm slide under her neck.

"Here, drink this," Bond's wife was saying in her flat voice. Diantha tasted hot, rank sassafras coffee at her lips, and then hot journey cake. She turned her head away from the second morsel. Bond's woman pushed it against her mouth again.

"Eat it. Don't take on so. He'll be comin' tomorrow; ye'll be a'right then."

The girl strained back, away from the smell of the corn cake. Panic welled up into her throat. She screamed at the shapeless figure stooping over her:

"No! No! No! Oh, please...."

"Ye plaguey fool! There's no manner o' use carryin' on like that."

"Please! Please! Let me go ... let me go!"

Bond's woman laughed, hard, dull laughter.

"Go, would ye? Go where? It's God's wonder the Injuns didn't get us a'ready, rammagin' straight up the Venango road. They'd have ye sure, ye little fool. Would ye rather be squaw t' some stinkin' Mingo when a white man wants ye, right an' holy?"

"Holy! Oh, God . . . holy!" Diantha's shrill laugh ran thin with hysteria. She fell back upon the grass, and saw the black bulk of trees above her begin to lean over, lower, closer, as if they were all falling at once.

"O-ohh!" Relief shuddered through her. They would fall and crush her. Her head went back, and her throat and breast yearned up to meet them.

When she knew, finally, that she had not been crushed, that the trees would not fall, her arms were bound again. They lay stretched out full length; under her neck was a pole; her arms had been pulled up to meet it, and her wrists were lashed to it with tightly drawn cords, in the Delaware fashion.

Moonlight lay over the swale like a thin skim of ice. A weight of silence pressed down upon the forest. Under it there were minor sounds—faint stirrings, a man's breathing, grass tearing where the horses grazed.

The girl's body moved. She drew up one leg, and found that her ankles were unbound. She drew the other leg up beside it, twisted over on one hip, rolled and twisted herself up to her knees. Kneeling, the pole dragged at her arms and the thongs tightened on her wrists; but she continued to kneel, her eyes searching the small meadow. Over against the trees, the blurred shapes of the horses blended into the deeper shadows. Closer, Bond and the *coureur de bois* were two black lumps. Diantha turned slowly. In her mind, thin and brittle as the moonlight, a hope began to shine. The swale lay empty and still, except for those faint breathings and those lumps of bodies, while she got to her feet.

She took a step, and then another. The green dress rustled. From the upper edge of the clearing came a whisper, hardly louder than the rustle of the silk. Diantha went steadily toward it, and found Bond's woman.

She was crouched in deep shadow, behind a fallen elm; the rifle lay across its trunk, a powder horn beside it. Diantha came to the rifle muzzle and faced her. Whispered:

"Will you let me go, now, while they are asleep?"

The woman put a hand to her mouth, and took it down again.

"Bullets," she husked. "Three of 'em; likely I'd not have time for more."

"Will you let me go?"

"No."

"Why? Surely . . . surely you are not like *them*."

"No."

"If I just slipped away . . . tied as I am. . . ."

"I would shoot you, if I could not catch you."

"Oh, why? Why?" The girl moved back a step. Two steps. Three steps. "Shoot. I would rather. . . ."

Awkwardly, because the long pole all but flung her down as she turned, she sped through the moonlit grass. The woman slipped deeper into the shadow, slipped under the fallen elm trunk, and caught her at the bottom of the swale.

"Fool!" She shook the pole so that it made the rawhide cut Diantha's wrists. "I said I'd kill you, or catch you."

The thin and brittle hope broke like skim ice; under it there was deep, hopeless water, cold as ice is cold. Diantha fought it, and came up out of panic again. Her breath sobbed, whispering, pleading:

"Why are you afraid to let me go?"

"He'd hang if I did."

Abruptly, there was hope again.

"Hang? You mean Bond? For . . . ?"

"For buying you when you were a free woman and he knew it. For taking your money. For killing the major." The dull murmur died under the weight of silence.

Diantha's whisper, when she tried again, was hardly more than a breath.

"Perhaps he did not kill Major Leslie." She knew that was futile; they had killed him—Bond had killed him; but she fought with every futile weapon. "No one could prove who killed him, if he is dead, and I said nothing. Listen: let me go. Go with me. I promise you Bond will not hang, will never be punished at all. I will pay you—money enough to do whatever you want to do—to go anywhere—to take him with you, and be safe, and never work."

Bond's woman jerked again at the pole. Diantha sprang backward, wrenching it out of her hand. Her voice rose.

"I mean it. You are the fool. Bond's squaw! You could be rich, in silks and a coach. I tell you, no one will be punished if you let me go, and I will make you rich."

"Have they scairt ye so?" The woman stooped, peering through the dark at Diantha's face. Her voice for the first time was gentle. "Touched, be ye, with their doin's? *Aiee.*"

She came closer and put her arm around the girl's back, under the pinioning pole.

"Come—ye'd best lie down."

"No! No!" Diantha struggled against her, her slight body helpless in the hard, tightening arm. "I am not mad. It is all true. I am not just Diantha Gail....I am Lady Diantha Gaillard, and there is money to pay you...and make you safe.....Oh, God, let me go! *Let me go!*"

Bond's woman put her hand on the girl's mouth and pulled her up across the silvered grass, into the tangled limbs of the dead elm. The ends of the pole, thrust under the branches, held her helpless until the brittle hope was broken utterly, and her sobbing ceased. Then the woman untied the cords, chafed the swollen wrists, and wrapped her in blankets under the shadow of the fallen tree trunk, and smoothed the hair away from her face.

In the morning, she told Bond harshly to leave the girl's arms unbound. Bond cursed her, and threw the leather strings into her face; when she turned away, her cheeks sucked in against her teeth, he picked up the cords and bound Diantha's wrists so brutally that her throat closed in a spasm of choked-back pain. The cry did not get to her lips; but she could not control the tears; they ran weakly, unrestrainedly down the smeared furrows on her cheeks. In the first mile through brush and brambles, her legs were bleeding again with fresh scratches, and her arms were numb to the shoulders.

The Venango road wound on and on through hardwood ridges and sunny swales, dipped through marshy fords of slowly moving streams, thrust itself through hazel thickets on bald hills and clung to slopes where bloodroots glistened against the brown leaf mold. Insects took up their droning; deer flies whirled in maddening circles around the horses' ears; hoofs cluffed through the soft dirt of the trail and sucked and slithered in the muck of the creek banks. Diantha rode oblivious to sight and sound. Only the thongs, cramping her ankles against the saddle girth and digging raw weals into her flesh, kept her from falling.

It was late afternoon when a figure in blue and scarlet stepped out from behind a great basswood into the path, and the horses, one after another, came to a halt, nose to tail in an ash-grown hollow.

Diantha hung doubled over in the saddle, her eyes dull with stupor, her mouth half open, her lips vivid in her gray face. She turned her head when Barent came and stood by the mare's shoulder, but her eyes made no sign that she saw him.

He had his cocked hat in his hand and a smile on his flushed face. Powdered and polished, with ruffles at throat and wrist, left hand on sword hilt and laced hat at his breast, he started to bow. And then his smile froze, and his bow stiffened before it was well begun.

"Good God in heaven!" He clapped his hat awry on his powdered wig, and plucked at the green gown drawn back across her naked thighs, all criss-crossed with angry scratches. "Diantha! Diantha, I never meant.... Do you hear me? *Bond!*"

Dimly, far away, she heard his hoarse voice cursing Bond in a choked and passionate fury. Dimly, remotely, she felt the rawhide loosen at her feet, and the saddle slip out from under her.

Barent sat down on the ground and held her on his knees, working at the knots between her swollen wrists. Bond came back along the bunched up horses and stood sullenly over them. The Swiss swore at him in tones that were deadlier for being low, and Bond answered him, blunt and surly.

"You said bring her, or I'd hang. There she is. Get it done with."

"By God, you are too much of an animal to hang. The cat ... by God, the cat to your back until you were flayed and bled to death! I'll pay you off for this one day," and cursed him again and viciously in foreign oaths that quivered in his throat.

"Ye're brash an' bold, *Mister* Captain Barent, hain't ye? Mind ye there's a rope f'r your neck too, along with mine, unless ye hush that gutter slut. An' hush her f'r good an' all, or I'll hush the both of ye afore ye come near Venango."

Barent was no coward. He looked up briefly at Bond's hand on his half-drawn hatchet and sneered at him.

"You're afraid to use it, Bond. Afraid of that name of yours.

161

You don't dare to die, Bond—you're Hellward Bound. God, they named you well!"

Bond laughed at him.

"Ye'll burn in the same fire, ye bloody-back. An' mayhap ye'll hang whilst I look at ye ahangin', too. Keep y'r Dutch dirt in y'r throat, Mister Barent; mayhap one day I'll tell how ye hired me t' kill the major."

Barent started. His lower lip thrust itself out, and his voice rose.

"You lie, you pig. I said: Don't hurt him too much."

"Phaugh! You said! Does it hurt to drown?"

The mercenary's ruddy color ran out of his face and left it gray as Diantha's against his scarlet tunic.

"Drowned?" His mouth worked.

Bond smirked and bowed.

"Over the bank, into the Mon," he gloated. "Ye'll be treatin' me right an' proper, Mister Captain, from now forward, eh?"

"Into the Mon ... right there at the town?"

"Ay. Ye're right brisk with y'r head, hain't ye? Into the Mon ... right above the sawmill, where the sojers work. If they find him, who'll they think done it, now? I hearn tell, seems to me, that ye tried to run y'r sword through his back right on the parade ground, wi' Captain Arnold alookin' on."

Barent cursed him with shaking lips, the girl forgotten. Bond laughed and slobbered, and wiped his beard and laughed again.

"Ye promised a deal of things, Mister Captain Barent," he mocked, "wi' y'r fine tall tales about Lady This an' Lord That, and money to burn in y'r pockets an' in my pockets too. I reckon now ye'll play fair an' square, an' no stabbin' in the back. Go on," he laughed again, "get it done with, an' we'll get ye hitched. Do y'r sighin' an' y'r lovin'; I'll see ye through, so long as ye play open an' proper. *An' ye'll do that.*"

He plucked the hatchet from its loop and drew the edge suggestively across his throat.

"Bond's my name. Ye see 't is as right an' proper as th' other. I've took my bond o' you, Barent; an' I'll hold it whilst ye live. Let's get agoin'."

Diantha knew dimly that the buzz of voices stopped, and that she was lifted and carried, and laid down again. She knew that she was bathed with cold water across her face; and that more cold water was set to her lips: and, after that, hot broth. She knew, after a time, that she was lying in the dark, on a bed that was softer than Bond's clapboard beds, and that she was no longer bound. She stirred, and heard Barent's voice close by her.

"Diantha...."

Out of her inertia of hopelessness, she answered him: "Yes?"

"Are you feeling better?"

She gave him the same faint "Yes."

"Will you hear me? I am sorry for what Bond did. I never intended that you should be hurt. I was mad with loneliness. Mad with love for you." She stirred again, as if in protest, and his voice pressed on eagerly. "When I knew I had to leave the fort, I could not hold it back; I loved you so much I had to have you, Diantha. I knew you would not have me ... there."

His hands fumbled with the blanket that covered her. She lay, inert, and did not move when they touched her arm and rested there. He leaned over her, his face a blur in the darkness.

"Oh, forgive me. I love you so madly, my lady."

"My lady?" The girl's head turned; her voice took on a fine edge—interest, surprise, understanding.

She heard Barent's breath catch and then go on again, louder, quicker.

His voice, too, was louder and faster.

"Oh, so ... what difference? Yes, I know who you are. That meant all the more that I must *take* you and *make* you love me. Diantha, do you not understand how terrible it is to love like that? To love so that a man takes his life in his hands, and his honor, and his freedom?"

"And takes the lady's freedom, too? You knew, on the ship, that day?"

"No. Not until afterward. It was Lawless thought he knew you. He was not sure until he saw you walk, with your hands straight at your sides, like a soldier's. He knew then. He had seen you at a masque, in London, in a hussar's uniform."

The girl lay so still that Barent leaned closer, emboldened by her calmness.

"What difference, Diantha? May I not love a fine lady, if she runs away like any peasant girl, and binds herself out to serve

163

five years? If any one is to have you, should I not be the one? Listen to me, Diantha Gaillard: Will you wed with me?"

There was a smothered sound in the blanket huddled about her face. It was a small and weary sound, but it was beyond any doubting a laugh. It angered Barent, and pricked him on.

"Will you wed with me, ma'm? You hear me, do you not? I offer you marriage."

Silence.

"Do you hear me?"

"Yes." A faint, weary "yes."

"Will you wed with me?"

"I should rather die."

Barent's face came down until she could feel his breath upon her mouth.

"I think," he whispered, the words slow-spaced as if he must stop between each one to draw that quick, panting breath, "that you will not die, but that you will wish much to be wed to me. Are you not here, with me?" His hand took her by the shoulder and shook her. "Are you not?"

"Oh, yes. Yes." As if it made not the slightest difference.

"I can do with you as I wish."

"You cannot make me wed."

"Perhaps you will wish to."

"No."

"So!"

The panting breath went away from her face. A hand took the blankets by their huddled edges and stripped them down. Then both hands were at her shoulders, fumbling at the puffs of silk. His fingers slipped under the froth of ribbons at her breast, and tore it and the silken shift....

Then, at last, welling over weariness and her abandonment to despair, panic flooded her. Her hands flew out and clutched at the ripping silk, and felt it tear again, and the rush of cold air upon her body. She thrust against him with both hands upon his shoulders, his ruffled stock and powdered hair a white blur above her. A white, formless blur...then, in a glare of red, she saw wig and stock and face between, with open mouth and staring eyes, and a great splotch of dark stuff spreading on it.

Her ears rang with stunning sound.

Face, wig and stock were gone again into a shapeless thing that fell swiftly toward her. Barent's body collapsed across her breast, heavy, smothering, twitching.

A hand fastened itself upon her arm.

Somewhere in the darkness that rang and rang with yells and shots, a voice plucked at her dazed brain.

It was guttural, grating. It said words that were noises a feeding animal might make. She jerked at the clutching fingers on her arm, and felt nails digging. Something dark, something that screamed, bounded over her. She saw it for an instant in the flash of a musket...a squirming copper body striped with yellow, a long yellow arm flung up, a hatchet glinting.

High, quavering, hideous, the scalp yell of the Ojibway pierced through the thick, pounding echoes of their guns.

The hand dragged at her. There was a foul smell. A thud. Barent's body was gone, his boots slipping across her knees as the hand pulled her clear of him.

CHAPTER XIV

*In Which a Stubborn Soldier of Fortune Burns Pitt's Town to Save It;
and Arnett Leslie Adds Desertion to His Other Follies:*

THE bite of raw whisky in the wound above his temple
gnawed at Leslie's brain until it roused itself out of stupor
and sent frantic messages to his body to fight back at the
pain. His hands struck out, only to be caught in an iron grip and
pressed down helplessly into some yielding substance that snapped
and crackled. In his aching head the crackling was like a running
discharge of musketry, every shot a fiery explosion inside his skull.
And then, mercifully, it dwindled into the crackling of dry sticks
in a fire; and that, in turn, dwindled into the noise that it really was
—the rustling and snapping of straw in the coarse, blanketed mattress on which he lay. Dizzy with pain, but conscious, he looked
up into Lieutenant Boyd's sober face. It lighted at the recognition
in Leslie's eyes.

"Lord love us, Major," he burst out, "ye're stubborn as ye're
troublesome. I thought ye'd made up that mulish mind o' yours
never to come back."

He daubed at the wound again with his whisky-soaked swab,
and nodded at some one out of Leslie's sight.

"Ye can be letting him go now," he commanded. The grip on
Leslie's wrists relaxed; the orderly who had held him helpless came
around from the head of the bunk and stood waiting. "By glory,
Major, we've had to spread ye out the way the Delawares spraddle
their prisoners for burnin', ye were that rambullious. Ye've been
tryin' to fight the whole garrison, so ye have."

Leslie turned his head on the straw pallet; for a minute the pain
blinded him, but as it cleared he saw scoured brick walls that met
a low plank ceiling, and a narrow window where yellowish light
fell slanting across a row of cots. His eyes turned back to the
surgeon.

"Where am I? How long...?"

"Faith, and where do ye think? Not prancing and frisking at the commandant's ball, for sure. Ye're in the hospital, where ye belong—our tight little hospital stuck away under the drawbridge like a bug under a chip."

"How long?" Leslie demanded again.

"Well, now," Boyd sniffed at the whisky bottle as if the room was not reeking already with the fumes, and took his time at putting in the cork, "well, now, 'twas close to sundown when we found ye hangin' like a bunch of grapes on those vines, half way between cliff and river, and plucked ye down. I'd be guessin' that was some fourteen hours agone....Here, now, none o' that, ye gamecock! Ye'll do no moving out o' that bed this day."

Leslie dropped back on the mattress and lay inert as Boyd bandaged the gash; the pain began to dwindle again, and he forced another question from his stiff lips:

"Have they found her...? Somebody said they took her away... she was gone..."

"Now, Major darlin', don't be goin' off into those crazy dreams again. All night it was *'Have they found her? Have they found her?'* And you not fit to be seein' anybody, let alone a petticoat."

Leslie got a hand out and seized Boyd by the cuff. His voice found strength enough to startle the surgeon with its fierce command:

"Drop your capers, Boyd! For God's sake, did nobody look for her? I told them and told them..."

"Told them what?" Boyd's face lost its forced gayety. "Easy, now. That's a bad head ye've got."

Leslie cursed him.

"Diantha...Diantha Gail! Damn you all for lumps and clods, they took her away last night! They tied her, and dragged her out ...smashed a musket into me...threw me over the bluff to drown me! Good God, and you've done nothing?"

"They? Who is *they*? I swear ye're ravin'."

"May God burn you all, Boyd!" Leslie's hand thrust the surgeon back so furiously he had to catch himself with a hand on the side-log of the bunk. "Are you *all* in it, hounding that child? By the eternal, I'll..." His head spun, but he forced himself upright on the bed and swung his legs clear of the blanket. "Boyd, it was Barent's doing and you know it. Barent's, and Bond's." He gripped the lieutenant fiercely by the wrist. "Where's Barent? Find Barent! I'll have it out of him!"

"He's gone. Hours ago. Captain Ecuyer sent him to Venango. He was in a rage—Ecuyer was—at Gordon there for stripping his garrison to send messengers." *

The grip of Leslie's fingers made Boyd wince.

"There...that's it! Barent has taken her with him." Leslie was not yet himself; he wasted breath and strength on oaths that startled Boyd with their deadly fury.

"Ye're daft," he told Leslie bluntly. It was, after all, a most unreasonable way to act over a tavern maid, no matter how alluring. "Barent went alone; I saw him go. Faith, it's daft ye are completely, Leslie; no man would take a woman into the wilderness, now the tribes are up."

He put his hands on Leslie's shoulders to push him down again upon the bed, and found, instead, a raging man springing up in shirt and drawers and starting for the door with lurching steps. It took both the surgeon and the orderly to stop him and drag him back.

"I tell you, Barent would risk his scalp and hers too, to have her. By God, Boyd, he has gone so far that he has no cause to stop. I tell you, he knows he will hang or rot in jail for a thief and perjurer. He swore her into servitude, and he'd take her to the torture stake to get her."

"Leslie! Leslie, be stopping now! I'll go see..."

"I'm going with you...."

"Ye're not. Be reasonable, Arnett, man. Ye'll kill y'rself with this ragin'. I'll go to Ecuyer..."

"Ecuyer, hell! Go to the Golden Eagle. See if she's there. If she's not, I'm going after her, and your whole damned garrison won't stop me!"

Boyd hesitated. Leslie lashed out at him:

"Now what? Now what? Will you be off?"

"But the Golden Eagle—she'd hardly be there now. She's here in the fort, like as not."

"Why? Why not at Bond's?"

* In a postscript to a letter addressed to Colonel Bouquet, Captain Ecuyer complains that Gordon is imprudent, stripping his fort to send soldiers with messages to Fort Pitt.

"Lord love ye, Arnett Leslie, there's hardly a cabin left in Lower Town by now. Ecuyer's burnin' them and tearin' them log from log, to keep 'em from being shelter for the redskins."

Leslie groaned, and his sick eyes goaded Boyd.

"So soon! Aghh!" The dread in his voice sent a shudder creeping along the soldier's back and the hairs prickling on his wrists. "Boyd, Boyd, have you ever seen a woman when an Indian war party had done with her? I have. Search the fort—quickly, quickly. If she's not here..."

Boyd moved at last, running for the door. Leslie raged at the orderly:

"You heard! Go! Help him! By the Lord, if you stand there gawping...."

The frightened private scurried up the stairs. Leslie sat down dizzily, groping beneath the cot for his boots. A wave of nausea swept him as he pulled them on, but he got it done; he knew, as well as he knew that his head was gashed, that Boyd would not find Diantha Gail in Fort Pitt, nor in the town. He did not mean to wait.

He followed the orderly up the dark stairway from the hospital, through the passage that led into a casement under the walls. It was strewn with blankets, where the gun crews slept, and littered with their gear. In a corner, match coats of the night sentries lay in a heap, and he snatched one up as he passed and got it somehow around him. At the door of the casement, he met the smell of smoke, and thought, by the dim light, that the blow on his head had partly blinded him.

And then he saw that Fort Pitt lay under a pall of smoke that let the sun through only in streaks, and that the streaks crawled with tendrils of the same smoke mixed with dust. It writhed and coiled upon itself, this way and that; through it moved a human confusion that twisted it constantly into new currents and eddies.

From the foot of the Flag bastion to the commandant's house where officers and ladies had played at hurly-burly, the frightened inhabitants of Pitt's Town milled and wept and shouted in a hurly-burly that had no gay cornets to rule it and no merry pranks to play. Household goods were piled helter-skelter over the parade. Cattle tugged at hastily driven stakes. Hobbled horses stumbled over heaps of bedding dumped down anyhow upon the dirt. Children ran wailing between the horses' legs or clung to skirts and the tag ends of bundles.

Through the covered way that led to the drawbridge poured a stream of refugees to swell the confusion within the walls. Over it, in the still atmosphere, ribbons of smoke hung motionless, like gray drifts suspended in midair. Only above the eastern parapet, toward the town, they moved a little, drifting on gusts of heat from burning cabins and crawling downward from the wall.

They had, to Leslie's aching eyes, the look of gray fingers reaching down into the panic-stricken mob. They had a smell, too, as choking as fingers on the throat, as smothering as a hand tight over mouth and nostrils. His eyes smarted with smoke and dust as he pushed through the crowd and into the covered way. A wagon drove him flat against the wall, and he cursed the driver in a blind fury, got a burly woods-runner by the thrums of his shirt and spun him headlong after the wagon, and burst through to the drawbridge. There was room enough there, for the moment; sentries with leveled bayonets were holding back clamoring men and terrified women at the entrance to the redan, pressing them back slowly to open a passage to the road. Behind Leslie, wheels rumbled on the logs, and a dozen artillerymen in rolled up sleeves and waistcoats came trundling a brass twelve-pounder, their bare arms straining at the ropes. After them marched a smart platoon of the Royal Americans, its muskets rigid at the carry, its white gaiters winking between the sharpened stakes of the *chevaux-de-frise* that ran along the outer earthworks.

All along the face of the eastern wall, Pitt's Town was coming down in ruins; gangs of men with mauls and crowbars were battering and prying at log walls. Half of the Lower Town was already strewn across its dooryards and alleys; for the most part, it was the upper half, cabin after cabin standing roofless, its log walls torn apart down to the door frames. Sweating townsmen were hoisting the logs to their shoulders and carrying them down into the open space in front of the redan; in the King's Highway, axmen were sharpening them into spiked points. Up on the walls, where the brick bastions of the eastern face ran into dirt walls faced with sod, other gangs were planting the sharpened logs, point up, to form a solid palisade along the ramparts. Pitt's Town was moving bodily into the fort, its houses literally becoming part of the fort itself.

Farther up the slope, the Upper Town was burning, column after column rising straight up in the still air until they spread and blended into a dirty ceiling of smoke that filtered the sunlight into sickish yellow. The tainted sun turned the whole valley sick.

Even the Golden Eagle was half gone. Gunners of the Royal Artillery were snaking its ponderous logs away with chains hooked to the traces of the gun teams. Inside the taproom, shirt-sleeved colonials were prying at the remaining logs with a fence rail driven into the chinking. They swayed up and down with a long-drawn "Ha-aah!" on the upswing, and a sharp, loud "Hah!" as they flung their weight upon the rail and forced it down.

Behind them, swaying on the swinging counter by the whisky barrel, one of Bond's cronies kept time with a slopping gourd. He hailed Leslie with a shouted oath.

"Yip-yip-eee!" he howled, and waved the gourd so that half its contents splashed at Leslie's feet.

"Thassa fancy buck was gonna do his wenchin' wi' Hellward's woman."

Leslie ignored him; spoke, instead, to the Pennsylvania corporal. "What's become of Bond?"

He jerked his round head toward the swaying tippler.

"Da rum-kag say dey go by Alleckany for make trade by Wenango. By Shertee's dey go, zur."

"Yip-yip-yipee-eee!" yelped the rum-keg over the rim of his dripping gourd. "Ay, ye fine macaroni, by Shertee's * to Venango. An' y'r wench, an' y'r horses, too."

Leslie crossed to the swinging counter in two furious strides and seized the pottle-pot by his be-dabbled beard.

"When did they go? When? God help you if you lie."

The tippler drew himself up in drunken dignity, too full of Hellward's whisky to realize that he stood in very real peril.

"Master Bond *an'* his lady frien' *de*parted yest'day, gen'ral."

Leslie jerked him savagely by the beard.

---

* Shertee's ——. The colloquial backwoods rendering of Chartiers. In Pitt's Town in 1763, Shertee's meant the crossing of the Allegheny River at Chartiers Old Town, settled by Peter Chartiers and his band of Pequa Indians on the present site of Tarentum.

"How did she go? Who went with them?"

"How? How? By God, wi' her foots tied under the horse's belly, that's how! An' she'd better gone willingly, wi' Master Bond. Ay, she'd better! An' she'd best be thankful he'd keep her for his bond wench, an' her beddin' wi' a man she's known a day; 'dentured women's been tied up an' flogged f'r that...."

Helpless as the man was with liquor, Leslie knew he was going to strike him. Leslie himself was helpless with a strangling fury. His fist crushed the ugly nose flat in the whiskered face. He was plunging for the door as the reeling body bounced back from the wall to sprawl across the overturned keg.

As he shouldered past the colonials, gawping along their fence rail, the greencoat corporal called to him:

"Bond's wife was wit dam, zur."

Leslie's hand flung thanks to him, a brusque wave that expressed little enough of the relief that information gave him. Bond's wife had gone, too. Her presence meant that Bond, at least, would hesitate before he went too far—might even embarrass Captain Barent, if, as Leslie was convinced, the Swiss mercenary had bulldozed Bond into taking Diantha out upon the Venango trail, beyond protection of even Pitt's Town's crude law. It flashed through Leslie's mind, as he ran through the courtyard, that the whole town and the whole garrison must know Diantha had shared his room with him last night—no, not last night—the night before that. Once more fear gripped him. Bond's pack train had been gone for a day and a night and half another forenoon. Thirty hours! And Bond had taken his horses. By the time the Indians raided the sawmill, the packtrain would have been twenty miles up the Venango trail. It was hardly possible that Indian warparties, closing in on Pitt's Town, would have left the road from Venango open. Already it might be too late.

Too late. Too late. The words beat at his brain as he stooped over the sailcloth by the tavern wall and flung it aside. Perhaps it was the wound across his temple that made his hands shake as they groped for the worn leather trunk. Perhaps it was the memory of what he had seen one morning when his patrol had stumbled across the bodies of the Simpson women....

He tried desperately to shut out that memory. But it came back again as he stepped across the doorlog of the room where Diantha had drawn up the flounce of her skirt to show him that her toes were clean. He saw again the hacked, burned bodies, obscenely dead in the sunlit grass, *and one of them was Diantha Gail*. He shut his eyes, shuddering, and a groan he could not choke back retched his throat. He flung the trunk down blindly and pressed his knuckles against his temples; the pain that shot through his head drove out the dreadful thing his imagination painted. He pressed hard on the bandaged wound. Better pain, if it would clear his brain, than those thoughts of what might be happening on the Venango trail. If he had needed a clear brain on the Cumberland road five years ago, he needed it far more now. With all the will power he possessed, he forced himself to think of what he must do—what he could do—what he must take with him—how he could get past the Indians lurking in the river valleys and in the underbrush above Massacre pond.

Slowly, because he knew he must if he hoped to save Diantha Gail, he drove himself back into something of the Leslie coolness —the remoteness that had made him a successful leader of border patrols where other militia officers failed.

He stripped off the artilleryman's match coat and the boots, and dressed himself swiftly in breechclout and leggings. The feel of those old, worn garments helped to steady him.

His rifle—he found it under the rumpled blankets on the bunk where Fritz had laid it. Powder horn, bullet pouch, knife. The empty loop on the belt of the hunting shirt reminded him of the hatchet in the trunk, and he slipped it into place, his hands closing fiercely on the small, keen head of it and the long, slim handle as it dropped against his thigh. In the trunk he saw, too, the black wooden case that had startled him and his father when he swung back the lid without thinking, and they looked at the brown steel barrels and the shining blades of Todd's boarding pistols. He reached for the case, then hesitated; they would be awkward things to carry. Then he opened the box, thrust the soft leather packets of flints and balls into the bosom of his shirt, shoved the flask of fine powder after them, and slipped the pistols under the belt of the breechclout, one against each hip under the skirts of the long hunting dress. He would carry them while he could; if, in his haste, they overburdened him, they would have to go.

Dressed and equipped for the trail, he felt stronger, clearer-headed. With something of his wonted calmness, he went quickly to the sapling shed to forage for food. There was beef in an earthen dish behind the chimney angle, and on a wooden platter, buckwheat souens left over from a meal. He shoved a handful of the cold lumps into his shirt. There was milk, too, in a dish, thick with unskimmed cream; as he drank it, he saw an army bat-wagon swing round the tavern corner and come to a stop.

Men in linsey piled out of it and ran into the rooms on either side. Some of them came out with oddments of household stuff in their arms, and one, almost empty handed, carried over his forearm the shift and the night-rail he had plucked from the pegs in Diantha's room. Others stood gaping in the opposite doorway, amazed by the glitter of mirrors and gilt and the sheen of blue harrateen. A sergeant in waistcoat and cocked hat cursed them through the door. The commandant, he told Leslie gruffly as he paused by the driver's seat with a question, was saving what household goods might be hauled into the fort before night.

"Strike me blind, them redsticks'll catch us with our arms full o' featherbeds an' plows an' warmin' pans," he complained, and swore at his laggard scavengers. "'Y God, they're swarmin' all along the river. Two fellows o' Croghan's tried to get through by Shertee's ford, an' a dozen red devils chased 'em within musket shot o' the King's Garden."

Leslie set his nerves against the fear that thrust through him.

"When?" he asked.

"Not two hours ago. Lookee, is that your gear they're draggin' out?"

Leslie looked at the dressing table, banging headlong through the doorway in two pairs of clumsy arms, and nodded.

"I hope you'll be alive t' use it, an' y'r lady too," the sergeant gloomed. "There's a curse on this bloody place—first Braddock, an' then Grant, an' now us, with the blasted fort slidin' int' the rivers, an' women and kids squallin' everywheres."

Up toward the stream that ran from the Massacre pond, shots rang out in a ragged volley. Standing on the wagon seat, the sergeant pointed.

"Look, the Injuns are helpin' burn the Upper Town!" He bawled with blanching lips at the men huddled in the windows. "I tell ye, get movin' wi' that stuff, or they'll scalp ye in y'r tracks."

He slid abruptly into the seat and seized the reins.

"An' Ecuyer gave orders nobody should leave the town," he laughed grimly. "The redsticks will see to that!" Leslie saw the sweat break out on the pale face in beads so close together they looked like woven wampum.

The horses jumped against the collars as the sergeant swung his whip, and jerked the heavy wagon around so that its tongue pointed to the alley and quick flight. The men in the cabin tumbled the virginal into it, jangling and tinkling, and thrust the brass-bound chest after it. The stool with the merry dolphins went flying over the side; a man came running with his arms heaped with blue stuff from the bed, curtains and quilts huddled together. Leslie slipped past him into the ravaged room.

The room concerned him little enough; but to step in and look at it gave him something to do. The column of dark smoke that rose from the top of Grant's Hill, and the shots from the ford on the King's Highway, told him that somehow he must keep a grip on himself and make himself wait...and wait...and wait, though every minute took Diantha Gail deeper into the wilderness, closer to danger. He could not help Diantha by walking into the cordon of Indian muskets and hatchets that hemmed in Pitt's Town on its narrow peninsula. *Wait. Wait, you fool, wait.* Fighting for self-control, he picked up the quilted blue gown where it had fallen on the puncheons, and folded it and smoothed it as if there was nothing in all the world more important than the neatness of that frothy finery. When he had it folded, he laid it away carefully in the leather trunk, and put the green slippers with it, and picked up the stays and packed them, too.

Wait. Wait. He might get through to Shertee's in the dark. In broad daylight, he would have the tomahawks on his trail before he crossed the hill where the Shawnees had set the heads of Grant's Highlanders on their painted stakes. They would be in his skull before he had gone a mile. *Wait...wait.*

Slowly, meticulously, he folded and packed the scarlet tunic, the boots and the cocked hat with its gold lacing, the sash and sword. When he had it done, he closed the trunk and locked it, and carried it out to the wagon. It slid over the wagon box on sacks of flour, slabs of bacon, smoked fish, powder kegs, bags of bullets and every manner of provisions stripped from Halbert

Bond's trading room and storeroom. In the brush beyond the pond, red devils were yelping as the flames burst through the roof of the Thompson house.

Leslie picked up his rifle and blew the old powder out of the pan. When he had it freshly primed, he went with easy strides around the end of the stable, out into the King's Highway, and up the slope toward Massacre pond. Where the road crossed the creek, a brass cannon stood by itself on a little knoll; around it, squatting in the bushes, matross men strained their eyes toward the thickets farther up and cast uneasy glances over their shoulders. Past them, trailing axes and muskets, came an unhappy file of town militia, headed for a cabin and a sapling stable that stood yet untouched in a weed-grown yard beyond the pond. The gunners looked at them apprehensively as they went by, and licked their lips, stirring restlessly.

The nondescript platoon of militia was battering at the eaves-logs of the cabin when Leslie joined it, and leaned his rifle against the corner of the stable. From the stable he brought an ax, and swung it against the upright logs of the door frame. When he had them cut through, he told the corporal who led the platoon to turn his battering ram against the wall beside the door, and saw the flimsy cabin collapse inward. Down somewhere in the flattened town, a drum began to beat.

"I'll burn the stable," Leslie told the corporal quietly. "Better get your men back. The cannon seems to be leaving us."

The detail went pelting down the road toward the comfort of the sentries along the creek.

It was easy enough to burn the ramshackle barn. Its walls of poles, set upright in double file and stuffed with grass and leaves, were dry and flimsy; its thatched roof was so much tinder. But it took Leslie an unconscionable time to get it burned. He had certain uses for it; and while the smoke from the other burning cabins of the Upper Town drifted down toward the Monongahela in darkening streamers, he perched himself on the crude manger, hooked his toes behind the forked stake that held it up, got out his pipe from its nest in the flap of his hunting shirt and slowly filled and lighted it.

Through the doorless entrance of the stable, he watched the matross men at the ford trundle their twelve-pounder back down the King's Highway; farther along the reedy edge of the pond, he saw the flash of a sergeant's halberd signal the pickets in.

Leslie took his pipe from between his teeth and rapped it on the manger. He did it slowly, deliberately, as if it required elaborate care. He looked carefully at the gnawed poles of the manger, and noted how each tap of the pipe bowl set a tiny arc of brown stain on the white scars left by the teeth of the beasts that had fed there and chewed the bark from uprights and walls. He looked hard at the glowing tobacco as it fell into the hay in the bottom of the manger. He marked each stem of the hay as it caught fire with a tiny red glow, and the first tongue of flame. While the fire flickered from wisp to wisp and finally puffed into a blaze, he rapped his pipe again and stowed it away with painstaking care.

To fix his mind on small things, to busy his eyes and his fingers with such trifles as the rapping of a pipe and a horse's toothmarks on a manger kept his eyes from seeing Diantha Gail's white shoulders writhing in the hands of fiends, and his fingers from trembling at what he saw.

The fire caught at the flimsy wall; the stable filled with smoke. Through the first swirls of it eddying out the doorway, he saw the artillery platoon dip out of sight into a hollow half way to the fort. Before its cocked hats came up on the next rise, he had picked up his rifle and slipped out, screened by the smoke from watching eyes in the underbrush on Grant's Hill. Behind the stable, last year's burdock and wild cucumber grew rank and tall. He dropped to hands and knees and thrust his way into the tangle of weeds, and lay at full length while the last of the pickets came by, swinging rapidly down to the ford.

For many minutes after the guard had passed, Arnett Leslie lay motionless, face down in the rank grass. He was weaker, he realized, than he had thought he was. In spite of himself, his thoughts began to range again, and he had to snatch them back; deliberately, because it was the lesser evil, he turned them toward the things he had tried for five weeks to forget. Leslie Hall . . . Evelyn . . . the great manor house of yellow stone on South Mountain, which now would never be built . . . boudoir furniture on packsaddles.

He had, he told himself, piled folly upon folly until the heap was ready to topple. Even his precious independence had gone; he had sacrificed *that* the morning he went dashing to Fritz Van Buren's rescue, and finished the job when he let a red-haired girl addle him into attempting to undo all the evil that a pair of lustful gentlemen could concoct. And now he was heading straight into the greatest folly of all. He knew, when he looked at it coolly, that following Diantha Gail up the Venango trail was the maddest of all the mad things he had done. Because of a girl's wistful mouth and shining hair he was about to put an end to Arnett Leslie and his follies. In all likelihood, Arnett Leslie would be dead by morning, and all because a tavern wench with mud-splashed ankles scrubbed her toes and showed them to him, and because her shoulders were more cream than white and ...

Leslie pressed his face against the earth.

Diantha Gail. Diantha Gail.

Barefoot and faded and alone, friendless, hunted of men and despised of women, trying to be gay....

Diantha Gail. Diantha Gail.

He loved her.

The realization shook him as no other emotion ever had had the power to shake him. He loved her, and he had failed her. He loved her, and she might be lying dead; she might be lying staked out as John Simpson's daughters had been staked out, naked, blinded, with fires kindled on their abdomens, dying in torment.

He burst out of the burdock and the cucumber tangle, the breath sobbing through his teeth and aching in his throat. He ran blindly up the slope, past the edge of Massacre pond, straight toward the scrub oak where the Thompson house had stood. As he passed it, it was still smoldering, the standing logs half burned, the wattled chimney leaning inward drunkenly as the slow fire ate at the timbers around the hearth. He barely saw it, barely felt the sting of smoke in eyes and nostrils, barely realized that where he ran a howling pack of Delaware warriors had swarmed all day. He never knew what saved him. Perhaps the sight of soldiers and townsmen, pushing through the underbrush along the Monongahela in a desperate sortie to sink the fleet of barges before the Indians took thought to seize or burn them, drew the savages off Grant's Hill in search of easy prey. Perhaps the orgy of burning and looting had tired them out, or the applejack and rum found in the outlying cabins took their minds, for a few hours, off the panic-stricken town. Undoubtedly, on that first day of the sixty-seven day siege, the Indian tribes surrounding Pitt's Town were in far less strength than they were a few days later; certainly, in midafternoon, they were gone from the crest of the hill and the oak scrub where they had massacred Grant's Highlanders five years earlier. Leslie got through.

When his frenzy left him and a little coolness came back into heart and brain, he was deep in the wooded hills to the north of Forbes' road; the Forks of the Ohio lay two miles behind. He was running along a hardwood ridge that dropped off on the right into a gloomy ravine choked with underbrush on both its banks and floored with willow growth so rank that the tangled tops had the look, from above, of solid turf.

Leslie plunged down through the brush into the twilight depths of the gorge. At the bottom, among the close-set clumps of willow, there was grayish, sandy earth, packed smooth and hard by spring flood waters. It made a firm footing on which his moccasins moved swiftly and soundlessly, and the grayish aisles twisted and twined among the willow growth like caves of a labyrinth, lined with springy brown stems and roofed with matted leaves. Slipping between yielding branches, running crouched over so that his passing would make no threshing of the green tops to betray him to Indians on the hills above, he followed the ravine downward toward the Allegheny.

Gradually the willow growth thinned out. Gray trunks of spindling swamp ash flashed by him as he ran; branches of buckberry snatched at his fringed thighs. Swinging aside to dodge a little swampy meadow, he saw three belated haw trees white with bloom. The slanting sun washed the grass below them with thin gold; across it something bright flashed, dipped, and was gone, like a gold nugget with wings. His eyes followed it to the tip of a young oak; for an instant a humorous shrug twitched at the corners of his mouth. Here, of all places, a Baltimore oriole! It brought back . . .

He stopped abruptly. Beyond the top of the young oak, a trail of thin blue vapor wavered against the bluer sky.

Leslie slipped into the cover of the nearest thicket, no longer running, his eyes darting down every twisting aisle, his finger lying along the trigger guard of the long rifle.

The ash and willow grew sparse. The bottom of the ravine spread out, and the trickle of water that ran through its deepest part fell into a rocky channel much too big for it. The brush-covered slopes of the ravine gave way to steep cliffs, bare rock for a hundred feet below their crests. Under the shadow of the eastern cliff, a round pool reached out into the open meadow, and the thin stream ran out to meet it, dropping over a rock ledge with an eager splatter. Beyond the meadow and the pool, there was no more underbrush. Leslie looked out between the gray-brown bluffs to the shining expanse of the Allegheny.

In the mouth of the ravine a fire was burning. The sun, reflected from the sparkling river, threw into sharp relief a dozen dark bodies moving about the fire.

Delawares in paint and feathers!

The Venango road was cut off.

CHAPTER XV

*In Which One Man Succeeds Because Three Others Fail; and Arnett
Leslie Finds What Is Left of Hellward Bound:*

LESLIE crouched behind the last thin screen of brush and
looked first at the painted Delawares around their fire and
then at the bare wall of the ravine.

He knew there was no alternative but to turn back. Even if
he waited for darkness, hours away, it would be a miracle to
creep over the shale and the loose bowlders strewn across the
mouth of the ravine without alarming the savages waiting there.

His eyes searched the eastern cliff, and his hands tightened on
the rifle stock: a scant quarter mile up the gorge, a cleft broke
the sheer brown rock. As if a stream ran out of it, scrubby trees
lined its lower end and joined the thick growth in the bed of
the ravine. They promised cover enough to let him climb up
unseen into the cleft itself. How far the fissure ran back into the
bluff he could not see, but it must lead to the wooded plateau
above.

The enforced pause had eased his laboring lungs. Ready to
push back up the valley and scale the cleft, he turned for another
look at the Delaware warriors watching the Venango trail, and
felt his hope shrivel and his heart sicken. Two of the savages were
coming toward him, the sun glinting on their musket barrels and
on the heads of the polished hatchets in their clout-belts. Already,
while he sought a way out of the ravine, they had come half
way from the fire, toward the round pond and the waterfall. The
tumbling stream had drowned whatever noise they made among
the rocks.

They came carelessly, their muskets cradled across their elbows—
so carelessly that Leslie realized they had not discovered him.
But they were too close for escape. If he tried to creep away through
the sparse young ash, even their clumsy trade guns must reach him
before he could get into the shelter of the willow copses. And if

he reached the willows unwounded, they would track him down on those damp paths; he had spent too much of his strength already to outrun them long.

He shifted softly to his knees and cocked the rifle, with the flap of his shirt over the lock to smother the sound. Over the dull barrel, he stared at the daubed faces and the shaven heads. The blood pounded at his temple, under the bandage—slow, insistent throbs of pain; the streaked, fantastic warpaint on the foremost Delaware began to run together into a red and black blob; the blob began to whirl. Leslie closed his eyes. Bond had not killed him with that blow on his head, nor by throwing him over the bank of the Mon'; but if the pain kept spinning those painted faces about, he would nevertheless die, and that very speedily—unless they caught him alive. He kept his eyes closed as long as he dared.

They were still closed when, dull and far away, a cannon boomed, and then another.

He peered through the bushes, and saw that the two warriors had stopped, listening, with their faces toward the distant Forks. Solid and sullen, the cannon boomed again, as if already Fort Pitt was fighting for its life. Then, thin and airy, the sound of musketry fluttered like lace on the thick fabric of cannon-thunder. In a moment, the lace blew away.

The two Indians turned and trotted back to join the others in the mouth of the ravine. Leslie, on his knees, saw a coppery body stoop over the fire and scatter it, and stamp out the embers in the sand; he thought, with a surge of hope, that the whole war party was preparing to take the trail down-river to join in the attack on Pitt's Town. Instead, they clustered among the tumbled bowlders under the shoulder of the western bluff and crouched there, waiting, hidden from the Venango road that ran along the flat shore of the Allegheny. It must run within ten yards of the Delawares in their ambuscade, Leslie told himself. Now, while the painted devils watched the river trail, he could slip away into the thickets and be safely hidden in the cleft of the opposite wall in ten minutes of brisk running and climbing. But he waited. That hasty crouching behind the rocks in the ravine's mouth must mean that there was life on the Venango road—perhaps only another band of Indians coming to help take Fort Pitt, perhaps couriers coming in from the outlying posts at Venango or Le Boeuf, or riding desperately northward with warnings from Ecuyer. Or, perhaps—and Leslie waited because he dared not go until he was sure—perhaps Halbert Bond had turned back and was trying to reach the shelter of the Forks before it was too late.

The chattering waterfall blurred all other sounds.

One moment, the brown bluffs framed only the flat strip of shore, a stretch of blue river, and green hills beyond. The next, there were three white men on three horses that ran with their heads low, straining for the last burst of speed as powder smoke sprang out in dirty gray patches from the rocks, and the gorge rang with the Delaware volley.

Then there were only two horsemen, firing from the saddle into the yelping devils that swarmed down upon them, and one riderless horse bursting through the ring of painted bodies, plunging among the bowlders. A naked warrior clutched for a flying stirrup, got it, slipped on a rock, and staggered back, his chest crushed by the lashing heels. The ring of bodies closed in on the two mounted men and the man who knelt on one knee to fire. The spurt of smoke from his rifle seemed to catch a leaping Indian in mid-air, lift him, turn him, and throw him kicking on his back among the rocks.

The horsemen turned somehow in the whirling, howling mêlée. Leslie saw one of them, erect in his stirrups, swing his rifle by the small of the stock in one hand and smash the muzzle down across a snarling face, then lean far over, reaching for the dismounted man who ran hobbling toward him.

Leslie stepped out from the fringe of bushes. The riderless horse, coming at a wild gallop along the edge of the pond, threw up his head, snorted, flung himself to one side into the spongy earth. His hoofs sank; he stumbled, lost his speed, and Leslie's hand grasped for his bridle. The leather of the head stall slipped out of his fingers, but his wrist slid over the flying rein; it caught in his crooked elbow.

"Steady. Steady, now." Leslie's voice was easy, reassuring. There was no waiting now to rack his nerves; for one headlong moment, the queer, remote coldness of Leslie men in battle possessed him. While the horseman at the ravine's mouth still leaned in his saddle, and the wounded man ran hobbling to meet him, Leslie was up on the snorting horse, swinging him, lifting him into a furious gallop straight down into the Delaware pack.

His left hand holding the reins, he swung the long rifle across his left forearm, fired, and saw a hatchet whirl out of a dying hand and gash the neck of another howling savage so that his shoulder and arm turned red in a gush of blood. Then he was into them, his empty rifle gripped with the reins in one hand, his own hatchet striking, lifting, striking at the clawing, panting things that wrapped their arms around the horse's neck, snatched at his legs and the dangling rifle butt. A narrow skull glistening with oil came up along his knee; black eyes burned at him through a mask of paint that was green on one side and black on the other. He drove his knee into it, saw a knife flash and drive for his thigh, saw it miss and slash through saddle and blanket and the horse's blood well up around the blade as it stuck there between Leslie's legs.

His hatchet whirled and the little blade went clear past its eye into the greased skull at the edge of the roached scalp-lock. The horse screamed and lashed out in terror and pain, and the Delaware hurtled aside, the hatchet still in his head.

Leslie had a blurred glimpse of a man in a coon-skin cap, his mouth wide open, yelling, a reddened knife in his hand. He saw the wounded man catch the other rider's belt and pull himself up behind the saddle, almost falling again as the horse reared and swung.

Then he was past them, out of the ruck of clawing, screeching devils, and his maddened horse was tearing through marsh grass and sumach scrub and the river was going by in a long, wavering ribbon of grayish blue. He felt the animal gather speed as his hoofs came out of loose sand into the packed earth of the Venango trail, and his frantic leaps smooth out into a reaching gallop. When Leslie wrenched the Delaware scalping knife out of the saddle, the pain of it brought another flurry of terrified running, and he saw the edge of the saddle blanket turning black with the oozing blood. Two miles upstream, the big bay settled into his swinging gallop again. Leslie talked to him and patted his neck; but he did not spare him. They crossed the Allegheny at Shertee's a little after noon. The huddle of bark huts was deserted; they dashed

hrough it in a flurry of flung gravel, and the forest closed above
hem and behind them.

Hour after hour, Leslie drove the wounded horse without mercy;
he did not dare to be merciful. While the tracks of Bond's train,
till undisturbed, led steadily northward along the old Indian path,
he did not dare to spare either the bay or himself. His eyes strained
ahead at every twist of the trail, hoping and dreading at once; but
hrough all the long afternoon, he found only one sign of Diantha
—a bit of green silk adangle on a long arm of blackberry. There
was a small, streaked spot of blood close to one edge of it, and a
urrow of torn threads across it.

Leslie groaned and kicked at the stumbling horse. "How did
he go?" he had asked. And Bond's drunken crony in the wrecked
taproom had answered, gloating: "How? How? Wi' her foots
ied under the belly of her horse...."

God! Through these bramble thickets that ripped at his legs
ven through the deerskin leggings. The blood throbbed under
he bandage on his head:

Diantha Gail! Diantha Gail!

There was blood on that torn fragment of her dress. Her feet
were tied. And her hands, too; they would not leave her hands
unbound. Brambles. Blood. *Bond. Barent!*

"Oh, God....God," he prayed through contorted lips, swaying
n the saddle. The prayer never got any farther.

Diantha Gail! Diantha Gail!

The bandage seemed to be tightening around his head, damming
up the blood. It beat and throbbed across the wound, until finally
e tore the bandage off and dropped it in the trail. A little before
usk, he saw where the hoofs of many horses had turned off the
ath, up a slope, into a small meadow like a saucer between two
ills, and where, a rod farther along, they had come back again.

He rode up into the swale and dismounted, running on stiffened
egs from the ashes of the tiny fire to the trampled grass where
odies had lain. All he found was the pole with which Diantha
ad been pinioned for the night. He guessed its purpose, and
roaned in agony of spirit a hundredfold more bitter than the
nguish he had known one night in Leslie Hall.

He ran down to the edge of the meadow and snatched up the
anging reins. When he put his weight to the stirrup to mount,

the big bay staggered, lurched sidewise almost upon him, and collapsed, the breath tearing at his nostrils and bloody foam dribbling. Leslie, the breath sobbing in his own throat in his fear and haste, stripped off bridle and saddle and left him there. Perhaps the gallant fellow would live; perhaps he would die there, slowly. He did not dare risk a shot to settle it; the blood beat at his head, and his feet beat on the earth of the trail, reeling northward. . . .

Diantha Gail! Diantha Gail!

John Simpson's girls. John Simpson's girls.

He followed the beaten Venango road all night, sometimes staggering, sometimes running furiously as the pictures in his brain overpowered his reason, sometimes—for a little space—walking because lungs and legs together rebelled at the merciless demands he made upon them. Always, after a few minutes, he put the rebellion down and trotted on through the dark.

Unseen brambles caught at the dangling thrums on his leggings and on the cape of the linsey shirt, or slid down the stock of the rifle, clutched across his body, and scored his hands. Twice, tripped on bare roots that lay across the path, he fell; and once, at a sharp turn of the trail, the rifle muzzle drove against a tree so hard that the barrel came back against his chest and winded him. And once a low branch struck him on the temple, and he saw again the flash of red lightning that had blinded him as he went down under Bond's musket barrel. At long intervals he dropped on one knee, his fingers making sure that Hellward's train was still ahead of him; each time he found the imprint of shod hoofs deep in the soft surface of the trail, and ran on again.

When the pitch darkness of the valley bottoms took on its first tinge of gray, he was still running, though his run was hardly faster than a fast walk and his feet fell heavily on the path. Every step was sending a jar of pain up his body, through the wound on his head. His fingers told him that the wound was swelling.

Morning twilight lay like cold ashes along the tops of the ridges when he stopped at last and turned off the trail along a tiny stream. A hundred yards down its course, he found a bit of open ground on a slope that faced the east. Here he flung himself face down, drank, and held his aching temple in the cold water; then he ate two of the buckwheat souens, and tore off a piece of his ruffled shirt to make a wet bandage for his head. Then, on his back with his face to a gap in the branches on the opposite slope, he slept until the sun came up.

The heat and light on his eyelids wakened him; he sat up stiffly, and at the first motion felt the muscles of his thighs tremble. They still trembled, the weak quivering of exhaustion, when he knelt again at the creek to drink, and when he pushed through the swamp ash and the creepers and stood for a moment on the Venango road to blow the powder out of the pan and reprime his rifle.

Here, in the creek bottom, the hoofs of Bond's horses had left deep tracks. Across them, at the water's edge, ran the pads of a panther, but nothing else; no one had passed, north or south, in the hour Leslie had slept. In the mud he found two sets of smaller hoof prints—the Nancy mare's, and the pony's. He followed them out of the low ground, around the turn of a hillside blue with violets, and saw the Nancy mare dead across the trail. Leslie's throat tightened, and the breath sucked through his clenched teeth. There was an arrow in the black neck, just above the windpipe—a short, thick arrow that stood out a bare four inches on either side.

Leslie broke off the thin flint head and pulled the shaft out, and looked at it with blurring eyes. It was cedar, winged with the tips of three hawk feathers dyed brownish-red, and marked with five parallel scorches like a brand—an arrow unlike any Leslie had ever seen before, thicker, shorter. It was not Mingo, nor Delaware, nor Shawnee. He read its meaning without any real comprehension of new peril. Its presence there, transfixed in the neck of a white man's horse on the military road between the Forks and the Lakes, meant that the attack on Fort Pitt was more than a border foray. It meant that the Ohio tribes had found allies among the western nations. It explained the audacity of the raid on the Fort Pitt saw-mill in broad daylight. It meant war.

To the man standing in the blood-stained path, his shoulders sagging and his head bent over the two pieces of broken arrow, those meanings were instantly clear; but they had no meaning for him at all. He looked at the earth beyond the mare's body, and saw that the fresh marks of her hoofs came toward him from the north, and that she had been weaving from side to side as she ran. The attack had taken place somewhere in the hills and swamps that still lay between him and Venango. He sped northward with long, desperate strides that took no account of weariness or pain. He was unconscious of anything except the mare's wavering, irregular tracks, and the dread of what might lie behind the next turning of the trail.

He had thought that he was close to Bond's second night camp, but mile after mile went by and still the prints of the Nancy mare's hoofs came to meet him, and the forest lay silent, flecked with sun and shadow. He passed, in a meadow, the ashes of a long dead campfire and the skeleton of a half-faced camp; the lush grass was thick with violets; above, on a bank, wild roses glowed against a glistening patch of rhododendron. Leslie did not see them, or see that his shadow wavered as it ran among the violets in the grass, like the shadow of a drunken man. He was realizing, in a bitterness of self-reproach that left no room for reason, that his body had betrayed him in the night; he had traveled more slowly than he had believed he was traveling, his legs shortening their stride and his dulled brain unaware of it. He drove himself now as mercilessly as he had driven the wounded bay.

The Nancy mare had run nearly six miles before the arrow in her neck had killed her. He saw where she had burst into the trail, the dirt torn up and flung by her flying hoofs. A little farther on, caught in the broken branches of a haw tree where it had threshed out its life, he found one of the pack horses he had bought from Tom Yeardley. And a little beyond that, the body of Bond's woman.

She lay face down, her head doubled under one shoulder and her arms flung out. Until he stooped and turned her by one arm, to make sure she was dead, he saw no wound, nor even a tear in the faded bed gown; then her head, flopping back grotesquely, showed the grass under it black with blood, and the white bone of her skull where the hair and flesh were gone. There was no other wound on her body. Scalped alive by some fiend who let her go when the skin on her head ripped loose—Leslie's eyes, searching frantically through the clustering alder thickets for other bodies, saw where she had plunged over a shelving bank above the trail and broken her neck in the fall. The dead horse in the haw tree had plunged down over the same bank; but there were three of those thick arrows sticking in the horse's side.

Leslie climbed the bank, and saw Bond staring with dead eyes at three buzzards circling just over the trees.

He had been scalped, and stripped to his clout. A dozen feet away, another naked body lay face downward, half hidden in bushes; Leslie drew himself up over the hanging lip of the bank, his eyes staring and staring; then, standing over the mutilated body, his breath ran out in a sound that was almost a laugh and partly a sob of unbearable relief. Stripped and scalped and shot twice through the body, Bond's woods-runner sprawled in the trampled and dabbled grass, his fingers still clutched on the broken handle of his hatchet.

Leslie darted across the bushy opening among the trees, and then circled it, careless that he trod on Bond's outstretched hand as he ran past his body.

There was no sign of Diantha; no sign, even, that she had ever been there. No packed-down grass to show where a fourth member of Bond's party had slept. No pole to pinion her at night. No footprints in the burned earth around the fire that could be hers. No sign, either, of Barent.

He darted across the clearing again and into the woods, and came to a larger meadow. There were three more horses dead in the bright grass; a buzzard stretched awkward wings and labored up to a bare oak limb; another buzzard came from the underbrush in the edge of the woods and joined it on the limb. Leslie thrust through the brush, and almost fell over Barent's legs sprawled out with the blue breeches and the polished boots still on them. A blanket was tangled around one foot as if it had tripped him when he sprang out of bed; another blanket still lay spread out on a rough mattress of pine boughs; the Swiss lay with his head among the protruding boughs, flat to the ground. Leslie, bending over him, saw that he had not been scalped; a musket ball had blown away the top of his head.

And still there was no sign of the girl. Leslie stripped the blanket off the pine bed, and jerked loose the one that was wound around Barent's boot, and found nothing. He dragged the stiffening body ruthlessly aside to search the ground where it lay, and saw the captain's high white stock lying, unbloodied, under it, and in the clenched fingers a scrap of green silk. He pulled it out, and with agony in his heart read the meaning of the pine bough bed, made so carefully among the underbrush away from the main camp, and of the unfastened stock and the torn bit of Diantha's dress. He knew where Barent's fingers had been to clutch that fragment of puckered satin—it was part of one puffed and gathered sleeve.

Barent had been here with her, alone, when the attack came. He had died instantly, never knowing what had happened. The savages who killed him had taken Diantha.

Across the swale, he saw the two buzzards launch themselves off their oak limb with a startled flapping, and realized that he was shouting; that he was storming at the body of the Swiss, cursing him for dying painlessly who had delivered Diantha into the hands of torturers; that he was praying to a calm heaven some formless, hysterical prayer.

The buzzards he had frightened gave their fear back to him. *Fool. Fool* ... to stand and curse when he needed breath and strength more than he had ever needed them. *Fool* ... to let his brain run mad when it must be cooler, clearer, steadier than it had ever been. *Think. Think.*

Bond had ridden out of Pitt's Town with at least seven horses; he had taken all of Leslie's; it was hardly likely that he would have taken none of his own. Barent must have had a saddle horse, at least; probably he had a pack horse, too, and perhaps a spare riding animal. But there were only three horses dead in the meadow where Bond had hobbled them; there was one more dead in the haw tree, and the Nancy mare dead six miles away.

Leslie pushed deeper into the underbrush and began to circle the camp and the meadow; if the rest of the horses had stampeded, the tangle of vines and elderberry and the thick leaf mold would show it; if the Indians had taken them, they would leave a trail that he could follow at top speed. A trail, he told himself, that he might follow until his lungs burst and yet arrive too late. If the marauders who had struck Bond's camp in the night mounted themselves on Bond's horses and rode swiftly, even a fresh, powerful runner would spend himself in vain to catch them; drive himself as he would, he knew that his strength was waning.

But the five dead horses, feathered with thick, short arrows, gave him a hope that slowly grew into conviction. Indians of the middle border would never have indulged in wanton horse killing; Bond's pack train would have been richer plunder for them than the garments they had stripped from his body. The strange arrows, the animals uselessly slaughtered, indicated a small war party from beyond the great lakes—a party of Indians little used to horses—taking what they needed to carry their plunder and baggage, and killing the rest for the sheer lust of killing.

His conviction grew so strong that he plunged out of the unmarked undergrowth and down into the Venango road again.

For a hundred yards along the path there were no tracks at all, except old ones half erased by rain. Then, north of the overhanging bank and the haw tree, he found fresh tracks again, coming into the trail from a patch of elderberry and young dogwood, in single file. The horses had been trotting. Leslie began to run. The big bay and the little mare had run until they fell; and the mare had died. . . .

Leslie lengthened his stride. A man could die, too.

Half a mile northward, the path dropped down into a marshy hollow where fallen trees had dammed a runlet and made a pond. In the spongy earth along the bank, he found what he had not dared to hope he would find—moccasin tracks, fresh, clear enough so that he could pick out the trails of three men. And the prints of the moccasins were trampled and blurred by the hoofs of the horses. *By God!* . . . it was more a prayer of thanksgiving than it was an oath. . . . Indians *on foot* were setting the pace.

Leslie stooped and drank from his cupped hand. He took time to reprime the pistols and his rifle. When he crossed the pond and followed the tracks northward, he settled into a long, swinging gait that spared his body as much as it could be spared.

There was a chance to close the gap of several hours between him and Diantha's captors, and close it in time. He must have strength left to fight when the gap had closed. If the savages who had captured her had taken the trail without harming her, she was safe until they made camp for the night.

He forced himself to believe that. He must believe it.

He followed the tracks all day. Late in the afternoon, he knew that he was gaining, that he had gained a great deal. Earth loosened by plodding hoofs and pushed over the surface of the trail was still moist. At midday, when he passed a stream and a trampled place in the grass where the Indians had halted to water the horses and strew droppings of parched corn and maple sugar from their own meal, the ridges of dirt at the toes of the hoof-prints had been drying and gray.

He cocked the rifle. The faint pad of his moccasins on the path became inaudible. His ears strained for the click of a hoof on stone, the rap of a hoof on a bare root; his eyes searched the greening twilight for the glow of fire.

At the end, he over-ran his trail. For suddenly there were no more hoof marks in the path, and he must turn and retrace his steps. Twenty yards behind him, at the edge of a rocky stream bed where no water ran, they began again. He could not tell, in the gathering dusk, whether the horses had turned off to right or left; the bare rock gave no sign.

With a chill of apprehension, he realized that he was farther behind than he had thought he was. Horses traveling up or down the stony stream bed would have made noise enough to be heard a mile away in the forest stillness.

He plunged westward, up the dry watercourse. It wound quickly into a deep ravine, with steep, crumbling banks.

Fifteen minutes brought him up against a jam of tree trunks and jagged projecting limbs, the débris of spring torrents heaped into a barrier impassable for horses, between banks equally impassable. It took all the self-control he could command to keep from plunging headlong down the ravine again, careless of crashing brush and clattering stones. He had lost time...time that might mean agony and degradation to Diantha Gail.

Diantha Gail. Diantha Gail.

The greenish light was greenish darkness when he came out again into the Venango road. Across the trail, the ravine where the dry stream ran was almost black, though a faint glow of sunset showed uncertainly through the trees on a hill beyond. He ran his hand across his eyes, wearily, almost hopelessly. In a few moments, even that vague glow would be gone.

He shook his head sharply; that dazed brain of his had tricked him again. The faint glow was not sunset light; he was looking east. It was the glow of fire, reflected in the tops of trees.

And then the forest was no longer still.

Out of the fire, a woman screamed. And screamed. And screamed.

CHAPTER XVI

In Which the Odds are Four to One, and a Man Must Keep His Head While He Watches the Woman He Loves in Torment:

FIRE searing the flesh...red-hot knives hung like a necklace on writhing shoulders...live coals in the arm pits and between the toes...splinters driven through young breasts and lighted....

He had seen John Simpson's daughters.

A shuddering cry burst from his throat:

"Oh, God...."

If he blundered now, those wails would go on and on, hour after hour, until Diantha Gail died as those other girls had died.

"God...."

Out of some deep reservoir of the soul, Arnett Leslie drew courage to endure the screams.

It rose within him to meet his need, a strong, cool tide to quench the fire that fanned itself to madness in his brain. It caught him up and carried him toward the red glow against the trees. He knew that his spent body was struggling among the tumbled bowlders of the dry creek bed; he knew that his legs were quivering with every step, that his hands were trembling, that his muscles were like water. He knew that his feet were feeling from rock to rock, from rock to log; that he was trying the footing under every step, lest a bowlder go crashing down or a dead limb break and crackle and betray him. He knew that his strength was gone; but the cold, deep flood that came welling up in him lifted him beyond the need of strength.

His body was fighting the darkness, the rocks, the broken, jagged limbs of drift, the snaring vines; but he—Arnett Leslie—was moving powerfully forward in the grip of a current that was strong as fate. He knew that he would come to the firelit trees before it was too late. He knew that he would have the strength to fight.

He was sweeping on through the whirling dark; the current

seemed to fill the dry ravine brimful, from bank to bank; it thrust him along as if it would hurl him bodily upon his enemies and blot them out. It was rushing him along too fast. He could not go hurtling headlong, without a chance to aim a single blow. He fought back at the too-powerful current, and it let him go. He dropped gently onto soft, deep sand; into silence. The screams had stopped. Below him he saw the fire that had set the tops of the oak trees aglow, and saw why the light from the flames had left the bed of the dried-up stream in darkness.

He was standing on a broad ledge of rock; behind him, a long, smooth slope of bare stone slanted down to the ledge. He had slid down the slope, into a basin hollowed out by countless years of torrents and half filled with dry silt.

Below him, the ledge dropped off twenty feet into a tiny meadow ringed with great oaks and dotted with young ash. In wet seasons, a roaring stream leaped over the ledge; it had dug out, at the edge of the meadow, a deep pot-hole. The bed of the stream where it ran away across the meadow was as dry as the rocky gorge above; but there was water in the pot-hole itself; Leslie caught the glint of fire reflected in it.

He stood as in a theater stall and looked down upon four Indians such as he had never seen before—short, broad-built, their heads grotesque in a barbarous war-crest that had the look of a crouching animal. They were naked to the waist, except for the wolf-tails that dangled from their heads and down their backs.

One of them was a little apart from the fire, stooping above the stump of a slim ash sapling that had been cut off three feet above the ground. He whittled at the stump with a knife, moving slowly around it, a thing of evil under the monstrous head-dress bristling above his painted face. He stopped, the knife blade lifted in the sheen of fire, as a figure came out of the circling trees; then the whittling began again.

Leslie's heart seemed to stop. The figure wore skirts that billowed and shimmered; and the skirts were green. Then the fire flared up, and he saw that the woman who wore them was an Indian. And that the girl who had worn them before her was crouched on her knees beside the fire. The bodies of the three half-naked Indians all but hid her.

They had stripped her, and tied her hands behind her back. One of them was kneeling in front of her, his hands moving about her face and breast. One sat cross-legged at her knee, facing her, his hands busy with something set up on a stick between his legs. As Leslie watched, sick with horror, he picked up the stick and thrust it into the girl's face and shook it; and Leslie saw that it was a scalp on a willow hoop, the dangling hair half-braided.

The girl's voice came up to him, faintly, a low whimper quickly stilled. The savage set his willow stick back into the ground between his legs and began again to braid the thick hair.

The Indian who knelt reached back and thrust a stick into the fire. As the flames leaped, he picked up another from the fire's edge and touched it to naked flesh. The whimper came again, broken. In the brightening flames, Leslie saw what they were doing.

The kneeling warrior was blackening Diantha's face and body with charred sticks still hot and glowing from the embers. And the clouted savage behind her was slowly plaiting her own hair into one thick braid to match the braid that grew from the human skin stretched on its willow hoop where she could not but look at it.

It seemed to Arnett Leslie that the last drop of blood was being squeezed from his heart. They were painting her for torture, and braiding her hair for the scalping knife while they made her watch the plaiting of the scalp they had ripped from the head of Bond's wife while she was still alive. In a sickening flood of realization, he knew the meaning of the slim sapling trunk whitening under the knife that stripped away the bark and sharpened the upper end into a long point. This was her torture stake. They were preparing to impale her upon it, instead of tying her as men prisoners were tied. She would stand there in agony while they whipped her with burning sticks, thrust splinters into her flesh and lighted them, girdled her arms and waist and legs with strips of dry bark and set them ablaze. They would give her not even the mercy of the rope at her wrists on which to run back and forth to escape, momentarily, the next fiendish cruelty.

Arnett's breath shuddered in his throat. He all but stopped breathing, lest the sound of it betray him. He prayed desperately, wordlessly. Two shots—he must fire two shots before he leaped. Pistol first; the rifle was surer for the second shot, at moving bodies. No matter how close other war parties might be, he had no choice. Two shots—leap—the other pistol. If one of them missed fire...

He dared not miss. He forced himself to prime one pistol from the flask of priming powder, to smother the sound of the lock in his hunting shirt, to powder the pan of his rifle afresh, to shift his feet softly on the rock to be ready both to fire and leap.

The Indian at the stake straightened and spoke. Diantha's body gleamed white against the fire as hands jerked her to her feet by the plaited scalplock they had made of her hair. Her face was black with charcoal; her breasts were ringed with it, and her body and thighs smeared and striped. She whimpered again.

They seized her from both sides at once, one by both arms from behind, two by her thighs and knees, raised her, and carried her toward the pointed stake. Her body, writhing, arched like a white bow bent.

"Oh, God...God...God," raced Leslie's brain. He realized that he was praying, but it seemed to have nothing to do with his body. His mind was frantic, but his arms and his hands were steady. He aimed the boarding pistol at the Indian who gripped Diantha's arms. He knew, as he pressed the trigger, that the Indian would shudder and stay erect a moment before he crumpled; that the other two would be too startled, for that moment, to release the girl. They would be together, away from their weapons.

Before the dying warrior fell, his hands dragging Diantha's body backward with him, Leslie dropped the pistol. Down the barrel of the long rifle, he saw the red-daubed face of the Indian who had sharpened the stake. The bullet knocked him backward. Leslie leaped.

He struck the meadow sod running, and kept his feet. The rifle, thrust out, drove past the front sight into dark flesh below a lifted arm. The shock of the collision wrenched Leslie's hand off the gunstock and tore it on the lock; he went to his knees on a squirming body, and felt nails gouging across his face. He got free —he had to get free; flung himself backward; lost the rifle; saw and heard a dark, squalling thing hurl itself at him.

He jerked the second of Todd's pistols from his belt and pulled the trigger. The lock clicked. The charging Indian spitted himself on the three-edged bayonet.

Leslie twisted away from the falling body, and felt the blade suck free. Blood, hot, gushing, drenched his hand. He knelt between one body that was still and one that flopped and made gurgling sounds, and looked at his battlefield. He had been one against four, and the four were dead or dying. He stared at them stupidly: it was hard to believe that they had died so easily.

The warrior who had impaled himself upon the misericord finished his dying; but one of the other bodies began to stir. Leslie was not sure that he saw it move; the whole firelit swale seemed to be rocking gently, and he shook his head to make it stand still. The wounded man kept on moving, wriggling away; beyond him, close to the fire, Leslie saw that the girl, too, was moving.

She was sitting up, unnaturally erect, her body contorted in a pose as wanton as a slave girl's in a bacchanalian frieze, her blackened breasts thrust out by the pull of the thongs that bound her arms. The crawling savage was moving toward her. Her knees drew up against her body, and her feet, thrusting against the ground, pushed her backward. Even as she hitched backward in the futile attempt at flight, she did not seem to see the dark body writhing toward her; her eyes, lifted, stared blankly past the Indian and past Leslie. Her knees came up again, her feet pushed frantically against the ground, and her body hitched a few inches. As she struggled she began to whimper again. Leslie crawled slowly over the body of the Indian he had stabbed and came down on the other side of it, on hands and knees. The dark, creeping thing was ten feet away, and the ten feet stretched out like the miles of the Venango trail. On hands and knees, Leslie took up the pursuit. Queer, disjointed notions went through his mind. He ought to get up on his feet, but he felt as if somehow he had no feet. He did not have even a body; it had sloughed away and run like water into the ground. He did not blame his body; it had been very tired—too tired, he could understand, to cling any longer to this Arnett Leslie who kept insisting that it run, and run, and fight, and crawl. His body, he decided, was like the big bay horse; it had run until it was too weak to stand up.

Close to the fire, he overtook the crawling Indian and crept up beside him. He saw the shine of eyes turned toward him, and felt the first rubbery yielding and resistance of the copper body;

then the three-edged knife slid in smoothly up to the muzzle of the pistol, as into a scabbard made for it. The pistol butt vibrated in his hand.

The air, too, was vibrating. He looked at the girl, and saw that she was screaming, her mouth wide open in her blackened face, her body hitching and hitching. The noise she made was making the vibration in the air; when her screaming crossed another scream, they made a thin tingling in Leslie's ears, like a saw blade pushed through a pine knot. He twisted half around, one elbow on the Indian's back, and saw that the other shrill sound came from the squaw.

He had forgotten about her. Now she was running along the edge of the trees. She had ripped off half the green skirt, and was waving it in front of her and crying out in high, chopped-off yelps, like a wounded dog. Between the yelps, Leslie heard bodies go crashing through the brush, and then, diminishing, the clatter and spatter of hoofs on loose stones. The Indian woman, he realized, had stampeded the horses; he had forgotten about them, too.

His brain, alarmed, told his body anxiously to get up. His eyes told him that there was still one horse, tethered within the shadow of the trees; his ears told him that it was snorting and pulling, and that, once, the rope on its neck choked off its wind.

The air had stopped vibrating; there was no sound at all except the trampling of the frightened horse. The Indian woman dropped the torn cloth and slipped out of the firelight, into the trees. Leslie knew that he had to kill her. If she got away, on horseback, there would be, before long, another torture stake for Diantha, and one for him.

He got up, ran in awkward, plunging steps across the grass, and caught her as she tried to mount the horse. The horse whirled and went threshing away. Leslie came back into the little meadow and stooped, swaying, to pick up the fragment of green silk and wipe the bayonet and the pistol barrel. Stooping, he saw the heaped-up baggage of the war party where the woman had been making camp. He picked up one of their blankets and carried it with him to the fire. As he crossed the swale, drops of rain fell hissing into the embers and raised the ashes in little puffs around the edges of the fire.

He knelt by Diantha and cut the thongs that bound her arms. His hands trembled, and the flesh was so swollen and ridged that one edge of the misericord cut the skin while the other edge cut the cords. When he unwound the rawhide strips, her arms dropped numbly at her sides; her body sagged a little, and tears began to run weakly down the smear of charcoal on her face. Under the charcoal, the skin was burned into white blisters ringed with red. She did not stir when he spoke to her; her eyes stared straight ahead, blank and dazed.

The hiss of rain in the embers quickened, and rain and wind together began to make a gusty rushing in the treetops.

Leslie rose shakily to his feet and raised his face to the rain. *God....* Rain to wash the trail and blur the tracks, and keep whatever other war parties were on the Venango road from turning curiously down the rocky stream-bed. Rain to give him time to rest. He thought that he could scarcely carry Diantha a quarter mile without falling.

He left her crouching by the hissing fire, and went weaving toward the overhanging ledge of rock and the pool of water at its foot, the blanket trailing behind him. Between the pool and the base of the ledge he found a patch of sandy earth, and spread the blanket on it.

When he bent over Diantha and lifted her in his arms, she cried out sharply and struggled against him, her eyes wide and staring.

"Diantha ... Diantha, dear." But she was still struggling, weakly, when he laid her on the blanket. Kneeling beside her, he unfastened his belt and laid it with its sheathed knife on the sand between the blanket and the pool, and untied the strings of the linsey hunting shirt and stripped it off. The chunk of beef and the buckwheat souens, crushed into a shapeless lump, dropped out onto the blanket and struck one of the girl's puffed arms. The cry it brought to her lips made a strident keening in his head.

He knew, and wondered at it dully, that he felt no surge of relief or joy at having her safe. His mind, in a detached way, told him that for the hours of darkness, at least, they were reasonably safe; without conscious deduction, he read in the conduct of the five Indians he had killed an assurance that they were an isolated band. If they had been otherwise, they would not have daubed Diantha in black for the torture; this first night's camp after the massacre of Bond's train would have meant degradation and the beginning of torture, but hardly the peeled and sharpened stake. Their failure to keep some rendezvous with other savages would not be likely to bring a search for them. If the battlefield below the ledge was discovered, he felt sure, it would be by chance, and the chance was slight.

He put the beef and the fried buckwheat mush on top of his pouch, and pushed them against the overhanging rock. Then, with an effort that drained the last of his will power, he went out into the little meadow again and found his rifle. The muzzle of it was fouled with blood; he cleaned it, standing and swaying in the rain, with thrums that he jerked from the leggings of the nearest Indian, and crept under the ledge to load it and prime it, and load and prime the pistol. Crouching there, the sight of the girl's body shocked him.

His mind, he realized, was staggering like his legs. He had taken off the hunting shirt to cover her with, and then forgotten. He spread it over her, lifting her hands gently to slip the edges of it under her raw wrists and swollen arms. She whimpered, but he did not heed it. The faint reflection of fire in the pool was beginning to move in fantastic dips and swoops. He lay down, and felt the rough blanket rush up to meet him. The packed sand under it rocked. With some half-formed notion that Diantha might be gone when it stopped rocking, he threw out one arm across her and curved it around her body.

CHAPTER XVII

*In Which Arnett Leslie Hears that He Is Dead, and Diantha Gail Rides
to the Governor's Ball Again:*

ARNETT LESLIE awoke cold and wet. There was a roaring
in his ears and a rushing in his eyes; the rain had turned
into a downpour; water slid in a gray sheet from the ledge
above into the pool beside him. Through the waterfall, as through
a moving curtain, he saw the tops of the oak trees tossing, now
dark, now pale as the gusts turned up the under side of the leaves.
It must, he thought stiffly, have stormed all night.

When he moved, his body felt as stiff as his brain. He did not
realize at first that he was not cold all over. Exhaustion had
dragged him down so deeply into sleep that when he did feel
Diantha's body pressed warmly against him, he thought first of
the little dog Robin, and the morning he had waked up, drenched,
on the Cumberland trail, and found Robin curled up in the curve
of his arm. It troubled him, when he realized that it was Diantha,
and not Robin, lying against him, to find that he felt no emotion.

He reached across her and groped for the beef he had laid away
with his pouch and powder-horn. He thought, numbly, that he
should feel ecstatically happy; he loved her; he had gotten her
back. The only feeling he recognized was hunger, and a weariness
that seemed to be inside his bones. He lay down again, quietly,
with his face to the clearing, and began to eat and to think.

Beyond the threshing treetops, clouds were driving in dark surf
across the sky; their ragged edges, gray against the dawn, curled
and feathered and blew away like dirty foam. Intermittent gusts
of rain spattered through the oaks. The storm, he decided, would
break up shortly; whatever he was going to do, he must do it soon,
while there was still rain to wash out his trail.

The water dropping from the ledge made a noisy lapping in
the pool, like a greedy dog. The pool itself had risen and spread
in the night; on the opposite side, toward the drowned fire, it

had overflowed into its old grass-grown channel and spilled out a stream that ran chuckling obscenely between two of the dead Indians. On the far side of the clearing, it scuttled down into the stunted cedars and the stony slope with a great commotion.

Leslie's eyes followed it until it was lost among the trees. It offered one way out. He considered it, his thoughts falling into ranks slowly, like soldiers on a forced march, wearily resentful at being aroused.

No matter how exhausted he was, no matter how helpless Diantha might be from her ordeal, they could not stay here; the Venango road was too close. Even though the rain kept on, there would be buzzards circling over the glade in a little while, and the first curious savage passing along the trail might come prying.

Leslie tore off a bit of the beef no bigger than two fingers and put the rest back on the bullet pouch. That, and whatever food he might find in the dead Indians' war bags, would be all they would have to eat; he would not dare to risk a shot until there was no other alternative to starvation. His mind trudged from one possibility to another.

He knew, in a general way, where he was. Lying with his back to Diantha and the rock, he was looking east across the little meadow. Behind him, within half a mile, ran the Venango trail. Eastward, perhaps five miles, perhaps twenty, lay the great bend of the Allegheny river—a huge bow with one tip at Shertee's and the other at Fort Venango on French Creek. The Venango road stretched like a bowstring from tip to tip—a bowstring nearly a hundred miles long.

There were half a dozen things he might do. He could press eastward through the unmarked forest until he came to the Allegheny; when he reached it, he could follow it up to the mouth of French Creek and so come surely to Venango, or build a raft and float down the great bend a hundred miles or more to the Forks of the Ohio and Pitt's Town. But the Allegheny would be the natural route for war parties of the northern Indians going to join the besiegers of Fort Pitt. To travel openly along the Venango trail would be hardly more dangerous than to float down the river or follow its bank northward to Gordon's post on French Creek.

He might cross the Venango trail and push west and south through the wilderness to the Ohio. But that way lay the Shawnee hunting grounds; and no matter which way he went, he must travel almost a hundred miles before he came to Pitt's Town. Alone, he might do it, and slip through the ring of savages around the fort. With the girl, it would be a miracle.

He came inevitably to the decision that he must find his way through the forest to Venango, avoiding both trail and river. If Venango had fallen ...

He put the last of his morsel of food into his mouth, and crawled out into the rain, rifle in hand. It was an effort to stand up. His body ached. But his legs, when he began to walk, were steady enough in spite of their stiffness. With methodical haste, he plundered the bodies in the glade, and the packs lying where the Indian woman had started to pitch their camp.

There was more food than he had hoped to find: handfuls of parched corn, maple sugar in two bark packets, a dozen strips of meat dried and leathery, and a hard, greasy mass that looked and smelled like sour tallow mixed with huckleberries in a bag of hide with the hair still on it. It was pemmican, though he did not know it; and smelled so foully that he was within a jot of tossing it aside. But it was food, and he kept it, and stuffed all that he found into the largest of the quilled and beaded pouches.

With his knife he cut one of the soaked blankets in two, and out of one of the halves fashioned a sling to hang across his shoulder, tying the ends together with the strings of one warrior's breechclout. Against a tree he found three muskets, with dangling powder horns; cheap trade powder, he saw when he poured a little out into his hand, but he filled one horn, and hung it with the pouch of food across his shoulder. Bowstrings, cut from the four heavy bows that lay in the tumble of blankets, he plaited swiftly into a sling for his rifle. That, with the flints from the muskets dropped in on top of the food, and a small and dirty kettle, made up his salvaging. He carried pouch and horn and sling to the overhanging rock and laid them beside the girl, and risked another five minutes to scramble up to the ledge where he had dropped the pistol after his first shot.

Then, though he told himself that it was a senseless waste of strength, he dragged the five bodies into the bushes so that Diantha would not see them when he woke her. Even in death, the painted faces were beastly under their wolf tail headdresses.

Stooping over the heap, he pulled off one of the war crests, stiff with projecting porcupine quills brightly dyed, and set it with grim humor on his own head. With his black, unqueued hair, that barbarous headdress might give him, in some headlong meeting in the woods, the instant he would need to put Diantha down and swing his rifle clear. He stripped off his ruffled shirt and rolled it into a tight bundle, went quickly to the powder horns he had discarded, and carried them across to the pool. With handfuls of wet gunpowder, he stained his neck and body and his back as far as he could reach, and stood up dark enough to pass as an Indian at fifty paces in the dark woods.

The sight of his belt with Diantha's braided hair lying across it reminded him that he had left his hatchet in a Delaware skull two days ago, and he went back into the bushes and tugged a tomahawk loose from its beaded loop. On hands and knees, he drank sparingly from the pool, and filled the birchbark cover of one of the sugar packets with water and set it at the edge of the blanket. It was only then, when he stood ready to depart, that he knelt beside Diantha and sought to rouse her, his hand slipping under her back to lift her, his voice casually cheerful.

She opened her eyes almost at once, and sat up quickly. The hunting shirt slipped off her shoulders and dropped to her waist, but she made no move to cover herself. Her eyes were startling, the pupils so dilated that there was no gray in them at all; they were black as the round charcoal center of a target in a ring of white—as black, and as blank. They looked at him without a sign of recognition. Her mouth, that he had seen firm and gay, angry and tender, roguish and arrogant in swift succession, drooped weakly open, and her tongue came out to lick her lips stiffly.

Holding her in the curve of one arm, he put the bark cup to her mouth; she drank thirstily, but spilled half the water, her tongue so swollen that she swallowed with an effort. As if it hurt to drink, she drew back against him, and one hand came up to push the cup away resentfully, like a sick child unable to understand. Her arm shocked him, it was so puffed and angry, the skin torn away to the quick where the rawhide thongs had gouged the wrist. She sat shameless, unconscious alike of her bared body and of the tightening pressure of his arm around her.

"Diantha ... Diantha, dear ... dear...."

The emotion that he had not felt and that had troubled him because he could not feel it, swept over him in an overpowering rush. He let the cup drop, and both arms drew her close and cradled her against him. For a moment, he forgot everything except that he loved her. He did not kiss her, or speak, or move. It seemed enough to press his cheek against her hair and hold her tightly in a sense of complete possession.

Abruptly, it seemed too much. Her body was hot against his rain-chilled flesh, so feverishly hot that it startled him. He spoke to her again, urgently, and his arms shook her.

"Diantha! Diantha!"

She stirred against him, and drew back, her mouth quivering.

"Don't tie me." Her voice and her eyes were empty, flat. "Please," they begged, "please don't tie me. I'll not try to get away, again."

"Diantha...." He shook her again, in the circle of his arms, and hurt her. The pain, for an instant, filled her eyes with life, and sharpened her voice into a cry. "Diantha, it's Arnett. It's Major Leslie."

She smiled at that, and looked at him so steadily that he thought she knew him at last. Her eyes half closed and a shrewd expression spread incongruously across her blotched face.

"Major Leslie is dead," she told him as if she had trapped him, cunningly, in a lie. "They killed him. He kept me by him all night, and they threw him into the river, and I ran away and came to America." Her eyes dulled again, and her mouth dropped. Arnett was suddenly more afraid than he had been when he heard her screaming. He could fight Indians; but the dazed eyes, the meaningless words, the slight body burning with fever, frightened him. He could not fight fever—or madness.

When he spoke to her again she did not answer at all, though she drank submissively when he put the birch cup back to her lips, and sat quietly while he pulled the hunting shirt clear where it was caught under her knees, and dressed her in it.

His hands shook as he eased her limp body to the ground and passed the blanket sling around her. When he stood up, she lay as in a hammock, high against his body. Naked to the waist, his face and body dark with gunpowder, the wolf-crest of an Ojibway warrior on his head, he waded knee-deep through the edge of the pool and turned into the run formed by its overflow.

Diantha roused as the first dash of rain touched her face and set the burns stinging; the blanket sling pinioned her arms, and she struggled to free them, moaning. Leslie stopped at the edge of the forest, resting her on one thigh while he pulled out the cape of his hunting shirt from around her shoulders and drew it across her face. Then he went on again, down a stony slope, the rushing water barely ankle deep; bushes whisped along his legs, and once he must balance precariously on one leg while he swung the other across a fallen log and twisted himself over gingerly, lest he leave telltale marks on the sodden wood. The motion made the girl moan again.

At the foot of the slope, there was a pool thigh-deep, and beyond it the stream went twisting through a slough fringed with willow and swamp ash, where mud sucked at his ankles and made progress laboriously slow. Twice he had to stop to rest, and ease the pressure on his shoulders by slipping his free arm under Diantha's knees. The second time, while he stood in swamp water over his knees and the rain hissed through the willows, she began to talk, and he thought with a surge of thankfulness that her mind had come back from wandering. He lifted the cape of the hunting shirt from her face and saw her smiling at him, like a delighted child.

"Truly, Major," she said gayly, though her swelled tongue blurred the words, "I did not know there was so elegant a chair to be had in all Pitt's Town."

His arms tightened, lifting her higher against his breast.

"Diantha ... Diantha, dear...."

But the brightness ran instantly out of her face and left it troubled.

"Are you sure they will not drive me out? Oh, I think I could not bear it." So that he knew she was still delirious and living over again the night when he had picked her up, all billowing green satin, bare knees and mud-splashed ankles, and carried her across the drawbridge of Fort Pitt to the governor's ball. Lord! It had been only four days ago! He had not loved her then.

But he loved her now, and his voice shook. "No. No. They'll not drive you out. Everything is all right, dear." The smile on her burned and blackened face was harder to bear than the burns.

"Truly, Major," she ran on, " 't is a quaint conceit to go barefoot to a ball. 'T would be the rage of London could they but know it." She giggled, and cocked her head. "Listen...."

There was no sound in the drenched forest but the rush of wind and rain, and the drip of water from the sodden branches beside them, but her feet began to beat time against his hip.

"I love violins," she said dreamily.

"Yes," he answered her gently. "We'll go that way."

For the next mile, though his cramped muscles rebelled, he carried her cradled in his arms, her head on his shoulder and her breath alternately warm and cool across his neck, her knees drawn high on his breast to save her feet from the whipping branches.

Her dreams changed. She began to talk soberly to some one she called Bob about a pair of crimson slippers with white satin ties. From the slippers, she went on to some unhappiness that made her twist and sob. Once she cried out angrily:

"He kept me by him, Bob. All night, I tell you!"

And again:

"Never! Never! Never!"

And stopped in the midst of her anger to look up at Leslie, her teeth set between her puffed lips and her eyes hostile.

"Bob will kill you," she told him fiercely. "Bob will kill you with his hands when he knows you have misused me so!"

Leslie went on steadily, wondering into what far places her delirium had carried her, and who Bob might be. At times the living pain broke through her dreams and her eyes went blank; once she cried out shrilly:

"Oh, it hurts...it hurts...it hurts...."

Leslie stopped, thigh deep in running water, and stopped her scream with his hand set hard upon her mouth, and felt tears warm between his fingers He began to search the wooded slopes desperately for some recess that might hide them. No matter how great the risk, he told himself, he must stop soon or he would kill her with pain and exposure.

The hills rose nakedly under the sparse oaks, and offered neither shelter nor concealment. The stream broadened over a smooth gravelly bed and wound through a meadow where marsh marigolds spread a dull glow in the blowing rain. Plumes of water weed clung about his ankles; the gravel bottom softened into silt; slogging through it, he felt the strength of his legs softening, too.

A kingfisher rocketed out of leaning willows just ahead, and his nerves jumped; a kingfisher made a noise like a boy drawing a stick along a paling fence, but it sounded, now, like the rattle of shots. A fish, heavy-bodied, blundered against his shin and was gone; the living touch made his whole body yield, like silt, to the quick thrust of fear. His arms tightened. *Diantha. Diantha.*

The meadow ended, and the stream entered a dripping woodland where underbrush stood darkly on the banks, and dead branches reached up out of the mud to trip him. It wound aimlessly, turning on itself, loooping, getting him nowhere.

But the hills flattened a little, and he found the water deepening. The stream lost itself finally in a sluggish back-water where sticks and dead leaves and matted grass drifted on the surface or hung soddenly beneath it, clogging his legs. He fought through it slowly and came to an opening among the hills where a beaver dam had made a slough; the storm had widened it; trees rose out of floodwater dotted with floating bark and brush. The water ran thinly over the dam; beyond it, between steep banks, he saw the land dropping away to the Allegheny.

He stopped, panting, at the lip of the dam, lifting Diantha higher on his breast to keep her above the water. Bracing one foot in the tangled logs of the dam itself, he freed one arm, and with it made marks on the topmost log, as if a man had lifted himself across it and gone on downstream toward the river. If the five Indians he had killed had been sought by other war-parties, and he was pursued, those tell-tale marks might lead the pursuit to the Allegheny. No Indian, he reasoned, would expect a white fugitive to turn back into the forest here, where the river route to Pitt's Town lay just ahead. He went back slowly through the slough.

It showed him, after half an hour, another opening in the hills, and another stream that ran down from the north. Diantha was moaning again as he turned into it. The current, pressing against his thighs, made him lean forward, his head and shoulders bent above her. They kept the rain from beating on the linsey shirt, stretched taut over her breasts. The soaked cloth defined small, ridged swellings where the charred sticks had blistered her. His legs felt suddenly as weak as water. Weaker than water; the rushing water tried to push them back; he had to fight both the current and his own legs. He began to watch the water, sliding toward him. There was a great deal of water; no matter how hard he fought it, it was still there, driving him back. He asked God to dam it. And then laughed. If God dammed it, he would have to climb over the dam, and he would be too weak. He asked God not to dam it, and laughed again.

Laughing, he almost missed the cloudy dance of sand about his knees.

When he did see it, he stopped and stared at it. The water was full of swirling sand; the current was no longer tearing at his knees, it was going around and around them crazily. He blinked at it, and looked farther on, trying to understand what had happened to the stream, wondering whether he was dizzy.

The sight of the forest startled him. For the forest was lying down.

CHAPTER XVIII

In Which Mr. Leslie Bathes a Lady, and Wooes Her, and Finally Weds Her, Although She Does Not Know It:

LESLIE stood in the swirling water and gaped at the crazy forest. The forest kept on lying down.

Rain ran over his face, into his mouth. He licked at the taste of salt on his lips and, bending, rubbed one cheek against the flesh of his arm to wipe the rain out of his eye. Then he looked at the forest again, and saw that it had not changed.

There were acres of it, prone.

No, not quite prone. Strewn, rather, in a huge windrow. There were hundreds of trees, thousands of trees, all leaning in one direction, slanting as if a gigantic hand had pushed them, bent them far over, and left them lying one upon another.

A hurricane had passed up the valley years before, swinging a freakish scythe.* On one side of the stream, ash and slippery elm grew at the water's edge, and behind them great oaks and beeches stood so close together that there was no underbrush, but a clean floor of leaves; on the other side, the oaks and beeches, and even the slippery elm and the slim swamp ash, lay slanted in a swathe that ran for three-quarters of a mile and then stopped as abruptly as it began. Most of the trees were dead, their roots ripped loose from the rock-filled soil, but between them grew a new generation of the forest, saplings five or six years old, their blowing leaves half hiding the ravage of the hurricane.

Leslie, staring at the grotesque hillside, had a strange feeling that he was looking at the roof of an abandoned cabin; the overlapping trunks were like shingles, warped and weathered; the green sapling tops had the look of moss; here and there the naked boles of the larger trees showed through the moss and the shingles

---

* Doddridge, in his account of the Pennsylvania frontier, speaks of such wind-ravaged woodlands as one of the phenomena of the region at which the early settlers marveled.

like bare rafters. A man could find shelter there. In that tangled ruin, he could lose himself, if he could enter it without leaving a trail. Leslie began to search the edge of the hurricane forest for a way to go in; but the bank was soft, and brush grew rankly there; brambles and creepers wove themselves into a mat among the sapling growth. His eyes came back to the sand that danced and whirled around his knees.

It came, contrarily, upstream. Leslie turned and went back, and found what, in his weariness, he had missed before.

A small, bright current came boiling out of the wrecked forest. It shot out under the trunk of a flattened tree so vigorously that it had gouged a channel of its own athwart the bed of the stream it joined. The two currents, forever struggling, churned the sand into its cloudy dance. Leslie dropped to his knees in the eddy. The small, stout current gurgled around his hips. It was cold—much colder than the main stream; when Diantha's bare feet touched it she stirred and cried out sharply. Leslie lifted the cape and looked at her face; the blisters were larger; the charcoal was smeared across her mouth; her eyes met his and did not know him. Grimly, knowing that it would hurt her burned body, he lowered her into the water, let one knee buckle under him, and sat down with his back to the cold current. He laid his rifle into the water beside the girl, holding it by the sling. Then he put both hands under Diantha's arms and began to push himself backward, bracing his feet in the sand, hitching his body along in jerks. When the fallen tree that lay across the stream was just behind him he reached back and slipped one hand under the trunk, digging his fingers into the bark. Pulling with his one hand, pushing with his feet, his body submerged until the current tugged at his long hair, he hitched himself under the tree and past it, into a dark space laced overhead with vines and alder branches.

He looked behind him, and saw more tree trunks prone or leaning sharply across the stream. But the banks were a little higher, and there was more space between the trunks and the surface of the water. He began to crawl backward, his rifle dragging through the water, the girl's body lying full length on his, the cold current pouring over them both.

The banks rose steadily, criss-crossed with trees. Some of the trees were still alive; the leafed branches of stout willows, of slippery elm, of ash and beech roofed the ravine until, in places, it was like a cave. A hundred yards from the main stream, the banks were high enough so that a man could stand upright beneath the roof. Leslie twisted over onto his knees and lifted Diantha into his arms again. He left the rifle leaning against the bank; it had grown in weight; it was too heavy for his spent arms. His leg muscles shivered as if they were cold; but the quivering, he felt, was inside, against the bones.

The going became easier, the creek bottom firmer. Before he expected it, he reached the end of the ravine. The banks spread apart a little, and then met; they made a bowl ten feet across, six or eight feet deep—a bowl with a lid of matted grapevines and branches. Near the bottom of the bowl, over a lip of projecting rock, spring water gushed into a bubbly pool. Above it, fragments of rock ledge protruded from sandy earth.

Leslie stood in the pool and considered the rocky projections. He might, he thought, climb them with Diantha in his arms; there was nothing else to do; she could not stay here in the bowl; the icy water made it cold. He began to climb the rock steps, slowly, with one elbow thrust out to touch the bank and steady him.

Half way to the top, he let Diantha's body hang altogether in the blanket sling while he caught a stub of dead branch overhead, and then the lip of the bank, and drew himself up. When he rested the girl's weight on the ground and crawled up out of the bowl and lay beside her, he saw that they were in the top of a great fallen beech. He felt, for a moment, dizzy; it was queer to look from the top of a tree toward its bottom—like hanging head downward.

He slipped his head out of the sling, straightened Diantha's sprawled body, and began to crawl away from her, toward the base of the uprooted beech. Twice he stopped, fearful that he would fall; then he went on again; it was hard to remember that the tree was lying on the ground, that he wasn't hanging head downward.

It was a giant of a tree. Falling, it had crushed two stout oaks and a whole group of lithe poplars. They made a jungle of branches through which he had to force his way; but when he was through the tangle, he came out on hands and knees into a clear space thick with dead leaves, roofed by the trunk of the beech tree, and walled on one side by the bent trunks of three poplars. The poplars were alive; their tops, caught under the beech, made a sort of canopy on the other side. Close to the base of the big tree, there was even a narrow space where the dead leaves that covered the ground were almost dry. Leslie crawled swiftly back to Diantha. He hurt her again, dragging her into the shelter he had found, and made her whimper. Then, so suddenly that Leslie's nerves jumped, she cried:

"Bob! Bob! *Ohh,* I hate you!"

And flung herself like an angry child, and lay sobbing on the ground with her blistered face pressed to the dead leaves.

Leslie went back to the spring and brought water in the bark cup. She drank it thirstily, noisily, pushing at the cup; her face, when it touched Leslie's chilled hands, felt hot as fire. The man went to work with anxious haste. He took out of the Indian war-bag his own ruffled shirt and soaked it with cold water and put it on the girl's burning head. He untied the ends of the half-blanket he had carried her in, and spread it over her. Crawling through the underbrush, under the slanting trees, he found a dead poplar, cut away the bark, and whittled off a handful of dry wood; foraging farther, he found smaller dead branches that had been kept dry under the matted ruin of the forest; back in the shelter beneath the giant beech, he shredded some of the driest wood into tinder. A little powder from the Indian horn, flint from his own pouch, the clink of his knife against it, a spurt of fire, and he had a tiny flame licking at the shredded wood. He fed it tenderly until it began to feed itself on the poplar branches; then he piled on more fuel, and scrambled back to the spring.

Squatting there, he scoured the Indians' filthy kettle furiously with sand, pouring the dirty water carefully onto the bank, lest grease and bits of soot float down into the main stream for a possible pursuer to see. By the time he crawled into the shelter again, the fire was going briskly; the space under the fallen beech was warm; the end of the soaked blanket was beginning to steam. With his knife he hacked down a sapling, thrust it deeply into the ground, and hung the kettle on it; into the kettle he dropped bits of the jerked meat he had pillaged from the savages' baggage. Then he went back to the spring and followed the little stream down to its mouth; warm from the fire, he shivered as he let himself into the icy water, but he set his teeth to keep them from chattering, and emerged in the eddy with his confidence growing. The spring was farther from the main stream than he had thought; he had found, he felt, the best hiding place in the whole Allegheny valley. The current, bickering with the larger stream, had gouged away every sign of footprints in the sand.

He crawled back toward the spring. Fifty yards up the ravine, he stood up, threw his arms over the bole of a slippery elm, and swung himself onto it. He crept along the leaning trunk until undergrowth, swarming over it, blocked him; carefully, taking infinite pains to make no cuts where they could be seen from the creek itself, he cut off strips of the bark and stuffed them into his pouch. He came back to the fire with the pouch full, his dripping rifle in his hand.

The kettle was simmering over glowing coals. Diantha lay as if she had not moved. He dipped out a bark cupful of the greasy broth; while it cooled, he took the ruffled shirt to the spring and brought it back, soaked and cold, and put it on her head again. Then, sitting beside her and holding her against his shoulder, he fed her the broth. She drank that, like the water, with greedy, childish noises, until she tired of it. He finished what was left of the broth, half a kettle of it, and went to the spring again to wash the kettle and bring back more water. Warmed, he realized that his muscles had stopped their quivering; he made good time, crawling on one hand and his knees, the swaying kettle held out in front of him. It even amused him to think how quickly he had learned to climb head first down a tree; he did not spill more than a little of the water.

Diantha was asleep. He touched her arm, above the elbow, where there were no burns, and took his hand away quickly. There was no time for tenderness. She needed surgeons, nurses, a bed, oils to ease the burns, medicine to break the fever....

He hung the kettle above the coals, and went crawling for more wood. There was plenty of that, dry enough, under the wreckage of the forest. By the time the water was hot to the touch, he had a heap of fuel in the shelter; his drenched leggings and breechclout were steaming, and the edge of the blanket nearest the fire was dry.

No surgeon. No nurse. He must be all of these. He lifted the blanket gently, lest he wake her, and hung it on sticks before the fire; kneeling, he drew open the flaps of the hunting shirt and slipped it down, drawing it clear of her; he had to lift her to free her arms from the sleeves, but she did not stir when he laid her down again. He tore off part of the ruffled shirt, dipped it into the warm water, and began to bathe her.

It took him hours, so fearful were his hands of hurting her. The charcoal was ground into her flesh where the hot sticks had left scratches as well as burns. He cleansed them all, though his hands shook before he had finished, and Diantha's moans made him catch his breath at her suffering. The burns, puffed white, with angry, blotched red spreading around them, looked worse when he saw them against her white skin. Once, under his breath, he told her that he loved her, and when she only moaned again he crouched over her, his hands on her shoulders, shaking her, asking her to hear him. Instantly, he was sorry; but she did not wake. He realized then that she was more in stupor than asleep, and fear came back. Dabbling at the caked blood where the brambles had raked her legs, he prayed again:

"God...God...." One word, repeated. He was not good at praying.

The blanket was dry when he finished bathing her. He lifted her, pulling the hunting shirt from beneath her, spreading the blanket in its place, and put her down again. Then he hung the shirt to dry, and left her lying in the steaming warmth of the shelter while he went for more water. She did not move while he was gone; the remnant of ruffled shirt on her forehead did not seem as hot as it had been; he wet it again in the fresh water and smoothed it over her head. In spite of himself, his fingers ran along her temples and touched her closed eyes. Kneeling beside her, he shredded the elm bark shavings in his pouch into the kettle and hung it above the fire. There was, he realized, only a little daylight left. What there was of it, he used to bring in more wood, to find dry grass and heap it into a pillow for Diantha, to cut brush with his knife and pile it against the trunks of the three bent poplars until he had a rude brush wickiup with two sides; the trunk of the beech made the roof, and its roots, still covered with torn-up sod, made a third side.

When the hunting shirt was dry, he dressed her in it once

more, and put the pillow of grass under her head. The space under the giant beech grew dark. Leslie let the fire dwindle to a handful of coals, and fed it with twigs, keeping the kettle simmering slowly. When the fire was low, he went to the far end of the brush wall and stripped off his own soaked clout, leggings and moccasins, and stealthily, lest he rouse the girl, hung them from projecting twigs. Then, naked, he sat down to his weapons, wiped them, cleaned them, and charged them afresh.

The familiar task eased his fear a little. It was easier, too, to think. But there was little to think about to any purpose, he found. He had done what he could. He had left no trail, except the signs he had made deliberately on the beaver dam, hoping to mislead any pursuit that might come. He did not believe there would be any pursuit.... Venango, Le Boeuf, Fort Pitt itself were prizes too rich to be neglected for the sake of pursuing one white man and one girl, even if a war party suspected they were hiding in the forest. If they were pursued, and found, he had chosen the best position he could. No war party could rush him through the tangle of fallen timber, nor creep up on him unaware except by way of the little stream. From the spring, they would have to come through brush and leaves; even an Indian must make noise enough to warn him. Unless they came in numbers, he would have a chance—as much of a chance as he had had when he looked down at Diantha's torture stake. There was nothing more he could do but wait.

His body waited, but his mind would not wait. It went racing up and down, as restless, he mocked at it, as the dog Robin. Robin....

It was not pleasant to remember that on the morning he adopted Robin, he had stood in Tom Yeardley's window and seen Diantha Gail flogged, and gone back to bed cynically pleased that a woman should suffer at the hands of a man. He would not think of it now; he had made—he would make such amends as he could. His mind ran on. It was at Leslie Hall before he could call it back. Leslie Hall, with its four chimneys marching black across the morning. The pungey, still loaded, nudging against the wharf. Evelyn Gentle's arms around his neck.... Evelyn Gentle's breast pressing against him....

Pagh! Evelyn Gentle....*Evelyn Leslie,* standing under the tree

216

they called after Judas Iscariot. He was glad he had remembered to tell her that. *Zooks,* he had been a rich man that morning... or thought he was. Now he sat here mother naked. He had hated women, that morning, too. And now he loved a woman so that he was willing to spend his life for her. No, it was more than that; he considered the thing somberly. He was startled, even now, to realize that if Diantha Gail did not live, he would not care for his life. He laughed inwardly. For a man whose pride was the cool Leslie blood, he had done strange things... wanting to kill Romney Clawther at Upper Marlboro because he laughed at a castoff lover ... and now, looking with approval on the end of his own life, on the chance that a bond maid might not live. *Gadzooks,* it took a cool head and a cooler heart to stand heat like that. The inward laugh forced his breath out harshly. Laughing, he heard other laughter...Dick Lawless' ribald laughter...and Kildane saying: "Red hair; neatest ankles west of London; rest of her to match, I'll wager. Whyn't you find out, Leslie?"

His restless mind pounced on that stray memory. Red hair. Ay, and neat ankles. But he had not bought her for that. He had bought her for the fear and the fearlessness in her gray eyes; for the sturdy tilt of her chin, defying them; for the drum-major courage of her slim shoulders. He had bought five years of her life...for a few guineas; he had paid more for a coat. Now he had nothing; and he would pay everything for her. Then he thought:

There is nothing to pay. She belongs to me. But not because I bought her. My father bought a wife; I wouldn't.

A wife! Queer...he had not thought of her as his wife. He had merely thought of her as belonging to him. Now he corrected the thought: he belonged to her. He loved her, he had followed her, he had fought for her, he was her surgeon, her nurse, her husband even—but she did not know any of that. He would have to wait to tell her. He would have to wait until she was well of the fever; no, until she was safe. He thought:

That is the way it is; it is complete, for me; I belong to her. But it is not complete for her, yet; she does not know I love her; she does not know she belongs to me. Until she knows, she doesn't.

He was strangely satisfied. His mind jumped ahead. He saw the limestone manor house and, a mile away on the next spur, the slate roof of Near-the-Navel shining in the sun. He saw the wheat fields rolling away to the Conococheague; the freighters' wagons and the pack beasts from the Forks of the Ohio winding up South Mountain to the new Leslie Hall; chariots and coaches and gay horsemen from Baltimore and Annapolis swinging in at a gallop between the stone gate-posts; hunting parties going out at dawn; a lovely woman, with no powder to hide the golden glory of her hair, ruling, in the limestone manor house, a bright world of her own.

He looked across the point of fire to the shadows where Diantha lay. He had told her about South Mountain, and the manor, but he had not told her about the golden-haired woman who would live there with him. He would have to tell her that.

He got to his feet and went to nurse the fire. His clout and leggings were dry, and he dressed himself slowly. When he had finished, he crept to Diantha and put a cautious hand to her cheek. It was definitely cooler. He took the remnant of linen shirt down to the spring and brought it back dripping, wrung it out, and laid it gently on her forehead. She moved restlessly, and he crouched motionless until she was still; by morning, he thought, he could soothe the pain of the burns a little; until then he hoped she would sleep. He went back to the fire and sat down, his rifle across his knees.

The wind strengthened, and new gusts of rain spat through the ravaged woods. Between them, wind and rain made so much noise he could not hear other sounds; he stayed awake, one hand balanced on the end of an upright stick. When he dozed, the stick slipped to one side or the other and his hand, dropping, woke him up. Toward morning, the rain stopped, and the wind went away; he let the fire die. He had to sleep, a little. In this retreat, he felt, there would be the least danger in the deep darkness before daylight; even for an Indian, the hurricane forest would be a veritable *chevaux-de-frise* in the dark. He lay down quietly beside the girl, his weapons at his hand. To make sure he would know it if she woke, he slipped one arm gently under her neck; there were no burns there. She moved, and turned her face toward him; then, with her cheek on his bare arm, she was still again. Leslie smiled at her. She did not know, yet, that she belonged to him.

No, that was not it. He belonged to her; he should not be getting

218

things mixed up that way. He was her husband; but she would not be his wife until they were safe in Fort Pitt again. *Zooks,* it made poor sense. But it was so. No matter. He wondered what the marriage service said; words; they could not change his sense of belonging to Diantha Gail, nor strengthen it. When she was well and safe, she would be his wife. He fell asleep smiling.

And it was Diantha who awoke first.

Her mind was clear. She was conscious of pain, like a garment, around her body; but the garment did not press as hot and tight as it had in her dreams. She was not surprised that Arnett Leslie lay there beside her. Feverish and raving, she had known that he was with her. Lying motionless now, she understood something of what had happened.

Leslie had followed her. He had fought for her, and saved her. She knew, vaguely, that he had carried her, how long or how far she had no idea. Far and long, she thought, as she lay watching his face. It was thick with stubble; and there was a wound on his temple, ugly and swollen, and crusted with dirt. Across one cheek ran three scratches, beaded with dried blood.

She saw, then, that he was naked to the waist; and realized, for the first time, that she was dressed in his hunting shirt. His chest was dark with powder stain, though she thought it was dirt. Across it ran a smooth streak, brighter than his skin; she put out one hand and touched it softly; it felt slick, almost brittle, like vellum. A scar; it was widest just above his heart. Some one had said, she remembered, that Major Leslie had fought the Shawnees, and a Shawnee hatchet had all but killed him. She put the tips of her fingers on the scar again. *If it had killed him ...*

The motion of her arm opened the hunting shirt on her breast. She saw that her breasts were white, with red blotches. When she had seen them before, they had been smeared with black ... they had hurt like fire....

She choked back the scream that came into her throat. *Foolish, to want to scream now.*

They still hurt, but the hurt was nothing to what had gone before. And her flesh was white. Arnett Leslie had bathed her, before he dressed her in his own clothing. Diantha lifted herself on one elbow and leaned toward the bearded face. It was thin ... thin ...

"Oh, I love you. I love you," she whispered, and kissed him on the mouth. His beard sent a shock of pain through her cheek, where the fire had blistered it. She kissed him again.

Then, softly, she lay down, her head where he had had it when she woke. She thought:

He gave me his fine bed, from London, and did not ask to share it. Now this.

She looked up wonderingly at the trunk of the great beech, and at the brush walls he had made. Smiling, she went contentedly to sleep.

When she woke again, Leslie was kneeling beside her. She lifted her arms to him. Lifted them, and let them fall, shocked.

The hunting shirt was gone. And Leslie's eyes, intent on her body, ignored her arms. His hands touched her thighs. She cried out sharply:

"No! No!"

To Leslie, it was one more of the cries of pain he had heard for two nights and a day. He put one hand firmly on her shoulder and pressed her back upon the blanket; her eyes, startled, seemed as black and blank as they had been when she talked wildly of going to the governor's ball in a riding-chair, and of Bob, and of a pair of crimson slippers. He went on with the business of being surgeon and nurse. And Diantha saw, finally, that he had a black kettle beside him. He plunged his hand into it and brought it out dripping and brown; some of the drops spattered on her body warmly. His hand brushed, warm and wet, across one of the burns on her thigh; went back to the kettle; brushed at her waist where the charred brands had girdled her with black.

Diantha, watching him, saw his face calm and still. It was not the face of a man in love. He worked briskly. His hands, intimate, were as impersonal as the dry leaves she lay upon. Her face burned with a rush of blood. Arnett Leslie had said he despised women. No; he had said that he despised one woman, and that he would let himself have no feeling at all for any other woman. He had followed her because he felt responsible for her; because Watson had not set her free. She was a duty.

Leslie, gently spreading on her burned breasts the thick elm-bark liquor he had brewed, saw her cheeks wet with tears. He wiped them away with the ruffled shirt before he began to smear the brown mixture on her face. When he had finished, and covered her again with the hunting shirt, he spoke to her. Her name, without an endearment to tell her the truth. She did not answer him, because she knew the answer would end in a sob. Leslie went quietly away.

Later on, he made broth again, and fed her; and she drank obediently from the bark cup. Watching him, when his eyes were on the cup, or the kettle, or on the business of laying her down again, she saw no sign that he loved her. The cool Leslie was in command; the compact he had made with himself, and with her, while she lay asleep, had left him content. *It is this way; I belong to her; when she is well and safe, she will belong to me.* He refused, sternly, to let himself go beyond that.

He realized, in the late afternoon, that her face was hot again. At dusk, stooping over the spring to wet the compress for her head, he heard a musket shot. It was not close; the hills and the woods dulled it. Then there were more shots. Coming swiftly through the tangle of branches, he found Diantha sitting upright, careless of the shirt hanging open, her face strained with fear. He made her lie down again; talked to her softly; smoothed the cold cloth over her temples. A little later, he heard the first scream. It was faint; it was far away; but it had unspeakable anguish in it.

Diantha, too, heard it. She sat up; twisted over onto hands and knees; Leslie caught her trying to tear her way through the brush wall with her fingers. The second scream was hers.

"Diantha ... Diantha, dear ... dear...."

She clung to him in terror, but the words he murmured to her meant nothing. Her body shuddered. Through the dark, the distant screams came one after another. Leslie left her long enough to smother the fire. When he came back to her, she fought him, and then clung to him again. He lay down with her, because she would not lie down alone. For hours, listening to the unceasing wails, he heard her voice, hoarse, unnatural, raving that she could not bear the pain; he knew that the burns still hurt, but that the pain she felt was the fierce bite of coals upon her flesh. She was back once more in the glade, with the braided scalplock on its hoop before her, and the stake whitening to a point.

Leslie, lying with his arms around her, wondered, with the emptiness of fear within him, what the distant screaming meant.

The torture stake, he knew, and a man dying there, or longing to die. But whether it meant that Fort Venango had been taken, or only that a white man had been caught alive, he could not guess. At daylight, the screams stopped. Diantha's body was burning with fever; he left her, that day, only to get cold water for her lips and head. He did not make a fire.

After dark, the screams began again. They went on most of the second night. After they stopped, a red glare rose and spread across the sky, northward, up the valley.

Leslie knew that Venango had fallen, and that he was closer to it than he had supposed.

He knew, too, that Diantha was growing worse. The shirt, soaked from the spring, turned hot in minutes when he put it on her forehead. Her cheeks and her neck were as red as the burns; her voice became a harsh whisper; her tongue fumbled at her dry lips and blurred her words so that he could not understand half she said. He carried her out through the hurricane woods the next morning, forcing his way through the matted brush, careless of the trail he left. His reason told him that the Indians who took Venango and burned it would be well on their way to Fort Pitt; his fear for Diantha told him that whether they had gone or not, he must hurry...hurry.... He did not dare to take her into the icy water of the spring, as he had before. He thought it would kill her.

He carried her all day.

Near sundown, he saw a beaten trail at his feet, and on it the tracks of many men. They all pointed south. He followed them, head bent above the limp body in his arms, his moccasins shuffling, his own body shuddering with exhaustion.

A hundred yards down the trail, hands reached out from the underbrush and seized him by both arms at once. He snarled at them, fighting with his feet, wrenching one arm free, striking out in blind despair. A voice said:

"Steady! Steady! Here, Braams, take the girl. Gently, now. God, she's been burned...."

He saw splotches of scarlet, a cocked hat, a white cross-belt vivid in the twilight. The voice said again:

"Steady, man. I'm Ensign Price, from Fort Le Boeuf. Are you from Venango?"

"No," Leslie croaked at him. "No. Fort Pitt."

"Good God, they haven't taken Fort Pitt!"

"No. No. She was...on way...to Venango." The ensign set a canteen at his mouth; Leslie swallowed, and licked his lips. "They got her. Started to torture her. She has fever...."

"Stab me, you've a pretty fever yourself. Do you know anything of Fort Pitt? How long...?"

"Four..." Leslie began. "Five...seven days ago. Attacked. Ecuyer burned the town."

"They burned Le Boeuf over our heads. Chopped our way out. Seven of us got this far. They've burned Venango, too; we passed it today. Can you walk?"

"Yes. She..."

"We'll carry her, turn and turn about. Planned to keep to the trail all night. Thought the red devils would look for us anywhere but there. Eh?"

"Yes. I was doing that, too. She needs a surgeon, soon ... soon."

"Your wife?"

"Not...yet."

He saw a giant of a man in a scorched red coat swing Diantha easily into his arms.

"Eighty miles, I make it," the ensign was saying.

The seven Royal Americans moved out along the trail. They marched all night. A little after daylight, they came to the skeleton of the Nancy mare, and saw two sated buzzards lumbering into the air. A soldier clubbed one down with his musket barrel.

"Pull the feathers," Price told him. "Got the notion from that beastly war-hat of yours," he added to Leslie. "We thought you were an Indian, when we saw you first. Came damnably close to giving you the bayonet. These feathers, now; maybe we can slip throught, at night; throw away these tricorns, eh?"

They marched the eighty miles in two nights and days, without food except the pemmican and the remnant of the jerked beef in Leslie's pouch. Price, pushing on ahead, found the bark huts of Shertee's town as empty as they had been the day Leslie rode through on his wounded horse. Hidden in the rank growth along the Allegheny at dusk, the eight white men saw the glare of the Indian campfires light the sky around Fort Pitt. Price came and squatted beside Leslie where he sat with Diantha's head and shoulders cradled in his arms.

"What is it, Major?" he asked. "You've more to lose than the rest of us. Shall we cross here? Or try it farther down?"

"Farther down," Leslie answered with stiff lips. *You've more to lose,* Price had said. Yes, that was it. That made it hard to choose. If he chose wrongly...His voice steadied. "All the way down, Price, I think; right across from the fort. We could get over the river here, or at a dozen other places; but there would still be the half mile of open ground to cross where the town was. The Indians will be there. The cellars are trenches for them, ready to use."

"What d'you want to do, Leslie, follow the river?"

"No. Back, just this side the crest of the hills. Their camps will be on the other side of the hills; the warriors will be down on the river bank, or across, in Pitt's Town. The best chance will be between them. What do you think, Price?"

"The hills it is. God, Leslie, it's quiet. D'you suppose they've taken Pitt, too?"

"With those walls?" He stopped. Price picked up his unspoken thought.

"Those walls...ay. Brick in front. But mud on the three river faces, and half the mud washed down into the moat. And the moat bone dry."

Hours later, stealing among open woods above the Allegheny, they saw that Fort Pitt had not been taken.

It was ringed with jumping flashes.

"Stab me, it's like fireflies in a circle," Price whispered.

The thuds of the muskets came faintly, a harmless sound; stones dropped into an empty wooden bucket would make a sound like it. The weary Le Boeuf men huddled together in a shallow ravine, waiting and listening. They had cast away their cocked hats; some of them had buzzard feathers in their hair.

Price put his hand on Leslie's wrist.

"Look!" A spark was climbing across the sky, arching in a graceful curve, dropping. "They're trying to burn the fort! A hundred women and a hundred children in there! Damn them! Damn them! Damn them!"

CHAPTER XIX

*In Which Is Told How Arnett Leslie Came to Fort Pitt Again, and
What a Strange Welcome He Found There:*

THE fire arrow winked out. Fort Pitt became only a darker
mass between the faintly luminous rivers.

"Shall we try it?" The ensign's whisper at Leslie's
shoulder was hardly louder than a drawn breath.

"If we had just fifteen minutes more...." Leslie felt his thighs
quiver with utter weariness. Perhaps the weariness was in his brain,
too, for he felt a surge of futile anger as he looked at the sky
above Grant's Hill.... "The moon's rising; by the time we can
get to the river, 't will be like crossing it in broad daylight."

He sensed the sagging of Price's body.

"I'd be for making a run for it...or trying to get one man
through the beasts. A sortie, now...or a few round shot to cover
the rush...."

Leslie knew they were thinking the same thought. Men—even
these haggard, exhausted men—might stake their lives on a rush
to the river and a hand-to-hand fight with the savages hemming
in the fort on the opposite bank. Neither Arnett Leslie nor the
ensign from Le Boeuf dared risk Diantha's life in that desperate
chance until there was no other chance to take.

"Best get as close as we can before it's too light," Leslie whispered. "They'll scarce be watching very sharp *behind* them."

"They'll be all along the river bank...."

"Ay. But not in the thick growth this side the bank. The willow
scrub grows rank there, just below the crossing."

Price's fingers on his wrist gave assent.

They stole back to the waiting men. The giant Swiss picked
up Diantha. In single file they followed Leslie down into the
rolling lowland.

He struck straight across the open ground; boldness had brought
them safely down the Venango trail; boldness seemed wiser here

as well. If there were savages camped in the river bottoms, they would be less suspicious of a file of feathered riflemen, hurrying toward the firing line, than of men crouching or crawling.

Back in the hills, dogs yapped and howled. At intervals the blunt explosion of a trade musket came from the Indian burrows across the Allegheny. Once—only once—the sharp crack of a rifle answered them; it brought a wild yelling and a splatter of firing from the besiegers.

Leslie stumbled into a dry gully cutting through the baked mud flats. He followed its meanderings, the column moving soundlessly behind him on the smooth sand of the cut. It twisted its way into dense growth. The rest was simple; it was easy to wait for a burst of firing, and push through the tangle, while the rolling echoes covered the noise, into the heart of the thicket where the darkness gave proof that the shelter was dense enough to offer complete concealment.

Leslie left the others there, half of them asleep, Price and the other half on guard, and wormed his way toward the Allegheny. It was close by—closer even than he had expected. Under the overhanging bank across the river, he picked out five savages. Lower down, a curve of the river hid the rest; but toward morning, cramped from his long vigil, he saw a dozen of them slip down to the shore and into the water. They got across, only their heads showing, one hand balancing musket and powder horn on their scalplocks. A little later, when the moon dropped behind the hills, the five nearest the fort crossed too, and ran slinkingly into the willows a hundred yards up stream. Leslie felt certain that they stayed there. He stole through his own covert to its upstream edge, and by daybreak was amazed by proof that he was right. With an audacity he had never seen before, the Indians in the willows built a fire. Apparently they had no concern at all about being fired on from the fort; the smoke of their fire was well within range of the cannon on the walls, but it rose in a thick blue column for an hour or more, and gradually thinned and wisped away.

Experience had convinced them, Leslie speculated, that the garrison would not waste ammunition by firing into underbrush without a target to aim at. It was not hard to guess that there was little enough powder in the magazine in Fort Pitt.

He crept into the heart of the tangle. Price nipped off a twig and chewed it reflectively when Leslie whispered his news of the Indians in the next thicket.

"I've heard it said the hinges of hell get devilish hot," he murmured, grinning, "what with the doors opening so often to let poor sinners in, but I misdoubt they get hotter than we shall get by noon. We'll do a proper simmer here when the sun stands over us, eh? Pho! You must be dead, Major; I'll slip out and keep an eye on them, Leslie. Get a few winks; there's nought else to do."

Price slipped away through the foliage. Leslie looked to the priming of rifle and pistol, and lay down. Even after hours of darkness, the baked earth seemed to give off heat; it would be stifling here in the river bottoms by midday. He slept with the smell of heated earth in his nostrils and the drone of insects in his ears. Arm's length away, as he closed his eyes, he saw the shapeless bundle of dirty rags that bound Diantha's feet.

He dreamed that it was burning coals, not rags, that covered Diantha's feet. He struggled to reach her, and woke with the smell of hot earth stronger and the drone of the insects louder. It was much louder—too loud to be insects at all. It was the drone of voices, singing. He sat up, startled.

The scarecrow soldiers were all standing, weapons clutched across their bodies, eyes fixed on the choked passages between the willow clumps. Diantha lay at their feet, her cheeks red as the raw scars, her lips pinched and white.

The willows toward the river stirred. Rifle barrels swung; out of the scrub, Price's corporal came, stooping, his hand beckoning Leslie.

"Dey be paradin' an' cavortin' by da ford," the corporal whispered. "Da ensign want you coom."

Price was kneeling in the edge of the covert. His eyes flicked up at Arnett, and back to the river bank.

Four savages, gaudy with paint and feathers, were stalking along the water's edge, singing. One of them flaunted a strand of wampum, shaking it toward the fort. Two of them had small British flags in their hands, waving them in time with the chant. Leslie knelt beside the ensign.

"Ottawas," Price whispered in his ear. "That's their way of ask-

227

ing a parley. I'll lay ten to one it's a trick. I swear there's more of them in the brush. Hah...look!"

Above the palisades on the Music bastion, a man in a hunting shirt stood out alone, bareheaded. He raised one hand, and his voice came across the water in a clear halloo.

"McKee, the trader," Leslie breathed.

The song stopped. The naked Ottawa with the blue wampum string flourished it overhead, and began a high-pitched harangue. McKee answered him in his own tongue.

"They want a canoe," Price murmured. "Want to go to the fort to talk."

A man in a scarlet tunic appeared beside the trader, briefly. There was a sudden bustle in the bastion. A gunport opened and the nose of a howitzer poked out. Around the angle of the bastion, outside the wall, two soldiers in waistcoats came running down toward the landing where three canoes lay drawn up on the bank. They came empty-handed, except for their paddles.

"They're coming over!" Price glanced at Leslie. Leslie nodded. "Corporal, go bring all our people to the edge of the underbrush here. Quiet...quiet, for your life." The corporal slipped away.

The two colonials got into one of the canoes and shoved off. Leslie's eyes and ears strained for some sign of the ambush he was sure had been laid in the rank growth of the flats.

The canoe was shooting swiftly across the current, the soldiers paddling as if they were anxious to have the job over and done with. The four Ottawas huddled together a little way from the water, waiting.

Leslie looked over his shoulder and caught Braams' eye; the giant's bristled face ducked in a quick nod as Leslie's glance went past him to Diantha....

The canoe slid its nose into the mud; the soldiers stepped out over the prow and came toward the Indians, side by side. They took six paces, and the Ottawas sprang. Two of them grappled the smaller man before he could raise his paddle to strike. The other beat down the reaching hands with frantic blows, turned, and ran for the canoe. The Ottawa who had flourished the wampum belt of friendship crouched, snatched a short knife from his moccasin, and bounded after him. The blade flashed once as it drove through the back of the waistcoat between the shoulder blades.

The colonial plunged on, three staggering strides. As the knife jerked out, he turned desperately and struck. The Indian leaped back and the blow missed. The wounded man took three more slow steps forward before he fell face down in the mud. The Ottawa sprang at him. The ensign raised his rifle; but Leslie put a hand on his wrist and he dropped it again.

"Wait . . . wait!" he whispered hoarsely. *"There . . . !"*

Out of the willows upstream burst a dozen naked warriors, yelling. The soldier struggling with three savages by the ford saw them coming; fear frenzied him; he got one hand free, drove his fist into a painted face, wrenched loose, and ran. His comrade wriggled futilely, face down in the mud, naked knees digging into his bleeding back as the Ottawa seized him by the queue and set the knife blade at its roots.

"Now!"

Price shot the kneeling Indian through the ribs; the heavy ball lifted him off the colonial and threw him into the dry reeds beside the path. He lay on his back, kicking, jerking. Leslie shot down the foremost of the yelling Indians running down the bank.

Over him, two of Price's regulars fired; and like an echo of the two big muskets discharged beside their ears, two more of Price's men fired from the undergrowth near by.

There were five painted bodies squirming or lying quiet on the river bank. The rest of the savages stood momentarily paralyzed by the ambuscade into which their own treacherous ambush had plunged them. Before they could move either to attack or fly, two more of the Le Boeuf men crashed through the willows and blazed into them, and the howitzer in the Music bastion caught them with a burst of grape-shot.

There were soldiers all along the palisades of the bastion now, and on the flanking walls, staring with astounded eyes at the bearded, ragged men who broke from the willows and ran in desperate haste for the river. They saw one man, naked to the waist, with a dirty bandage around his head, stop in the open path, whip his rifle to his shoulder, and fire; saw two warriors, braver than the rest, rush down the bank with hatchets in their hands; saw him thrust the muzzle of his rifle into one vermilion stomach like a spear, and meet the other Ottawa with a sidewise leap and a circling blow that did not quite block the tomahawk.

Then a tall soldier with a bundle in his arms ran out of the thicket, tumbled his burden into the canoe, and went leaping up the bank to join the fight, his musket by the muzzle in both hands.

The ragged men on the shore shoved the canoe out of the mud. Two of them got to the paddles. One, his rifle clutched across his body, stood facing the willows, waiting. The rest plunged into the river and started across, wading, swimming, floundering.

A bullet cut the water beside the canoe, and the waiting rifleman fired into the puff of smoke that rose in the bushes; then he, too, ran for the Allegheny and plunged in.

Behind him, Braams' musket whirled, and the trigger guard cut like an ax blade into a shaven skull and the stock broke off and flew into the willows. With the splintered remnant, Braams beat down a savage who clung to Leslie's arm with one hand while he drove his hatchet again and again at the white man's face.

"We go now?"

Leslie jerked his leg clear of the squirming body on the ground. He was panting, and trickles of blood were running down from a long gash across his chest; Braams saw that he was smiling.

"Come on, they're going to make it across." Together they sprang down the bank. The howitzer banged again, and its canister of bullets ripped and whistled just over the heads of the two running for the river's edge.

Braams ducked, and Leslie laughed aloud—a startling sound in the bloody, trampled flat. As they splashed into the shallows, the giant turned his bristly face toward him across one ripped shoulder, and showed his teeth in a slow grin.

"I stoop down yust in time," he observed mildly, and Leslie laughed again.

It was a relief to laugh—to dare to laugh. The current received him, lifted him, carried him along easily. They went toward the mud fort on a long, slanting course across the river. Leslie laughed again as the howitzer sent another canister of screaming balls overhead, and a chorus of furious howls rose from the western bank around one high-pitched, astonished yelp of pain. Braams, a yard ahead of him, set his feet firmly in the silt and waited for him.

"You be sick in da head, no?" he inquired. "*Ja,* so; poot your hand on my shoulder. I saw how he w'ack you on da head. *Ja,*

girl needed...Damn them, they were jostling her from one to another again. He began to run, up the slope. A private of regulars grasped at his bare arm, and Braams growled and struck the soldier's hand down. Running, the two uncouth figures came to the single log that lay as a bridge across the moat, below the Music bastion.

Braams would have plunged on across, but Leslie stopped him.

A man in a blue coat with gold lacing on the sleeves was taking Diantha's limp body out of Arnold's arms. His pale, drawn face bent over hers, and his red hair, all awry, fell forward over his eyes as he yearned toward her.

"There..." Leslie heard Arnold's voice, thin, triumphant over something he did not understand. "There, that's one of them! That's Leslie!"

Across twelve feet of ditch, he looked into bloodshot eyes, deeply sunk between cheekbones on which freckles stood out in harsh splotches. And heard a low, deadly voice saying:

"Let no one touch him. If he does not hang, no one shall kill him but me."

Leslie began to laugh. The red-haired man took one furious step toward him, then turned and went at a shuffling run through the tunnel under the bastion wall. Leslie did not look after him. He merely stood and laughed, weak laughter that he had no will to stop. It was, after all, very funny. Now that the furious young man whose red hair and freckles matched Diantha's had gone, he saw who had been standing there beside him in the sally port; and he could not help laughing.

He bowed, and found that the empty ditch started to fly up in his face; so he put out one hand and steadied himself with his fingers in the torn place on Braams' shirt. With the shirt to support him, he found that he could bow without danger of toppling into the moat.

"My Lord Lawless, your humble servant," he called, and essayed another bow. "Did ye come for that second shot? And all those miles, too! And Tom! Don't tell me ye've wrecked that noble coach already, and come hunting for a new one. 'Y gad, Tom, I'm just out of coaches!"

He heard Dick Lawless squealing:

"Stop him! Stop him! He's still a pistol to his hand!"

233

And saw Tom Yeardley run out upon the single log that spanned the moat, his heavy face thrusting forward, his mouth wide open as he shouted:

"Steady, Arnett! For God's sake, don't make it any worse!"

Which was nonsense, and Leslie decided to say so; the feeling of relief was strong upon him, and he resented this dramatic commotion, this bursting excitement. He wanted to rest. He was conscious of resentment toward his own mind as much as toward Tom Yeardley and Dick Lawless; he wanted his mind to rest, but it insisted on staying wide awake, alert with a strained intensity that took in every detail of dry-mud wall, of the sharp points of palisades ranged above it, of faces peering between the points. After days and nights when it had been torture to keep his eyes open, they persisted now in telling him that Valentine Arnold's white crossbelts were in need of fresh pipe-clay, that Dick Lawless had tricked himself out in a hunting shirt of yellow buckskin all adangle with foppish red thrums and stiff with beadwork, that Tom Yeardley had cherokeed his hair so that it stood up in bristles like a worn and faded harness-brush.

Tom was almost across the moat. Leslie saw his roached hair looming up, larger, impossibly larger; he could not tell Tom's hair from the wavering line of the palisade behind it. Tom, and Lawless, and Arnold's red tunic and the black wall became hopelessly mixed up; they became huge, and they would not stand still. All at once, so slowly that he thought they were bowing to him with grave politeness, they all leaned forward and fell into the ditch, and the fort toppled in upon them.

Somehow, Arnett was underneath, where the bottom of the ditch should be. But the ditch had no bottom at all; he went down and down. The Allegheny river began to run into the ditch. When all the water in the Allegheny was gone, the Monongahela came down from the other side of the fort and tried to fill up the ditch, too. But there really was no bottom to it. It struck Leslie as being a very foolish waste of water, pouring the rivers into a bottomless ditch in that way; he tried to tell somebody about it. If the siege went on long enough, the people in the fort would need that water to drink.

Then he remembered that the fort had fallen into the ditch, so it was all right. They wouldn't need water any more.

He went to sleep very comfortably.

234

CHAPTER XX

In Which Mr. Leslie Learns Somewhat of the Faith and the Faithlessness of Women; and Mislikes Both the Lessons:

LATER—a long time later—Leslie saw that something would have to be done about the river that was pouring into the ditch. The ditch, he discovered, had a bottom after all; he was lying on it, and it was hard; and the water was rising and wetting him. It was exasperating; he did not want to be disturbed. When the water, dark and stifling, came over his mouth and his eyes, he protested petulantly:

"Let be! Let be!"

Somebody laughed, a low, throaty laugh. He opened his eyes, and saw a hand poised with a dripping towel just over his chin, and beyond the hand a plump brown arm and a brown, merry face intent on some task that seemed to be highly amusing. He felt some rough covering being drawn up along his body. The sopping towel dripped on his face and neck, and he said *"Peggy!"* very loudly and impatiently.

The brown face turned toward him, and Peggy Sargent, between laughing and crying, put her lips where the cold drops had fallen on his cheek, and then put them on his mouth, warmly, with her hands cradling his face.

"That," said a grumpy voice somewhere overhead, "will either kill him or cure him. Come away, ye flibbertigibbet."

"Boyd!"

"Good morning to ye. I'll come an' pay ye a professional call when this shameless hussy let's ye be."

"Shameless!" Peggy straightened up, arms akimbo, the blood beating hotly along her throat. "I take shame for all of you. The best man in the whole dirty garrison, and you clap him in the guardhouse...!"

"Hm." Boyd came around the head of the bed and pushed her aside with a roughness that was all but affectionate. "He may be the best, an' then he may not; but I'll lay a month's pay, Leslie, that ye're the cleanest. She's scrubbed ye an' scoured ye an' tended ye like a babe in arms. How's that head of yours?"

Leslie shook his head gingerly, and then explored it with his fingers. One side of it had grown enormously. He spoke with rueful humor:

"Ugh, it feels a deal like a pudding bag that's been left overlong in the oven. It didn't burst, did it?"

Peggy laughed, and rubbed her hand across her eyes. Boyd sat down heavily on the side of the bed opposite her, and expelled his breath with a grunt.

"No. Ye're the luckiest devil I ever saw, Leslie—and the unluckiest. When ye took French leave ten days ago, all the rules said ye should have died of it. Ye come back with a fresh crack on the noddle, and damme if ye aren't cured; all ye needed was sleep, an' ye've had that. And *baths!*"

Leslie's fingers told him that some one had put a clean, smooth bandage on his head; exploring further, while Boyd and Peggy watched him, he found that his chest, too, was swathed with bandages. He lay relaxed on the hard bed, and breathed deeply. With each breath, some of the strain seemed to run out of his body and leave it soothed. He turned his head experimentally on the folded blanket beneath it and found, instead of rough beard tearing at the wool, a sense of smoothness; he was shaved and even—he sniffed the blanket suspiciously—perfumed with bay rum. He essayed to stretch, and then, when it did not hurt, he did it again, luxuriously.

"Peggy," he smiled, "is there any of the river left?"

"The river?"

"I dreamed I had fallen into the ditch, and the fort on top of me, and that the Mon was running in. I was furious about it, because the ditch had no bottom, and all the water was going to waste." He chuckled, and stretched again, like a lazy cat.

"You did fall into the ditch," Peggy told him, her face sober.

"No! Did I now? But the fort did not fall on me? Lord, I've had the wildest dreams. People from Maryland all over the place—Dick Lawless, that I had the duel with, and Tom Yeardley, who stole my coach to fetch me home." He lay a moment silent. Peggy

Sargent smoothed the blanket meticulously across his chest; Boyd fussed with a roll of lint.

"Diantha . . . ?"

Peggy's hand pressed heavily for an instant, and went on with its folding and smoothing. Boyd looked at him sharply.

"She's well," he said. "Shaken. Damned nervous." He got up and went across the guard room to his medicine chest where it stood on a bench. "Not even a scar from the burns, in a week or two. What did you use, Leslie? Ye're quite a quack, aren't ye?"

"Slippery elm," Leslie told him. "How soon can I see her?"

"Eh? See her?" Boyd swung around at him. "Stab me, did ye say *see her?*"

"Of course. Good Lord, man, I . . ."

Peggy stood up abruptly, her lower lip caught between her teeth, her face stormy.

"Oh, tell him!" she burst out.

"Tell me what?" Leslie raised himself on one elbow. "What is it, Boyd? Did you lie when you said she was well?"

Boyd came toward the bed, and stood glowering down.

"No. She is well, or will be soon enough. There will be not even a mark on her body, I told you."

"Her face, then. Is that it?"

"No."

Across the pallet, Boyd's eyes and Peggy Sargent's met. Leslie felt grateful for the sense of coolness that enveloped him. Felt, too, that he was about to need it.

"Go on, Boyd. Get through with it."

"Oh, damme, she's had a fearful fright," said Boyd, fidgeting. "She is not over it, quite."

"Ay. She has been where few have been and lived." Leslie looked down again into the firelit glade where the slender stake whitened and thinned to a point, and a half-braided scalp hung on its hoop of green willow. "She would have gone mad if she were not so brave."

"Mmm. Ye know, then . . . mmm . . . ye know a fright like that does things, sometimes, to the brain?"

"Boyd! Not mad? You don't mean she has gone *mad?*"

"No. . . ."

"Will you tell him?" Peggy blazed again.

237

Boyd sat down solidly on the bunk, and plunged.

"I told ye, Arnett, that ye were the luckiest and the unluckiest devil I have ever seen. Outside of fightin', y'r luck's all bad. Ye see, ye're in the guard house...."

"Ay. I am not blind. Get along, will you?"

"The guard house, now—'t is not the worst place ye might be. It's cool. Anyhow, it's cooler. And we're packed into this damnation fort like queue hair in an eelskin."

"Damn you, Boyd, will you make an end of it, and tell me?"

"I will that. Ye're under arrest, an' there's a court to try ye, soon as ye can walk, for desertion...."

Leslie lay back on the odorous blanket and laughed in limp relief. It was, after what he feared, so small a trouble that he could not help but laugh.

"...and cowardice."

"Cowardice?" The tight bandage on Leslie's head made his astonished frown lop-sided. Then, still frowning, he began to smile. "I'll lay you my last shirt, Boyd, if you can find it, that I can name the man who made that charge." He was able now to sort out the true scenes from the dreams; he remembered that it was Valentine Arnold who had been so insistent about taking Diantha out of the Swiss soldier's arms. "Tell me, Boyd, it was Captain Arnold, was it not?"

"Ay."

"Ay." Peggy Sargent took up Boyd's word and made it quiver. "Cowardice. And Val Arnold brings it, because he is mad with love for her and thinks to ruin you. And who is to be witness against you? Leave me be, Mr. Boyd; I will tell him, and be damned to you. Who but this same fine Lady Gaillard who would have died if you..."

"*Who?*"

Leslie lifted himself again on wrist and elbow. Expecting to be shocked, he was, nevertheless, taken by surprise. Peggy flung herself down on her knees beside the bed.

"Oh, I told them and told them, Arnett Leslie! I swore you did not, any more than I knew, that she was not Diantha Gail at all, but Lady Diantha Gaillard...who lies, and is cold, and cruel...."

Boyd leaned across the blanket and pulled her by the sleeve.

"Peggy! I told you..."

"Oh! Ay! You told me! You told me to keep my tongue between my teeth, and let you cozen and trick him! You, pretending it is her mind. Her mind is clear. And hard. You went into hell to find her, Arnett Leslie, and she spits on you. She ..."

Boyd jerked her roughly by the arm.

"I told ye, Peg, I'd throw ye out if ye acted so. I am throwin' ye out now. Be gone, Peg! I swear ye've done harm enough. No"... brutally ... "I mean it. Out with ye."

The girl got to her feet, tears running unchecked down her cheeks, her teeth biting at her full lip until the skin was white, and then blood red, and then white again. She went sullenly to the door; it grated shut behind her.

Boyd looked at Leslie, and past him at the floor.

"She is *Lady Diantha Gaillard?*"

"Ay."

"Why, then she is. Why all the pox and pother about it? I knew she was no ordinary tavern wench. My Lord, Boyd, ye all knew that! Ye saw her that night, at the ball."

The surgeon's glance flicked toward him, and away.

"D'ye say ye knew her for a fine lady?"

"For a fine lady? Dammit, man, d'ye think I should have left her at Bond's an I had known that?"

"There are," said Boyd slowly, "those that think it."

"To what purpose? God's breath, have done with this fencing and mincing. Out with it! Did Peg speak the truth?"

"Peg? Hell's hinges, she does not know what she is saying. 'T is not the other that suffers; 't is Peg. She's watching a man with her heart in his hands squeezing it and twisting it, and throwing it out to the dogs. Women! Women! Oh, damn women! There's nought but love, love, love. She is jealous as hell, and out of her head with it. D'ye see, Leslie, she has been mistress to this top-lofty Arnold for three years now, and Arnold has cast her off. He was a-doing it when you came to Pitt's Town, and would have done it, too, had you not run off with the other. And now that she's back again, and a lady, I think he would hand poor Peg Sargent over to the first redstick that came seeking white flesh to roast at the stake. Ay, damn him, I do. I saw him strike her when he found her waiting for him by the door as he came out from asking for Lady Diantha's health. So . . ."

Boyd blew out his breath between pursed, nervous lips. Leslie let himself down on the bed and looked at the ax marks on the beams above. Beyond the guardhouse door, a sentry challenged hoarsely. Boyd pursed his lips again and blew, and got quickly to his feet.

"There!" he said in undisguised relief, and went to open the door. It swung back with a shriek of hinges, and Leslie saw that his fantastic dreams had not been altogether dreams. Tom Yeardley stood in the guardroom doorway, his big face half eager and half solemn. He had a musket in his hands; Boyd took it, murmuring, and leaned it against the wall. Tom came heavily across the room, through the grilled light from the barred window, and stood grinning beside the bed.

"I told you," said Leslie, remembering, "that I was just out of coaches. What brings you here, Tom? And will you tell me what devil has bitten this wild Irishman of a surgeon?"

Tom's placid eyes lighted and his wide mouth made creases in his cheeks.

"Pinch me, you're better. Pinch me black and blue, you are."

Leslie pinched him.

"Sit down, Tom. Zookins, 't is scarcely a fair trade. I rescued you from Master Grannis' cardroom floor, and you come to rescue me from Pitt's Town jail. You can smell trouble a thousand miles, Tom. What brought you? Have they heard already, across the mountains, that the tribes are up?"

"No." Tom sat down and cuffed Leslie's jaw with one huge fist. "Why didn't ye tell me, Arnie?"

"Tell you what?"

"That you'd put cockleburrs in the king's drawers."

"Hm. So I did that, did I?"

"Why didn't ye say ye'd bought y'rself a red-headed wench, and turned London upside down?"

"London? You've never heard from London since April."

"Ay, London. Ye plaguey fool, d'ye think ye can raddle-daddle me? Ye did buy her, didn't ye?"

"Yes. For a reason."

"By the holy poker, it had best be a good one."

Leslie sat up and pulled the blanket around his shoulders. It slid up over his knees, and he locked his arms around them.

"Tell me, Tom. Boyd says she is no bond maid at all, but Lady Diantha Gaillard. I wish," he smiled without humor, "that I had known it sooner."

"Gad, d'ye mean ye thought she was a common slut?"

"No, a most uncommon girl to be indented. That is why I bought her of Todd, to set her free."

"Pinch me, why didn't you, then?"

"I did. Watson perjured himself, and sold her again."

"Ahh! So that was it? Can you prove it?"

"Prove it?"

"Ay, prove it. A pretty pottage, you may call it. A pretty pottage, with a hangman's rope cooking in the midst of it."

"Because, after all, she was Lady Diantha Gaillard, and not a plain man's daughter?"

"Lady Diantha Gaillard! Riddle me, Arnett, even you might have played fast and loose with Lady Diantha and got off with a twigging, but when you settle on a countess...."

"A countess!"

"...countess of the Austrian empire...."

"Tom, you're serious?"

"By God, Arnett, I was never more serious in my life. She's not just Diantha Gaillard, daughter of a little viscount. She's Frances Charlotte Diantha, granddaughter of a duke, grandniece of a prince, niece of a king's admiral, baroness in her own right, and since April 1 when her grandfather died, Duchess of Strangden, and sole heiress to Strangden Castle in Northants, and half the county besides. Gad, I can recite them backwards, in my sleep. I've done it, so her brother tells me."

"Her brother? So that was her brother—the one who said he would kill me, if I did not hang. And Lawless—I suppose he is here, too." The ridiculous, wavering vision he had been so sure was part of his dreams was coming true with a vengeance.

"Ay. It was Lawless insisted on the cowardice part of it."

"I see." For the first time there was a note of anger in Leslie's voice. "Has he, by any chance, taken command in Fort Pitt?"

Tom Yeardley snorted.

"Ecuyer would like to drown him. Plague on it, Arnie, don't

you understand what a kettle of trouble you've been brewing? You might better have kicked my lord Amherst in his backsides than kidnap the Duchess of Strangden."

In spite of himself, Leslie began to laugh. It was serious enough, in all conscience. But it was humorous, too; he had been so sure that nothing worse could happen. Tom looked at him gloomily. After a while, he dug one fist into the skirt pocket of his coat and pulled out a paper.

"Laugh at this," he suggested, and passed it over.

Leslie, with quickly sobering face, read the royal warrant ordering the king's officers everywhere to seize the person of one Arnett Leslie, sometime of Leslie Hall in the colony of Maryland, and hold him securely to answer charges of conspiring to kidnap and do violence to the person of Frances Charlotte Diantha Gaillard, Duchess of Strangden in Northants, and so on, and so on, and so on. And read, also, the names of Captain Walther Barent, Halbert Bond, and John Watson as his fellow conspirators.

He read on to the end, and handed the warrant back.

"Barent and Bond are dead," he said. "That leaves only two."

"That leaves only one," Yeardley corrected him. "Watson hanged himself in Annapolis jail."

Leslie sat silent while Tom thrust the paper, crackling and rustling, into its pocket again.

"That's done," he grumbled, and forced a smile.

"Oh, *you* are the magistrate who seizes my person, eh? I thought the magistrate read the warrant aloud to the condemned. The king shall hear of this."

Tom's smile collapsed.

"Joke, plague take you, Arnie. But there's a king's cruiser riding in the stream at Annapolis, and her captain is here in Fort Pitt, itching to tear the heart out of the man that wronged his sister. And what can you say against it? Are there any to swear you didn't buy her?"

"I did buy her."

"Ay, your name stands on the papers they took from Watson."

"Lawless heard me tell Watson to free her."

"Lawless! That monkey, in his beads and quills. He'll make you a fine witness. He's been egging Captain Gaillard on to shoot

242

you down, with neither duel nor trial. And they'd give him a barony if he did."

"Bond dead. Barent dead. Watson dead. Todd, I suppose, is on his way back to England." Tom nodded. "That leaves only Robin Stuart."

"Who is Robin Stuart?"

"Captain in the Black Watch. He was my second when I fought Lawless; and he saw me give Watson money to give to the girl we called Diantha Gail, and heard me tell him to deliver her papers to her."

"And where is he?"

"He was under orders for Philadelphia, to serve with Bouquet."

"Arnie, ye'd best pray that no Indian lifts Robin Stuart's scalp. If Stuart dies, you die too. Todd can't save you, with your name on the papers, and Lawless swearing that you wanted the girl, and a dozen here to swear that you took her to your room and kept her there the night."

"That." Leslie's mind flashed back to the dark room of the Golden Eagle. A feeling of unreality oppressed him. There was no sense to any of it. He said so.

"Sense to it!" Tom grunted. "Ye read the warrant. There is that much sense to it."

"But grant that I bought her. Grant that I knew her for a duchess..."

"They do not say ye knew her for a duchess; she did not know it then herself. Just that ye knew her for Lady Diantha Gaillard. Lawless swears he told ye, on the ship, the day ye bought her. He swears she angered ye when she refused to be y'r mistress, and so ye schemed with Barent to buy her and send her into the backwoods to be Barent's plaything. And when ye went home and found what had happened there, ye took the notion to have the girl for y'rself, and so followed her to Pitt's Town, and quarreled with Barent when he would not give her up...."

"And killed him in the woods, I suppose," Leslie finished for him.

"I've heard it said," Tom told him, and showed his amazement when the man huddled in the gray blanket began to laugh.

There was, Leslie discovered, a good deal to laugh at. The whole wild business was too preposterous for anything but laughter. He even accorded to Sir Richard Lawless the first jot of admiration he had ever felt for that unpleasant pottle-pot. Mr. Lawless, it appeared, had in him an unsuspected capacity for mischief, and a very gift for lying. Ay, and a gift of audacity, too. It took a vast quantity of rattish courage for Sir Dick to bring himself face to face with the girl he had sworn into Halbert Bond's gentle hands. It took, in all conscience, more courage than the evil fellow owned. Arnett Leslie came abruptly to the realization that there was more to the affair than was yet apparent.

"Tom," he asked soberly enough, "do you know who it was that hatched this scheme, that had the constable take her out of her room at The Three Balls, that swore she had never been set free and that the buying of her on the *New Adventure* was only a drunken joke? It was this same Dick Lawless."

He had, he saw, shaken Tom Yeardley out of his placid look. Tom's eyes bulged, and his mouth opened and closed twice before he could get two words out.

"Not Lawless!"

Leslie nodded and hugged his knees. He had begun to contemplate with satisfaction the reckoning he would exact from Sir Richard. He would not repeat the error he had made on the knoll across the Severn from Annapolis; he would not, this time, shoot a leaf out of a tree. Mr. Lawless had earned killing.

"Yes, Lawless. God knows how he made Watson come to his scheme; bribed him or bulldozed him, I suppose. Barent wanted the girl, and Lawless helped him with his money and his false oath that I had not freed her and had not meant to free her."

"So, that is the way of it? Do ye not see, Arnie, 't will take a miracle to prove it?"

"No. Not a miracle, Tom; just a word. 'T was Diantha told me Lawless swore against her. A word from her, and it will be Dick Lawless sitting here, instead of me."

"Will she say it?"

"Of course."

Yeardley stirred uneasily on the bed and looked down at the white boot-hose rolled above his knees. The tops of them did not suit him, and he fussed and fiddled with them while he spoke.

"There is more to it than that, Arnie. Boyd put it to her only this morning: she has been too ill before. He thought to find out whether she felt ill toward you, and asked her if she would want to see you, and thank you for saving her. And she said: 'Don't let him touch me! Don't let him touch me!'" His troubled eyes met Leslie's uncomfortably.

"Boyd says she is not herself. She was in hell, Tom. The fright..."

"Ay. That is what they all think."

For the first time, Arnett Leslie felt afraid. It was not fear of the trap Sir Dick had set for him, though he began to see that it had been well set. It was fear of the days and nights in the hurricane woods, when he had been nurse and surgeon, and Diantha had wept and whimpered at the touch of his hands bathing her body, and screamed, clinging to him, while shrieks from the torture stake at Fort Venango rang through the darkness. *You know,* Boyd had said a little while ago, *what a fright like that does to the brain sometimes.* He had, again, the feeling that had come over him as he stood in his old room at Leslie Hall, fronting his father —the feeling that he was alone in a high place, and that the high place was cold. God, what a jest it would be if Diantha, out of those nights and days of fever, had come back to reason with the belief that he had been another Barent!

It was a very funny jest. He looked at it until the bitterness would not be denied and burst out of him in a laugh so ugly that Tom's hands jerked at their silly fiddling with his woolen stockings.

"I'll tell you about it, Tom," Leslie told him, and laughed again. "I'll tell you, and you shall laugh with me. Ay, and at me, too. Listen: I, who swore I would not look at any woman, knowing too well how treacherous they be, looked at a woman before six weeks had passed. Yes, looked at her, kissed her hand, and all but died with an Indian knife in my ribs again. Listen, Tom: I, who have not so much as one shirt to my back, I who am a major of backwoods militia, fell in love with a duchess! Is it not a noble jest? Come, laugh! I had, a fortnight ago, six shillings in my breeches; now I do not even know where those breeches be. And I, with neither shirt nor breeches, thought to wed with the Duchess of Strangden, Tom. There, by God, is a jest for the coffee house. I think Master Romney Clawther should burst his seams at it."

Tom sat silent, his hands helpless on his knees, his tongue helpless in his mouth. Sullen anger grew and darkened in his face.

When he spoke at last, his voice was as bitter as Arnett Leslie's laughter:

"Ye're not even a major of backwoods militia, Arnie. This foul Sir Dick went screeching to the governor, and the governor broke you. He's taken back your commission."

Leslie found that a good jest, too, and would hear more about Sir Dick and the governor.

"D'you say, Tom, he screeched?"

And Yeardley, to humor him, rehearsed the story.

"Ay, screeched. He screamed like a peacock, all aflutter to shame you and gain the king's grace, until the governor gave in. The way he screeches, the Indians should have him."

"You've heard him, then?"

Tom looked wonderingly at his friend. Leslie's tone had fallen suddenly as calm as if they were discussing a new style of wig. His lips curled, and Tom felt his own gloom lift a little. He had seen that smile before.

"Ay. At Near-the-Navel. D'ye see, Captain Gaillard, who is her half-brother and so missed the title when her grandfather died, would stop at nothing. When he found Lawless in Annapolis, and had the story out of him, he must drag Dickie with him to Fort Pitt." Leslie's smile tightened and his brows went straight; his eyes withdrew into dark slits. The story interested him. Tom went on: "He gets the governor to sign the warrant, and goes galloping off into the hills, with my lord Monkey-on-a-Stick bouncing along behind him because he does not dare to do otherwise. They came to South Mountain one evening, and stayed the night, and Sir Dick tells me over the brandy cups how he browbeat the governor into lifting your commission, and what he will do to you if ever he can come up with you. He screeched for me, and scared Anstice into fits. She thought the redsticks had us by the hair.

"And in the morning she said I must come along with them, because you might have need of me."

"I think," said Leslie pleasantly, "that when you die I shall marry Anstice."

Tom's face creased.

"Pinch me, that's more like ye. Ye'll fight them, then, and we'll have the truth out of this duchess jade if we have to squeeze it out with our fingers to her noble neck."

"No. Squeeze Dick's neck an you do not mind the soiling of your fingers, Tom. But I love Diantha Gail."

He said it so casually that Tom blinked at him and set him straight:

"Not Gail, Arnie. Don't you understand? She's Lady Diantha Gaillard. Does y'r head pain ... ?"

Leslie smiled faintly.

"Duchess or no, Tom, I love her. I think I understand what is at the bottom of all this. God knows why she came away to America, a bond maid indented for five years. 'T was some good reason, or she would not have kept silent and let them perjure her into Bond's hands, when she knew she had but to name herself and be set free. They'd not have dared to do otherwise but investigate. I misdoubt Lawless had some inkling why she had run away, and knew she would keep silence. Now, don't you see, 't is Lawless that is in the soup. When Gaillard came, he had to concoct some tale; and when Gaillard dragged him out here to Fort Pitt, he has no choice but to bluster it through if he can.

"Pshaw, Tom, I will not addle my brain with thinking of it. When Diantha is ready to do it, she'll have him up by the scruff of his neck like the mangy puppy he is. Mark you, Tom, there'll be no court-martial, and no trial for kidnaping, either."

Tom, stubborn, would not be convinced.

"They're using her as a witness in the court-martial, Arnie," he argued. "Whatever reason she has for keeping silent, as ye think, they know she will forswear you. Stab me, there's the scheme, I'll warrant you. Bob Gaillard told me a little of why she ran away. There was some business of a lord who tricked her and kept her by him in his rooms all night, and sought to make her wed him, and she would not and so ran away. They think she will do anything to keep that secret, Arnie. And if she bears witness against you in the trial here, why, 't will stand in the record when they try you for a kidnaper, too."

But Leslie only shook his head and would have none of it. He was thinking, instead, how many things were made clear and reasonable by the fact that Diantha Gail was Lady Diantha Gaillard, Duchess of Strangden, countess of ... whatever it was. It told him why she had set her teeth against crying out when Bond's whip bit her flesh. It told him why she faced him with her chin up and her eyes more curious than afraid, the day he bought her in Todd's cabin. It told him why she had been the loveliest woman he had ever seen, that night at Ecuyer's ball. It told him she would never lie to save herself.

"There'll be no court-martial," he repeated.

But ten days went by, and Arnett Leslie was still in the Fort Pitt guardhouse, with the oak beams in their slots across the door and a sentry on the bench outside. On the twenty-third of June, Captain Ecuyer named the members of a court to try him for desertion and cowardice, with Captain-lieutenant Burns as judge advocate to prosecute the charge.

Yeardley, coming to the guardroom in the evening with the news, told Leslie with savage violence that Captain-lieutenant Burns had spent two hours that afternoon with Lady Diantha, and come away smiling.

CHAPTER XXI

n Which a Red-headed Girl Proves that a Duchess in a Borrowed Night-rail and Bare Feet May be a Duchess Still:

DIANTHA lay in the blue-curtained bed and looked across her cubby-hole of a room into the triple mirrors.

The three mirrors were better than the window. If she urned her head on the pillows and looked through the window, he could see a patch of black dirt in the middle of the parade round, and part of the red-brick barracks beyond it. But if she y still and looked into the mirrors, she could see everything that appened, from the door of the governor's house to the covered ay under the Flag bastion, and from the Flag bastion to the two ud-and-brick ovens and the forge on the other side of the parade. Peggy Sargent had set up the dressing table close to the bed, nd arranged the mirrors so that Diantha could lie back on the ft pillows and watch the life of the besieged fort move back and rth in their bright surfaces.

Just now she could see three Peggy Sargents coming toward er; the mirrors had a fascinating trick of multiplying people by ree if they came close enough to the open window. Diantha niled drowsily. It was amusing to see three Peggys carrying three ooden trenchers, each one with an astonishing number of mugs nd gourds and porringers upon it. Each of the three Peggys had er lower lip tucked under her teeth, and an air of intense con-entration on her flushed face. In a minute, the three flushed faces ould turn into one, and Peggy would be coming in with break-ast, and she would have to get up. Diantha curled deeper into e feather bed, and thought of the hot nights when she had wakened, ice cold and shivering with terror, and Peggy's arms ad soothed her and cradled her.

They had been terrible nights—the dreams worse than the eality that they brought back.

She counted sleepily on her fingers, tapping off the nights on

one hunched-up knee; it had been two—three—*four* nights sin[ce]
she had dreamed at all. *Dear* Peg.... "Please, God, be good to her[,]"
she murmured into the pillow.

And then she laughed, and caught herself. A prayer that ra[n]
right on into a foolish laugh probably wasn't the best kind [of]
prayer. But it was hardly possible to see three Peggy Sargen[ts]
backing gingerly through the doorway, with three bare feet dab-
bing out backward to push the stubborn door wide open, an[d]
not laugh a little. It felt good to laugh again. Sometimes, becau[se]
she was still tired and weak, it was hard to stop.

The door banged against the wall, and Peggy turned cautious[ly]
around, all but cross-eyed in her absorption. The two mugs o[n]
her beechen platter were full to the brim, and steaming.

"Coffee!" she announced triumphantly, and set the trencher dow[n]
on an upturned keg beside the bed. "It's mostly rye and it's part[ly]
wheat, but there were five coffee beans, too. I saw them. I eve[n]
held them in my hand, and dropped them into the pot one b[y]
one. I had them of Captain-lieutenant Burns"...she wrinkled he[r]
nose..."but that needn't spoil the coffee."

Diantha wriggled up among the pillows and hugged her knee[s.]
"Why should it?"

"Why? Oh," Peggy bent busily over the trencher, "he has bi[g]
ears."

"Oh."

Peggy glanced sharply at the thin face behind the mosqui[to]
netting of the blue bed. It was smiling and sweet; except for th[e]
worst of the burns, still faintly red along one cheek, and the gra[y]
eyes too big for it, Diantha's face showed only a little of the suffe[r-]
ing she had known. It showed no sign at all of concern at th[e]
mention of the judge-advocate who would be prosecuting Arne[r]
Leslie in a few hours; Diantha had been as silent about his tw[o-]
hour visit with her as if she never had heard of Captain-lieutena[nt]
Burns.

Peggy bit her lip again as she stooped to pick up the slippe[r]
beside the bed.

"No more breakfasts in bed, Mistress Gail! What with Captai[n-]
lieutenant Burns' coffee, and two journey cakes from Lieutena[nt]
Donnellan, and two bowls of rye porridge from the refugees' ove[n,]
and a piece of bacon big as your two thumbs straight from Captai[n]

Ecuyer's kitchen, you're getting three times as much as any Royal American in Fort Pitt."

"Captain Ecuyer has been marvelous kind, has he not, Peg?"

"Pooh! Ecuyer nothing. You may be the Duchess of Strangden at the *front* of the governor's house, but it's Peggy Sargent that's royalty in the kitchen at the back. I dare say I'm compromitted with half the garrison by now, begging tidbits for her ladyship. After today, *you* can help with the flirting. 'T will make a merry tale at court when you go back, Di." Peggy crossed her eyes and pursed her lips. "Tell 'em how a duchess went begging for a pone of cornbread, and the captain's cook made her pay for it with a kiss."

Diantha laughed happily, and slid to the edge of the bed. With two thin white knees and two plump brown ones to brace it, the shaky keg did very well as a breakfast table. Peggy chattered between mouthfuls, and amidst of them, too. It made no difference to her that the girl who shared her bed, and wept on her shoulder when dreams wakened her in shuddering terror, was duchess and countess and what-not besides. The officers of the garrison might find time between watches on the walls and cattle guards and patrols to powder their hair, and pipe-clay their belts, and bow and make a leg when they passed Lady Diantha Gaillard's window; but Peggy clung sturdily to Diantha—and even shortened it to Di.

She thought, this morning, that Diantha looked a good deal like a duchess, with her red-gold hair streaming over the coarse night-rail and turning it into beauty—but a good deal like a very pretty camp wench, too, with her bare knees hugging the keg and her fingers busy tearing the bit of bacon into equal portions.

"Lud, I be minded to eat this morning, Di. I almost starved, waiting for the porridge. And you should hear the women gabbling around the ovens." Peggy held her share of bacon daintily between thumb and forefinger, and squinted up at it before she nibbled at its lower end. "Poor Captain Ecuyer is in worse case than the hen that hatched out the ducks. He's the widowed hen's-husband, and he tries so hard to mother the whole pondful. And all he gets for it is a devilish quacking and scolding. God knows how long we'll be pent up here, no food coming across the mountains, and the woods full of red imps; but last week when he ordered the women out to help cut the spelt, he had to threaten that he'd lock them up in the guardhouse before some of them would go."

Diantha blew on a spoonful of rye porridge.

"Did you go?" she asked, her lips as close to the steaming stuff as they dared to get.

"Oh, la, of course not. I, a nurse with two patients on my hands?" She gobbled the last of her bacon, and licked her fingers greedily. "But the rest of them went, except those that have had the smallpox and can nurse the men in the hospital. I s'pose you can't blame the women for fretting. They're hungry, and they're scairt. But they bedevil Ecuyer so it's a wonder he doesn't order half the women in the place muzzled, the same as he ordered the dogs to stop barking! But, my dear, he *did!* Posted it in orders, and there's a reward of half a crown for any soldier who kills a dog running loose. Poor Fritz is in a stew about his precious bear."

"Oh, did he ... ?" Diantha's eyes questioned Peggy eagerly.

"La, yes. Didn't I tell you? Fritz slipped out with the cattle guard two days ago, the first time they'd let him outside the gates, and he found his bear ... where do you think? In the cellar of Bond's tavern! He'd smelled honey, and crawled down through the loose planks and got at two whole kegs of it. My dear, he was plastered with it—and so fat he bulged. Lud knows what Fritz can feed him, though he won't need to eat for weeks, he's so stuffed with honeycomb."

"Fritz ..." Peggy, glancing up sharply, saw Diantha's face very sober over the rim of her noggin, and her gray eyes dark. "He was so brave!"

"Braver than Major Leslie?" Softly as Peggy said it, the question was a challenge; but the bare-legged duchess ignored it.

"I remember the first time I saw him," she said, and Peggy knew she was thinking of Fritz, and not the man Fritz adored. "He looked such a mouse. It was right outside this barracks, Peg. I was running away from Barent, and I passed Fritz. He was crying, because he was so frightened. But he kept on coming. Oohh!" She shuddered, and put down the untasted coffee. "Will I *always* remember?" Her hands came up and covered her face, her bandaged wrists pressed tight against her chin. "I want to forget! I want to forget!"

252

Peggy Sargent opened her lips to speak, and then closed them again, firmly. She wanted to say that Diantha had found it easy enough to forget Arnett Leslie and what he had done. It was hard not to lash out at her with angry, scornful words. Little fool, she did not even realize that she was sitting on the blue-curtained bed because Leslie, from the guardhouse, had told Boyd that it was hers, though Arnold had given it to Peggy when Leslie disappeared and the wrecking party from Bond's tavern brought it in, all mixed up with sides of bacon and powder kegs and bolts of cloth. Day after day, time after time, Diantha had shrunk away from the mention of Leslie's name, with her eyes aloof and that queer, childish rigidity in her arms.

As if, Peggy thought angrily, she actually hated the man who had risked his life for her. Peggy took a spoonful of porridge with an impatient jerk that crammed it all into her mouth at once, before she realized how hot it was. Between pain and anger, she broke a promise.

"Arnett gave you this furniture, didn't he, Di?"

"No."

Peggy felt an almost overpowering longing to shake the calm smile out of Diantha's still face, to grip those creamy-white shoulders and shake the stiffness out of them, to make her realize that she was a cruel, ungrateful minx. As cruel, as ungrateful as a—as a *duchess*.

"You took it, then," she flashed. "You slept in that bed, the night they tried to kill him."

"The night Bond took me away," said the Duchess of Strangden, in a small, stiff voice. "I wondered why they came to that room, not knowing I was there."

"Di!" Peggy sprang up, a plump brown fury. "Are you trying to say *he* helped in *that*?"

"I don't know." Cool. Hostile.

"Yes, you know." The fury boiled over in tears. "You know you are being vile! You know he almost died for you. Boyd says he should have died of that wound on his head. Do you think you have had that bed to lie in because you are a tuppenny duchess? Or because you've taken away from me the man who loved me, once? Be still! Maybe Fort Pitt will hold out. Maybe you'll go back to England, and trample decent folk with your dainty satin slippers. Maybe you'll take Val Arnold with you. Take him! I despise him, and you, too!"

Diantha was sitting very straight, her hands tense on the two ends of the trencher. The scar on her cheek was redder than it had been for days. She sat silent as the storm of words came at her in breathless gusts.

"Did you know that after Bond took you away, Val Arnold gave *me* the furniture Arnett left behind? Did you know that he lived with me, here, in this room, until Arnett brought you back? Did you know that Arnett Leslie, ill of wounds he took for *your* sake, thought of you even when they put him in jail? Ay, that he did. He browbeat Boyd into finding this furniture, and into carrying you here, out of the hard soldier's bed they had laid you on. Did you know that he asked me to nurse you, when I would rather have stayed with him there in the guardhouse than live with a *duchess?*" She made the title an insult.

And the duchess laughed.

She thought, for an instant, that Peggy would throw the trencher at her.

But just throwing a wooden platter and its half-emptied dishes was not enough for Peggy's trembling passion. The trencher and its porringers and its noggins of precious coffee went clattering and splashing to the floor; the keg fell over and ran quickly under the bed; Peggy's hands took the Duchess of Strangden by her shoulders and shook her. And shook her. And shook her.

Until, through her own blinding storm of tears, she saw that there were other tears sliding down the raw scar across Diantha's cheek; and realized that somehow Diantha's arms were around her neck, and that the slim young duchess who could be so cold and cruel was sobbing as if she would never stop.

Peggy's hands stopped shaking her, and slipped around her shoulders. They sat together on the rumpled satin quilts and wept with their cheeks touching and their arms clinging to each other. The keg stopped its hollow rocking beneath the bed; the porridge cooled in splotches on the floor, and the rye-wheat-coffee went trickling in aimless courses over the uneven puncheons. One of its trickles came and made a pool against one of Peggy's bare feet and cooled there, and reminded her at last of the havoc she had made. She drew back a little, and saw, in the triple mirrors, a fi of Royal Americans marching toward the guardhouse. She watched them a minute, and saw that they were merely relieving the sentinel there; but she slid back toward the foot of the bed, away from the arms that had turned her cherished indictment into futile weeping.

"You know he didn't kidnap you," she accused. "How can you shame him so?"

And then she saw that Diantha Gaillard was really a duchess, and not a pretty camp wench. For the shoulders in the linsey nightrail stopped shaking, and the pointed chin went up like a small drum major's. There were tears on it, all ready to drop, but they could not keep the chin from being stubborn, imperious, a little ruthless.

"Now you listen to me," and Peggy, because she could not, somehow, help herself, sat quietly against the foot-post of the bed and listened, and looked with growing wonder at the arrogance in the thin, pale face. "Have you ever seen a duchess? In a carriage, with footmen? And linkboys running ahead with torches? Didn't she look proud, and cold, and as if she didn't care for anything or anybody, except herself? Well, then. I'm a duchess. See?" The bandaged wrists darted out and the slim hands gripped the quilt and dabbed it recklessly at the tear-wet cheeks and chin. "See? I *will* be a duchess, mean and willful. I *will* scrub my face on the only blue satin quilts in all the wilderness."

Over the huddled silk her smile flashed out.

"Oh, Peg, I can be mean and cruel and vile if I have to be; but that doesn't mean I haven't a reason for it. Don't you see?"

For the first time since she had seen Bond's pack train come ambling down the King's Highway into Pitt's Town with a red-haired bond maid perched between salt sacks on a rawboned horse, Peggy Sargent felt awed by her, and bewildered. There was an air of power about the red-gold head now, a look of daring, almost a look of malice, in the gray eyes. They meant more to Peggy than all the titles she had heard rolled under excited tongues on the parade ground. She sat biting her full lip, retreating into sulky silence.

"Don't you see?" Diantha asked again. The dark head against the bed curtains shook reluctantly. "Tell me, what has happened in Pitt's Town since Bond took me away?"

"They burned it." Slowly, like a child whose fingers have just been rapped.

"Hasn't any one been hurt?"

"Hurt!" Peggy's quicksilver temper began to bubble. "The Indians scalped two of our soldiers right at the sawmill. They shot a trapper who tried to get through to Venango with warning, and he barely got back; and they scalped poor Jim Thompson yesterday afternoon, with the whole garrison looking on from the wall. And Sergeant Miller was killed just a week ago to-day—shot on Grant's Hill, with his platoon around him, in plain sight of the fort."

Diantha nodded.

"And another soldier shot on the Monongahela bastion, by an Indian on the island in the river," she added. "The judge advocate told me yesterday. And still you don't see?"

"No, I don't."

"Goose! What's the good of being a duchess, if she can't *do* anything? At least, *this* duchess is keeping Major Leslie from being killed."

In spite of her imperious air, there was a small-girl smugness about Diantha now. Amazement and indignation chased each other across Peggy's face as the meaning of that satisfied little smile dawned upon her.

"You mean ... you'll keep him there? You'd shame him so, to keep him out of danger? Di, you can't do that!"

"I've done it," Diantha triumphed. Then her face sobered. "Peggy, he has done his share. Time after time, those last three days, I saw him stagger, and catch himself. Peggy, Peggy, did you really think I had no heart at all ... after all he did?"

"But, Di, you *can't* do that."

The pointed chin went up again. No duchess in her ducal hall could be more arrogant than Diantha Gaillard, in a borrowed night-rail, in Arnett Leslie's bed. But Peggy had lost her awe.

"You can't brand him a coward, Di. He'll hate you."

"He does already."

"He does not," hotly. "He loves you."

The red, tousled head shook itself gravely.

"He might have, once, I think. It's too late now."

"Oh." The girl sitting cross-legged in the tumbled quilts was, after all, duchess and countess and grand-niece of a prince. Peggy could understand that it was too late. She saw the faint smile and a wistful look in the gray eyes, and wondered whether Diantha was sorry; she did not quite dare to ask, and bit her lip because she wanted so much to know. As if her thoughts were written in her face, she heard them answered:

"No, Peg, you can't tell him. Silly, of course you can't tell him. I think he would tear the guardhouse down to get out, if he knew that I was keeping him there. Promise?"

It was not a question; it was a command. There was something about this new Diantha that insisted on being obeyed. Peggy promised. But a minute later, on her knees over the wreckage of their breakfast, she was reminding the duchess who swung bare feet happily over the side of the bed that Arnold would be coming shortly to escort her to the court-martial.

Diantha slid out, a little-girl avalanche of haste.

"Oh, and I must scrub me, and comb me, and dress me in my best. Peg, is there flour enough so I may powder me, and cover this ghastly scar? Burns gave it you? Bless him. . . . I could fall in love with him. . . ."

"And he the man who's trying to bring disgrace on Arnett?"

"Pho! Take that top-lofty temper of yours and use it for a stool; it needs sitting on, darling. He's but doing his duty."

"Di?" Peggy sat back on her heels, her fingers sticky with porridge gleaned from the floor. "You'll never testify against him?"

"I must testify." Diantha's voice came lightly, gayly, from the depths of the brass-bound trunk. "Captain-lieutenant Burns assures me there is no other way, and Captain Arnold says so, too."

She came up out of the chest, her arms overflowing with the blue sarcenet, all stiff with quilting and side-hoops, that Leslie had shown to a bond maid with grimy toes, one night at the Golden Eagle. Over the stormy blue folds, her hair glowed brighter, and her eyes took on again the sheen of malice.

"What will you do, Peg? Will you throw me out?"

"I think I'd hate you."

The crumpled gown dropped a little.

"Peggy, do you love Major Leslie?"

Across the bed, the two girls looked at each other through a long moment of silence. When Peggy answered, her voice was low and quivering:

"I would to God I did, Di, though he would never look at me."
She got up, her body drooping over the trencher and its cluttered
gear. "I love a man I despise. When you're in love, Di, you can't
help it; you can't help anything. I love Val, and I am ashamed of
it—not that I followed him here, knowing he would never wed me;
that doesn't count, either, if you are enough in love. I love him,
and he loves you, and you love..."

"Don't say it, Peg. I don't. I must not, ever."

"I know. They say love is beautiful. It's a lie. A hateful, ugly
lie. Twice Val has thrown me off; and I lie awake at night, praying.
Do you know what I pray for, Di? I pray that he will be shot; I
love him, and I want him to be hurt...oh, badly hurt, so that
he will need me, and call for me, and want me again. And when
I think of him hurt, suffering, my heart stops." Her knuckles
whitened over the edges of the wooden platter. "I'll fetch some
water."

"You're a dear, Peg. Fetch plenty of it; whole rivers full. There
be two of us to scrub. You're going with me, in that other London
gown—the yellow one, with the flowered brocade."

"Oh, no..."

"Oh, yes. A duchess can't go unattended! Look, Peg, this Fort
Pitt of ours has not fallen yet, and neither have you stopped fighting. Captain Arnold has never seen you in yellow, has he? La,
dear, we'll make him stare at you!"

Peggy was smiling again as she started for the door.

On the step, she paused, and looked back over her shoulder:
"Di?"

"Yes?"

"What are you going to say when they call you? Will you say
he is innocent?"

The blue gown tumbled down anyway upon the bed.

"Stars and garters, Peg, I shall say no such thing! And have
him freed, and on the walls to be shot at? What an addle-pated
minx you are, sweet. There, don't glower at me. I warrant I shall
flummox the gentlemen of the court much worse, my dear. Look
you, I shall tell them he bought me at a drinking party—that is
the truth—and that he must be kept safe in jail to answer for it.
And then, Peg, I shall make Captain Arnold stare at me, too, as
well as at you. Ay, and choke for very fury at me. I shall make

such a fool of him that he will never come a-wooing me again—
no, nor that mincing Lawless, either. I shall swear Major Leslie
is no coward, but the bravest, most self-possessed, coolest man in
all the colonies."

And then added, as the door swung shut behind Peggy:
"And the coldest, too."

CHAPTER XXII

*In Which Major Leslie Frustrates Both the Man Who Would Destroy
Him and the Woman Who Would Save Him:*

VALENTINE ARNOLD saw to it that such ceremony as
Fort Pitt afforded was provided for the court-martial of
Arnett Leslie. Every captain of the regular line in the garrison was detailed already for the court itself; but Captain Arnold,
in his capacity of adjutant, found it possible to detach a squad
of the Pennsylvania Provincials as a headquarters guard. They had
been on duty in the Ohio bastion until daylight; but at ten o'clock
they were turned out with fixed bayonets and freshly pipe-clayed
crossbelts, and marched smartly across the parade ground behind
the tump-tump of a single drum. In their green tunics and breeches,
with black cocked hats and long black spatterdashes, they made a
brave show against the red brick wall of the governor's house.

A few minutes after ten, two sergeants dressed a file of Royal
Americans in front of their barracks.

From the officers' quarters opposite, a knot of scarlet uniforms
complete to sash and saber moved slowly along the barracks wall
to the governor's house and filed up the steps between the rigid
muskets of the guard. Behind them, alone and unhappy, Captain-
lieutenant Carre came out of a doorway not far from Diantha's;
almost in front of hers, he met Captain Arnold, coming with Captain Gaillard and Sir Richard Lawless to escort her to the trial.
Carre's salute was impeccable; but his gaze was toward the barracks
roof. He crossed the parade with rapid strides, acknowledged the
salute of the shining halberds as the sergeants presented arms, drew
his sword, and snapped a command. The file of grenadiers went
briskly past the clustered women and children, packed between
the ovens and the well, and halted in front of the guardhouse with
a crash of musket butts on hard-baked earth.

Diantha, standing in the doorway between Arnold and her
brother, saw the sentry lift the bars and swing the guardroom door

open. She heard Arnold mutter angrily, and Lawless' loose voice chatter excitedly. At her shoulder, Peggy Sargent giggled.

"La, did you see that?" she whispered. "There's Major Leslie, coming out of the guardhouse to be tried, and the guard presents arms!"

There was a flash of steel, halberds and bayonets and sword. The scarlet squad wheeled toward the governor's house. A drum took up, timing the march with solitary beats. Behind it, Carre walked with flushed face; he walked so slowly that his prisoner was almost abreast of him, at his shoulder.

Arnold muttered again. The ceremony was going wrong. Arnett Leslie was not wearing the scarlet and buff of the Maryland troops. He was dressed in a sober brown hunting shirt of linsey, with short brown thrums but without even the swagger of a cape.

"Pinch me! Pinch me blue!" Diantha heard Sir Richard piping. "We'll have that red jacket of his back on him, and the swords snipping his buttons off with the whole garrison looking on! He can't get off by hiding in a dirty shirt, eh, Gaillard?"

Sir Richard, in his yellow doeskin hunting dress, stiff with beadwork and quills and all adangle with purple thrums, was a gaudier spot of color than even the blue gown and the yellow brocade when they moved down the barracks wall toward Ecuyer's headquarters. Altogether, the greencoated guard and the scarlet escort, the London gowns, the naval uniform, and the fantastic hunting shirt adorning my lord Lawless, they made a gay show for the refugees to watch. The three groups met at the foot of the steps. If Diantha realized that Captain Arnold had timed his ceremony so that she must see Arnett Leslie walk past her, under guard, a scant arm's length away, her calm face did not show it.

Leslie saw her, and bowed gravely; and she gave him the barest, stiffest inclination to acknowledge it. But the prisoner, quite undisturbed, flashed a smile at Peggy that told her, as clearly as a dozen phrases, that the yellow gown was made for her gypsy beauty. He went by, between the bayoneted muskets of the Pennsylvanians, up the steps, into the long hall where he had led Diantha to the governor's ball.

Then the girls were walking into the balconied hall, past an anteroom where an armed sentry stood guard over prospective witnesses, past a long table where the officers of the court sat in a double row of powdered wigs and scarlet tunics, to a bench against the wall. Arnold bent over her, whispering:

"The president of the court consented that you should sit here, instead of with the witnesses. It will be hot in there. And nothing they have to say concerns your testimony."

"You are too kind," she murmured.

She saw Leslie, an inconspicuous figure in the gaudy setting, rise from his chair to hear the formal charge read aloud, and heard him say "not guilty." He sat down, and slouched with his head a little to one side to hear Yeardley, beside him, and Boyd, just behind him, when they whispered. Both Yeardley and Boyd were smiling.

Near the head of the table, a little to one side, Captain-lieutenant Burns fiddled with the point of his quill as he called his first witness, Captain Arnold.

Arnold's testimony was precise, unhurried. If he did not state exactly the circumstances under which Major Leslie helped a demolition party wreck a cabin in the Upper Town on the day he disappeared from Pitt's Town, Major Leslie seemed not to care. He waived his right to question the witness. Arnold came and sat beside Diantha. His attitude, as he left the witness chair, was that of a man who had performed a painful duty.

Captain-lieutenant Burns spoke to the president of the court:

"Although he is not logically the next witness, I am calling next one Peter Lanness, a resident of Pitt's Town, who was wounded by Indians in a vain attempt to carry dispatches to Fort Venango. He is still under the surgeon's care, and Mr. Boyd is desirous that he shall be spared the heat of the day. The guard is bringing him."

Burns fussed and fussed with his thumb at the end of his quill. Yeardley sat with the back of his neck on the back of his chair and gazed intently at the ceiling. Boyd sat and grinned toward the spectators' bench, until Arnold began to fidget and fiddle, first with his sword knot and then with the jabot at his neck, and then with the hat on his knees.

Leslie's faint smile settled itself a shade more firmly on his lips as the wounded messenger came hobbling up the steps between two grenadiers and sat down in the witness chair. One of the soldiers lifted his splinted leg and laid it stiffly on a stool; the witness squirmed uneasily, and shot quick looks up and down the

262

stiff rows of judges, his black hair in his eyes, his unshaven face ducked into the neck of his hunting shirt.

Captain-lieutenant Burns put down the pen he had almost ruined.

"Your name?"

"Peter Lanness."

"You are a trapper and trader?"

"A *coureur de bois*." Lanness used the French word sturdily, though some of these redcoated officers had fought at the Loyal Hanna, and marched with Forbes to drive France away from the Forks of the Ohio.

"You are a resident of Pitt's Town?"

The black stubble on Peter Lanness' cheeks rippled in a rueful grimace. He spread his hands wide.

"I have a cabin, one time. Now I think maybe I have—what you call?—one cellar."

"You volunteered to ride to Fort Venango on June first, with a message from Captain Ecuyer?"

"For sure. Joe Neron and Black George, they go too."

"Did you get to Venango?"

Peter Lanness' leg slipped off its stool onto the floor in his indignant squirming. The grenadier who stooped to lift it back for him ducked his head too late to dodge Peter's excited arms; his hat went flying across the room; and Boyd grinned delightedly at the laugh that circled the table.

"Excuse, please," the Frenchman sputtered. "That is one damnfool question. Do we get to Venango? Maybe if we are birds we get there; maybe if we are fish, we swim there. I bet you no man go from Pitt's Town to French Creek this month, eh?"

"One did," remarked Burns, and looked at his inky thumb. Arnold stirred impatiently. "Tell us why you did not get to Venango."

"By the flat host, look at this leg!" The *coureur de bois* patted the splints with both angry hands, leaning forward and shouting at the prosecutor. "You know damn-well for why we do not get to Venango. I think you make fun with me, no?"

"Not at all," Burns began, and out of the corner of his averted eyes saw Captain Arnold jump to his feet.

"This is wasting the time of the court," he snapped at the president. "Some of the officers here have duties elsewhere."

Captain Phillips looked mildly surprised.

"It seems better to let the witness tell his story in his own way, Captain Arnold. I am assured the trial will be hastened if he does. Go on."

Arnold sat down, his saber clattering.

"Peter Lanness, tell us what happened on the road to Venango." Burns went back to the fraying turkey quill. The Frenchman hitched forward on the edge of his chair. "By God, there is nothing happen. Two, maybe three mile, there is nothing happen. Then, *bang!* Everything she is happen, all at once. The big ravine she is lie there wit' her mouth by the Allegheny, like snake in sun. We ride in front of her—*spwagh!* She is spit Delaware like a snake she is spit out baby snake—four—six—maybe ten. *Bang!* I have no more horse. I am on the ground; my leg she is broke. The horse, she is run, run, run." His galloping hands showed how the horse ran, swerving through the clutching savages. Though he sat in a chair, he seemed to crouch; his hair dropped farther over his eyes; he looked up at death, rushing down upon him.

"Black George, he is shoot. Joe, he is shoot. The Delaware, they jump like tree-cat, they squirm like snake, they yell—*yough-yough-yough!*"

Peggy felt the slim body beside her shudder, and put her hand warmly over Diantha's where they lay clenching the blue sarcenet.

"I think I have in a minute no more hair," Peter Lanness said in a frightened tone, and Diantha shuddered again. "Joe, he is turn round and ride back to me; there are four—six of those red devil all round him; he is hit with hatchet. *Wooish! Wooish! Phlogh!*" His arm rose and fell three times, and the fascinated men leaning toward him across the table saw the hatchet fall and heard it swish, and then heard the sound it made as it bit into flesh and bone.

"It is no good. They are too many. There are two of them on Black George's horse. There is a knife, so hungry, just by my hair." His lips slavered to show them all how hungry that knife had been. "Then I see! By the good God, I see one miracle. I see that a man has catch my horse and turn him round and come like hell." For a second Peter was astride a galloping horse, on the edge of the witness chair; in another second, he was hobbling, crawling, reaching up to grasp a hand reaching down to him.

"This man, he is shoot while he ride. The Delaware, they are round him like the rattlesnake in the den, all twist' and curl' up, so thick they are. This man, he take the rein and the rifle in his one hand. He hit these Indian with tomahawk. Wooish, *phlogh!* Wooish, *phlogh!* By God, that man, he is ride through them all!

"While they fight with him, Joe is get me by the hand. I am on the horse behind Joe. Black George, he is go by me like sturgeon in the river, so fast he ride. Joe and me, we are sturgeon too. When I look back, this man what catch my horse, he is ride fast, fast, upstream. I say, 'Joe, that is fine man. It is too bad he go that way. By and by he be dead, eh?'"

Peter Lanness settled back into the chair. A sigh like a breeze brushing past the eaves ran through the room.

Burns cleared his throat.

"Do you know who the man was—the one who caught your horse?"

"No. By God, I would like to see him."

"Would you know him if you did see him?"

"For sure. He was so close to me like you."

Burns spoke again: "The prisoner will rise."

Leslie stood up quickly. Across the powdered wigs and the shoulders of the red tunics, his eyes passed slowly along the group against the farther wall. His faint smile met Arnold's furious face and the still hate in Gaillard's without changing; it warmed a little at Peggy's eager smile, and chilled again. It seemed to Diantha that he had not looked at her at all.

"Mr. Lanness, is that the man?"

The Frenchman screwed himself around, both hands on his leg to hold it on the stool. Then the leg slipped down with a thump. Peter Lanness crossed himself.

"He is a fish then, or a bird! That is the man, for sure." His hands spread themselves wide; then his arms opened as if he would embrace the tall man in brown forest dress, even though he must take the whole intervening court in his arms to do it. "Nom d'un nom d'un nom, did you go then to Venango?"

One of the guards told Peter gruffly to be still.

"I think," said the prosecutor slowly, "that Mr. Lanness has established that Major Leslie was *not* in Pitt's Town, on the afternoon of June first. We shall establish further by other witnesses that he was assigned to duty there, and that in departing he was guilty of desertion."

Boyd bent over Leslie's shoulder, whispering.

"My next witness," Burns began. But Boyd, unwontedly solemn, stepped forward a little.

"There will be no need for more witnesses," he said gravely. "It has been proved that Mr. Leslie departed from Pitt's Town, and he admits that he did so without authority. He desires also to plead guilty to the charge of cowardice."

There was a sharp cry from the group against the wall. The stiff line of scarlet along the table stirred; powdered wigs jerked up in amazement; boots scuffled; Captain-lieutenant Burns crumpled his turkey feather altogether and pressed his lips tightly.

The president of the court looked from Arnold's face, where triumph was intruding on blank astonishment, to Leslie's. Leslie was still smiling, his cool, detached smile. Phillips shrugged his shoulders, and started to rise. Boyd grinned.

"Before the court passes sentence," he began, "it should be made clear that Mr. Leslie is not subject in any way to the findings of this court-martial." He stopped, and waved a hand at Arnold to silence him. Arnold's face was flushing, his mouth working.

"Mr. Boyd will have to explain that," Burns snapped.

"I will do that, and enjoy it," Boyd snapped back. "It is very simple. I marvel it was not thought of when the charges were brought." He grinned again at Arnold. "Mr. Leslie was commissioned a major of militia by the governor of Maryland four years ago. Like as not ye've forgotten it, but ye'll recall that in the late war there was much to-do about those colonial commissions, until His Majesty settled it. If ye'll think a bit, ye'll recall that by his order a colonial field officer may do the duty of his rank when he is serving with colonial troops, but when he is serving with royal troops, *he shall have no rank at all.*"

Boyd stood and beamed at the startled court.

"Ye see, being with a garrison under a captain holding a royal commission, Mr. Leslie is no major at all, at all. He's just Mr. Leslie. He didn't desert; he just went away. It's that simple. And a-top of that, the governor of Maryland went and took a notion that he wanted a major nearer home, so he took back Mr. Leslie's com-

266

mission, and on the first of June Mr. Leslie wasn't even a soldier any more, let alone being a major.

"He's just a private gentleman, an' ye can hang him for thar if ye like; but ye can't hang him for being a deserter, for he had nought to desert. And if a gentleman says he's a coward, why, ye can't hang him or shoot him for being over-modest."

It was obvious even to Arnold that the trial was over; he read it in the relieved faces of the court. Boyd was grinning from ear to ear; Carre, standing rigid behind his prisoner, appeared to be on the verge of choking because he could not laugh at Boyd's abrupt turning of the tables. Captain-lieutenant Burns addressed the president of the court gravely, but his lips twitched; and Captain Phillips agreed without a moment's hesitation that the prisoner should be removed while the court discussed the unexpected turn of the case.

Arnold looked at Gaillard's set, angry face, and then at Diantha's; she was paler than she had been when she came in, and there were tears in her eyes. Arnold saw the very ceremonies he had devised to make Leslie's disgrace more glaring turn into a perfect setting for his triumph. Leslie was marching across the hall, side by side with Carre; the captain-lieutenant with his drawn sword looked more like an escort of honor than a guard.

The adjutant's thin lips sucked in between his teeth. Then, his sword banging against the arm of his chair, he got up quickly. His plan of campaign had gone amiss, but there was still time to change it. He went briskly across the hall to the commandant's office, and the door closed behind him.

Peggy Sargent slipped her hand over Diantha's listless fingers where they lay on the lap of the blue dress.

"Don't worry, sweet," she whispered. "See, they're smiling, there at the table. They didn't *want* to convict him."

Diantha stared miserably ahead, her fingers limp and unresponsive.

"Di . . . Di, dear. What's the matter?"

"He thinks I would have testified against him," the girl whispered, and rubbed one bandaged wrist across her eyes to keep back the tears. "He *must* think so."

"But, Di, you can *tell* him."

"Tell him!" The gray eyes were quick with scorn, as a duchess' eyes might be. Then they were blinking and miserable, and not like a duchess' haughty eyes at all. "He'd know I was lying. Oh, he couldn't believe that, ever!"

An orderly came out of the commandant's office and spoke respectfully to Captain Gaillard. He leaned to his sister and told her Ecuyer had asked him to come to the orderly room. The affair of Arnett Leslie, deserter, was not yet over, he assured her grimly.

Diantha sat in woebegone silence, hardly hearing Peggy's cheerful chatter. The room blurred, but she could see it clearly enough as it had looked the night Arnett Leslie had set aside his own troubles and brought her to the governor's ball. He had dressed her, a slattern in a tavern kitchen, in the London gown he had bought for the girl he loved; here, now, she was wearing another of the dresses he had meant for that faithless, heartless woman. And she herself had been as faithless, as heartless, in Arnett Leslie's eyes. How he must despise her! She could not tell him, now, that she had never meant to hurt him, but only to keep him safe; she could not tell him that she had meant to shame the men who called him coward. She could not explain *that* unless she explained also that she did not mean to swear, later on, that he was innocent of selling her to Barent. If she told him that, she must tell her brother, too, and have him freed; or Arnett Leslie himself would lay her whole pitiful scheming bare.

Her hands moved with a sudden fierce gesture under Peggy's comforting fingers. Her shoulders stiffened against the chair. She could not bear it to see Arnett Leslie standing again in the way of death. He was scarred already with blows that might have taken his life...for her. He had leaned over her, soothing her, bathing her, and she had seen the mark of the Shawnee hatchet on his breast. She had slept in his arms. She had loved him. But he had been cold and calm. He had not cared at all. She had been his duty.

Diantha knew that the blood was sweeping up her neck and face in a surge that seemed to drain her body and leave it weak and trembling. The room went out in a mist of tears. Through them, she saw the door of Ecuyer's office swing open. Captain Gaillard stood in the doorway; his hand rose, and dropped in a gesture of futility and anger. Then he came toward her, his heels loud on the sounding-board of floor. His face, when she could see it, was dark red—so red that his unpowdered hair looked bleached above it.

"What ... ?" Her throat closed, and she put her hands up to it. "What ... ?"

"They turned him loose," Gaillard said bitterly. "A cheap, slimy trick, and they turned him loose. Why, damme, they gloried in it! Shook his hand. Took his parole. Diantha, by God, they offered him command of the militia!"

He thought, for a bit, that his sister was going to faint; his arm slipped around her shoulders, and held her against him.

"I know, 't is shameful. Good God, I would not have believed that British officers could hold themselves so light. But," he swore savagely, venomously, "there's my lord Amherst still. I warrant you 't will be a different reckoning when he hears of it."

"You mean," faintly, "he is free, and *fighting?*"

Gaillard laughed harshly.

"Fighting! Militia never fights ... it runs. And this scum of the earth here ... faugh! ... he's well placed with them. He showed his colors, even when they turned him loose and kow-towed around him. He would not be commander. I do not wonder; he'd not have the gall to face us at the mess table. No, they enrolled him as a gentleman volunteer. Mark that, a *gentleman*. He's a private, like any pottle-pot out of that pig-sty of a town.

"Come, Diantha. I do not wonder you are shocked. You'd best lie down a while. There's no fear he'll get away. Arnold will watch him like a hawk. He'll go back to England and be tried, and hanged, too, and you'll forget all this. Come away, my dear."

Diantha let him lead her to the door and down the steps, where she had sat on Leslie's knees to bathe her feet, and had a soldier dry them before she put on the satin shoon to dance at Ecuyer's ball. As they moved slowly across the parade, a solitary shot rang out on the eastern wall. Somewhere, thin as a knife edge and as deadly, the yelps of the Shawnees slit through the echoes.

On the ramp that sloped down from the Flag bastion, a man in waistcoat and white breeches stood out, hatless, shouting:

"Indians in Lower Town! They're driving off the cattle!"

On the bench by the guardhouse door, a drummer boy sat up and fumbled for his drum. While it lay on the bench, he began to pound it wildly, and the sentry cursed him. The two sticks thrudded into the long roll, and shirt-sleeved men with muskets in their hands came pouring out through the arched entrance of the casement under the Flag bastion.

They formed, in front of the guardhouse, a ragged, unmilitary line.

"Look at them!" That was her brother, Diantha knew, mocking the linsey-woolsey militia. She rubbed the tow cloth bandage on her wrists across her eyes, but the parade-ground and the guard-house and the motley line kept dimming. Then the line moved, curled like a crawling snake in the sun, twisted around the corner of the guardhouse. A man in a green coat ran ahead of it, a bare sword flashing in his hand. The militia platoon, a brown snake with a green head, plunged into the covered way and was gone.

Diantha felt her brother's arm insistent around her waist, but she would not move.

"Did he go with them?"

"Yes, but it makes no difference; he'll not get away. The Indians will finish him if he tries it."

CHAPTER XXIII

*In Which Mr. Leslie Is Informed He Must Dance at the End of a
Rope or an Apron String, and Grossly Insults a Lady:*

THEY said, in Fort Pitt that night, that it was Arnett Leslie
who smelled the Shawnee ambush outside the walls.

Militiamen, digging two shallow graves in the ditch
beside the King's Highway, thanked God that the court-martial
had not lasted ten minutes longer. If the damned regulars had
bundled Leslie off to jail again, there would have been more
graves, they swore, and felt goose-flesh prickling through the sweat
on their arms because they had been so close to lying in these graves
instead of digging them. Or so close to roasting.

There was a suggestive odor of roasting flesh in the hot dusk.
If Arnett Leslie had snatched the militia platoon back from massacre, he had not been able to save the cattle and the horse herd.
The Shawnees, stampeding it in broad daylight to draw the garrison out, had killed only two white men; but no one in the besieged
fort failed to understand that death had come measurably closer
to them all. The cattle and the horses were half their food; and
most of the herd was gone. They smelled the beeves roasting on
the spits, and sickened; when they had eaten the meat of the animals
killed that afternoon by Indian bullets, they would be that much
closer to starvation; when they had starved long enough, the Shawnees would come over the wall, and the burning flesh would be
human, and alive.

After the attack on the cattle herd, the specter of hunger was
never absent.

Captain Ecuyer, at his table in the orderly room, saw it grinning
at him. His thick fingers folded slowly and heavily the message he
had just written to Colonel Bouquet, somewhere beyond the Allegheny mountains. Slowly, heavily, his mind plodded over the hundred miles of wilderness trail a messenger must travel before he
came to the doubtful safety of Fort Bedford. For every mile of that

trail, four men had died. The Swiss soldier of fortune, listening to the shots racketing in endless echoes along the river bluffs, knew that the man who carried his message to Bouquet probably would die.

He looked up as an orderly came in and stiffened to salute in the doorway.

"Mr. Leslie, sir, wishing to speak to the captain."

Ecuyer grunted, and got up, buttoning the scarlet tunic he had loosened against the heat.

He met Leslie with outstretched hand.

"Come in, Major. I am glad to see you. That was a good fight today, no? Come; sit you down. Here."

The governor pushed a splint-backed chair along the table. The orderly came in with two candles in the necks of bottles, and went out again.

"Now I can say something, Major," Ecuyer said abruptly, his blunt fingers pushing the bottles so that the light would fall on the brown hunting shirt and the thin face above it. "That governor of Maryland, he is a fool."

"The Royal Americans never had much love for him," Leslie returned dryly, and Ecuyer chuckled.

"That is right. You set your Maryland cavalry on our recruiting parties; you steal our recruits because, you say, you own them. Like black slaves, no? Um, excuse, please. I forget you are accused of buying a duchess and selling her again. By God, that is damned nonsense!"

"Thanks. Some people think it is sense."

"Bah! I have done what I can, Major. I do what else I can do, maybe, when we finish this war. What do you think?"

"I think I can get through to Bouquet with that letter, Captain."

"Letter? Letter! How do you know I write a letter to Bouquet?"

Leslie nodded toward the folded dispatch.

"I thought, after today, you would write one."

"*Ja! Ja!* The governor of Maryland takes your commission; but that does not make you a bad officer. You know what today means. We shall have bad times unless relief comes."

"They have never been so bold since Braddock's day," Leslie said quietly. "Even with the French behind them, they were never so persistent."

"They cannot take this garrison, Major."

"No. But they can wait."

"Six weeks, you think?"

"Six weeks? As bad as that?"

"On half rations, and less than that for the women and children, there is food for six weeks."

"Then, sir, may I go to Bouquet?"

"Why you?"

"I know the Monongahela country, Captain. Better, I imagine, than most of the traders and trappers here. A man might get through by Red Stone and Great Meadows where he could not get through to the north."

Ecuyer's fingers drummed on the table planks.

"You wish much to go, Major?"

"I wish to see Fort Pitt relieved, sir, before it is too late. Bouquet is not much west of Carlisle, if he has found any troops at all to bring that far." Leslie hesitated. "You do not think, sir, I am seeking to escape my trial?"

"*Peste!* I know you are not. Orderly!" The commandant looked apologetically at Leslie. "I shall ask Captain Gaillard to agree. It is ..." his hands flattened themselves on the table in resentful helplessness ... "a royal warrant that he has. He has promised already that the king shall hear how I set you free. Free ... to get yourself scalped, eh? Orderly, go ask Captain Gaillard to come."

"And Lady Diantha," Leslie's voice cut in, sharply.

Ecuyer glanced at him, and the orderly stood uncertain in the doorway.

"She knows the charge is false, Captain. That should settle it."

"Good! Good! Orderly, the lady, also." He leaned across the table, between the candles. "In God's name, why has she not said so? Will you tell me that?"

"I do not," said Leslie, smiling faintly, "know a great deal about duchesses."

"Or women! Any women!" the Swiss agreed with vigor. "Who can know them? That wench of Arnold's, now. By God, I should have put the cat to her many days, she set these officers of mine in such a stew. Now you see, she is worth a platoon, all by herself. By God, Leslie, she keeps those women in order where a general

273

could not do it. And Arnold ... you have seen him, eh? Head over heels about this red-headed duchess. Pah!"

Leslie's faint smile deepened a little. He rose, still smiling, as Diantha and Captain Gaillard came in and stood questioningly at the foot of the table. Ecuyer invited them bruskly to sit down, and the girl let Gaillard push a splint chair under her; except for one flashing look at Leslie, she kept her eyes on the commandant's red face. Leslie sat down calmly, one hand and elbow on the table edge, and made no pretense not to watch her. The blue sarcenet was vastly becoming. She had the chin of a duchess. And the air.

Ecuyer was blunt. Gaillard heard him through, and said one word as bluntly:

"Impossible."

"Do you realize, Captain Gaillard, that this post is in grave danger?"

"I do not." There was more than bluntness in the sea captain's tone. He was frankly and outrightly scornful. "You have three hundred men, half of them regulars. A hundred seamen would rout these naked savages."

"A hundred seamen," Ecuyer told him patiently, "would name another hill for us." The beads of perspiration under the edge of his wig ran down his forehead as his head jerked. "That hill up there—Grant's Hill—was named for a brave fool who tried it with good Highland troops. Not a hundred of them, either. Grant had five hundred."

"You imply, sir..."

"No. I do not imply. I tell you, as a soldier, that unless this garrison is relieved within six weeks, the women and children we have here will begin to starve. They are on quarter rations now. In six weeks... *finished*. This dispatch to Colonel Bouquet must get through. I ask you to accept Major Leslie's parole to take it."

"I have no reason to believe Mr. Leslie's parole is good. He is a cashiered officer of colonial militia, and he is under charges that mean hanging, sir. Your responsibility..."

Ecuyer got to his feet. Diantha's eyes followed him.

"I know my responsibility, sir. You are accepting a heavy one yourself, Captain Gaillard."

Leslie, sprawling in his chair, spoke carelessly to them all.

"The charge is false, and can be proved so."

"Then prove it!" Gaillard shot the words at him.

"Diantha can tell you." He smiled at her, a wide, unconcerned smile. The smile and the name together set a match to Gaillard's quarter-deck arrogance of anger.

" 'S breath! Ye'll not name her so! Ye'll not foul her with y'r damned backwoods manners, ye . . ."

Leslie waved his hand.

"Oh, let be, Gaillard, let be. 'T was Diantha I bought and paid for. Ay, and Diantha who took my bed and shared my room." He was laughing, his head back on the staves of the chair, his careless hand waving Gaillard back. Diantha stared at him unbelieving. Gaillard took two quick strides to pass around the foot of the table.

Ecuyer's stern voice stopped him.

"None of that, Captain Gaillard. I'll hold this man for your royal warrant as I'll hold this fort. Mr. Leslie. . . ."

"My regrets, Captain Ecuyer, sir." Leslie rose languidly, and bowed a little. "I thought that perhaps Captain Gaillard might be wiser than he is."

"By God . . . ! Wiser? What . . . ?"

"Why, d'you see, 't will all be bound to come out in the evidence, in any trial there is. I thought, now, maybe you'd let it drop, and let me be on the road to Bouquet. It seems a vile thing to do, to dirty a woman's name for a charge so shallow."

Gaillard roared at him, and would have rushed in and struck him but for Ecuyer's hand hard on his shoulder. The commandant spoke harshly, angrily:

"Mr. Leslie, you've gone too far."

"But you've not asked the lady whether the charge is false," Leslie suggested, not moving.

"Well?" Ecuyer's flushed face swung to the girl.

She rose, a shimmer of gold-red hair and stormy blue gown, and faced Leslie across the candles, and the candles set sparks burning in her eyes. Sparks like gunners' matches at dark gunports, he thought fleetingly; in a second, her indignant fury would explode and scorch him. He had insulted her as grossly as he knew how; perhaps, in her anger, she would blaze out with the truth. But the explosion did not come. She said, clearly:

"I know that Mr. Leslie bought me as a bond servant."

Leslie's lips curled.

"I bought you in order to set you free, and signed your freedom," he told her coolly, a little contemptuously.

"I do not know that." Coolly, too. "My lord Lawless swears this man bartered me for a jest. The man who helped him hanged himself because he knew his guilt." Her voice weakened. "I think," she went on, faintly, as if it cost her pain so to condemn an otherwise brave man, "I think Mr. Leslie would never set me free."

She had never seen Leslie's face so drawn and so withdrawn. He bowed with rigid politeness to the governor.

"My regrets for an embarrassing mistake, sir."

"You may report to your barracks, Mr. Leslie." The commandant's voice was gruff, his stiff shoulders hostile. They were more hostile, Diantha thought, as he swung about to make her an elaborate leg and bow her out. She had need of the arrogant thrust of her brother's chin to help her keep her own chin up while they followed the brown hunting shirt down the steps of the governor's house. There was a contemptuous swing to the very thrums of Arnett Leslie's forest dress.

When Gaillard left her at the door of her room, she stood for long minutes staring through the dusk. A tall figure passed blackly through the glow of the ovens, and disappeared into the dusk toward the militia barracks.

Up on the Flag bastion, a sentry's hoarse voice bawled the hourly hail:

"All's we-el-ll!"

From the Music bastion, a clear, boyish voice took up the shout:

"All's well!" And round the five points of the star-shaped ramparts, from the Ohio bastion, from the Monongahela bastion with its walls of barreled earth, and from the Grenadier bastion to the south, the comforting cry went up through the still dark.

Five times. . . .

And then a sixth time, and a seventh. Again. And yet again—high, uncanny, mocking the assurance of the sentries' calls—"All's we-e-ll-lll!" In the ruins of burned cabins, in the willows across the Allegheny, and on the towering bluffs where warriors looked down as from a balcony into the beleaguered fort, Indian voices picked up the cry and turned it into a fiendish taunt.

Leslie, dropping down beside Tom Yeardley on the bench by

the barracks door, looked up toward the invisible bluffs as the eerie cry mocked the sentinels.

"Cheerful," he commented.

Tom took the stem of his long clay from between his teeth, and rapped the bowl gently on the bricks behind him.

"As cheerful as you are," he agreed placidly. "I surmise you're stopping with us in Fort Pitt a while."

"Ay. I blundered it."

Tom filled his pipe in serene silence.

"She wouldn't let you go," he concluded aloud, when he had the tobacco packed to his liking. "I marvel you're so witless, Arnie."

"Witless! Gad, I put it to her, face to face."

"And face to face, she said you were guilty as hell," Tom finished for him.

"I have never," softly, bitterly, "heard a lie told better. She convinced Ecuyer."

"Plaguey, she convinced *you,* and that's more."

"She convinced me I am an utter fool. I am so much a fool I cannot see yet what she gains by lying."

Tom murmured amusedly to his pipe, and took the stem from his lips to chuckle.

"Ay, you're a fool about women, Arnie. You'd not believe it if you were told what she gains." He laid a heavy hand on Leslie's knee. "You're bad as that top-lofty brother of hers, expecting these red devils outside to fight fair and square, like civilized folk. A woman in love is not civilized; she fights like any greasy brute of a Mingo, teeth and claws and a knife in the back. Arnie, did that knock in the head leave you no wits at all?"

"Damnation few, Tom. Too few to see where hanging Arnett Leslie will help a duchess with her loves."

"Flog me, you're a precious numskull. There's no wonder a tomahawk can't break that head of yours." Leslie slumped against the barracks wall, too bitterly weary to be annoyed at the recurring chuckle. "You'll never hang, Arnie, unless it's to a duchess' apron string."

"I'll have the rope, if you please."

"No. You'll have the apron string, and tie it to your neck yourself. Did you ever take thought that every day she can make Ecuyer and Arnold and her brother believe you the rankest scoundrel unhanged, she gains a day of safety for you?"

Leslie made a faint, impatient gesture. It was too preposterous for energy.

Yeardley thrust the pipe into his listless hands.

"Puff," he commanded. "There's no more than two fillings left in this pouch of mine; you'll smoke sawdust when that's gone. I'm breakin' my word to speak so, but I'll not have you throwing your life away for any woman. If Diantha Gaillard can lie for you, Tom Yeardley can break a promise. She lied to keep you in the guard-house, Arnett, and she wept when they let you out; she lied tonight to keep you inside these walls, because she loves you—and that wildcat wench of Arnold's will claw my eyes out if she knows I've told you. She gave her word she'd not tell; and I gave mine." Silence. The tobacco glowed red and redder to Leslie's nervous puffing. "You don't believe that, do you?"

"No." The rim of the clay bowl took on the red glow of the tobacco. "If that were it, I ended it tonight."

"Eh? Ended it?"

The pipe bowl bobbed to an emphatic nod.

"I told her, before Ecuyer, that I would dirty her name if they tried me. I told her brother she took my bed and shared my room."

"And she held her post like a soldier," Tom triumphed at him. "Gave you volley for volley, didn't she? Ay, I'll lay you my thousand acres at Near-the-Navel she stuck to her guns, and made Ecuyer find another courier to take his message to Bouquet." He laid one clumsy arm across Leslie's shoulders. "What ye said to her did no harm. But ye shame her when ye think she's no better than Evelyn Gentle. I tell ye, Arnie, I'll dance at y'r weddin', and kiss a duchess, too, when I kiss the bride."

"You'll dance at a Shawnee stake, more likely," Leslie told him, and let the pipe go out.

CHAPTER XXIV

In Which Sergeant Peggy Washes a Soldier's Shirt and Earns the Envy of a Duchess; and Mr. Leslie Loses His Temper and Two Friends:

D AY by day the shadow of the torture stake crept closer to the fort.

On the twenty-eighth of June, it came so close that men and women could feel the bite of the flames on their fear-ridden nerves, and see their own bodies writhing under the fire-brands and the red-hot hatchets. For at nine o'clock that night, the startled sentries behind the palisades on the western wall heard Indians in the moat below them. Frantic drums sent the whole garrison rushing to the loopholes.

In the morning, patrols crept over the wall to look, and came creeping back again with grim, portentous faces. The soft earth of the moat was thick with moccasin tracks. The besiegers had found the weakness of Fort Pitt.

From that day on, half the garrison manned the firing steps day and night. At two o'clock every morning, the half who slept were shaken from their bunks and mustered by companies on the parade. From two until five, every man who could hold a weapon stood at a loophole, one musket in his hands, another leaning against the wall beside him. Eyes stared blindly into the fog; ears strained for the whisper of moccasins in the ditch; gunners stretched prone in the embrasures, watching and listening.

Morning after morning, the sunrise burned away the fog, and the attack did not come.

Day after day, men who had guarded the flimsy palisades half the night must work with ax and mattock to strengthen the barriers. At the forge near the ovens, the blacksmiths hammered odds and ends of iron into crow-foot traps, three-legged contraptions with sharp spikes sticking up an inch or two above the legs. Under cover of darkness, volunteers crept over the walls and planted them in the moat to pierce the Indians' moccasins. Ecuyer seized every bear and beaver trap in the refugees' belongings, and the militia set them on the slopes of the mud walls. Gunners of the Royal Artillery planted mines among the traps. Bales of deerskins came out of the traders' stores and were piled up behind the weakest parts of the stockade. An order, posted on the hoarding beside the door of the governor's house, forbade any one to use a nail for his own purposes. Every nail, every bit of iron must go to the sergeant major to be turned into canister for the guns, against the day when the cannon as well as the women and the children must go hungry.

On the morning of July third, the Indians crept within thirty yards of the main gate in broad daylight to fire at the lookouts. When the dozen cows and the few poor horses that were left were let out to graze, a full company must go as bullock guard, lest savages ambushed in the cellars attempt a massacre under the very walls.

Ecuyer posted another order: every able-bodied woman must bear her share of the fatigue parties; any who refused could starve, there would be no rations for her. Women went out with sickles and knives to cut and bind the spelt, with half the garrison in skirmish line around them and brass cannon straddling the furrows. On Mondays and Thursdays, a company of militia threw a screen of pickets from the main gate, through the ruins of the Lower Town, to the bateau shed on the river bank, while a score of women filed across the drawbridge with dirty clothes in baskets, or in bundles on their heads, and knelt on the log wharf to wash them.

The brunt of the outguard duty—the trap setting, the herding, the protection of the reapers and the washing parties—fell to the town militia. Their skirmish line, in linsey and buckskin, sank out of sight in the weeds and found shelter in folds of ground where the bright uniforms of the regulars and the Pennsylvanians betrayed every crouching soldier. Some of them died; but the motley companies acquired a fierce esprit de corps of their own. More and more, as the siege dragged through July, the militia fought the deadly little skirmishes in which a life or two bought a few more blanket-loads of spelts or saved a few more rows of corn and beans from the choking weeds.

More and more, Arnett Leslie, without rank or title, became the commander of the town companies. The woodsmen, the trappers and traders, the backwoods farmers who formed their ranks had all the borderer's distrust of officers in lace and ruffles. They had not forgotten the sheeplike slaughter of Braddock's regulars seven years before; nor that the Highlanders who survived the massacre on Grant's Hill owed their lives to backwoods riflemen. They gave Leslie, who had led militia, the confidence they could not give a subaltern of the Royal Americans. Peter Lanness, hobbling about the fort on home-made crutches, told and retold the story of the fight on the Venango road until it became a sort of heroic legend. Boyd pestered Leslie for details of Diantha's rescue, and when he failed to get them cobbled up a story of his own.

A private in the homespun ranks, Leslie found himself thrust into authority. Yeardley dropped naturally into his old rôle as second in command, and managed, whenever he met Valentine Arnold or Robert Gaillard, to give them a placid smile more tantalizing than the occasional arrows that came whizzing over the walls to skitter along the parade ground or stick quivering in the barracks roofs. Fritz Van Buren, clinging to his two muskets like any full-grown man, became not only Leslie's shadow but his orderly; obedient in everything else, he refused stubbornly to sleep in the militia quarters, and insisted on curling up beside his bear, tethered and unhappy in the hot cranny between the ends of two adjoining barracks.

Tom, Fritz, endless duty, and dour little Robin wriggling on his leash at the foot of a bunk, gradually eased whatever wounds the red-headed duchess in the governor's house had left Leslie. He saw her at times, at a distance, busy at a table by one of the open windows. Tom told him, casually, that she had gone to Ecuyer with a demand to be treated as any woman of the garrison; but Ecuyer, or Arnold, or her brother had seen to it that she was assigned to work that kept her off the walls and inside the gates. With a dozen of the older women, she labored at improvising lint and bandages, and food for the children sickening in the damp heat. But when Arnold would have moved the blue bed and the dressing table into the governor's house, where the officers' ladies were quartered, she was as stubborn as Fritz about his bear; and the commandant was curiously unconcerned at her brother's plea that Peggy Sargent was no fit roommate for a duchess. He suggested, bluntly, that Lady Diantha Gaillard was capable of judging for herself; and might have added that Captain Gaillard was much in the company of Valentine Arnold, had he seen the humor of it. What he did see was that Lady Diantha's open friendship for Peggy Sargent gave the girl a standing with the refugee women whose fears and clamorings tormented him. For Peggy Sargent was Sergeant Peggy now in earnest, sturdily ruling the twenty stoutest women and girls who had been detailed to the task of keeping the water barrels on the walls filled. The shingles of the barracks roofs were dry as tinder; fire arrows were a ceaseless peril; there were not men enough in the garrison to spare for the water detail—and none to protest when Peggy went recklessly along the walls, two heavy buckets swinging from her yoke, while the bullets pattered on the palisades.

Tom Yeardley complained mildly that she was at the militia barracks oftener than at the well; and winked at Fritz because they both knew that she came to get first-hand news of Leslie to take back with her to Diantha.

She told Leslie, once, that Diantha was well, and that the scars were entirely gone; but his brittle smile and the black brows pinched into a harsh line above his eyes kept her from saying so much again. Daily, when Captain Arnold took his station at the steps of the governor's house to receive reports from the officers on guard, she sat on the bench outside the militia barracks or perched on the log frame of the well to watch him with eyes that made no effort to veil their hurt. At night, on the parade ground, when the muskets were silent and the women and children clustered outside their hot quarters for a breath of cooler air, she sang and danced and laughed, the gayest person in Fort Pitt; but even the smallest drummer knew that the girl watched Valentine Arnold with tears in her eyes. There were tongues a-plenty to remark the difference between Arnold's cast-off mistress and Lady Gaillard's cast-off suitor—for every one knew how Major Leslie, in scarlet and yellow, had brought Bond's tavern wench to the governor's ball and introduced her as his promised wife; and knew, too, that she accused him now of buying her as a bond servant and selling her to Bond for a drunken jest. There were hot quarrels about his guilt, and one fierce fist fight behind the barracks that went on until Braams, the Dutch regular, knocked a matross man senseless against the brick wall.

If Peggy Sargent wore her bruised heart where all might see it, Arnett Leslie kept his securely hidden. If he cared one lead shilling what the Duchess of Strangden did, or with whom she flirted at table in the officers' mess, no one could read it in his face or in his crisp, cool bearing. He even walked with Peggy, one day, across the drawbridge and the parade, as the militia detail came in from escorting the wash-women down to the river and back. He carried her bundle of damp clothes in his arms while she carried his rifle, and bowed, over the bundle, as unconcernedly as any polite stranger, when Peggy waved to the red-headed girl at the window of the governor's house, and the red-headed girl waved back. Women about the ovens, watching avidly, saw him stoop with Peggy and open the bundle on the doorstep of her room, and heard them laughing gayly together. After a minute or two, he walked briskly to his own quarters, trailing over his arm the shirt she had washed for him.

Passing the gaping women at their spits and kettles, he had no means of knowing that their tongues were busy over the spectacle of a red-haired girl leaning out a window to watch Peggy Sargent roll up her washing again. Nor that they were reminding each other that this red-head, who had turned so amazingly into a duchess, had delivered a bundle of washing not two doors away, to that swaggering Dutch captain, Barent, whom she also accused now, though he was dead.

The siege dragged through July. Heat, monotony and the ever-present specter of starvation sapped the morale of the pent-up refugees and the haggard men who guarded them. Fifteen hours a day the sun blazed down full upon the fort, and there was no shade. It turned the barracks into stifling ovens, where half-starved children cried sleeplessly through nights that were all but as hot as the days. It fired the precious corn in the garden, and baked the parade ground until it cracked into a dizzying pattern, and men with mattocks must fill the biggest cracks lest soldiers trip in them in the dark and set off their muskets.

The rivers fell lower and lower, and a sickening smell arose from the exposed silt to join the stench of packed humanity in the fort. The faces of men on the walls burned almost black, while their hair bleached, and the bloodshot whites of their eyes gave them a staring, haunted look. Nerves dried and snapped. Dogs howled, and a harried commandant set a squad to bayoneting every loose one. One hot evening, when a sobbing militiaman had died of three frightful wounds and a Delaware Indian had crawled up close to the main gate to howl tauntingly that Fort Ligonier had fallen, an orderly posted on the notice board an order that read: "The wolf and the bear are to be immediately killed or put out of the fort."

The lank backwoodsman whose children had made a pet of a cub wolf drew his skinning knife with a grin, and invited another family to supper. Leslie and Yeardley, coming down from guard duty on the Ohio bastion at dawn, read the sentence on the hoarding and looked for the bear in the angle of the barracks behind the ovens, where Fritz had tethered him handy to scraps from the cooking. The bear was gone, and so was Fritz. Leslie, searching with weary anger in his heart at the needlessness of it, found tracks down the earthen wall. A startled grenadier on guard at the sally port facing the Monongahela would have barred his way until he saw the cold fury in the strained face. Leslie followed the mingled tracks of moccasins and shambling paws down to the river bank; they crossed the drying ooze and disappeared, and the man came back with bitter oaths on his lips.

He watched the grenadier drop the bars of the sally port gate into place, and walked slowly through the narrow tunnel. Half way to the inner face of the wall, he heard a shot; the earth dulled the sound of it, and dulled the sharp cry of a woman's voice. Leslie's taut nerves snapped him into a run; a shot, a cry, a clamor of voices might mean anything, in that tense atmosphere of constant dread.

He saw, as he came out onto the parade ground between the ends of two barracks, an officer in a scarlet tunic and a woman in a wine-red dress, facing each other by the well. Around them was a growing circle of women in shapeless linsey gowns and men of the militia companies half naked as they had sprung from their bunks in breech-clout and leggings. From the farther fringe of the circle, a shirtless villager raised his rifle in his naked arm and flourished it, hailing him:

"Leslie! Look ye here, Major, the lousy scuts have..."

A new burst of clamor blurred the rest of it. He thrust through the crowd, and saw Peggy Sargent confronting the man she loved, tears running down her sun-blackened cheeks and words stumbling over each other on her shaking lips. There was blood in a wet, black stain on the wine-red dress, and blood on her bare arms.

Across her arms, limp and lifeless, hung the body of the dour little terrier.

The stir Leslie made pushing through the circle turned her toward him.

"Arnett! Arnett! He killed Robin."

Arnold's lips were white.

"Leslie, get this rabble still!" His voice, tight with strain and weariness, quivered like a strumming wire. "You know the orders ... dogs running loose ... get this rabble into barracks."

"Arnett, I went to ask you ... about Fritz. When I opened the door, Robin was loose. He ran out. This ... this brave officer shot him. *Ohh* ... you evil ... cruel ... !"

Arnold swung on his heel. The circle gave back a little, but it did not open.

"Captain Arnold," said Leslie, gently, and those nearest saw that he was smiling.

The clamor stilled itself, and the circle pressed in again. Leslie put one hand into the breast of his hunting shirt and drew out his pouch; out of the pouch he plucked a meager jingling of silver coins, and counted them, slowly, while Peggy's sobbing breath made the only sound in the deadly hush.

"The reward is a half crown, is it not, Captain Arnold?" Cool, smiling, taut, Leslie stepped toward the adjutant and put out his hand.

"Oh, the devil!" Arnold snapped, his eyes wary, his fingers creeping toward his saber hilt.

"The devil," said Leslie softly, "would take shame at this, and would not take his pay. But you will take it." His lips parted in a smile that bared his teeth. Arnold, like a man bemused, put out his hand and took the half crown Leslie held out to him—the reward offered in garrison orders for the killing of stray dogs. Then, with a hysterical oath, he dashed the coins into the crowd and began to shoulder the women huddled behind him. A townsman cursed him in ripping oaths.

"Silence!" said Leslie sternly. "Let him through."

He reached out for the furry body sagging between Peggy's arms.

"Thank you, Peg." His breath choked in his throat. "Poor little rogue of a dog. I bring all my friends bad luck."

"Arnett ... *don't*. Oh, not that. You're *crying*."

CHAPTER XXV

In Which a Duchess Gets Down On Her Knees in the Dust; and a Humming Bird Sings a Death Song in the Garden:

THERE was mutiny in Fort Pitt. In fact, two mutinies.

One was on the parade ground, where men and women stormed against Ecuyer's orders forbidding them to venture outside the walls. Weeds were choking the garden; the untended corn was dying; villagers with the pinch of hunger in their faces pressed clamoring around the officer of the day.

"Name of a name!" swore Joe Neron, who had ridden with Peter Lanness on the unsuccessful attempt to break through and warn Fort Venango. He flourished his hairy bare arms under the lieutenant's nose. "Shall we sit here and starve, then? By God, there is not food here for a week. Do we sit here and leave those corn, those melons, those potatoes for those red devils? By God," as the jostling, shouting crowd approved him, "I will not sit here until I am so weak they walk in and scalp me lying down!"

"Nor I!"

"Not me, nuther!"

"Where's Ecuyer? Fetch Ecuyer!"

The subaltern sent a runner to the commandant. Ecuyer turned in relief from one mutiny to another, and left Captain Gaillard to cope with his rebellious sister.

Diantha, bare-footed, in the skimp blue dress she had worn as Bond's kitchen wench, did not clamor or storm. She merely announced that she was sharing the dangers of the other women, whether they went into the fields to cut the spelt, or down to the bateau shed to wash, or up onto the walls to fill the fire barrels.

Having made the announcement, she would not argue. She simply said "No," calmly and gently, to every protest and plea. To Captain Ecuyer, called in by her brother, she smiled, and curtseyed with outrageous impishness, the ragged blue hem tweaked halfway up to her knees.

" 'T will make the women feel easier to see a duchess washing shirts," she told him, and smiled again at his astonished Swiss oath.

In the end, both mutinies gained their objects.

Toward noon, one of the militia companies fell in before the guard house with muskets, knives and tomahawks. Leslie led the forty out through the main gate in double file and flung them in a long, slowly creeping skirmish line out through the garden and into the underbrush of the abandoned common. They pressed past the end of Massacre pond, climbed the rail fence at the far end of the pasture and disappeared into the woods. After half an hour, a runner came back to the gates to say that the forest edge was clear.

Fifty women and half as many men, released from duty, trooped out of the fort with hoes and spades, with scythes and sickles for the corner of the spelt field still uncut, and with baskets and blankets to bring back whatever vegetables the weeds and the drouth had allowed to grow. As they scattered through the over-grown garden, the picket line dropped back out of the woods to form a long semi-circle of sentinels, from the north end of the garden where it faced the Allegheny to the upper end of the old French cemetery where weed-grown wheel tracks marked the Allée de la Vierge of the old regime.

The villagers who had plantings of their own hurried to them. The scythes and sickles began to swing through the brittle wheat. The rest of the working party attacked the grass and weeds in the corn and potato plots.

The sentinels sank out of sight in the brush and the rank grass. Garden and pasture and grain field lay as quiet as if there never had been war, or siege, or death. After a time, the nervous lifting of heads stopped; there was nothing to see except the parched grass of the common, the zigzag of fence, the sagging crosses on the French graves.

It was breathless and still among the corn rows—so still that every weed plucked from the dry earth made a little, dry sound as its roots pulled loose. Even where the weeds grew rankest and the corn was sickly yellow from choking, the soil was baked and cracked, and the edges of the corn were burned crisp. The weeds themselves were limp and wilted in the heat. Between

Diantha's bare knees, the pile of weeds she had just pulled looked already as lifeless as if they had been uprooted hours ago.

She reached ahead and pounded at the hard earth with one grimy fist. In the next row, Peggy looked up at the sound of thumping and her dark head came peering through between the stalks.

"Paint and patches, darling, what are you doing?"

Diantha thwacked the dirt with both small fists at once, and rubbed a thumb across her nose.

"Making beds for my poor knees, sweet," she answered. "This ground is like hot stones. I'll need patches, for my knees, if I stay here saying my prayers till sundown."

"You've a patch on your nose now. A nice black one."

"A new fashion for the macaronis, my dear." Diantha hitched herself along and settled her knees gingerly into the two dusty hollows she had thumped into the ground. She sank back on her heels.

"Consider, Mistress Sargent," she minced, while Peggy's teeth flashed in a growing smile, "how Mistress Jones will lead the grand march at our next rout, in the exclusive new fashion of Pitt's Town. She will wear dainty shoon of rich black mud—if it rains that night, you see—tastefully adorned with one large blister; and stockings of the same material, with clocks, my dear, cunningly confected of mosquito bites and pink scratches. I think pink is so much more becoming than red—mine are red. And her gown, h-mm, her gown is a problem, Peg. By that time, you see, we shall have no gowns in the present mode; we shall have used them all for bandages and for swabbing out cannons. How would a nice deerskin apron do? And the very latest powder to her face, my dear—the kind just becoming popular...."

"The new dirt shade," suggested Peggy, and wiped some of it off her forehead with a damp wrist.

"You smudged it," said Diantha critically. "And the dirt shade is too dark for candle-light. I favor that lighter, clay tint, with a cast of yellow to it—say Virgin Alley dust. Has that not a London sound, Peg? And a black patch on her nose, arranged in the new conceit introduced by Mistress Peggy Sargent, with its lower edge daintily shaped to adorn the nostrils."

"Is my nose dirty?" Peggy snatched at a puffed sleeve and scrubbed anxiously.

"If it isn't it's the only clean one in the King's Garden, sweetling. Don't interrupt. We have to dress her hair. Let me see.... We might choose that plastered effect so much in vogue in Pitt's Town; it's very becoming to ladies with dark hair. No, it will be out of style by that time. Mistress Rawbones-Jones will wear her hair in a hoop."

"In a hoop?"

"Certainly." Diantha's voice went flat. "In a hoop with plaits, and pictures painted on the skin. Ugh—I'm sorry, Peg. I can't ever forget watching them plait that woman's scalp."

"I know." Peggy's hand came through between the stalks and touched Diantha's cheek. "Try not to think about it, darling. It's all past and gone."

Diantha's fingers touched Peggy's.

"I don't know what I'd have done without you, Peg."

"You'd have married Arnett Leslie, and you will yet."

Diantha flung Peggy's hand down and bent again to the weeds, her fingers plucking furiously. Peggy smiled down at her dirt-streaked neck.

"Goose," she said gently. "You know you stay on your knees so you'll not be looking for him up there on the hill. I saw you staring at him when the guard went out. Lud, you'd not have treated him so unless you loved him. Snort, then," as Diantha made an indignant small noise. "You'd rather go around down-looked and miserable than admit that you love him. What's the good of being a duchess if you can't do as you wish? You'd no such pride when you took his gifts...."

" 'Pride ... !' "

"And what else may it be, then?"

Diantha huddled over the dry seed stalk of a plantain, examining it as if it were the most fascinating object in the world.

"Would *you* wed with him?" Her fingers stripped off the lowest rings of the seeds.

"I?" Peggy laughed. "He'd scarce want *me,* my dear."

"He has been kind to you. And you washed his shirt." The seeds flew in a small shower over Diantha's knees as her thumb and forefinger stripped the plantain bare. Peggy's laugh rang out so merrily that heads came poking up over the corn rows to look at her.

"There's a deal more to the marriage service than the washing of a shirt," she said. And added: "I've heard so," soberly.

Diantha sat back on her heels.

"You mean," she began resolutely, "that no man would wed a girl who..." Her voice trailed away.

"...had belonged to another man," Peggy finished it for her.

"Peg!" Diantha jumped up in quick contrition, her hands scrubbing themselves in her skirt to rub off the dirt, and took Peggy by both shoulders. "Peg, I'm sorry. Oh, I'm such a devil...selfish ...cruel..."

"And in love," said the smiling face between the rustling stalks. "Don't be sorry, dear. I'm not. Diantha Gaillard, what's worrying you so?"

Diantha shook her head slowly.

"I don't know, Peg. I...I...Oh, Peg, I think he would not have me even for a mistress, now."

The brown hands took her firmly by the elbows and shook her.

"What nonsense are you talking? Silly minx, I vow I think your head is not right even yet. If he would not have you for a mistress 't is only because he loves you too much."

"And knows too much of me."

Peggy looked searchingly into the woebegone face and the shamed gray eyes that turned persistently away.

"Di, sweet," she began; and found the girl suddenly in her arms, murmuring against her damp shoulder:

"Oh, Peg, I can't make it seem wrong for you. You love him so, and you don't try to hide from God, or anybody. I love him that way, too, and I have to hide...and hide...and hide. And still I know that he knows, and he can never want me...!" Which altogether made so little sense that Peggy Sargent did not try to answer it at all, but stroked Diantha's braid where it lay across her shoulder and whispered small nothings to the top of her head.

"I couldn't help it! I couldn't help it!" Diantha cried stormily. "You loved Val, and it seems all right to me. I...I don't believe even *God* minds. But it's so *different*. It's so *different*. Oh, Di, what am I going to *do*?"

"Tell him."

"Tell him what?" Diantha's voice was small and puzzled.

"Lud, how do I know?"

At which, for some incomprehensible reason, Diantha straightened up, pushed her hair back from her temples, and smiled.

"Am I dreadful?" she demanded. The smile disappeared. "I know I am. I love you so, Peg, and I say things that hurt. I'm sorry, truly."

"*I'm* not. Look, Di, the flag's coming down."

On the nearest bastion, a drum rolled sonorously into the rumble of the retreat. Arm in arm between the corn rows, they watched the red cross slide down the staff, its blue field lost against the blue of the river beyond. Where the Lower Town had stood, the heat haze danced and shimmered and waves of it rose to make the fiery cross dance and shimmer also, like a dropping flame.

Up and down the garden, men and women straightened. Heads turned toward the cemetery where one or two dots marked the presence of a sentry prone behind stump or hummock. A scarlet tanager flashed across the corn, the whir of its wings faintly audible. There was another whir, louder and closer, a vibrant humming, quickly gone.

"A humming bird!" cried Diantha, and stood on tiptoe in the dirt to look.

Behind them a man shouted hoarsely. Peggy's arm gripped Diantha's.

"Look."

In the potato patch, the men who had been digging were standing in a cluster. One of them ran a few steps, stooped, and stood up with an arrow in his hand.

"Injuns!"

The cluster broke, running. A woman screamed. Diantha felt Peggy's arm dragging at her, heard Peggy's voice crying out at her. She stood on tiptoe again, her eyes on the deep grass beyond the burying ground. The air was full of vibrant humming. In the thickets along the Allegheny, a musket banged, and then a dozen went off in a fusillade that slammed against the ears with recurrent shocks of sound. Diantha saw smoke blossom and hang in black puffballs along the river bank; saw men spring up along the pasture fence, heard Arnett Leslie's voice, shouting at them to lie down, to hold their fire; felt her cheeks go cold as ice and her lips pinch and her body shrink as the Shawnee yell ripped through the shots and screams. She knew that bodies were tearing through the corn.

A man with a red beard and staring eyes went past, his breath rasping in his throat as he ran. She saw the picket line leap to its feet and run for the cornfield, its rifles trailing. And then the river thicket was alive with naked savages, and the scalp yell rose in beastly, freezing yelps.

Peggy's hands gripped Diantha's wrist, the wrist still red from the rawhide thongs. The familiar pain shot into Diantha's brain and filled it with panic. She was screaming as Peggy dragged her through the corn, sobbing screams that hurt her throat and set up a ringing in her ears. Her whole head rang. Her legs felt limp. She knew she was running, running in a world that rocked, toward a red and black fort that rolled crazily from side to side, toward a river that stood up like a high hill one moment, and sank away into a yawning pit the next, toward brown hills that rose and fell like waves, sickeningly.

The parched meadow between the garden and the fort was dotted with running figures, women in skirts that stood out like sails, flying sunbonnets, streaming hair. The bright flag was climbing again. Below it, between the gray faces of the gate, a long column of men in scarlet coats four abreast was coming on the run. Between it and the flag, a bundle of black smoke shot out from the bastion and floated there. Out of it came a shock of sound that blotted out the yelping, and ran like rolling thunder along the cliffs. On the Grenadier bastion another smoke cloud burst out and hung suspended, and another thunderclap of sound jarred the hot, heavy air and the hot earth underfoot. The shells screamed over the heads of fleeing women and burst in the underbrush at the river bank. The bushes spewed out more naked bodies. They came in a howling rush that crossed the open ground and gained the corn before the howitzers could fire again. Out of the cornfields, pickets burst helter-skelter, a dozen men running for their lives.

Diantha wrenched her wrist out of Peggy's grasp and turned to look. An Indian leaped out of the corn, his mouth open, his body shining like a copper snake in the sun, his arm up, a stone maul swinging. He was a dozen yards behind the last of the pickets. Diantha's throat closed convulsively. The white man stopped, glanced at the pan of his firelock, swung on his heel, and shot the Shawnee down.

"Di!" Peggy's voice screamed frenziedly. "Di! For God's sake, Di!"

Diantha ran again, toward the tall white man now trotting alone behind the fleeing guard, coolly biting the top from a cartridge as he trotted. The air crackled and rang, a hideous clamor of shots and yells. Peggy's voice was lost in it; Diantha's was lost, too, but she screamed at the too-cool runner:

"Arnett! Arnett! Arnett!"

The guard passed her. The nearest of them, a big man in green breeches, made toward her as if to stop her. He shouted at her as he came; and then his mouth jerked shut and he fell heavily, his musket flying from his hand. Diantha tripped on the long barrel and went down on hands and knees across the big man's back.

He squirmed under her, and groaned. Diantha crouched beside him, her eyes fixed on the tossing corn. It was alive with Indians. As she stared, a dozen of them broke into the open, and their yells rose triumphantly:

The big man plucked her skirt.

"Mistress Gaillard, they mustn't take you. Listen to me! Listen! If you can't run, get my gun. I didn't fire. Get it. Let me shoot you." His voice rose to a scream. "I've got my knife. I'll kill you with that. I saw them with a woman once. O God, let me kill her!"

He hitched toward her, his legs dragging, his hands tugging at his belt. Diantha neither saw nor heard him.

"Arnett!" she wailed, and got to her feet again. "Arnett!"

Leslie was running now. His arm caught her around the shoulders and spun her about and lifted her.

"Are you hurt?" he shouted down at her.

"No. No. Oh, Arnett. . . ."

She heard him groan, felt the lift of his arm relax, saw him thrust his rifle toward her.

"You fool, you little fool!" His voice was harsh. "Take that and run!"

He stooped over the wounded colonial, swung him to his back by one arm and leg, and ran on, staggering with the weight of him.

A thrown hatchet flashed past and struck the packed dirt of what had been a dooryard, and went whirling end over end.

Ahead of them rose a shouting. Behind them, through her own

gasping breath, Diantha heard the thud of feet. Leslie was crying out at her:

"Drop! Drop! Lie down!"

She saw him fling himself headlong, the man on his back rolling like a bundle of clothes across his head and into a dusty hollow. She let her knees go, and fell. Face down in the dirt, she felt the rifle snatched from her hands. There was a flash of fire, a rolling smash of sound. Clear and sharp in the sudden silence that followed it, a precise, soft voice said calmly:

"Half-cock firelocks!" There was a stir, a quick clicking noise. "Handle cartridge! Prime!"

Men came running, men in scarlet coats and white gaiters. Hands lifted her, dragged her. She fought them, struck at them with her nails. Across the shoulders of the red coats around her she saw Arnett Leslie running in great leaping strides, his rifle by its muzzle in both hands; saw a glistening body, its right half yellow, its left half green, its head hideous with green spots, rise up in the ruins of a cabin to meet him with tomahawk and knife; saw the thrown knife strike the rifle barrel between Leslie's hands and fly aside; saw the stock whirl and fall, and the painted monster reel away with its green spots covered by a sliding mask of red.

Then Leslie was running back. The Pennsylvanian was hobbling away with his arms across two scarlet coats, and the company of Royal Americans drawn up in the King's Highway was opening ranks to let them through. The soft, precise voice was calling Leslie by name:

"Prettily done, Major Leslie. We might have picked him off from the wall, but he's better out of the way. I'm going to give them another volley before we go in.

"Present firelocks! *Fire!*"

Again the rolling smash of sound. Then feet thudding on planks that gave back a hollow drumming; chains clanking; timbers groaning. A vision of brick walls rushing by, of a man's sweating neck against her chin, of air bitter with powder fumes, of a covered passage filled from wall to wall with soldiers at the double.

Behind the running column, the ponderous drawbridge of Fort Pitt swung slowly up, and the log gates closed.

CHAPTER XXVI

In Which the Tempest Bursts Upon Fort Pitt, and Men Fight for Their Lives Behind Barrels of Earth and Bales of Deerskins:

IT was quiet in the covered way. The log gates shut out the din. For a moment there was only the scuff of feet on soft dirt, the phruff of jostling bodies, the noise of breathing.

Then the running column came out into blinding glare and confusion.

The parade ground was pandemonium. Men shouted and cursed, women moaned and wept, dogs yapped. A tow-haired baby girl, stark naked, trotted wailing from one seething group to another, lost and frantic with terror. A black heifer ran round and round its picket until the rope pulled it down upon its knees, nose against the ground, and it crouched there bawling. Over against the Grenadier barracks a hatless drummer boy beat the long roll endlessly.

The howitzer in the Flag bastion fired again, a blunt smash of sound that shook the fort; and as its echoes rolled and broke along the bluffs, the redcoats shoulder to shoulder along the north wall leveled and fired. In the hot, heavy air, the cannonshot was like a blow upon the skull; the crash of the volley, sharper, flatter, was like a hand swung hard against the ear.

The soldier who carried Diantha loosed his hold and slid her to the ground. Her skirt caught on the frog of his belt as she slipped down, and she stood for an instant bare-legged to the thighs. Jerking at the cloth, she looked up into his face—a grave, boyish face, turned steadily away. The boy was blushing. Diantha thought suddenly of Arnett Leslie, kneeling over her, bathing her. The dress pulled loose, and the youngster ran to catch up with the running column, half way across the parade. By the well in the middle of the square, he stopped, his head bent back, a gaitered leg swinging in a grotesque arc as he spun slowly on one foot, blood spurting around an arrow in his neck.

Diantha's breath caught on a choking sob. She ran and knelt beside him.

He was strangling with the blood in his throat; it flew in drops from his lips and spattered on his face and on Diantha's hands and breast. He died while the air around them whirred with arrows. One struck and splintered on the baked earth beside them. From the east wall came a frantic cry:

"Fire! Fire! The roof's on fire!"

Sergeants with halberds were clearing the parade ground, herding women and children into casements under the South bastion. The air was full of crackling and whirring; a wave of smoke drifted down as a company on the firing step above the gate blazed away with another volley; through the smoke three fire arrows came curving, the burning bark at their tips flickering pale red. They dropped harmlessly in the dirt. But others had struck the shingled roofs of the barracks against the northern wall and stuck there. Two men in red coats were crawling over the peak of the roof, targets for a storm of bullets and arrows, to reach a flame that had begun to lick along the shingles on the inner slope, where water thrown from the ramparts could not reach it. They beat out the flame with their hats, and started back. One stiffened, then relaxed, and came sliding horribly down to the eaves, his fingers scratching at the shingles. He fell into the parade, limply, and lay motionless.

The parade ground was empty now except for the cattle staked out at one side; women and children clustered at the windows of the barracks, their strained faces peering out, row after row of them from the sill almost to the tops of the windows. Across the square, an arrow broke a pane in the commandant's house and glass fell tinkling on the brick steps. A sergeant looked at the broken window. Then he ran quickly along the barracks, swinging the solid shutters tightly shut. Diantha saw an arrow strike and stand quivering in the wooden blind where, a moment before, a child's face had been. Up on the wall behind the barracks a man began to shout again:

"Fire! The roof's caught again." And then, higher and shriller, "Water! Somebody get more water! The barrel's empty! Somebody. . . ."

Diantha ran for the well and the pile of wooden buckets.

She had two of them filled and the yoke on her shoulders when a door in the shuttered barrack wall flew open and two women came running—Peggy Sargent and Captain Jones' raw-boned wife. Peggy seized her by the shoulders, heedless of the slopping buckets. Diantha pulled away.

"Let me go," she cried. "Let me do *something!*"

"Di, dear, you can't go up there now!"

"I can. I'm going. What difference does it make what happens to me? I've just done harm to everybody. Let me *go!*"

Diantha backed away and swung the dangling bucket past her. With tears running down her cheeks, she sped toward the ramp that climbed to the eastern wall, the buckets swinging and splashing. The spilled water made black spots on the baked dirt. A man in a linsey hunting shirt dropped back from the firing step, smoke wisping from the muzzle of his rifle.

"Got him!" he shouted, and jerked out his knife to gash a long mark on a log in the palisade. There were two other marks alongside it. "I'm agoin' t' leave that knife there. Them bastards is crawlin' int' th' ditch." He drove the long blade into the log and reached for his powderhorn.

"Good Lord!" he cried out. "Gal, don' waste thet water. We're all like t' have our tongues hangin' out f'r water b'fore this here siege is over. Gimme them buckets!"

He came across the firing step to seize the pails.

"No!" Diantha flashed at him fiercely. "Get back to that loophole. Don't you dare touch those buckets."

"Jumpin' gees!" he swore delightedly. He nipped the stopper from his horn between his teeth and poured powder down the rifle barrel, swearing softly between clenched jaws. "I'm aputtin' your name on this one!" he called after her, and rammed home the bullet with a hard thrust.

The air was breathless and biting with powder fumes, and hot as an oven here on the wall. The sun, beating full against the inner side of the parapet and the row of sharpened logs that ran along its top, threw its heat up into the faces of the men who stood at the loopholes.

Where the firing step turned past the Grenadier bastion, Diantha had to step around a pile of scarlet coats thrown down in the dirt. The gunners of the Royal Artillery were fighting their howitzers stripped to the waist, sweat running in streams down their reddened flesh. While the gun pointers crouched at the embrasures, seeking some movement among the ruins or in the cornfield and the bushes beyond to betray a hidden marksman, the rest sat on their haunches between the wooden gun-carriages and their neat mounds of solid shot.

It was hotter still along the northern wall, where the barrack walls crowded close to the ramparts and penned in the heat. There were black and brown patches on the shingles where fire arrows had set the roof ablaze.

The men along the palisade here were militia. Occasionally a man fired; for the most part they stood with one shoulder against the logs and peered through the cracks between the palings, their rifles leaning beside them. An officer came hurrying down the firing step, a small black pot in one hand, a gunner's slow-match in the other. Where the water barrels stood, he sprang quickly upon a bale of deerskins, glanced over the palisade, and sprang back. Behind him an arrow struck with a thud in the barrack roof. He looked at it with a grimace, and touched the match to the fuse protruding from the iron pot. When it sputtered, he swung back his arm and threw. Along the wall, men thrust their rifles through the loopholes, waiting.

The grenade burst with a clanging bang, and a puff of black smoke welled up. Instantly a dozen rifles cracked, and a shout ran along the pales.

"That routed 'em out," said a man whose lank black hair hung in sweat-drenched strands around his cheeks. He dropped his musket butt to the ground and blew smoke from the muzzle. "They came out like seeds from a bursted melon."

"Did the boys hit any?" asked the officer. He looked at the deerskin bales and then at the arrow in the roof behind him, and did not climb up again to see beyond the wall.

"There's one of 'em lying in the weeds in plain sight. That's *one* we got." He put his cheek to the logs and stared out through a crack. "An' one tryin' to crawl into the gully." He lifted his rifle, cried out sharply, and staggered back. An arrow came in between the logs as he drew back, its point buried in his jaw.

"God damn 'em," he shouted hoarsely, the shaft waggling and dangling. "God damn 'em!"

He pushed past the officer and leaped to the pile of bales and pushed the long barrel over the logs, the arrow sticking out across his thumb as he gripped the stock. Bullets thudded on the palisade and another arrow passed with a gobbling noise, and still he stood there, sighting. His rifle cracked and jumped, and he crouched down quickly.

"By the Etarnal!" he swore, and raised a hand to steady the twitching shaft, "they paid for that one!" He slid down from the bales and set his rifle against them. Diantha, standing fascinated beside the water barrels, started forward with one half-emptied bucket.

"Water, by God." He set the bucket on the palm of one hand and raised it to his mouth. Water trickled down his leathery jaw and washed the running blood over his chest, between the flaps of the hunting shirt. He drank and drank, the mottled feather on the end of the arrow jerking in crazy arcs with each gulp, and poured what was left in the bucket into the nearest of the barrels.

"I'll carry 'em down f'r you, m'lady," he said, and picked up the yoke and the other bucket. "Reckon them redskins c'n spare me till I get this sliver cut out."

There were more women around the well when Diantha and the rifleman came down into the parade. Peggy was sending them in relays along the walls, some to fill the fire barrels, some with gourds to serve the thirsty men. Diantha filled her wooden pails, hooked them again to the heavy yoke, and went back to the northern wall. On the ramp she had to stop, and stand with her back against the bricks while two soldiers of the regulars came down from the Grenadier bastion, an officer riding between them on their clasped hands, his arms around their shoulders. Diantha saw Ecuyer's blunt face drawn with pain, and an arrow protruding from his thigh; his blue breeches were splotched with blood. In the bastion, as she hurried by, the men around the guns were standing with their backs to the howling storm outside, staring anxiously after the two who carried Ecuyer through the fluttering women and up the steps of the governor's house.

Diantha emptied her buckets into a barrel, and went back. She had to wait her turn at the well. There were a dozen women there now. One of them tipped a freshly filled pail as she stooped over it, fumbling for its handle with the hook of her yoke, and Captain Jones' grim wife swore at her.

"If this well runs dry, ye'll be prayin' for that water while they roast ye," she stormed.

Diantha felt the hot earth reel crazily under her feet and her lips suck in hot air that had the taste of a burned copper pot. She thought she was going to scream again. Just in time, she heard a shrill voice shouting her name.

A boy, shorter by two inches than the musket he dragged, was pelting toward the well.

"Miss Gaillard!" he shrilled, and stopped, panting, while Mrs. Jones cursed the girl at the windlass for letting the rope swing idly in the well so that she might listen. "Mistress Gaillard, y'r brother's hit! They taken him to y'r bed. I been lookin' ever'where for ye, 'long the wall."

She was surprised. Bob hit ... and she felt no such shock as she had felt when she saw Arnett Leslie trotting coolly at the rear of the guard. She loved Bob.

"Is he badly ... ?"

"Naw," the boy reassured her with the calmness of a veteran. "He taken an arrow in his leg, like Ecuyer. He can swear noble. Ye'll hear him, soon's ye getten to th' door."

CHAPTER XXVII

*In Which a Red-headed Gaillard Quarrels with a Red-headed Gaillard,
and the Lady Confesses She Lied:*

CAPTAIN ROBERT GAILLARD had stopped swearing from sheer exhaustion; but even before he stopped, Diantha had heard only a little of his loudest and choicest. For her room was full of sound that beat down every other sound. The savage attack, blasted away from the northern wall with hand grenades and musketry, had shifted to the opposite side of the fort, where the steep bank of the Monongahela afforded shelter to a swarm of Indians.

Just now, the weight of the firing beat back and forth between the river bank and the section of the stockade behind the governor's house and the officers' barracks next to it. It hammered in recurrent surges against the eaves of the barracks. Before one surge washed back, another broke over it, swallowed it, drove it in a louder, harder shock against the brick wall of the room, against the shingles, against the eardrums.

Diantha sat on the leather trunk at the head of the bed and listened. One hand lay in her lap, the other on the quilt, touching her brother's hand without holding it. He did not want her to hold his hand, except at first when Boyd spoke of poison on the arrow head that had pierced his leg; that had frightened him.

The wound was through the tendons behind his knee. It was the devil's own nonsense, he swore at the surgeon, to be crippled by a sliver of stone; and Boyd, cutting the flint out by the light of a single candle in Diantha's hand, had said cheerfully that it would be something else than nonsense to lie with only the stump of a leg and see a Shawnee warrior come bursting through the window after his scalp. Gaillard, in spite of himself, had been thoroughly sick; and as shame-faced, afterwards, as a small boy who had disgraced himself. There was something about the thought of a knife stripping off his hair that squeezed his stomach.

He lay without moving now, on the blue satin quilt, on the canopied bed, his wounded knee drawn up to ease the pain. His face, the white bandages, and the length of his bared leg made a vague profile of white against the farther curtain of the bed. The shutters were closed against the fire arrows, and it was dark in the room. Dark, and hot. Breath was tarnished metal in the nostrils; it drew a rasping taste through the back of the mouth.

Bob Gaillard stirred restlessly, jerking his head toward the recurring surges of sound, toward the eaves above and behind him. Diantha leaned forward a little, and felt her soaked dress pull away from her body and a slow rivulet start just below the hollow of her throat; it ran jerkily, queerly cool, between her breasts. Her hand, moving against Bob's, felt the smooth satin beneath it. She thought: *This is Arnett Leslie's bed. He meant it for another woman.*

Her fingers pulled the silk into themselves and held it. The waves of sound came, and fell, and came again. She was conscious of them; but she was more conscious of herself, more conscious of her body than she had ever been. She thought: *It was dark, like this, under the trees where the hurricane had been. If this were Arnett, here, wounded, instead of Bob? Why do I feel...the way I feel?*

She put the hand that was in her lap up to her heart, against her breast, and raised her head toward the eaves and the roaring. She could see, as if the room had no walls at all, just how the stockade looked; she had passed along the firing step only a little while ago with buckets for the fire-barrels. The eaves of the barracks were knee-high to the men at the loopholes; the knees would be green, with the tops of black gaiters just below them; the Pennsylvanians held the wall behind the officers' quarters, with a platoon of the town militia on their right, toward the Forks. They were all firing furiously, in platoon volleys; the surges of sound were coming closer together, with deeper, sharper spaces between them. Like waves, rising under a rising wind, with deepening troughs.

Sometimes, between the surges, she could hear a thin yelling. It was like looking down into the trough between waves and seeing jagged rocks just break the surface and then vanish. Each time the sound washed over them again, but the yells were still there, waiting. She began to wonder whether there would always be another wave to smother them. She strained her ears, listening for a silence. Perhaps there would be one tremendous wave of sound, and then silence, and then the scalp yells breaking through, breaking through the stockade, through the closed shutters, through everything.

Her body pressed against the disordered quilt. She thought: *This is his. I want to be close to what is his. This must be the end.* Her brain said it with finality, without emphasis. *That must be why I feel as I do. He is out there fighting; no matter who else fails, he goes on, fighting. I want him to go on. I want him to be immortal ... through me.*

Hot as it was in the stifling room, she felt the blood sweeping hotly up through her breast and neck and through her face.

"O-oohh!" That was her voice; she did not hear it. Instead, she heard her thought, loud, inside her: *That is why I feel ... the way I feel!*

"Di!" Gaillard was shouting it at her. Startled, she realized that he must have shouted it more than once. His hand closed impatiently on her wrist. "Di!"

"Yes, Bob?" The tide of sound welled up against the eaves; her voice, straining to rise through it, hurt her throat, and her mouth was full of brass ... warm brass, with tarnish on it. Gaillard's hand pulled her harder against the bed, so that she felt the wet dress tug and tug at her breast, in time to her heart. Perhaps it was in time to her breathing; she was breathing, she thought, almost as fast as her heart was beating.

"Di, you lied about Leslie."

She could see, by the changing blur of his face, that he was shouting. She could feel, by the grip on her wrist, that he was excited. She bent over him:

"No. No. Why?"

"You lie!" That was plainer, even too loud, in the space between waves of musket fire. "I saw you. God's breath, the whole garrison saw you!"

"Saw me?"

"Stop your play-acting! I said *saw* you—saw you run to your lover, to Leslie. By God, you have been sly about it. Pretending to hate him. Pretending to accuse him. Lying..."

The sound surged up again. She had to scream at him, leaning over the bed, her arm twisted under her:

"Bob, be still! You're out of your mind. You're all a-fever."

"A-fever!" Oaths. "Pah! You told the whole town today that you love him, that he has had you. Burn me, it was like seeing my sister standing stripped in the stocks, like a strumpet ready for the flogging, and the whole fort staring at her... laughing."

"Bob!" Shamed. Refusing to believe. Believing.

"Ay, laughed, I said! I stood there on the wall with Arnold, and Helm, and Burke and the rest, when you turned and ran to him. I heard Helm whisper: 'He found her naked in the woods, and had a week with her. Some men have all the luck.' I struck him while he laughed. He chose pistols, after the attack is beaten off."

"Oh, you're wrong! You are so wrong!"

"Wrong! That brazen Peggy could have been no more shameless, throwing herself at Arnold. You did lie, did you not? You lied to hide what happened between you. By the Lord, I'll have it out of you...!"

His hand dragged at her. It was hot, there on the bed, pulled down against Gaillard's shoulder, his angry breathing in her face. The room seemed to move a little, swaying. She thought: *This is why I thought today was the end. He is tearing up my lie. Arnett, I put a lie around you, to protect you a little. Now...*

She tried desperately to think. She must find an answer that would prove she had not lied; but she knew that there was no such answer. Words could not erase what Bob Gaillard had seen when she flew to Leslie, instead of to the drawbridge and safety.

Instead of Gaillard's face, so close to her, she saw a swale among the oaks, a fire, a plaited scalp, a stake. If she admitted that she had lied, they would let Arnett Leslie go out again into that howling horror beyond the walls. They would let him risk his life to find Bouquet. She heard herself screaming:

"Bob! Bob! I love him so! I love him so!"

"Ah... now we have it, eh? You *are* a strumpet?"

She thought: *It is wicked to scream so. Ugly. It was so still under the trees, when I woke and loved him. Still, and beautiful.* She felt a blind wish to hurt the man who profaned that.

"Bob, is it so hard to be half-brother to a strumpet?" She said it hoarsely, bitterly, against his ear. "You only laughed when it was

Aldersea—and told me to ask him on my knees to wed me. It was you who laughed that day...."

He pulled himself up, cursing at the pain of his leg; and sitting against the pillows, shook her with both hands on her shoulders.

"You little ...!"

"Go on. Go on," she stormed at him, and struggled until his hands slipped down to her elbows and held them to her sides. "If you do not like lies, have the truth. Do you know why I ran away? Do you know why? Because you laughed—you, my brother, when I had no one else to turn to. Because you would have me plead with his grace of Aldersea to make me an honest woman. Oh, I know. He could have made you an admiral; and so you laughed, because he had played me a clever trick to make me wed him...."

"Diantha! Be still! Be still, I say!"

"Still! I will not be still! Shall I be still because a pig of a noble lord, all silk and mire, drugged my wine and kept me by him all night? I wept for that. 'T was you who laughed. You want the truth. Here, have it: Because you laughed, I sold myself for five years to buy my passage out to Maryland, where I should never see you more, nor any one who would know, and laugh. Arnett Leslie would have freed me; he bought me, and that other pig you are so fond of swore me away behind his back. You love to run with pigs, do you not, Bob Gaillard? Aldersea...and then Lawless ..."

"Lawless!"

"Ay, Lawless. Now you are listening, are you not? Sir Richard Lawless knew me on shipboard. 'T was he swore I lied when they arrested me, in Annapolis, and I said Arnett Leslie had bought me to set me free. Lawless paid Watson, the agent, to forswear me too. He told Barent who I was. Together they pretended to sell me to a beastly, drunken trader—him they called Hellward Bound, because he was so. Listen: they *gave* me to Bond, to carry west, to Pitt's Town, and *paid* him to hand me back to Barent when he came. Oh, Barent told it all, gloating, when he had me by him in the forest. He would make me glad to wed him, he said; make me *beg* to wed him. And then he would pay Sir Richard Lawless one hundred thousand pounds when I should be Duchess of Strangden."

She broke off, sobbing. Gaillard's arms left her elbows and went around her shaking body.

"Diantha...." His voice was low and husky, but the girl heard it. So did Gaillard. They had been shouting, screaming at each other; and it had been hard to hear. Now the least murmur was clear, almost loud. The room was still dark, still hot; but it was empty; there was no more noise.

They raised their heads and looked toward the ceiling, toward the eaves, and then at each other.

"We've beaten them off," Gaillard said. "This time."

"Yes." With one hand, leaning on her elbow, she pushed the wet hair back from her cheek.

"Diantha ... why did you lie?"

"I love him."

"But to disgrace him so. Why? Why, unless you had that which you would hide? Did Barent ... ?"

"Oh, I do not know. I do not know. It is all so clear, so hideous clear, until just there. I do not know what he did. He was there, taunting me, telling me the whole evil plot, and then the Indians came...." She turned her head on Gaillard's arm and hid her face against his neck.

"And Leslie?"

"No. Oh, no."

"No? Then why ... ?"

"No. Oh, I would to God he had. He nearly died for me. He dressed me in his own clothes, and went naked himself in the storm. He bathed me; he nursed me; he fed me. I slept in his arms. And when I would have had him love me, he put down my arms and would have none of me."

"Then, again, *why?* Why accuse *him?*"

She sat up, suddenly fierce and defiant.

"Why did I lie? He is alive, is he not? You would have sent him out again, you and Ecuyer, after all he had done. He starved, and fought, and carried me day after day, with his blood dried on his wounds and would not care for them. And you would have sent him out, alone, to find Bouquet, to save you...."

"There are children, Di, and women...."

"God's breath!—that is your brave sea oath, is it not, Bob?—and there are men, too. Why he? Oh, Bob, he has done enough,

306

and I would not have him go again. Yes, I lied." Her hands took him by the loosened collar of his shirt and shook him in her turn. "Yes, lied! I didn't let you send him, did I? I made you keep him here, safe, so you could hang him for my honor's sake."

She laughed a little, high, hysterically.

"Diantha...stop! You do not love him, or you would not do that."

"I did it."

"He will hate you for it, when he knows." And heard her wail that he must hate her anyway.

"You cannot use him so, Di. No matter how much you love him, you cannot dishonor him, to make him hide behind a woman's hoops. Burn me, Di, is it not enough that he has lost his rank, for you? That he nearly died, for you? You cannot..."

She jerked away. The featherbed shook as she slid off, and her bare heels thudded on the loose floor. Amazingly, from across the room, Gaillard heard her humming.

"Di," he called, frightened. "Di."

"Yes, Bob," as cheerily as if she had never wept. "I am only a-hunting of the shutters. 'T is hot as hell in here. Oh, swear at me, an it pleases you. May I not say 'hell,' who have been there, and come back again?" He heard the bar slide back from the shutters, and a small, pleased laugh. "You see, I have thought of something. You shall not make me let him go out to hunt Bouquet."

Gaillard could not know that she was standing with the oaken bar in her arms, clutching it across her breasts until they hurt. Her voice ran on, lightly, almost gayly.

"You see, all I have to do is to keep on lying. And if you tell the governor that I am lying, I shall tell him it is you who lies, because you wish Leslie to go out and die."

The shutters swung open, and the light sprang in. The parade lay empty under a thin, dirty haze that was part evening fog, creeping up from the rivers, and part dusk. The feel of tarnished metal pressed on the nostrils and on the back of the tongue. Somewhere a child was crying. A distant, spiteful shot cracked out; and up on the wall, a derisive shout answered it. In the silence that came behind it, Gaillard spoke slowly:

" 'Gad, what fighting fools we Gaillards are! Can you think,

Di, what admirals your sons will make? I'd like to see a red-headed Leslie. By God, I would. But I'd hate to see one boarding a ship of mine with a cutlass in his fist."

He heard her feet slow and soft on the puncheons, and then their quick rush as she came and threw herself down beside the bed and buried her face in the quilt, huddling it about her mouth. Through it, he heard her choked cry:

"Bob...don't. Oh, Bob, I think I cannot bear it. There will never be a red-headed Leslie. Never. Never."

A vicious crackle of musketry ran down the northern wall. An officer, shouting, cursed the man who began the firing. Echoes. A confused bicker of voices. Silence. Gaillard spoke again, slowly:

"Do you love him so much?"

"Yes," faintly.

"Enough to give up Strangden castle, and all the titles, and thirty thousand pounds a year?"

"I wish you wouldn't," plaintively. "What good to plague me so?"

"Why, d'you think to wed him and take him back to England, and give him macaronis for his diet? No, my lady, you'll be duchess of some limestone farmhouse, with a heathenish name like Near-the-Navel, when you wed with him."

The flushed, hurt face came up out of the huddled quilt.

"Bob, you are cruel to tease me so," she reproached him. "You know he hates me, and will hate me more."

"Um...ay, he will. Unless you tell the truth."

"Never!"

"Never? Not even if it meant, perhaps, that red-headed Leslie?" He smiled, and reaching over, tweaked her nose, and swore to find it damp. "Di, listen to me. You said I laughed at you once, when you needed me. I'm not laughing now. I think I am not the same brother who laughed at you, that morning, and you are not the same Diantha, either. If you love him, Di, and hope to have him, tell the truth, and he'll not hate you. He'll love you."

"Love me! Oh, he might have, once. When I was a bond maid, for all he knew, and he scolded me because my feet were all a-smeared with mud, he might have. But..."

"D'you mean he'd ask a bond maid to wed with him, and not a duchess?"

"Never. Oh, you do not know him. He could have had me. He

could have had me for the asking, and without asking, too, and he did not want me. He will never ask me, now."

"So. Well, then, would you run away again if I said the same thing I said before?"

There was little enough of the duchess about the wistful face that looked at him doubtfully.

"I'm saying it, no matter what, my dear. Did you ever know a Gaillard who was a coward?"

She shook her head, smudging a bare arm across her tear-wet mouth.

"Well, then, I'm telling you: You'd best go to him now and ask him on your knees to marry you."

The bed shook again as she sprang up. For a moment, she was a small, quivering fury. And then a small, wistful girl, stretching out her hands to him, crying:

"Bob, you'd not cozen me to tell him, just to send him out ... there?"

"Di, you're not the only Gaillard in this room. I'm not a coward, though I'm only half your brother. I'll lie here and drink a toast— in river water—to the first Shawnee that comes through that door. But you're in worse case than I; don't you see? Could you ever tell a red-headed Leslie that his father hid behind his mother's panniers at Pitt's Town siege? Look you, Di: You said Aldersea could make me an admiral. I dare say the king can make me a landed gentleman, and will, too, when he knows I've wed a duchess to a plagued colony farmer. But I'm telling you, though I lose my ship for it, that if you love Arnett Leslie you must go and tell him."

He heard the girl's breath draw in, sharp and hard, and saw her take one slow step toward the door, and stop.

"Bob, it's not the duchess, nor Lady Diantha Gaillard, neither," she said shakily. "He never knew them. All he knew was Diantha Gail, who had neither pride, nor shame, nor shoon. See, I am just as I was then ... the day he bought me. I'm ... I'm going now. He bought me. He cannot ever set me free ... wed ... or unwed."

She ran to the door and swung it open. He saw her outlined against the failing light, head up, arms at her sides, straight as a small drum major on parade. The door closed.

CHAPTER XXVIII

In Which a Duchess Forgets That She Is a Lady; and a Lady Is Forgiven for Being a Duchess:

THREE men played at mumblety-peg in the dirt of the Ohio bastion, pretending a cheerful absorption in the game. Over them rose the grotesque bastion wall—two tiers of barrels filled with dirt. Between the warped staves, the dirt showed powdery gray, like ashes; dry, like ashes.

Carre flipped the knife past Leslie's knee, into the side of a barrel; it stuck there, quivering, and a cascade of dry earth ran out between two staves. Falling, it made a dry, rattling sound. Carre imitated it with his breath—a harsh gasp, rasping in his throat. Price put out his arm in a torn sleeve and plucked the clasp-knife out of the wood.

"Ugh." He handed it back to Carre. "If it's all the same to you, don't practice your death rattle in company. Have you no manners?"

Under his bleached eyebrows, Carre shot a glance at Leslie, and flipped the knife again.

"Manners," he repeated. "It's the major who should mend his manners. Telling us to our faces he is bored with us. . . ." He pulled the blade loose and struck it impatiently into the baked earth between his boots. "Listen to them out there, Leslie."

It was quiet in the bastion—so quiet that Carre's cross-belt, creaking in its frog, was profanely loud. From the misshapen wall to the eaves of the barracks, it was quiet—a thin, stretched tympanum of silence. Through it ran an unceasing vibration of sound that the pent-up garrison had not heard before.

Leslie, listening, heard it like the muffled *rrrmm* of insects, and grimaced at Carre. The sound was the mingled noise of voices, of moving bodies, of digging. For two hours, since the second rush at the wall had been beaten back, the sound had been growing. It came from behind the banks of the two rivers; in places, the bold voices and the scrape of metal against clay were a bare sixty yards from the palisades. At the loopholes of Fort Pitt, haggard men stood helpless, listening; the river banks gave the besiegers more cover than the makeshift stockade, the casks of earth and the piled-up fur bales gave the white men. There was nothing to fire at.

Carre pointed the knife at Leslie.

"Listen to them," he said again. "They've come down river by hundreds. You're mad to think of trying to get through them. It's suicide, and I'll not help you."

Talking, he felt futile. Leslie sat there, within arm's reach; and yet he was too far away to touch. He was like a man shut up in some fortress of his own, gates shut, drawbridge up; his face was as still as the faces of the brick bastions old Forbes had built here, and as impregnable, Carre thought. The trouble with Forbes was that he had finished his fort with dirt, and the dirt had mostly washed away. But the reserve that Arnett Leslie had built around himself these last few weeks was solid brick all around. Carre had a feeling that he was sending words against it uselessly; they would bounce off; the man inside would hardly hear them. But he tried again:

"I grant you, Leslie, this looks like the end of things. We'll starve; and when we're too weak to hold a gun, those red brutes will break in. But we're not cannibals; we can't eat you. All you'll do is get yourself killed, or burned, and your carcass will do us no good, frying at a stake out there on the bank."

"Some one has got to get through," Leslie answered. He had been answering Carre and Price with those same words for almost an hour.

"Great God, Leslie," Price burst out at him, "four men have tried it. Tried it when there was a chance to get through. Halleck and Meldrum were the best we had, and they didn't make it. Ay, and Meldrum was as good a woodsman as you are; where you've been over the mountains twice, he's crossed them forty times. But he never came back."

"Some one has got to get through," Leslie repeated mildly. "If you'll not help, I'll try it anyway."

Carre dug savagely at the dirt, and saw Leslie smiling faintly, watching the random knife-strokes.

"Damme, will you force me to tell Ecuyer and have you under

311

arrest again?" The knife sent a shower of dirt over a pair of sweat-blackened moccasins that came suddenly around the angle of the barrels; they covered an unbelievable space of ground, and Carre addressed them without looking up: "Hello, Tom Yeardley. Come and talk sense to this crazy galoot. He's stirring up mutiny."

Yeardley set his musket against a cask and wiped his face with his sleeve; his lips were ringed with black from biting cartridges, and his sleeve smeared the powder grime across one cheek. He sat down heavily in the dirt.

"Mutiny, is it? If you can eat it or smoke it, I'll take six."

"Major Leslie wants to break his parole and try to get through for help...."

"That isn't mutiny. That's damn' foolishness; I've been expecting it."

"I'm going," Leslie told him. "I asked Carre and Price to waste a little powder on me, to clear the way. There's still a chance for a man to slip down to the river and swim for it."

"They've got camps all along the far bank," Carre protested for the dozenth time. "Even if you got through the mob on this side, you'd never get up the cliffs on the other. You'd stir up a hullabaloo from their dogs and their squaws, and they'd have your hair before you'd gone a mile."

"I'm not going to climb the bluffs." Leslie's dogged face turned from the regulars to Yeardley. He had not intended that Tom should know he was going until he was gone—and gone too far for this loyal friend to follow him, or to stop him. "I'm going to swim up the Mon' two miles...three miles...maybe four if necessary; then I'll strike straight across country to the Forbes road."

"The Forbes road!" That was Carre again.

"Ay, the Forbes road." Leslie swung to Price. "*You* know that's sense. 'T was you marched straight down the Venango road, knowing that no Indian would think a white man crazy enough to use the open trail. They're not watching the Forbes road now, any more than they watched the Venango trail two months ago. They're all here, waiting—Shawnees, Mingoes, Delawares, Wyandottes and God knows how many of the northern cannibals. They know this fort can't hold out much longer; they're not going to watch a mountain trail when they see five hundred scalps here, ready for the lifting. You know them, Tom. Isn't that the truth?"

Yeardley nodded, heavily, unhappily. Leslie went on, not rushing headlong, but with precise logic; a general, comfortable at headquarters, might have mapped a sortie for other men as coolly as this man in draggled linsey planned the risking of his own life. He took the knife from Carre's hand and drew a diagram in the dirt.

"Look, Tom: Here is the Grenadier bastion. The carronade there can fire down the moat, all the way to the river. You know the Indians will clear out of the ditch and stay out, for a few minutes at least, if the gunners put a few rounds of grapeshot into it. All I'm asking Carre to do is to order the gun crew of that carronade to fire three or four times. I'll slip out through the sally port into the moat, and run for the river after the last shot. I'll be through them in two minutes. It's a chance. It's the *only* chance!"

Tom blinked.

"Whyn't you ask Val Arnold to do it?" he asked.

"Eh? Arnold . . . !"

"Why not, now?" Tom drew his soiled sleeve across his face and blinked again above the soaked cloth. "Val Arnold will be so tickled to be rid of you that he'll give you every gun in the whole blessed mud heap. He'd stand court-martial forty times over to get you out of here, Arnie—after today."

Leslie's hands, hanging limp between his knees, clenched in a gesture of sudden anger. Tom fumbled uncomfortably at his fringed cape; and his thick lips turned outward in the deprecatory smile that gave him the look of an embarrassed baby.

"'Gad, I'd think Leslie would want to stay, after today," Carre blurted. "Stab me, if a woman like that loved me I'd not leave her for those butchers out there. I'd be with her to the last gasp, and I'd kill her with my own hands. . . ."

"It's no good, Carre," Tom broke in upon him. "He knows ye too well. Ye don't mean that; ye're but trying to anger him into staying, and ye might know better. It's wasting breath." He looked at Leslie's unmoved face. "Don't ye see, Carre, he's got to go, after today. It's the one chance of saving her."

Carre stared at him, amazed.

"D'you mean you *want* him to go?" he demanded.

"He's going. If ye'll not give us the guns, Carre, we'll go ask Arnold, who will." He got clumsily to his feet. "Well?"

Carre nodded.

"I'd rather go myself, after seeing *her* today. Damme, I would, Leslie, and I'd like you to believe that. I see why you will go in spite of us. I'll make a bargain with you: If by this hour tomorrow we have no word from Bouquet, I'll give you anything you wish, and the governor may court-martial me and be damned."

Leslie, seeing his grieved and stubborn face, said shortly that he was content. Carre clicked the clasp-knife shut and sprang up. His hand brushed Leslie's arm.

"You plagued, gallant fool! God bring you back, Arnett Leslie. She is more queen than duchess."

He swung away with a quick salute, and Price followed him, his smile fading as he saw the unhappiness unmasked, for an instant, in Leslie's bloodshot eyes. Yeardley stood looking down at his friend's hunched shoulders.

"So, Arnie," he said slowly, "you'll throw yourself into the fire for a woman, after all. And I'm helping you do it."

"It was not needful to say that, Tom."

"About what happened today? Poh! D'you think they're talking of aught else, down there in the women's barracks? The whole fort saw her turn and run to you because she thought you were in danger."

Leslie got up, his face once more the dark, aloof mask he had learned to make of it. Tom put a hesitant hand on his shoulder.

"I'd not let you go, Arnie, if I hadn't seen her do it."

The reddened eyes looked at him dully, and then past him at the piled-up barrels, and the sentries crouching at the peepholes beside the two brass guns.

"I called her a fool," Leslie said harshly, and let Tom see the misery in his face. " 'T is I have been the fool, Tom, thinking somehow she is no duchess at all, but only the frightened child I bought on shipboard. I am a cursed, clumsy oaf, Tom. Each time I might have helped her, I failed. Today, when she ran to me, I called her a fool."

"D'you think that matters, Arnie?"

"No," steadily. "Not at all. I have my senses back. I'll not see her again."

Tom's big, red face took on its look of a benign baby, and his lips pursed in a grave smile.

314

"Not even if she wished it?"

"No," Leslie told him shortly.

"Heigh-ho, you're a grand soldier, Arnie, but as a lover you're no better than any cask of dirt in this plagued bastion."

"There's more need for soldiers. She'll have lovers enough." The mask slipped into place again and hid whatever Tom had seen of emotion. "We'd best look to the cartridges again. We'll be getting another rush when the sun is gone." He moved briskly around the angle of the bastion wall, into the narrow space between the stockade and the barrack eaves. At the first loophole, a barefoot giant in breechclout and nothing else lolled back from the palisades to give him room; Leslie looked out toward the river bank and the forks where the two streams merged.

The sun was almost down, sinking into a level band of haze between the Ohio hills. The haze had turned blood red.

Sunset meant blessed relief to the men standing to their loopholes in that sweltering space between log walls and brick barracks. But sunset was coming too fast today. Leslie, listening to the sound of digging and the hubbub of voices behind the river banks, heard also the stirrings of nervous riflemen along the palisade, the shuffle of feet lifting and shifting, a high-pitched curse.

The loopholes here looked out upon the strip of bank where the prisoners of Braddock's disaster had died, inch by inch, screaming in the fire. Now, as the sun went down, the glow of fire was lighting the same bank again. The clouted giant beside Leslie put out a hand and plucked a splinter from a palisade and munched it.

"They're cookin' out yonder," he said, and spat out slivers. "Couldn't ye give 'em a blizzard with the cannon, now? Right at the lip o' the bank, say?" He spat again. "I'd as leave burn as see 'em cookin' and eatin' under our noses."

"All we'd hit would be the river, Bleese, and have them laughing at us. Didn't you get supper?"

"A dozen hominy grits ... *agh*. I been slobberin' myself, lookin' out at them patches o' nettles on the bank. Nettles makes good soup, Major; they're better'n hominy grits. D'ye think, say, some on us c'd slip out a night an' get us some nettles?"

At the next loophole, Peter Lanness drew back piping:

"There's side meat in those nettle', eh, M'sieu Leslie? Maybe M'sieu Bleese he get nice Mingo steak, no?"

"I'd as leave eat rattlesnake as Mingo," growled the woodsman Lanness came hobbling over, using his musket as a crutch; Leslie staring out at the darkening weed patches on the river bank, heard him gabbling shrilly:

"Rattlesnake, she is not bad to eat, no—if you have rattlesnake. By gar, those rattlesnake out by river, I skin them 'live one day. They owe me one big debt for bite me in leg."

There was a blur of motion in the nettles. A weed top dipped against the reddened sky. Leslie stepped back and raised his voice:

"Look out! Here they come!"

The giant flung himself against the wall; the logs creaked under the impact; his rifle thrust out; the stock came up against his cheek; his shoulder jerked to the recoil. From the river banks a dozen shots answered the crack of his weapon. The palisade blazed out, hushed, blazed again. Smoke hung along the stockade, thick gray-yellow. The air turned sour. Smoke and air—thick as clabber, sour as whey—as if the hideous yelling in the weeds had curdled them. A red spark leaped up from the river bank, curved, arched downward toward the wall, vanished. Three more shot up together, arched, and fell. One went out. Two struck in the shingles of the barrack roof. Leslie, running, kicked them loose and stamped out the tongues of fire that licked around the arrow heads. Still running, he came down from the steep slant of roof to seize a shrieking man by one fat arm and tear him away from a loophole where he was firing furiously first with one musket and then with a second. Both muskets were empty; the fat man did not know it. His round, frightened face peered up at Leslie, piggy with blond bristles.

"Py helzige Himmel...!" His mouth quivered. "Ach, Mister Leslie, dey be commen oop!" He broke away and flew to his loophole again. Leslie pulled him back and took the musket out of his fist.

"It isn't loaded, Doctor Muller."

The missionary gaped at him, whirled, and snatched up the other gun.

"That one is not loaded either."

Johann Muller's eyes rolled. He set the musket against the palings, at arm's length, as if it had betrayed him. Leslie found his powder horn adangle on its string, under the tail of the churchly coat, and put it in Muller's hand.

"*Danke! Danke!*" One shaking paw worried at Leslie's arm. "I load goot now. You do not tell, *bitte?*"

Leslie ran on along the firing step. Carre met him; each hung on a heel long enough for a quick question and reply.

"I've been in the Music bastion," Carre shouted, close to his ear. "The damned smoke's thinner there. They're swarming into the ditch from the Allegheny...."

He dashed on. Leslie went to a loophole and peered out, seeing nothing but the curling smoke. After a minute, the smoke turned red underneath, and the blast of a six-pounder churned it. Carre had told the gunners they had a target in the ditch; the ditch spewed up frantic howls, and then more howls as a fierce crackle of rifle fire ran down the wall. The six-pounder blazed again.

After it, there were only random shots. But between them, the panting white men heard the noise of digging begin again. And then a new sound that was partly a silky ripple, like a snake crawling on dry earth, and partly a crackle like running musketry, far away. In the women's barracks, a child screamed wildly; a babel of screams and cries poured out onto the parade. Militiamen, turning from the rifle ports, saw a red glare lifting and spreading from the barrack roof behind the Ohio bastion, and the lick of flames crawling swiftly up the shingles. The flames hissed as water struck them; but they crawled higher. Shouts:

"Water! More water...quick! The barrel's burst!"

Men came running along the firing step, deserting their loopholes. Leslie drove them back.

"Will you let the red devils walk in while your backs are turned?" he stormed at them in a blaze of anger. "Hinks...Stookey...you know better! Lovatt, your wife's safe—but she'll not be if you leave the wall. Get back to your loopholes!"

He pressed them back, hungry and nerve-racked men on the verge of panic, watching the roof burn above their children's beds. Behind them, Tom Yeardley's great voice boomed, and his great hands plucked them by cape and belt and ears and arms and scattered them by main force along the wall again. The mounting flames lighted the parade and a group of women at the well. Feet pounded along the wall; buckets thumped; water went hissing across the shingles; the fire died and left the fort in darkness.

"They're at the digging again," Tom said in Leslie's ear. "Is it a tunnel, d'you think, Arnie?"

"They took Pres'que Isle that way."

"God, where *is* Bouquet? We're getting shaky. Too damned shaky." His hand closed on Leslie's wrist. "Look, Arnie: let *me* go. You belong here, where she is, if they break through."

"No," sharply. Then: "Tom, if it comes to that, will you kill her yourself?"

"Ay." Tom's hand slipped away. "I'll be getting back to the men. You'll not raddle us, Arnie? You'll not slip out tonight?"

"I'll wait one day. I'm a coward, Tom. I do not want to go. I'm like those men—Lovatt, and Stookey, and the rest; the only chance they've got to save their women is to hold the wall, but they left it. I keep hoping we'll get word from Bouquet tonight."

Heels gritted along the firing step—harried, official heels. The man who wore them sent his voice ahead:

"Leslie! Major Leslie!"

"Price?"

"Ay. Looking for you, Leslie. Message from headquarters. Report to the Ohio bastion." The ensign jerked it out, his voice as harried and hasty as his heels.

"Price, you didn't go to Ecuyer?"

"Not I." Price fidgeted with his words. "Not I. Not Carre, either. You'd best hurry, Leslie. Urgent. Come along, Yeardley, I need you." He pulled Tom with him; Leslie went toward the Ohio bastion on a run, a formless dread hurrying him. Price, fleeing through the wilderness with the survivors of Le Boeuf, had been steady as a rock; only something so seriously wrong that it approached disaster would make his voice shake. It was a scant thirty yards to the bastion, but as he ran Leslie saw, in flashes, a dozen things that might have happened: Ecuyer dead. The water in the well poisoned. The powder gone bad in the magazine. A message from Bouquet that relief was impossible....

"Halt!" Carre's voice, smothered. The barrel wall loomed just ahead; its shadow hid Carre altogether.

"It's Leslie."

"Give the password!" Carre jerked it out nervously. "The password, man!"

"Annapolis," Leslie said impatiently. Plague take the fellow, it was no time for Tower-of-London folderol. He waited, and heard, first, a faint whispering, and then a voice that certainly was not Carre's, giving him the countersign:

"Job."

Soft. Low. A shy, breathless voice. And then a whisper that was neither words nor breath, but the ruffle of bare feet in dust and the faint stir of knees against clinging linsey. A smaller, darker shadow slipped out from the shadows of the ungainly wall.

"You *are* Job, are you not?" Still shy. A little tremulous. Very determined. It caught Leslie's throat with a quick tightness, slipped, and caught an instant in his heart. "You *are* Job? I am...I am your plague of boils. Will you...speak with me?"

"Diantha!" The man did not say it aloud; the pent-up longing of weeks shouted it at him. For a moment, the tightness in his throat and heart was like the squeeze of a small hand, warm and intimate. Then the hand slid away. He felt, instead, the constraint that he had forced upon himself slip over him again. He found only one word to say:

"Yes." Then he found two more and added them to it: "Yes, your grace."

The small shadow said "Dammit!" and moved closer.

"I came to thank you." The small voice caught, but the catch ran quickly under a laugh and hid itself. "You see, I have not forgot my manners." She came still closer, so that her face and her ankles were two white blurs against the dark bulk of the wall. "'T is a most unfashionable hour to call, is it not, Job?" she ventured.

Leslie did not help her. The words he had said to Tom Yeardley on this spot an hour ago were saying themselves again in his brain: "*I have been the fool, thinking she is no duchess at all, but only the frightened child I bought on shipboard.*" He would not be a fool again. His hands closed hard upon each other above the muzzle of his rifle.

"Truly," Diantha tried again, "it was not my fault I am so late in thanking you. Men have such quaint conceits about their wars; this afternoon, when there was no shooting anywhere, I tried to

come and find you, and a sergeant with a halberd told me, very
fierce, that it was dangerous. 'No women,' he growls, 'on the walls.'
I had to wait until all the guns were going again and the barracks
were on fire before they would let me come. Then I fetched me
two buckets from the well, and the only man who noticed me said,
'Hurry. Hurry!' Men," she concluded solemnly, "are funny. But
I am here to thank you . . . for this afternoon. You saved me."

There should be words to answer her. Leslie could not think
of them; the words that came to his tongue were not polite words;
they were the words a man said to the woman he loved, when he
held her in his arms in the dark, under the trees where the hurricane had been. They had nothing to do with constraint. When he
had said them to Diantha Gail, she had not heard them; he could
never say them to Diantha Gaillard. He said, instead:

"I didn't save you. There were forty men there to do it."

"But not forty to call me a fool!"

The constraint tightened its hold on him. He said, stiffly: "I'm
sorry."

"Oh," airily, "I would not have you sorry. It is for that I thank
you most. I came to tell you what a truly great fool I am." The
small shadow took a breath that seemed too big for it. "You know
I lied about you."

"Yes."

"I have let them think vile things of you—that you knew me
when you bought me—that you bought me to make sport for your
drinking party."

"Yes."

"That you gave me to Bond."

"Yes."

"And followed me to Pitt's Town, and kept me by you all night
in your room."

"Yes."

"Oh, Lord, have you no other word but 'Yes'? Can't you say
zooks! or zounds! or stab you! or burn you! or *something?*" She
stamped one bare foot on the ground, and swore and wailed because he vexed her, and the ground was hard. "I warrant you'll
not be so calm when I tell you why I lied about these things!"

The tightness filled Leslie's throat again.

"I'll tell you why! I lied to keep you here! Did you know that?

320

I lied to keep you safe. Oh, I would have kept you in the jail if I could, to keep you safe. Did you know that? I lied because I love you! Did you know that?"

It was Leslie's turn to lie. He lied without thinking, scarcely knowing that he lied:

"Yes."

"O-*ohh!* You didn't! You couldn't!"

"Why did you come?"

Another breath too big for so small a shadow.

"I—I told you. To thank you."

"You have thanked me," he said coldly. "What else?"

"O-*ohh!*" She backed away from him. "I—I see. You are always cool, and strong, and sure of yourself, are you not? I should not have been afraid. It is perfectly safe to tell you what I came to tell you. No, stay where you are; I do not care who hears me. If they laugh at me and mock me, it will teach me, perhaps, never to be so great a fool again. I came to tell you that you bought me, but you cannot sell me, nor give me away. I came to tell you I was yours the day you bought me...that I am yours now, wed...or unwed." She was sobbing now. "I came to ask you...to forgive me ...for being a duchess."

The white blur of her face disappeared; the blur of her ankles diminished. Her feet made small, stumbling noises in the dirt.

"Diantha!"

She ran blindly into a barrel in the dark, and swore, and pummeled it with both fists. When Leslie caught her by the shoulders and turned her around, she pummeled him, and swore, and said: "I hate you! Let me go! Ohh, I *hate* you!"

"I know that, too," Leslie said, and, stooping, swung her up into his arms and held her. "Diantha...Diantha...you know I love you. I have loved you ever since that night I carried you, like this...."

Diantha sniffed, and rubbed her face against the cape thrums on his breast.

"I loved you first," she told him plaintively. "Much the first. Ever since the day you glared at me, standing with Sir Dick's arm about me, and bought me for eighteen pounds. Do you think, Arnett, I shall be worth it?"

His arm hurt her, until she discovered that he was trying to reach her face, with his hand, and turn it toward him. Then it was his mouth that hurt her; but she did nothing to avoid that hurt. Her arms went up with a rush about his neck.

"Oh, Arnett, Arnett, I almost died," she whispered against his lips. "Of loving you, I mean. And hating you."

"I knew you hated me."

"Because I loved you so much, and knew I could not resist you if you would have me. Oh, I was so wanton; I waved at you, standing all naked and dripping from my basin, through the shutters of The Three Balls. And you looked, and went on. I hated you for that." Her lips hurt again; her hands, clinging, made the hurt last and last. "But I hated you more in the woods, in the dark, under the fallen trees. If you had loved me you would have kissed me, one little kiss . . . and you only washed my face."

She tweaked the long hair that lay over the collar of his hunting-shirt.

"*Oh,* I hated you, that morning. And then I thought you were like all the rest, and would have your way with me, loving me not. I hated you, and feared you, and loved you until I could scarcely breathe—and you spread mush on me as unconcerned as a . . . as a . . . as a *midwife*. Oh, I was afraid then, really afraid. I knew then that you would never love me . . . never want me, even, like the others."

Her face hid itself altogether in the smoky fringes of his shirt.

"Oh, Arnett, you looked at me . . . all of me . . . and you did not want me. I could have *died*. You do want me, do you not?"

There was no Leslie coolness in the voice that answered her. It trembled.

"Yes. *Yes. Yes.*"

His rough chin bruised her face. His arms, hungry, filled themselves with her body, lifted her, drew her up high against his breast and cradled her there.

"You want me, Arnett . . . thin as I am . . . more boy than woman? I who nearly killed you with my foolishness? I who am all burned and scarred?"

"Want you! Oh, my dear . . . !"

She squirmed in his arms and found a place for her chin just under his. Her lips moved against his neck, a tremulous motion that was partly sigh and partly caress and partly a small, passionate repeating of his name. His face turned slowly against her cheek, so that her lips must touch it as it turned, and their mouths met. As if his arms could not hold her close enough, she pressed against him until even her soft, round breast hurt the unhealed hatchet gash through shirt and bandage. And then, like a mischievous imp, her slender tongue darted out to touch his lips, and darted back again, terrified at such unheard-of boldness. Her body, possessed of the same imp, wriggled around so that her legs hung a-dangle across his arm.

Somewhere between laughter and tears, she pulled up the tattered flounces until her knees were bare, and waved her naked feet.

"You cannot see them, Arnett, but they are all begrimed again, like any dirty urchin's. Will you have me so? Will you wed with me, Major Arnett Leslie of Maryland, and take me away to that great mountain of yours, and build me a limestone manor house, and let me be your scullery maid? And give me a kiss each night and morning for my wage?"

Somehow, holding her in one hollowed arm, he freed one hand to slip down over her splashed ankles and cradle both grimy feet within his palm.

"No, Diantha—that I will not."

"You will *not?*" Her hands took his face between them, and her eyes searched it, though it was only a paler shadow in the dark. "You will *not?*"

"No. But..."

"Oh, there is a but? You will have me for your mistress, rather? I...I do not care, Arnett. In whatever way you want me...."

He shook her gently.

"I cannot forget that you are a duchess. And I will not wait. And I will not have you for my mistress, either, in ragged gown and muddy feet."

"Then...then *what?*"

"Why, then this: That day I bought you, dear, you were a fine lady, though I knew it not; and I, though I knew it not, was a penniless vagabond without a home. I would not wed with you in such false colors, Diantha. But, if you will, a poor, dirty fellow called Arnett Leslie, who should not look so high, will wed with Diantha, Lady Gaillard, Duchess of Strangden..."

"Arnett!"

"...in a blue London gown and satin shoon, with linstocks for candles and musket shots for wedding bells, here, in Fort Pitt, tonight."

"Here...in Fort Pitt...tonight?"

"Yes." His arms, tight as they held her, tightened around her as if they never could hold her close enough. Her hands trembled on his cheeks. Her face came nearer, her quick, startled breath upon his mouth. With a low cry that formed no words at all, she pulled his head down upon her throat and breast.

"Oh...you are not cool, and stern, and sure of yourself, are you? Arnett, your arms shake so...oh, yes! And yes! And *yes!*"

They kissed again.

Ten feet away, the ensign who commanded the two cannon sat on his gun platform, his head turned steadily away. They did not know it. Around them, the artillerymen crouched at their peepholes or sat propped against the gun carriages. But to Diantha Gaillard and Arnett Leslie, there was no fort, no hunger, no waiting death. Their lips clung; their bodies touched.

A single musket shot struck heavily against the silence and shattered it. As the pieces fell in rattling echoes, a cohorn bellowed farther down the wall. Leslie, looking with dazed eyes above Diantha's head, saw the flicker of rifle fire run down the northern rampart.

"Diantha. Diantha, dear. You'll have to go back to your room."

"No." Her breast pressed hard against him. "No. Find me a place—any place—here on the wall. I will not go, until you marry me."

Bodies, crawling, made the gun platform creak; the red glow of a slow match showed for an instant the polished barrel of a carronade. The night burst into red light and thunder, and the air jumped. When the red light went out, the sky was full of red sparks, curving, dropping. Along the stockade rose a crying:

"Look out! Fire arrows! Oh, God, it's *raining* fire!"

Across the bastion, there was an empty space where a third gun was to have been; it had gone to the Music bastion instead. A man with a musket crouched there, behind a plank gunport that had once been a cabin door in Pitt's Town. Leslie put Diantha down beside him, in the corner where the plank shield met the barrel wall. She knelt there obediently.

"Come back, Arnett. You are not just yours, now."

"Yes. Yes." Her hand slipped through his. Bullets pelted against the barrels. Behind them, the shower of fire arrows thucked into the barrack roofs or fell, grating and rattling, on the dry earth within and without the stockade. Leslie, finding his rifle, moving quickly down the militia line, sensed that this was the worst attack of all. There were no surges of sound; the firing was a steady roll. From the river banks, from the weeds and brush, from the outer trenches long since abandoned, rose a howling like that of all the beasts.

A roof caught again, and a man with a bucket, pouring water on the mounting flame, took a fire arrow between ear and shoulder and fell screaming, beating at the fire with his hands. Along the palisades the gun smoke hung. When the six-pounder fired, the roll of smoke showed like a writhing snake, monstrous, with a red belly.

Then, strangely, its red belly showed continuously, just level with the loopholes. Through the smell of powder came the smell of burning. The long, dead grass on the dirt walls of the fort, kindled by fire arrows that fell short, blazed up suddenly in a long rank of yellowish flames, black-tipped with smoke. The scalp yell rose triumphantly. The tongues of flame climbed swiftly toward the palisades. The palisades began to burn. Men must drop their muskets and dash water between the logs; load; fire; run to the lowering barrels for more water; load and fire again.

Leslie had one glimpse of Diantha. She had left the shelter of the embrasure. She passed him, running, with two empty buckets.

"I love you!" She was gone.

Then there was a moment when the fire burned unhindered, and every man stood to his loophole, firing, loading, firing with grim desperation, while barbaric figures danced and howled in the rising glare. Hands clawed at the palisades. Tomahawks struck through between them. Men fought for their lives in a red and black nightmare. Then the nightmare exploded in stunning shock and blinding light. The fire had touched off one of the mines planted in the outer face of the wall, to be used as a last resort. It blew up, shaking the stockade, shaking the earth. Through the flash a nude body hurtled crazily. Clods of dirt rattled down. Inside the fort, men rushed to brace leaning palisades, shaken loose in the mud wall by the explosion. Outside, the yells went mad with fury.

But the attack was over.

Leslie, running along the wall, found Peter Lanness crouched half way to the top of the stockade, on a pile of fur bales.

"Hark," he whispered down to Leslie. "You hear dat, no?"

There was a scrabbling noise in the ditch, a clink of metal, hoarse breathing. Before Leslie could put out a hand to stop him, Lanness leaped crablike for the spiked tops of the palisades and flung himself over. Leslie climbed up on the bales. A moment later he was leaning over the wall, pulling Peter up and in. As the Frenchman tumbled across to safety, Leslie felt a spatter of warmth on his face. Lanness mumbled, and took something from between his teeth.

"By gar, I have pay dem back now. Me, Pierre Lanness. I pay dem for break my leg." He chuckled and spat. "Dose trap in bottom of ditch, dey are good t'ing, no? One of dem catch fine buck. He sit dere, try for open trap wit' he's tomahawk. Pouf! Here is he's scalp."

Leslie left him chortling and tying the hair to his clout belt.

In the shadow of the barrel wall, he found Tom Yeardley and Carre, with Diantha between them. They put out their hands eagerly.

"I'm glad, Major," Carre said, gripping his hand in both fists. "Damnation glad. 'T will bring us all luck."

Diantha came frankly into Leslie's arms.

"Darling, you bathed in a bucket, and dressed you in the dark, in Hellward Bound's kitchen, that other night. I have brought a bucket especially for your bathing and shaving, and your uniform, too."

"Fiddlesticks, my lady," Carre broke in headlong. "We'll relieve him from the walls for the wedding, surely. Ay, and burn candles for it at the governor's house, though it takes the last stub he owns."

"No, please. I wish to wed him here. And for my wedding march, I wish him to come and meet me just down the wall a little, and carry me here. You see," she laughed, faint with happiness, "I came to the governor's ball in a fine, brave chair that carried me so

326

gently, and I but a bond maid then. La, Captain Carre, I am a duchess now. You would not deny me my marriage wish? Nor have me come to my wedding in a chair less elegant than I rode in to your precious ball?"

She had her way, though Tom Yeardley swore, with secret tears in his eyes, that she was a sentimental, headstrong hussy, and Carre blustered against a wedding in the dark, where none could see the bride in her London gown. Diantha silenced them with her hands upon their lips, and brought her hands down again with a kiss in the palm of each, and laughed at them for their gallantry.

And so, an hour later, Arnett Leslie waited for her at the head of the ramp that led up from the parade-ground. The grenadiers who held the wall there turned curiously at the rustle of silken petticoats. Phillips, who had been president of the court at Leslie's trial for cowardice, gave him a sweeping saber salute, and crossed blades with the lieutenant of the grenadiers, so that Diantha went to her wedding, after all, in style, beneath an arch of swords.

With her walked Peggy Sargent, and behind them Bob Gaillard, hobbling, with his arms across the shoulders of two stout village girls. Not even for the wedding of a duchess could men be spared from the wall that night. Leslie went forward soberly to meet Diantha's brother; he had, in this hour, forgotten him; he remembered best, about Gaillard, the deadly look with which he had greeted the fiasco of Leslie's court-martial. But the frigate captain met him with outstretched hand and a "Damme, Leslie, I'd rather see her yours than any man's I ever knew."

Diantha's hands squeezed Arnett's arm.

"Aren't we nice, we Gaillards?" she murmured. And pressed his arm the tighter when he whispered in reply:

"You'll be no English Gaillard in ten minutes, dear. You'll be a Maryland Leslie."

Gaillard, steadying himself with one hand on the shoulder of the scarlet coat he had persuaded Governor Sharp to strip from Leslie's back in disgrace, told them with a chuckle:

"This red-headed spit-fire doesn't know yet why I told her to ask you, Leslie. I found that pistol case of yours in her room one night, when she was raving that you had bought her for a joke. 'Y gad, I was ready to kill you that night. Then I read the plate in the cover; d'you know, Leslie, that Tom-ox of yours had never told me 't was you fought the *New Adventure's* poor little gun and drove the Frenchies off. Damme, I was on your side from then on; I knew the wench was lying."

"And the wench knows *you* are lying now," his sister told him happily.

Leslie picked her up, all billowing skirts and clinging arms, and carried her along the brick parapets and the pointed logs of the stockade, past the silent, waiting men. And Phillips forgot his dignity enough to vow that the maid of honor should not walk when the bride rode, and bundled Peggy up into his arms and followed them half around the circuit of the wall to the Ohio bastion.

There, with the barrels of earth looming over them, and the red glow of the gunners' matches for candles, fat Johann Muller married Diantha, Lady Gaillard, Duchess of Strangden, to the man she loved, though he stumbled over the marriage service, and made up queer, Dutch-English phrases to take the place of those he could not remember. And then, when she had kissed her husband, Diantha Leslie let them all know that she could be a soldier's wife.

"I'll go now, Arnett," she said quietly. "I would not take what other wives may not have. I think I shall not sleep, dear; I am too happy. When they do not need you, come."

Her arms went up around his neck in a quick, fierce hug. Her body clung to him.

He saw her move away, a small, sturdy shadow, erect as a drum major. When she was lost in the dark, Leslie spoke in a low tone to Carre:

"You can tell Ecuyer about the guns, now. I would like to have some firing from the other bastions, too, so they will not watch the Mon' side especially."

"Good God, Leslie, you're not going, after this?"

"Of course I'm going. There is no other way to save her, or any one. You know that."

"Ay." Carre said it heavily. The sound of digging was louder than before.

Toward morning, they saw what the digging had accomplished. Through the mist, the flicker of musket fire ran up and down the river triangle. The air was full of the whine of bullets; they drummed on the palings and smacked the shingles with dry, brittle sounds. As the sun rose and the mist thinned, the watching men thrust rifles grimly through the loopholes, straining their eyes for the first target in that persistent ring of fire.

The fog burned away. The bullets continued to whine overhead and spatter on logs and roofs. But there was no feathered head, no copper shoulder, no slightest movement of the weeds at which to aim. The besiegers had dug burrows into the river banks, with slanting tunnels through which to fire. Sheltered, untouchable, they lashed the stockade with lead. Occasionally they found the cracks between the logs and the crevices between the barrels. Three times, in the first hour after dawn, the bullets found white flesh.

Then, abruptly, the firing ceased.

A white flag waved in jerks on the farther bank of the Allegheny. A shrill hail came across the water. Leslie sent a militiaman to call Ecuyer and McKee.

By the time they came, it was light enough to see that there were four figures on the distant bank. Three were Indians. The fourth was a white man, naked, his hands bound at his back.

One of the Indians waved the flag. Beside him, another flourished a smaller object that was also white. While he flourished it, he shouted, and McKee, listening, translated swiftly.

"He says the white man is a messenger from Bouquet, with a letter. No, two letters. He is willing to bring them if we promise not to fire."

"Promise," said Ecuyer.

McKee mounted the barrel wall and shouted. The Indian with the letters left the group and came down the river's edge. He dragged a small canoe out of the willows and paddled across. McKee, risking his life, went out through the postern under the Music bastion and met him at the landing. When he came back, he handed Ecuyer two sheets of paper, torn and sweat-stained.

They were Ecuyer's last letter to Bouquet. The white man on the bank was Meldrum.

CHAPTER XXIX

In Which a Page from the Official Journal of Fort Pitt Tells What Transpired on Diantha Gaillard's Wedding Day:

A DRUMMER BOY in a red coat lay asleep on the bench inside of the governor's office, one arm curled round his drum.

The trim orderlies were gone; the loopholes needed every man. For two days and a night, the tow-headed drummer had been the governor's whole staff.

Now, across the stump of a candle on the table, Ecuyer looked at him heavily. The greasy light gave the boy the face of a corpse—yellowish, with hollows where his cheeks should be. The soldier's lips moved as his mind moved, slowly, putting into orderly ranks the words he would set down in his report for the day. There was no one to read the report; it had become very plain, these last two days, that unless help came quickly no one would ever read it. But his majesty's regulations called for those daily entries in the journal. Captain Ecuyer began to write.

"29th July,
"Continued firing on the fort, the whole day, from the Ohio bank, they kept up a very smart fire, this day a number of shells thrown to disperse them, but they only shifted places, this day and yesterday about 1,500 small arms fired on them from the fort. Wounded this day: Marcus Huling's leg broken, Sergeant Hermon shot through the lungs, a grenadier shot through the leg, fired three shots from a six pounder, as they were passing the river in canoes; obliged them once to throw themselves into the river, one of them said to be cut in two by one of the shot. These two days killed several of them from the fort, one of them wounded and drowned in the river, attempting to swim over and five more seen carried out of the canoe on the farther side of the Ohio, supposed to be

wounded. The roofs of the Governor's House and the Barracks much hurt by the enemy's fire." *

He turned the page; his lips began to move again, helping his brain trudge on through its clogging weariness. His eyes, having no part in the task, ran to queer scenes; they made him see feet in column, feet in gaiters, trudging through a road that was deep mud. The mud clung to the feet, pulling them back, clogging them. His mind, for a moment, played him tricks; he saw his thoughts plodding along, absurdly, in muddy gaiters; it took an effort to lift them and move them forward. The desire to sleep clung to them.

He shook his head, jerking his thoughts, shaking off the sense of thick, sticky weight. His eyes turned to the sleeping boy again, and saw that he was smiling in his sleep; then, peering intently, they saw that it was not a smile at all. The drummer's face was so thin that the skin seemed stuck to his cheek bones; sticking there, it pulled his lips up from his teeth. Thin...

Ecuyer's quill began to scratch on the fresh page:

"I have at present four legs of beef and no flour. (A relief expedition must) bring a great deal of it or the jaws will rest immovable."

Fort Pitt, with its three hundred men, its hundred women, its hundred children, was just that close to starvation on Diantha's wedding day. The commandant's lips twitched as he sanded the page; he looked, for a moment, as if he smiled. Then his mouth set itself and hid his teeth. He got up, supporting himself with his hands on the table edge, easing his weight to his wounded leg, listening to the muffled thudding of muskets beyond the walls. The besiegers in their burrows were still at it. Sixty days...by the good God, for sixty days they had been around him, and they were still at it. He thought of the musket flashes he had watched through the past night, circling the fort, closing in. It was asking much of a man...to ask him to go out there, alone. He grimaced again, and walked slowly, limping, past the bench and the sleeping drummer boy, through the door into the outer office. His hand, fumbling, touched the shoulder of a man who lay on a plank bed against the wall.

* From the official journal of Captain S. Ecuyer, commandant of Fort Pitt, preserved in the British Museum.

"Major Leslie...."

"Ay." The puncheons creaked. "Good evening, Captain. Are we ready?"

"You have not slept?"

"A little. Enough." Leslie swung his feet to the floor and stood up. "The firing stays about the same."

"*Ja*. They are a little closer on the garden side, where Captain Bassett's house was. No rush yet tonight. You are sure," he hesitated, "you do not wish to tell your wife good-by?"

"No." Leslie moved toward the lighted doorway. "Let her sleep. I have left a letter for her, with her brother. And a will. You will remember, if neither he nor I get through alive, that I leave everything to her." He chuckled. "Everything. A bed, a trunk, a dressing table, and three thousand acres of wild land, to the Duchess of Strangden. How much time is there?"

Ecuyer tugged at the fob adangle under his tunic, and looked at his watch.

"Ten minutes, Major. Carre will open on them at a quarter to ten, and then Phillips on the opposite wall; no volleys, every second man firing five rounds as he pleases. Five minutes after Carre starts it, the Ohio bastion will fire three rounds of canister to sweep the ditch. Then the Flag bastion three; then the Ohio again, so they will not see that we are concerned especially with the ditch where it runs down to the Mon'. Nine rounds, you understand, Leslie. After that, the two howitzers in the Grenadier bastion will put four rounds of canister into the moat, toward the Mon'; if they are in the ditch, that should clear them out, for a little while."

"Long enough," said Leslie cheerfully, "to get down to the water."

"Remember, Major... nine rounds before the Grenadier bastion fires at all; you had best slip into the tunnel then. Captain Arnold is waiting for you at the sally port."

"Arnold?"

"*Ja*. He feels that he has done you ill. He asked, himself, to go out with you, to make some amends. These women, they set us a little wild inside, no? I think, Major, he has regrets now. He said, if there should be some of the Indians left in the moat, a man going with you might keep them off until you should have time to get away."

Leslie shrugged. It was, after all, Valentine Arnold who had killed Robin; it was Valentine Arnold's order to put out the bear that had driven Fritz over the wall; it was Arnold who would have branded Arnett Leslie for deserter and coward to aid his own wooing. It was hard, now, to think of him as wanting to make amends.

"The canister will clear them out," he said curtly.

"You will have a little help, too, from the south wall," Ecuyer told him. "A few shots—not enough to stir them up; enough to hold their attention, only. I thought, if that side of the fort did not fire at all..."

"Yes. Yes. That is better. Thank you."

"Your friend Price picked the men to fire."

"Good. Thank him for me, will you? The pack...?"

"Arnold has it. Ha...! It commences."

Behind the closed shutters, the glass rattled in the windows of the governor's room. The first cannon shot from the Ohio bastion slugged the close air and pushed it against the eardrums, a dull shock. Ecuyer blew out the candle and opened the door. They went together down the steps of the governor's house, where Diantha had sat on Leslie's knee to wash her feet and put on her stockings, where she had stood and watched Leslie pass by, a prisoner, on his way to be tried for a coward. The Flag bastion began to fire.

They walked quickly along the front of the governor's house and past the officers' barracks...past the door where Barent had made love to a bond maid and drawn his sword on the shabby stranger who intervened...past the door where Diantha lay asleep across the foot of the canopied bed, at Bob Gaillard's feet. Duchess of Strangden...niece of a prince...countess of the Austrian empire...Mrs. Arnett Leslie of nowhere. Arnett Leslie walked steadily past the closed door. At the end of the barracks, he said:

"Captain Ecuyer, tomorrow, please, tell her I was thinking of her. Say I thought it was easier to go this way—that I will get through safe."

"Ja! Ja!"

They turned into the dark space between the brick buildings and saw Arnold waiting at the entrance to the tunnel under the south wall. Arnold held out a small pack, rolled tightly.

"I tried both pistols," he told Leslie. "They have fresh flints, and the muzzles and the vents are plugged. The quartermaster cut the plugs, and we tried them; they will keep the charges dry. Prime them, and they will fire, if you have need of them quickly."

"Thank you."

In the pent-up, triangular space between the two barracks and the rampart, the heated air was vibrant. The successive shocks of the cannon made the ears ring. It was difficult to listen, or to talk. Leslie cared to do neither. He loosened the strings of his hunting shirt and stripped it off; untied the leather latchets that held the tops of his leggings to his breechclout belt, and stood naked in clout and moccasins. His body, blackened again with gunpowder, remained invisible in the dark; Arnold's face and Ecuyer's made fleeting blurs when they moved, but Leslie's dark skin was as little white as any Indian's where the sun had touched it.

Ecuyer took the bundle and tied it firmly to the beaded belt, behind. Absently, without enthusiasm, Leslie heard Arnold speaking of moccasins, powder and ball for the pistols at the center of the small pack, food. Without enthusiasm, he saw the Royal American stoop and slip off first one boot and then the other.

"Ready?"

"Ready."

Arnold's stockinged feet rustled on loose gravel; Leslie bent double and followed him into the tunnel.

"God be..." The first blast from the howitzer sweeping the river end of the moat cut the governor's good-by in two. It was cooler in the passage under the wall, and quieter. At the iron-bound door that opened into the moat, Arnold was waiting, and his hand, fumbling, closed over Leslie's forearm.

"...damnation sorry," he was saying, in a high, rapid whisper. "...make public apology when you get back...."

"Yes. Yes." Leslie was impatient. What Valentine Arnold thought concerned him so little he did not know what he was saying. He had never, he realized, been so reluctant in the presence of danger. He did not wish to go out through that safe and solid door; he wanted, just now, to live. The captain began to undo the bars that fastened the door, and they slid back with the faintest scraping of wood on the iron hasps. *Lord,* it was through the sally port that he had gone out one morning seeking Fritz, and come back to find that Valentine Arnold had shot poor Robin. He thought, coldly, that if he got through the savages on the river bank and came safely ashore upstream under the bluff he had in mind, he would look to those fresh flints Arnold had set in his pistol locks.

Where the door had been, a dully luminous rectangle took shape in the solid blackness. Then it glowed red, and lost itself as the night snapped back behind the flash of the howitzer. Together, they stepped out into the moat.

Flash . . . *jar*. Shocked air buffeted their faces. Echoes beat themselves to pieces on the cliffs across the Mon'.

Leslie moved quickly along the base of the brick rampart, around the rough stone blocks that marked the first angle of the Grenadier bastion, into the largest section of the ditch. The officers of the garrison had played at bowls there the day he came to Pitt's Town. Now the Royal Artillery, twelve feet over his head, was playing at bowls with whatever savages were lurking in its deep shadows. He stopped, close under the gunport, waiting. Seventy yards to the right, the moat ran out through the river bank onto the open shore. On either side of it there were burrows where the Shawnees lay; he had marked, last night, that the line of rifle flashes ran far up the Monongahela, almost beyond range of the fort. There were so many warriors in the besieging army now that there was not room for all of them on the firing line that circled the walls; they spread out wherever they could find a hiding place from which to shoot, though their balls fell short of the palisades.

Flash . . . *jar*. The gunners overhead fired their fourth shot.

The red glow lighted the bottom of the ditch; winked out. Leslie, running for the river, heard the clang and screech of fragments tearing at the baked earth; heard the slough and slither of falling dirt; a long-drawn howl, more animal than human; yells. Behind him, he heard Arnold carom into the wall of the ditch. *Damn him!* He might be sincere about making amends, but the naked man running soft-footed toward the river bank and its crackling rifle pits cursed him for not keeping them inside the fort where they belonged. *Fool!* If he fell and made a clatter, he would have the Shawnee pack jumping down onto their backs. Raging inwardly, he stopped. Two strides away, he could hear the regular's loud breathing. He put out his hand and clutched Arnold by the tunic.

"Back . . . go back!" he whispered.

There was the beginning of a whispered answer. Arnold never

finished it. They knew, a split second before the knife drove at Leslie's ribs, that they were not alone in the moat. There was a place where the darkness was darker, solid; it leaped at them. Arnold's arm, flung up, missed the Indian's blade and struck his wrist. His other hand, clutching, felt bare skin sticky with paint.

His voice was a hoarse breath:

"Go! Quick! I'll take this one!"

Leslie left him there. Heard, as he began to run again, the sound of strangling.

Ten yards from the river bank, the bottom of the moat was no longer smooth. The canister had gouged it and strewn it with clods. They crushed under his moccasins with a gritting noise and made him stumble; he stopped running; ahead, close, he saw the black sheen of the Monongahela sliding by.

Abreast of the firing line, the din of the Shawnee muskets told him he had a chance; they were blazing away at the fort in a frenzy of haste, shooting at the flashes as Price's picked riflemen let go at random. Leslie walked out of the ditch onto the flat shore so close to a warrior that he could have touched him; the Shawnee, plastered against the bank, was staring along his musket barrel toward the stockade, waiting for another flash to give him a target. The high bank blunted the battle noises; the white man, walking steadily across the dried silt of the shrunken river, heard minor sounds in undertone—the tump-tump of a ramrod on a ball, a skitter of clay down the bank as an Indian squirmed in his burrow, harsh voices. A little way down the stream, some of the Indians had built a fire and were standing around it, eating; it cast a glow over the sliding water, and made objects blackly visible along the shore.

Leslie walked slowly into the water. He did not dare to hurry, or make a splash. He was wading. Knee-deep; thigh-deep; waist-deep. Then the river took him soundlessly.

He began to swim with the current, edging out little by little from the shore; it carried him below the fort, well out into the joined rivers, before he passed midstream. Sinking, he untied his moccasins and kicked them off. Then he settled himself into the dark water and swam with all his strength up the Monongahela.

For half an hour he could see the red, darting flashes drawing their circle around Fort Pitt.

CHAPTER XXX

In Which Sleigh Bells Turn a Hot Night Hideous, and the Army Sent to Save Fort Pitt Is Ambushed 20 Miles Away:

ARNETT LESLIE had no very clear idea how he had come to Tomahawk. He saw it, lying below him, no larger than a dirty handkerchief dropped in the immensity of the great valley.

Old Iron Head had cut that square patch out of the wilderness years ago, and hemmed it with a palisade of logs. Leslie recognized the place; he had camped there with Fritz, and Fritz' thieving bear had stolen the last of the cornbread while they slept. He looked down at it with a dull surprise; it should not be there, it should be farther to the east, miles farther, hours farther. It was quite impossible that he should have come, before midday, to Tomahawk. He watched the dirty handkerchief grow as he ran down the mountain. Running had become a habit; it was easier to run than to walk; when he walked, his body had acquired a queer, annoying trick of weaving from side to side, making his feet stumble on the edges of the wheel-track. Running, he was able to work a counter-trick on his body; he simply let it hang forward, as if it was going to fall; each time before it fell, one foot or the other swung ahead and caught it. The trick made running automatic; he thought, foolishly, that if he found Bouquet and the army he would not be able to stop and tell them about Fort Pitt; he would go running past, first one foot and then the other catching his body just before it fell down.

He considered the problem seriously. Half way down the mountain, he decided what he would do when he met Bouquet. He would simply make his feet stop, and let his body fall down. Colonel Bouquet would have to pick him up out of the road to let the army go by; when the colonel picked him up he would tell the army that it would have to hurry to keep Diantha from worrying.

When he came out into the clearing, among the stumps, he saw why Tomahawk had looked like a dirty handkerchief. The Indians had been there, too, and burned it; even the grass was scorched and yellow, and smeared with black splotches that had been cabins in April.

Leslie passed at his shuffling run. He felt, for a moment, exultant. It had been midnight when he climbed the bluffs above the Monongahela, with the warm river water streaming down his body into the fresh moccasins he had donned from the pack at his belt; it had been daybreak when he had swung away from Forbes' road, plunging through the forest in a great semi-circle to avoid Ligonier and the savages lurking around the stockade; by the sun in his face, it was yet not much past ten o'clock. He had come, in ten hours, more than sixty miles. Ahead, miles ahead, hours ahead, the Allegheny Mountains stood purple-blue against the sky. He saw them now, immense as the valley had been immense when he looked down into it from the ridge above Tomahawk; when he crossed the valley and the mountains, he would come to Fort Bedford, and find the army.

Yes, the army would be at Bedford. It had to be.

Arnett Leslie put out his tongue and tried to moisten his dried lips. Lips and tongue, they only scraped each other; he grimaced, contorting his cheeks, trying to squeeze out the saliva. *God,* the army *must* be at Bedford. Today or tomorrow, the women and children in Fort Pitt would eat for the last time. After that...

He ran on. He must climb that mountain. He must get to Fort Bedford, and find Bouquet, and the army. He must find them quickly.

But the army was not at Fort Bedford.

Arnett Leslie came to Stony Creek a little after noon. He knew it was past midday because his shadow got to the creek before he did and was lying in the water when he dropped down on hands and knees to drink. Kneeling, he could look up through the swamp grass on the opposite bank and see the mountain. The mountain had come definitely closer; it was more green than blue; across it on a long slant ran the dark scar of road. Leslie drank again, sparingly, and thrust head and face into the water; when he raised his head with a jerk to throw the wet hair out of his eyes, he saw that the scar had changed. It was no longer dark; it moved.

It was, he decided, very much like the scar of the Shawnee hatchet on his own breast—the old, dry scar, not the new one. He looked down at himself, mildly curious, mildly pleased to find the comparison was not inapt. The long, slanting scar was lighter than the rest of his body; the skin that covered it had a thin, brittle look, like parchment, and when he moved his arm and the chest muscles moved with it, the parchment-like tissue rippled and glistened. When he looked back at the mountain, he saw that its scar was rippling and glistening, too. It was brighter, if anything, than the gash on his own flesh. He was on his feet, wading, half way across the stream, before he realized what had happened to the road to make it seem to move, to flow, to ripple and glisten in the sun. He stopped, dead still, knee deep in the tugging water.

The brightness on the mountain side was made of the white covers of baggage wagons. The glistening was bayonets. The flowing was men...men...horses...more men.

The army was not at Bedford. The army was there on the mountain, thirty miles closer than he had dared to hope. Bouquet was coming! Arnett Leslie floundered through the water and began to run.

He seemed, in the undulant immensity of valley, not to run at all. To crawl, rather. His shadow lengthened ahead of him until it was as tall as he; and he took a queer notion that his body finally had tricked him and had fallen down. It required, now, a deliberate effort to move his feet, as much of an effort as if his body actually lay there on the ground ahead of him and he had to push it. He watched the shadow's head, measuring how far it moved with each push, picking out marks along the road, saying to himself: *Ten pushes will put it past that tree*. And after the tree: *Four pushes will bring it to that plantain stalk*. Sometimes it took five pushes instead of four, and he swore, croaking, hating the useless burden of his shadow.

He was watching it when it crawled grotesquely up a fringed legging yellow with dust, up over a dangling powder horn, into a fringed beard yellow with tobacco drip. He stopped, swaying, but he did not fall down; it was fortunate, he thought, that the man with the yellow beard was there to hold his shadow up. Looking past him, he saw Forbes' road full of kilts and bayonets.

"Name o' th' Lord!" said the scout. "Be you from Ligonier? Have they took it yet?"

"No. From Fort Pitt," Leslie mouthed at him, and heard nothing. He tried again: "From Fort Pitt. Where is Bouquet?" This time he heard the words.

The bearded man raised his rifle arm's length above his head and flourished it. His mouth, wide open, showed four black snags of teeth. His voice rose in a shrill hail, and Leslie saw other riflemen trotting toward them, thrums bobbing, weapons at trail. They passed with quick, curious glances, with flung questions.

"From Pitt's Town," the scout told them. "It's still holdin' out."

They trotted on, keeping their distance ahead of the kilted column. After them came a horse, galloping—a gray horse with a red rider, red and black kilt flapping, red jacket perking up at every jump. Leslie took a step to meet the gray horse.

"Ye've taken a bad sun scald, Robin," he croaked. "Have ye no goose grease handy?"

Robin Stuart gaped at the naked wretch who called him by name and pulled his lips back from his teeth, smiling horribly through dust-caked hair that dangled down his cheeks.

"Arnett Leslie! It's never Major Leslie?"

"Ay. For God's sake, Robin, have them to hurry."

Stuart flung himself out of the saddle.

"Arnie, man, I canna believe.... What have they done to ye?"

He did not wait for the answer. The urgency in the blood-rimmed eyes was answer enough. He got his arm around the sweat-streaked back.

"Here, Arnie. Can ye mount? Bouquet's just down the road. There...foot in the stirrup. Man, ye're barefoot; there's nought but rags o' leather, and y'r feet all bloody."

Leslie looked down at them curiously; they had not hurt at all. He shoved them hard against the stirrup iron as the horse began to move, and saw black blood well from a cut he had not known was there. Stuart's hand lay on his grimed thigh, steadying him. The ground rose and fell in waves. At the top of the first wave they passed more of the shirtmen, a straggling squad, long rifles criss-cross against the sky, eyes squinting into the sun, watching the thin fringe of scouts flung out ahead.

Riding up the next slope, Leslie saw the crest of it break suddenly into blinding, sparkling foam. The foam ran down to meet him, all polished steel, two hundred steel blades flashing above the polished muskets. They flowed by. From the saddle, he looked down between them and saw, underneath, a dark current of black knapsacks swaying above dust-dark kilts. Through the current ran dull gleams of red as the highland jackets swung unbuttoned from the bent, plodding bodies. From the highland bonnets, long feathers danced in a dizzying, criss-cross pattern, bobbing along on the current. The naked man on the horse closed his eyes to shut out their dancing; it made the mountain and the valley and the horse dance too.

There was an empty place in the road, and then more sparkling steel, more swinging kilts, a gleam of Lochaber axes swaying, a turgid current of tired legs and drifting dust. Then the road was empty again, except for clumsy bat wagons heaving in the ruts, and two strung-out lines of pack horses. Leslie thought he had dozed. While his eyes were closed, the army had gone by. He put his hands together, tight, on the saddle horn, and leaned to Robin's bonnet:

"Is that...all?"

Stuart looked up.

"Ay. That's all. Four hundred thirty, and half o' them more fit for bed than marching. Here comes the colonel."

Bouquet came up at a gallop along the crawling baggage train.

"What is it? A message, Stuart?"

Stuart saluted; Leslie lifted one hand from the saddle horn and put it back quickly; the gray horse stood still, but the ground would not.

"Major Leslie, colonel, from Fort Pitt," Robin said.

"Pitt! After five weeks...When did you leave the Forks?"

"Last night."

"*Last night?* Seventy miles?" He swung to Stuart.

"Look at his feet, colonel. He's not lying. Do ye not recollect him from '58, with the Maryland men?"

Bouquet ranged his black mount along the gray's neck.

"Leslie! Yes. Yes. I ask pardon, Major. We have all been frantic Rumors. Rumors. Fort Pitt holds on?"

"Yes." Leslie closed his eyes to shut out the scarlet coat and black horse. Red...black; red...black; fire...night...

341

crackling...hatchets licking in between the scorched palisades...
a girl crouching against the flimsy wall....

"It can yet hold on?"

"Yes." *It can yet hold on!* Leslie felt a blurred rush of hatred for
the calm, calculating Swiss. It was easy to say "Hold on," sitting
there in trim bright tunic, in ribboned wig, in crisp white spatterdashes. He forced his eyes to stare at the full, handsome face. "Yes.
There was food, yesterday, for one day more. There has been a
continuous assault for three days. The barracks were on fire five
times yesterday. Ecuyer is wounded. Yesterday they brought our
last messenger and showed him to us, naked for the stake, on the
river bank, and sent Ecuyer's letter back to him. There are six
hundred of them...."

"Six hundred. So. And Ligonier...you came that way?"

"I heard firing there this morning."

"Good. Good."

The wagons, stolid, crept like snails. The soldier, stolid, watched
them creeping.

"Good! Good!" Leslie heard his own voice, croaking, mocking.
It would take those crawling wagons weeks to reach the Forks of
the Ohio. He said so, furiously.

"You say they have no food," Bouquet answered, his eyes on the
creeping rear guard. "To go there without food is impossible."

"There will be none left to eat it," Leslie told him harshly. The
Swiss soldier of fortune put out one hand and touched his shoulder.

"Good. It is so bad as that. That is what I wish to know. We
will go there in time. See to him, Captain Stuart." Even then he did
not move, sitting there massively calm, watching the red jackets
of the light infantry toiling through the dust cloud behind the
baggage train.

Robin hailed a wagon. Heaving, complaining, it lurched up out
of the ruts and came to a halt in the brush alongside. The wagon
box was filled to the tops of its high sides with sacks of corn meal.
Robin and the teamster plucked Leslie out of the saddle and laid
him on a blanket spread across the sacks, and the wagon jolted
down into the ruts again. Stuart, squatting in the low space under
the canvas cover, produced from his sporran a gnawed heel of
wheat bread and a slice of bacon.

"Here, Arnie. Lie back; I'll feed ye." He broke the bread. "Man,

342

man, I canna believe.... D'ye recall, Arnie, I said I would think of
ye when I rode through these mountains ye had fought in?"

"Ay." The sun came strained and thin through the wagon
cover; the rakish highland bonnet set dour shadows on Robin
Stuart's face and sunk his eyes deeply into their thickets of black
hair. "Ay. I named a dog for you, Robin."

"Did ye, now? A snappin', snarlin' beast, I warrant. Look ye,
Arnie: ye haven't said, but the sweet lady ye were goin' to wed...
she'll never be yonder, in Fort Pitt?"

"Ay."

"And ye came away. That wanted courage, man, hers and yours.
I remember that day, on shipboard, when that wastrel Lawless
railed at ye for a coward, and ye had the courage not to fall in
with his wicked dueling until he misnamed y'r lady, and then
stood his fire and put y'r bullet in the air. Be easy in y'r mind,
Arnie. Bouquet is a grand soldier, for all he sits like a mountain."

"Lawless is there, too," Leslie told him.

"Yonder? In Fort Pitt? Damme, did he quarrel with ye again,
that you scared him out of Maryland, and sought him...?"

"No. 'T was he came hunting me. You see, Robin, I did not
wed the lady I told you of."

"Ye did not?"

"No. She was already wed. And I am wed to that girl I bought,
that day on the *New Adventure*."

"Ye're never! And Lawless came seekin' ye, to do ye hurt for it?"

Leslie smiled, and took what was left of the bread and bacon
out of Stuart's fingers.

"He did me, first and last, the two best services of any man. I
would not have bought her but for him; I would not have wed
her had he not come hounding me and let her see I was not the
beast she thought me."

While the floundering wagons inched their way across the valley,
Robin Stuart heard how a bond maid became a fine lady, a duchess,
a countess and a wife in the midst of hunger and death; and must
clamber out over the corn-meal sacks to tell the tale to Bouquet.
He came back, hours later, to tell Leslie that a flying column would
ride for Ligonier that night, and that Bouquet would leave the
baggage wagons and press on with such food as could be carried
on the pack saddles of three hundred horses.

Thirty men rode out of Tomahawk after sunset on the night dash for Ligonier. Somewhere in the darkness on Laurel Ridge, they became thirty-one. At daybreak, when they broke from the forest edge and rushed for the log gates of the beleaguered fort, they were only thirty again. Two miles beyond the stockade, Arnett Leslie turned on the bare back of his stolen horse and listened to the distant rattle of musketry as Bouquet's flying column ran the gauntlet of the besiegers. The firing lasted five minutes, and ceased. The thirty men were safe. Leslie kicked his horse into a shambling run up the valley of the Loyal Hanna. No matter how hard Bouquet drove his little army, it would not get to Fort Pitt for three days. When they got there, they would be outnumbered. The three hundred men inside Fort Pitt could help them, if they had word in time. He rode with a growing eagerness, a growing exultation. When he came to the weed-grown ovens and the old log breastworks of Twelve-Mile Camp, where Bouquet had fought the Shawnees seven years before, he was seeing again the limestone manor house he would build for Diantha. He heard her whispering against his cheek:

"... and let me be your scullery maid, and give me a kiss each night and morning for my wage."

They had had, so far, only such hasty kisses.

He saw, too late, the roached scalplock rising from the laurel smother between two cat-clay ovens; saw brown smoke jetting; felt, instantly, the sag and quiver of the horse. While the beast staggered a dozen steps, he searched the brush, the breastworks, the encroaching forest growth, and saw only the one warrior rushing toward him. A youngster, Leslie told himself, unblooded and thirsty for his scalp. He let himself fall with the horse, drawing his pistol as he fell; lying with one cheek to the grass, he saw the Shawnee leap a stump and plunge at him with lifted hatchet. The misericord slipped softly through the gay band of yellow that ran like a belt around the copper belly. The hatchet cut the sod six feet away. The yellow paint turned red. In cold anger Leslie took the scalp; he was not sure whether he or the tyro warrior had been the greater fool; altogether, they had almost destroyed the limestone manor before it was even started. Reluctantly, Leslie left the road, running southwestward through the hills, fiercely resentful of the delay.

In the end, it was the delay that saved him.

Two miles from the trail he turned north again. From a hazel copse, late in the afternoon, he looked out across a rolling valley and saw the road far ahead, winding westward through Crab Tree Bottom. It vanished into distance, into a purple gash between blue ridges. Fifteen miles beyond the ridges, through the twisting defiles of Turtle Creek, lay Braddock's battlefield; beyond that, four miles northwestward, lay Fort Pitt. Leslie wiped the streaming sweat out of his eyes and ran on; the linsey leggings and the fresh moccasins Robin Stuart had found for him were drenched black; the deerskin shirt Robin borrowed for him he had discarded hours before, except for a long strip cut from the skirts of it to bind his feet when the moccasins gave out.

He ran cautiously, from cover to cover, following the windings of dry creek-beds, seeing the sunset a red glare above the gap at Turtle Creek, seeing it fade and leave the ridges charred black against the sky. A ravine with steep banks shut out the hills; stars came and looked down at him between the leaning willows. When the ravine lost itself at last in a dried-out swamp, he saw that the charred ridges had been rekindled.

A red glare hung again over the deep gash of Turtle Creek. Through the hot, pressing night he heard the jingle of sleigh bells. He stopped running. Began, instead, a stealthy creeping up the steep ridge. Came, step after slow step, to the brink of the defile. Saw the red gut of valley teeming, churning, swarming with savages.

Their fires stretched for a mile, staining the dark reaches of the creek, dancing on the dark walls of the ravine. Around the fires, the warriors were dancing also, whorls of black bodies, blackly shadowed, redly lighted. Each writhing, leaping circle swirled around its own vortex of leaping flame. A phrase leaped into Leslie's brain. He had heard Peter Lanness describe a war dance of the Ottawas:

Hell gone for a sleigh ride!

Out of the hellish ravine, out of the obscene yelling, rose the jingle of the bells. Fire glistened on them where they hung to the clout belts of howling Delawares. A naked, copper leg, thrust suddenly into the glare of fire, showed anklets studded with a double row of white man's sleigh bells. Leslie crept over the brink of the

345

defile, crept down the rock-strewn bank. When he was close enough to be sure that there were no white men pinioned, waiting for death, no fresh scalps dangling on coup sticks in the frenzied dances, no white women's clothing on the squaws banked beyond the fires, he crept up to the brink again.

He had been, once more, too confident—so confident the Forbes road was unwatched that the lone Shawnee had almost shot him from his horse, so confident Bouquet would save Fort Pitt that he had begun to dream again of South Mountain, and Diantha, and the wage she had bargained for.

With a groan, he turned his back on the distant Forks and slipped down the ridge. If he would save Diantha, he must warn Bouquet.

A little after daylight, at a turn of road beside the Loyal Hanna, a startled scout threw his rifle to his shoulder, and dropped it at the sound of a white man's voice. Leslie, shuffling past him, saw black snags of teeth above a yellowed beard.

Under a burning sun, in moving dust, the army dragged itself seventeen miles in one forenoon. After the first three hours, its canteens were empty. The springs were dry; the streams were twists of bare sand, of mud baked and cracked into mosaics. At intervals the red-kilted pipers of the Black Watch flung their wild "Come to the Feast" into the hills ahead; at intervals the big drum tolled the marching cadence; behind the pipes and the drum, the colors drooped, moving as the men moved, bent forward, listless. Around them hung the dust; the regimental flag, buff silk with the gold "XLII" upon it, took on the hue of the dust; the very roses and thistles, twined around the Roman numbers, turned brown as if they were wilting in the heat.

Half a mile ahead, the fringe of scouts appeared out of the valley, moving slowly up rounded hills. They made a ragged line of dots; the dots seemed to jump about, now here, now there, though actually each dot barely crawled; a dot vanished into a fold of earth, and abruptly, away to one side, a similar dot came out of a clump of trees. Watching them was a dizzy business. Leslie, riding with Robin Stuart in the gap between the rear of the Black Watch and the leading company of the Seventy-seventh, found the dots blurring and losing themselves against the parched brown hills. The Forty-second began to climb. "Are ye sure there *is* any Bushy Run?" Robin asked him, the burr of his voice thicker with the dust in his throat.

"Just over this line of hills. We'll be atop it in ten minutes, and drinking in half an hour. How long d'you think Bouquet will wait there?"

"Only until dark, Arnie. We'll march off and leave the campfires burning, to make y'r red friends think we're set there for the night. Did I not tell ye, man, he is a grand soldier? *Whush!* Did ye hear that?"

The two plodding regiments heard it, a single shot. Heads went up. A quick stir ran down the column like a shiver. Then the files stiffened; the ripple of bayonets above the feathered bonnets swung into a tight, quick rhythm. Over the hill, another shot cracked out ... another ... another. A dozen burst in a straggling volley. Up ahead, the knot of shirtmen who marched behind the fringe of scouts spread out, like a fan flipped open, and went running into the brush. Bouquet whirled by at a gallop. The pipers wheeled out to the side of the road. Two companies of the Forty-second, light infantry, went up the hill at the double. Just under the crest, still running, they wheeled, one company to the right, one to the left; wheeled again, up the slope into line. The line, steel tipped, went out of sight.

The shots blended into a crackle that was like flames crackling through dry brush, uneven but unceasing.

Panting, with sweat streaming, with claymores clacking against their thighs, with bearskin helmets slanting forward, the grenadiers of the Black Watch left the column and swung into line of battle. They met, as they crossed the hilltop, a fusillade that hung the scrub oaks to their right with balls of smoke. Steadily, precisely, the double rank of bearskins turned on its flank, hung an instant, fired once, and charged. Behind them, from other scrub oaks, a volley blazed into their backs. Panting, half blind with sweat, the light infantry that was left of the Forty-second deployed in the hazel brush to the left of the road and charged the woods from which the volley came. On both sides of the hill the firing redoubled; smoke rose above the stunted oaks; out of the smoke came a frenzied yelping.

"Come to the Feast!" shrilled the pipes of the Black Watch, playing the Seventy-seventh up the slope. As it came, the woods on both sides blazed and spewed smoke. Men fell. The column shrank in upon itself. A line of naked, bounding bodies broke from the cover of the hazel scrub and came on, yelling.

Commands. A stiffening. A level flash of light as the muskets of the Seventy-seventh came up together. A rolling crash. A roll of smoke smothering the road. Out of the smoke a rush of men.

The Montgomery Highlanders, charging, met the Shawnee hatchets with the bayonet. Grenadiers to the left of the road, light infantry to the right, they cleared the scrub oaks for three hundred yards. Bounding, howling, the Shawnees fled before them. Bounding, howling, they came back again as the Highland line drew off.

Up the road at a gallop came the pack train. Behind it burst a new clamor. Two companies of the Seventy-seventh went down to help the hard-pressed rear-guard; between them, plunging, squealing, colliding, the loaded horses stormed up the hill. Packs, ripped open, strewed corn meal in the trampled road. Shots from the forest edge tumbled beast after beast out of the jostling herd.

A teamster on a tall bay galloped through the brush to check the stampede at the hill top; a ball gouged through the horse just back of the ribs; he reared, spouting blood, and swung at a mad run toward the crackling woods. The teamster, sawing at the reins, tried desperately to stop him, gave up, flung himself out of the saddle. His foot caught in the stirrup and he fell and was dragged. His jacket pulled up over his head, and then his shirt. When a second shot stopped the horse, he got up blindly, clawing at the garments about his face, his back streaming from a dozen gashes. Three Indians pounced upon him as he stood there pawing; two struck him with their hatchets, but the third jerked off the coat and shirt and scalped him while he stood erect. He fell, still shrieking, and a grenadier, prone behind a stump, shot down the warrior who held the scalp.

Soldiers and shirt-men, wagoners with long whips and sergeants with bright axes swinging, they got the remnant of the horses into the scanty shelter of a locust grove to the right of the road. Firing, loading, firing again, the Highlanders got themselves somehow into a circle around the hill, half way down the slope, their backs to the pack train, their bayonets to the swarming woods that hemmed them in.

Arnett Leslie, a dead man's musket in his hands, came back with

348

Robin's company from a headlong charge and dropped where a tree, uprooted, had left a pocklike hollow. Along the fallen trunk, a squad of the Black Watch crouched. Toward them, through the hazel clumps, a flood of painted Ottawas welled up across the ground the white men had abandoned. They fired as they came. Behind the log, the ramrods slid home, the musket barrels slid out; the grenadiers fired, scrambled over the fallen trunk, and charged with a wild, high cry. Leslie, running with them, saw a head with horns and fur above a crimson face, fired from the hip, and saw the horns root the grass as the Ottawa kicked and flopped about in dying. The pack fled howling; the grenadiers turned back; after them, when they had reloaded, came the horned, daubed warriors.

That was the battle.

There was the round knob of hill, parched and waterless. There was the road, running across its rounded top, running down to Bushy Run and plenty of water, half a mile away. There was the locust grove, a little below the crest, where frightened teamsters fought to hold the frightened horses, stripped off the packs, heaped them into a crude fence, a crude barricade. There were the clumps of stunted oaks, the tangles of laurel, the patches of hazel brush. There was, below them, a strip of open ground, and then, at the bottom of the hill, thick woods whence came a ceaseless yelling, a ceaseless fire; whence came, also, one rush after another that must be driven back.

Through the burning afternoon the two regiments—they were, actually, not one full regiment—endured the fire, the thirst, the certainty that they were surrounded and outnumbered. They knelt, fired, rose, charged down the open slope. The long, dry grass was slippery; the men's shoes were worn slick from a hundred and eighty miles of Old Iron Head's road. Charging, they slipped and staggered; turning when the savages fled before them, they slipped and fell, clawing at the grass, squirming for safety. Some of them died under the Indian knives and mauls before they could gain their feet, and those who survived looked down from the thin firing line at their scalped and bloody heads.

Men's bodies ran with sweat. The white, red and green checkers of the Highland bonnets turned black with it. The scarlet jackets turned black; the kilts hung soaked and clinging around sunscalded thighs. Dust caked on streaming faces, and the streams dug furrows through it; bloom from the dry grass caught in the sweat drops under the eyes, under the lower lip; the cartridges drew black rings around straining mouths. There was the taste of fur, the bite of powder gas in the throat and nose. The sun slid down behind the Bushy Run ravine and left the four hundred men inside the ring of death.

Not all of the four hundred were thirsty. There were more than thirty dead. But the wounded made up for those who were dead in the agony of their thirst; there were more than forty of the wounded; they lay among the sacks of flour and corn meal, among the trampling horses, and moaned and cried for water.

In the dark, Bouquet called his officers together. They sat on the sacks and talked. Not much; there was not much to say. Without the food and the wounded, the men who were left might cut their way through to Fort Pitt, or back to Bedford. If they left the food behind, Fort Pitt would starve, and they with it. If they retreated to Bedford, Fort Pitt must surrender, or fight on until, starving, its men grew too weak to stop the rushes, the women too weak to quench the fires. There was no talk of leaving either the food or the wounded; the Black Watch, the Seventy-seventh would not save themselves. There was a word or two about the thought in every man's mind: Braddock's battlefield lay off there to the west, a short day's march away. Braddock had gone into the battle of the Monongahela with twelve hundred men, with cannon; four hundred savages had destroyed him. Bouquet had now on this hill above Bushy Run something less than three hundred and fifty men. He asked Arnett Leslie, calmly, how many warriors he thought were around them.

"All the Shawnees, probably," Leslie answered, "from Fort Pitt, with all the Delawares and all the Mingoes. Say five hundred men. The Forty-second had Ottawas in front of them this afternoon."

"The jolly fellows with the horns," Robin said from the next meal sack. "They sounded hoarse."

"Their voices are harsher," Bouquet put in. "Gladwyn * should be glad to be rid of them. Who else?"

"Wyandottes—not many, probably—and a few young bucks from the Miamis. Perhaps," his throat tightened at what he saw when

---

*Gladwyn, commandant at Detroit, in the Ottawa and Ojibway country.

350

he thought of them, "a few Ojibway from Major Gladwyn's neighborhood. I saw none, but they have been at Pitt's Town."

"Altogether?"

"Altogether, six hundred warriors."

"If Ecuyer could strike them from the rear with the Fort Pitt garrison," a captain of Montgomery Highlanders suggested.

"I will try to get through," said Leslie, and felt Robin's hand objecting, plucking at his arm.

"No." Bouquet spoke decisively. "If the attempt failed, it would doom Fort Pitt."

"It is doomed," some one said grimly out of the dark, and went unrebuked. Around the foot of the parched hill, the yelling burst suddenly into a triumphant chorus.

Leslie turned to face Bouquet across the faint sheen of Robin's crossbelts:

"I am not a soldier in fact, Colonel. I am only a former major of militia, here by your courtesy. May I recall to you how you beat the French Indians at the Loyal Hanna?"

"Of course, Major. The Maryland men earned the right to speak at any council. Did you know Shelby, who fought and killed a chief outside the barricade that day?"

"Ay. It was outside the barricade I was thinking of. You fought them first outside, and then retreated, and when they came on, hot and yelling, you turned on them at the palisade and whipped them. Both you and Shelby were audacious that day."

"Which is to say, Leslie, that you would risk a retreat here to draw them on and trap them, eh?"

"Something like that, sir." Startled voices jumped out at him. Bouquet said, in his blunt, calm way:

"Good. Good. We shall talk about that."

There was no sleep on the hill that night. The yelling and the moaning never ceased. At dawn the moans were fainter, but the howls redoubled. Men looked to the priming in their pans, looked down at the ring of woods where painted bodies capered just out of range, looked at each other, croaked, swallowed at their furred tongues or at the hearts in their throats. Leslie, walking with Bouquet and Stuart along the firing line, saw the trim Highland regulars dirty and unkempt as his hard-bitten militiamen behind the palisades of Fort Pitt. Before the sun was level with the tops of the scrub oaks, the hill was hot. It was possible, in the clear, bright air, to see a long way.

The Forbes road, running through the circle of beleaguered men, stretched away east and west, empty, peaceful. Standing in the wheel tracks, it was difficult to believe that to walk along them down the brown hillside was to die. The road, homely and familiar, strengthened the sense of isolation. It was as if, still alive, these two regiments were already in the region of the dead. Beyond them, along those ruts they had trod, was the land of the living, remembered, almost visible, but out of reach. Even the water was out of reach, and thirst intensified to torture.

The sun mounted, the heat increased, the fight began again. Rush, counter-rush, retreat, it repeated itself. There were more dead, more wounded. Sure that their trapped prey could not escape, the Indian warriors would not face a charge. They ran, yelping, ahead of the bayonets; and when the bayonets went back to fill the gap they had left in the firing line, they sucked the Indians back with them.

"We beat them every time, but we never win," Robin panted. He looked down at the blood dripping from his finger ends, and held out his left arm to Leslie. "Damme, they burned me, Arnie. Ye'd think I was a gentleman, fighting a duel before breakfast. 'T was in the left elbow y'r noble Lord Dick furrowed ye, was it not?"

"Ay, and we had a drink on it," said Leslie, smiling.

"The devil fly away with ye! Will ye have done with speakin' of drinks, man? 'T is all right for Bouquet to tease these red devils into thinkin' we're about to howl king's cruse, but I canna stand teasin' concernin' liquid."

"I think," said Leslie as he cut away the sleeve of Robin's jacket and bound a strip of shirt around the gash in his elbow, "I think Bouquet's about done with teasing them."

In the locust grove where the pack horses jerked at their pickets and the wounded who could still hold a musket lay waiting with their shoulders to the barricade of sacks, the pipers of the Black Watch began to play:

> *Fareweel to Lochaber,*
> *Fareweel to my Jean,*

Where heart-some wi' her,
I hae mony days been....

Around the firing line, men licked their lips, loosened the claymores in their scabbards, wiped sleeves across their eyes to see. High and plaintive, the pipes sang:

> *Lochaber no more.*
> *Lochaber no more.*
> *We'll maybe return to Lochaber no more.*

From the woods below the north slope, a surge of naked bodies swept up the hill; a company of grenadiers fired, charged, and swept it back. The pipes played on.

Stuart spoke softly to his crouching men. The lament changed, the music quickened; the pipers went screaming into the shrill defiance of "Come to the Feast."

"They're coming," Robin said hoarsely, and drew his claymore clear.

Out of the woods that lay between the white men and Bushy Run leaped another howling rush. Stuart waved his hand; behind the next company a bearded officer waved back.

"Present, *firelocks!*" The pipes stopped on a high, wailing cry. "Remember, it's fire and run this time. Take aim ... *fire!*"

The two light companies got to their feet in the hanging smoke. Instead of charging, they began to break and fall back. They straggled, drifted along the face of the hill, began to run. Behind them, the rushing warriors raised a yell of triumph. Around them, the companies that had not broken began to move back, shortening the line, closing the gap in the circle. The whole front facing Bushy Run bent in, retreating as the torrent of painted bodies poured up the hill. The whole front gave way ... except that on one side of the hill a company of grenadiers, crouching, running, sped through the hazel coverts *toward* the oncoming savages ... except that on the opposite side of the hill, a company of light infantry did the same thing.

Between them, pell-mell, rushed the howling pack, straight for the baggage train.

Ahead of the rush, in full flight, Robin Stuart's company and the other that had broken with it ran headlong to the rear, toward

Ligonier. They met, those two broken companies, at the far end of the baggage park. Met, fell with the cool discipline of veterans into line, wheeled, went at a dead run southward along a wooded spur that stuck out from the knob of the hill.

The white man's two traps were set.

Bouquet sprang one of them as the Indian charge reached the flour-sack barricade.

From both sides, the companies that had run crouching into ambush in the hazel brush rose and fired point-blank into the huddled mass, loaded, fired, and charged with the bayonet.

On the wooded spur Robin Stuart's two companies wheeled right again to face the west. As the second volley from the ambushed companies crashed into the trapped Indians inside the circle, Stuart sprang the second trap. In close order, with leveled bayonets, the light infantry burst out of the woods along the spur and struck the flank of the Indian firing line outside the circle.

There was, ahead of them, a strip of brush, a scatter of stunted oak, an open space, and then the woods. High and fierce as the Shawnee scalp yell, the Highland pibroch rose above the crash of firing. Thrusting, stabbing, the two companies ripped through the brush and the oak scrub. They swept into the open ground a score of screeching, hacking Delawares. The left flank company, plunging into the woods, drove out another score. The Black Watch had them hand to hand at last. Feathered bonnets flew to meet feathered scalplocks. Under tartan kilts, bare legs locked with legs that were bare from breechclout to moccasin.

Leslie, fighting with clubbed musket, saw a Shawnee dodge a soldier's bayonet thrust, knock up the gun barrel, and throw the man off his feet with a hand grappled in the badger fur of his sporran. Striking with the butt, Leslie missed, went to his knees, and got the savage by the buffalo hair of his own war-sack and wrenched him clear. The Highlander's bayonet ripped the red throat open.

Up and down the brown slope the mêlée spread. Knife against claymore, gun butt against gun butt, it swirled west around the turn of the hill toward Bushy Run. It met, in full retreat, the horde that had rushed the baggage train and found itself caught between two fires. There was, for a headlong moment, a crush of two hundred men fighting body to body.

354

A sergeant of the Black Watch took a Delaware maul full in the face and went down, his Lochaber ax flying from his grasp. His hand, groping, closed on a dry mullein stalk. As he dragged himself toward it, scrambling for a footing on the slippery grass, a greased and red-daubed warrior snatched up the ax and whirled it. The blade fell once on the clutching hand and severed it, fell again on the neck of the red jacket and stuck there. The sergeant sprawled face down, twitching, the severed hand still clenched around the mullein stalk. Robin, his broken claymore in his fist, broke through the press and snatched up the ax; whirling, it crushed the head of the Delaware stooping with his knife at the sergeant's hair. Three warriors closed in; the reddened ax swung again and sent one of them staggering; the others leaped under the haft and gripped Robin by the arms and waist. Leslie saw him fight free of the mêlée, the ax gone, his fingers on one painted throat; saw him break the other's grip and swing away; saw that the reeling Indian had his kilt gripped in both hands. The kilt, unwinding, spun Robin full about; his fingers slipped; spinning helplessly, he flew down the slope like a boy thrown loose from a children's game of crack-the-whip.

"Robin!" Leslie cried at him. "Robin, I'm coming!"

The stock of his clubbed musket broke off short on a shaven skull. A knife drove for his ribs. A hatchet, whirling, struck him on the head. Falling, he saw Robin go down under another lifted hatchet.

The grenadiers of the Forty-second, roaring, came down the hill and swept the mêlée into the woods below it.

CHAPTER XXXI

THE silence, for most of the men and women in Fort Pitt,
was harder to bear than the waiting.

They knew, after the seventh day of August, that something stark and terrible had happened in the hills beyond Braddock's field. On that day, a horde of Indians poured past the fort.

They flourished scarlet jackets and feathered bonnets. They carried, on long poles, fresh and ghastly scalps. They waved like banners the long tartan kilts of Highland soldiers. They shouted, brandishing their trophies, taunting the haggard garrison that lined the palisades. But they did not stop.

Men, women, horses and baggage, they streamed across the Allegheny a half mile upstream and vanished into the hills.

Ecuyer, stubborn and cautious, kept the gates closed and the drawbridge up. The five hundred pent up inside the walls lived on with their hunger, with the sickening stenches, with the burning heat. After the days and nights of ceaseless musketry, the silence was unbelievable. Women, face to face at the ovens where there was nothing to cook, screamed at each other to make themselves heard, and felt their nerves jump and quiver when the sound struck their ears and pierced them.

Diantha smiled wanly at her brother and shook her head.

"Please, Bob. Don't argue. There can be no more danger. I shall go mad if I stay here, listening, listening."

She pulled the limp skirts of the blue gown out through the pocket holes, and heard Bob rally her:

"Primping again, though your feet are bare. D'you mean to crape your hair, too, so that you may pick nettles in style?"

She made a face at him, and sobered.

"I keep thinking of Peg. The day Arnett was tried for being a coward, she said to me, here in this room: *I lie awake at night,*

356

*praying that Valentine Arnold will be shot; I want him to be hurt,
so that he will need me and want me again.* Now she has her wish,
and I envy her. I envy her, Bob. I keep praying for Arnett to be
wounded—oh, even terribly wounded—so they will bring him back
and let me care for him. Even with that awful gash across Val's
face, she is happy; she has him . . . safe. I have nothing but
the listening."

She went out into the unbelievable silence.

Tom Yeardley sat on the wood frame of the well, one foot drawn
up across his thigh and cradled in both hands. He untangled himself and came lumbering to meet her.

"Will he . . . ?"

Tom shook his head, his face screwed up into wrinkles, like a
baby on the verge of crying.

"No, Diantha. I've just come from Ecuyer. He'll not let a man
go out of rifle shot. He says, if there is any army to be found by a
scout on the Forbes road, it will come marching in sooner or later.
He'll not risk another man to go looking for it."

"I knew he would not. No . . . no . . . I am all right, Tom."

She smiled, and went quickly toward the covered way.

In front of the guardhouse, Captain-lieutenant Phillips stood
with heels precisely together, watching while a sergeant with his
coat in rags and his halberd polished to mirror brightness dressed
a company of the Royal Americans into rigid perfection. The Royal
Americans were very gaunt and very threadbare, but they were
regulars. Such buttons as they still possessed shone like the sergeant's halberd.

Phillips, facing about, saw Diantha in the group of women clustered below the Flag bastion, and raised his hand in salute. As
he brought it smartly down, he called out to her:

"Today. I feel it."

" 'T is the soup you feel," she flashed at him. "They tell me the
king himself will have nettle broth for his dinner when he hears
of it."

Phillips gave her a silent cheer as he went by at the head of the
rhythmic column. The steadiest regiment that bore the king's
cypher could teach Diantha Leslie nothing about courage.

The drawbridge swung slowly down with a great clatter and
shriek of chains. The musket stocks struck with a precise slap

against hands weak with sleeplessness and hunger; threadbare gaiters swung in unison through the gates and out across the cracked mud of the King's Highway. After them trooped the women with baskets on their arms, with knives and shears and sickles. The regulars wheeled smoothly toward the river bank, deployed, and ran into skirmish line among the naked chimneys.

Between the picket line and the watching gunners on the walls, the women fell to snipping the tops from the nettles growing rank behind the ruined cabins. They talked a little. Once there was a laugh, quickly smothered. It seemed, in the unnatural quiet, like blasphemy.

There was nothing, no loud talking, no heedless laughter, to keep out the sound that came, faint and far, across Massacre pond and the hills above it. The click of shears stopped. The baskets lay forgotten among the nettles. The picket line heard it and stood staring toward Grant's Hill. The women came out of the weeds and stood behind the pickets.

High and clear, the music of bagpipes came out of the forest and shook the silence to pieces. The walls of Fort Pitt filled with men; the drawbridge swayed with the stampede of a shouting, weeping, jostling crowd. From the walls and from the baked roadway where the women stood rose a murmur that swelled and swelled.

Out through the forest wall came the swing of red kilts. Behind them came the glint of steel.

The murmur rose into a formless sound that was like a great laugh and a great sob at once.

The red kilts came down over the hill, between the first skeleton chimneys. They came with a jaunty, victorious swing, the big drum thundering ahead, the pipers blowing with all their might. Wave after wave, shining in the sun, the bayonets of the Seventy-seventh dipped down to the ford and poured along the King's Highway. Behind them, wave after wave, the Black Watch filled the road between the ruined cabins, steel blades like a burnished hedge above them, feathers cockily aslant, red jackets bobbing, sporrans swinging.

The formless shouting grew into a roar. On the crazy, jack-straw walls, men swung their hats, flourished their muskets overhead, and cheered in a paroxysm of relief.

In the rutted earth that once had been the dooryard of Hellward Bound's Golden Eagle, a girl in a limp blue dress pushed between two pickets. One of them, flushing, offered his arm. She put her hand on it, and he saw that her fingers were puffed and blistered from the nettle stings. The red-kilted pipers were coming, the drum booming, the pipes gone mad. Arm whirling over arm, the drummer's sleeves made a red blur as he swung past.

A mounted officer trotted slowly by, his eyes scanning the crowd. As the ranks of the Montgomery Highlanders rolled along the picket line, he slapped his horse smartly and rode to overtake the pipes. Pipers and drummer wheeled to the right and came marching back. Across from the yawning cellar of the Golden Eagle, they halted. The drum stopped. The music went tumbling hilariously into another tune.

The officer dismounted and stood waiting. When the last files of the Seventy-seventh passed, he crossed the road and bowed to the girl in the blue dress.

"Mrs. Leslie, your humble servant. Have you forgot me, ma'am?"

Diantha stared at him, her gray eyes wide, her fingers closing and unclosing on the picket's sleeve.

"I saw you," she began, and faltered. "I saw you . . ."

"On the *New Adventure,* ma'am. May I wish you happiness?" His red, somber face broke suddenly into creases. "Law, Mrs. Leslie, he's safe enough. Did ye not recall the song they're playing? I'm daft . . . clean daft. I planned it these twenty miles, and never thought ye might not know it. Listen: it's for you they're playing."

Beaming, he raised a bandaged arm that had no sleeve and beat time to the piping.

"Listen . . ." The pipes played on:

> *"I love a fine lady,*
> *She's bonny and brave. . . .*

"Ay. Bonny and brave. God bless ye! Here he comes."

The last bearskins of the grenadiers were going by. Behind them came the pack train, the precious sacks of corn meal bobbing, bandaged men swaying above them, the walking wounded clinging to the wooden saddles alongside. Here and there in the column, the worse wounded rode in blanket litters slung between two horses.

A wagoner, his leather shirt ripped from belt to shoulder, his hands at the halters of a stretcher team, led them out of the column.

Arnett Leslie lifted his swathed head from a folded jacket and saw Robin's face one great smile, and Diantha's lifted, questioning.

He called to her:

"Diantha. . . . Diantha *Leslie!*"

She came with a rush and knelt with her bare knees in the dirt. Her arms went around his neck in a tight, fierce hug.

"Arnett. Arnett. Arnett." Over and over.

"Diantha. *Sweet.* Barefoot again. . . ."

"Oh*h!*"

"May I not plague you, dear? I have counted on it."

"And I so worried. . . ."

"Thinking you might not have your limestone manor after all?"

"O—*ohh!* I never thought of the manor. You know it. Oh, I am caught again in your plaguing. . . ."

Leslie's hand tangled itself in her unbraided hair. Against her cheek he whispered, reproaching her:

"You did not think of our fine manor, on our own fine mountain? I think, perhaps, you do not want it."

She would not be caught again.

"Oh, I want it," she said coolly, "but . . ."

"Oh, there is a but?"

"But I want . . . oh, I want a part of my wage to be paid *now!*"

He paid it, though the whole Black Watch, halted in the King's Highway, watched him do it.

THE END